The Death
of
Clara Willenheim

The Death of Clara Willenheim

Charlotte M. Lesemann

The Gothic Literary Society, LLC

Acknowledgments

This book would not have been possible without the support of so many others. I owe a huge debt to my parents who very patiently encouraged and aided me while I chucked a perfectly good career in favor of pursuing what I have believed to be my life calling since I was old enough to hold a pencil.

Thank you to my friends, fellow writers and beta readers. I greatly appreciate your interest and feedback. To Elena, my cover designer, whose vision and skill is everything I could have hoped for in a designer, thank you for your patience as we worked out the final product. To Angela Brown, my editor, I am so blessed to have you on my team. Thank for going above and beyond and for encouraging my work so enthusiastically. Your support means so much to me.

And lastly, but most importantly, I want to thank the Lord Jesus Christ who is our Justice and for whom this book is written.

"Vengeance is Mine, and recompense;
Their foot shall slip in due time;
For the day of their calamity is at hand,
And the things to come hasten upon them."
Deut. 32:35

Slumber

"In death—no! even in the grave all is not lost. Else there is no immortality for man. Arousing from the most profound slumbers, we break the gossamer web of some dream. Yet in a second afterward, (so frail may that web have been) we remember not that we have dreamed."
—Edgar Allan Poe

Chapter One

1865, Bavaria

Every house is an extension of its occupants. It absorbs their secrets, clouding its windows over time, in an attempt to veil the hypocrisy and lies. Bricks and stones grind against selfish ambition and settle under the weight of apathy. But in the end, no house can withstand its own history. The larger the house, the greater the fall.

Waldensee stood in a rolling valley, its proud stone towers and crenellated roofline dwarfed by the surrounding mountains and forests, outshone by the shining waters of its namesake lying still and dark at the eastern edge of its sloping lawns. It had stood there for more than four hundred years, enduring the Willenheim family, preparing its testimony.

On a November night, Clara Willenheim, Waldensee's youngest encroacher, stepped back from the edge of the roof as the house shifted beneath her feet. The blood pumped down her arms, the nerves in her fingers itched. If she could have flown from the stone edge of the house, above the harsh geometry of her grandmother's gardens, then up over the timbered peaks in the distance, she would have. To the north, the sky glowered, sharp with energy as a first jolt of lightning struck the horizon. White light divided the past from the present, turning the rolling gray into shades of bruised, fading twilight. The air smelled of death and new life. Of the moist earth mixed with the frail afterlife of fallen leaves. She shivered as the damp breeze lifted her blond hair.

Movement caught her eye, pulling her gaze down the edge of a stone turret to the ground eighty feet below. There a hooded shape astride a horse broke from the shadows, galloped along the farthest edge of the formal gardens, and made for the cover of the dense forest. Clara clutched at the stone teeth that bordered the roof and leaned out, her brow gathered in concentration. As she did, the shifting fog snaked its way across her line of sight, blocking the rider from view. By the time it scudded past, he had disappeared into the timberline. A sour tang, mixed with the moist air of the gathering storm, filled her mouth. Rain began to fall. She turned away from the edge, gathered her skirts, and ran for the tower door.

It fell shut behind her, the noise reverberating against the stone walls. Clara leaned back against it and brushed a damp strand of hair from her cheek. Her sleeve, tattered and wet, clung to her arm. She rolled it up, then the other. Beside her, a lantern hung on the sconce where she had left it. For a moment the wind still gusted about her, casting looming shapes on the stone walls. But then it died to an intermittent whistle and the light stilled.

Centuries of foot traffic had worn the surface of the stone stairs to a low dip in the center of each tread. She hugged the walls of the tower, her fingers brushing against the rough stone, as she circled down through the darkness. Thin gasping breaths of chill air crept around the gaps in the masonry, snaking under the surface of her fingernails.

She stopped at the closest landing. Below her, the stair spiraled into the depths of the house. As she peered down into the darkness, she heard a high keening—a sound like the desperate cry of a child. It rose and wound around her, echoing in her mind. She shuddered and drew open the landing door. Beyond it lay a narrow passage where her candlelight flickered off cobwebs and speckles of mouse pellets. When the heavy door fell shut behind her, she breathed a deep sigh of relief.

Throughout the house, hidden corridors wound like arteries between rooms, passing over halls and pooling under stairways. Her own highway that, to the best of her knowledge, lay forgotten in time and unknown by the rest of Waldensee's inhabitants. She traveled swiftly from one passage to the next until she reached her destination. Her lantern illuminated a small pattern of circles she had carved in the wall. She pressed her ear to the wall and listened.

Silence.

Beside a long split in the wood framing, she reached for the familiar latch and pressed it down. The wall slid open. She stepped through the paneled wall into her boudoir, a small rectangular room bound by a worn gold Aubusson carpet patterned with faded red flowers and green tendrils. Tall arched windows lined one wall, their curtains drawn against the oncoming night. Gold mirrored sconces shone with newly lit gaslight.

Jutta had been there already.

Clara sighed and pushed the panel silently into place. She crossed through a narrow door into her bedroom. The sheets of the bed were folded back. Her nightgown and robe lay over the back of a chair by the fire. The logs were just beginning to catch from the fresh kindling.

A low rustling sounded from the maid's room, which adjoined her sitting room. Clara set the lantern on her desk. There a wide swath of parchment paper lay, the shadings of a capercaillie's wings partly drawn. She picked up the drawing, rolled it carefully, then hesitated. Silence. She held her breath and waited. The sound resumed.

Glancing back toward the door, she strode around the bed, stooped, and drew out a heavy leather bag. She opened it and set the rolled drawing on top of her already-packed clothes and toiletries. Drew the latch and buckled it, carried it into the boudoir, and set it on a stool. She opened one of the mirrored armoire doors. A reflection swung into view. She cried out and slammed the door. Jutta stood just behind her, her dark eyes piercing.

Though she stood several inches shorter than Clara and only a few years older, Jutta's penetrating eyes radiated the intensity and certainty of a slowly gathering fire. Her hair, the color of roasted chestnuts, shone from under her white head scarf, tiny curls edging her forehead. She held a stack of clean white towels that stood out starkly against her soot-colored dress. Drops of moisture lay scattered across it, like inkblots, staining the surface.

For a moment they stared at each other. Jutta's gaze traveled to her sleeve, which hung unraveled and torn. She took in the bag, frozen in Clara's grip, met her eyes, and turned into the bathroom.

Clara glanced back to the hidden panel in the wall, heard footsteps, and turned back in time to see Jutta's hand grip her arm. "I've made up your bed, Fräulein." Clara winced and started to pull away, then thought better of it. She allowed herself to be led to a chair beside the fire, the bag still held fast in her hands.

"Sit here. It's a cold night. Cold and damp. Best to be away from the draft on a night like this." Jutta stood before the chair, her hands folded. "I could brush your hair if you wish. You'll be wanting to be in bed soon."

"It's not that late."

Jutta took up the brush from the dressing table and stood behind her. The brush pulled too lightly at Clara's hair, a terrible tickling sensation. She shivered.

"Stepan said there's talk of another one missing. Taken from an inn in Fussen. Her father said she was impatient and wandered off while they were packing. She was too young to know. *A danger foreseen is half avoided.*"

"Yes. Foreseen," Clara echoed. The skirt of her dress had absorbed the fire's heat and seemed to sear her fingers. Still, her shoulders trembled. She buried her hands in the folds of her dress, clutching the fabric in sweaty palms. And started to rise. But then Jutta cleared her throat and turned to face her. Clara collapsed back into the chair.

"Your mother plans to renovate the rooftop conservatory." Jutta brushed the hair back from Clara's face.

Clara raised her eyebrows. "It's too late in the season."

"Perhaps. She must believe that there's always something that can be done in any season, if only preparing the space. Repairing and replacing what's been broken. She gave me a list of supplies to order. Seeds and such."

Clara's face grew hot; she pulled away from the brush. "That's enough. Really. I'm too close to the fire." For a moment she faltered, then, seeing her nightgown lying over the opposite chair, gestured to it. "Help me into my gown."

As Jutta turned, Clara gripped the leather bag and turned to run.

Later she couldn't have said whether Jutta had anticipated her move or had simply been quick and unfortunate. Regardless, the girl's hand shot out and grasped one of the handles of the bag. For a moment they were both held fast, opposing forces equally determined. But then desperation rose in Clara's chest, and she wrenched the bag away.

Jutta's arms flailed for a second before she fell back, hitting her head with a crack on the edge of the fireplace surround. She lay still on the floor, the flames coloring her still face and smooth olive skin.

"No, no, no," Clara whispered." But when she crouched beside the girl, she felt her breath between her lips. She pulled a lap pillow from the chair, gently lifted the girl's head, and slipped it underneath.

She bit her lip, hesitant, but there was nothing else she could do. She took up the bag again, retrieved her black wool coat from the armoire in her dressing room, and strode to the panel in the wall. The hidden latch gave instantly. She pushed it open and slid into the dark passage without looking back.

It was dark, too dark to see her way, and she had left her lantern on the desk. But there was no way to go back. Not now when Jutta could awaken at any moment. She could raise the alarm and bring Berend, her grandmother's manservant and Clara's omnipresent jailer.

She moved carefully through the labyrinth of the house, pausing to anticipate stairs up or down. Finally she rounded the bottom of the last stair and felt the cool, settled air of the ground floor. Here the house felt damp, close to the rain-drenched earth beyond.

Clara breathed a sigh, her step livening as she traversed the passages between the main rooms. Until, at the faint sound of muffled voices, she froze. She ran her hand over the wall, feeling for the cover of a peephole. When she pushed it aside, light streamed into the passage. It was the western drawing room. A fire glowed in the fireplace. Her mother and grandmother sat in armchairs across from one another, their usual position after dinner until they retired for the evening.

Her grandmother held a book in her lap, but her gaze was fixed on the fire. Clara's mother bent over her herbal notebook, making occasional notes. *Renovating the rooftop conservatory...* Clara didn't doubt that her mother planned to do just that. She divided her time between her garden and her laboratory, spending countless hours poring over pharmaceutical books, notating her findings in her journal. Mixing tinctures as meticulously as she rendered their forms beside her notes.

As if she heard Clara's thoughts, her mother raised her head and, seeing her grandmother's eyes turned toward her, nodded lightly then lowered her eyes back to her notebook. A slight smile, acquiescent, deferring—the smile she'd always had for Clara's father—played about her lips. Clara felt the pressure rise behind her eyes. She breathed deeply, dropped the cover, and moved on.

Several turns later, she came to what should be the library, but when she ran her hands across the walls of the passage, Clara came away with nothing more than dust. No seams divided the wall, no latches. She reversed her steps to the corner and retraced them. Nothing. Frustrated, she moved down the wall, picking up her pace until she collided with a dead end. She had rounded one turn too many.

Backtracking, Clara felt her way along the passage walls until her fingers brushed a familiar gap, long and unbroken. An entry point into the house. She felt the uneven surface of a peephole and slid the cover aside. The room lay in darkness, devoid of sound or movement. She let the cover fall back into place and walked her fingers back to the gap in the wall. She pressed the latch, releasing the door.

The smell of old leather and sweet smoke hung motionless in the cold air. Clara stepped through the opening. Groups of sofas and chairs lay like irregular, shadowed bodies. She blinked back tears. A limestone fireplace stood neglected along the far wall. Rows of bookshelves rose to a coffered ceiling high above. All lay shrouded in silence.

She took another step. The floor creaked, piercing the silence. She froze as a cold wave of fear shot through her limbs. Her heart pounded in her ears. No sound came from the hallway beyond. A jagged streak of lightning raced across the sky, illuminating the room in stark and unnatural shades of white and gray.

Out of the corner of her eye, she caught a glimpse of something. A shadowy form in the balcony above her. She turned, her breath caught in her throat. But then another spark of lightning lit the room. The balcony stood empty. She steeled herself and hurried across the floor to the windows.

Clara grasped the iron handle and turned, but the window stuck fast. She let go then tried again. Still the window wouldn't budge. She moved from window to window, trying them all. Each one was secure, unyielding. The heat spread through her body—tinging her fingers and toes with an incongruous mixture of cold fear and hot determination. Tears welled in her eyes. She fought them back and tried the windows again. Nothing. They were unassailable. No bars or nails held them fast, yet they refused to give way.

No. They're open. They should be open now. They have to be. She fell against one, her face pressed to the cold glass. She imagined she could feel the rain misting the pane. Outside the gardens lay in mazes of boxwood and spiring cedar, springing to life in the light of the storm.

The garden. The sight of green—even in its stagnant, autumn stupor—flooded her with insight. She knew what to do. Fortitude coursed through her. She dashed across the floor and slipped back into the dark passage.

When she reached the south side of the estate, her hand coursed along the rough, dusty wall of the passage until she felt the latch. Taking hold of it she pushed. And then realized she hadn't looked or listened first. Her heart lurched. But as the door opened, the only light she saw was the occasional flash of lightning. She waited. Twenty-two counts before the thunder. The storm was moving on. She smiled to herself.

Stepping out, Clara quickly took in the space. The solarium was an elongated ellipse, entirely encased in glass and steel. Long palm fronds cast fanlike shadows on the black-and-white tile floor. Cold, damp air hugged the thin shell.

Clara wove through potted ficus and philodendron and stone benches until she reached the far perimeter where three sets of double-doors beckoned her. The first was secured fast. But the second wasn't. She took hold of the handle. The cold steel stung her hand and sent a shiver of excitement through her body. It stuck briefly before the bolt loosened in its casing. As she pushed the door open, a mist of rain struck her in the face. She laughed lightly.

Her last thought was of the veranda beyond the solarium, bordered by a low stone wall. Of the stone pillars topped in carved eagles, their wings tucked in as if in perpetual rest. Of the north lawns, stretching down to the lake. Of the oak and beech and elm trees that stood like swaying sentinels posted around the marshy shore. All this she could see and feel through the glass door. The smell of wind and rain. The shadowed land. And a face reflected in the glass above her own.

Before she could cry out in shock, an arm encircled her, pinning her arms against her body. A hand reached over her face, holding something pungent. It smelled of mulberry and tobacco and the sharp odor of a nest of mice.

A cold darkness overtook her.

Chapter Two

Berlin

"That's a hell of a tale!" Jan paced around the dark office, a compass in his hands. He reflexively snapped it open and shut as he passed back and forth over the worn Turkish carpets heaped with piles of papers and leather portfolios.

"Hmmm." Richter, lost in thought, sat at the oversize desk, his hands steepled before him.

Jan nearly tripped over a stack of umbrellas, calling Richter's attention back to the conversation at hand. "If it's true, it would be the most extensive—and the most insidious—intrigue that I've seen in almost thirty years of work."

"Can we trust him?" Jan asked, reorienting his small spectacles from where they'd slipped.

"I believe we can." Richter inhaled deeply. "He has no incentive to lie. If anything, the opposite is true."

"I suppose..." Jan had recommenced his pacing. "He's quite a figure, though. I suppose it will be sensitive."

"Undoubtedly." Richter raised heavy eyebrows at his youthful apprentice. "And dangerous. Not a word of this can leak out to anyone before we're ready to move forward."

Jan grinned conspiratorially. "We have a good starting point, though. It seems like he has the whole story."

Richter leaned back in his chair and stared out into the room, his eyes fixed on nothing in particular. He thought he had seen it all in his years of service: from petty disputes to violent crimes prior to 1851 and then, after that, every shade of political machination one could imagine. But this would top them all.

And Jan was right. If their source could be trusted, they already had much of the story in hand. Richter had no reason to doubt his informant's credibility. However, the individual was, understandably, somewhat removed from the situation. Much could be misconstrued or exaggerated—a case of hearsay. Despite that, though, something about the entire affair rang true.

"...put it back, can we?" Jan was saying something to him.

Richter quickly inferred his drift. "No, no. We certainly can't *put it back*, as you say. We can't discredit any of it out of hand. Particularly in light of the looming unification. That would be disastrous, in more ways than one.

"Of course, if we follow this lead and discover what our source has said is true...well, that's an entirely different matter. That would be the defining moment for both of us. The minister president would be keenly interested in a matter of this magnitude."

Jan approached the desk opposite Richter and sat on the edge of it, selectively choosing a file from the pile. "I've already confirmed the details about the baron's daughter. Herr Willenheim...um...Edgar was nineteen at the time. Her father received a handsome payout—far more than his annual salary—to keep the matter quiet. She was sent to France for a time, where they don't have such..." Jan paused, searching for the word. "Such *particular* standards. I believe...yes, here it is...a friend of the family resides in Paris. She remained there, 'gaining an appreciation for the arts,' until her conspicuous condition was, well, less conspicuous. The child was given up for adoption.

"Meanwhile, Edgar remained at the school in Vienna, virtually unaffected by the entire incident, thanks to his father's extensive wherewithal. Where he…" Jan set that file down and rifled through the stack, retrieving a second one. "…where he continued his *distinguished* tutelage in such things as…" Jan held up his hand, ticking off the items on each of his fingers. "…gambling, shooting and excessive spending on just about any worthless pastime one can imagine."

"That's not terribly different from any of his peers or their own fathers. It's the rest and the extent of it that concerns me." Richter interjected. "A loose purse here and there, a dalliance on the side…not ideal, but not uncommon. But the other reports…"

"It lends a lot of credence to our source," Jan said.

"It does." Richter agreed. "It certainly does. It also calls into question the purported activities of those with whom Edgar was so closely tied. Their loyalties are already in question. Many of their closest associates, even Edgar's own mother, hail from Austria, a region reluctant to embrace Prussia's rule and on which Bismarck's efforts to unify the region are increasingly focused. If their involvement in the case at hand is verifiable…" His voice fell off as he retreated into thought.

Part of him was reluctant even to voice such a possibility. Yet some other part of him knew it was, at least to some degree, a likely reality. It was that part of him that felt the most conflicted. The entire case threatened to upend his established convictions.

For twenty-eight years, Richter had labored faithfully for the Prussian government, executing justice in the name of order and the king's interests. He had served under Wilhelm I, whose tight-laced standards had kept both citizens and budgets in check. Then, in 1848, the revolution. The country had shifted dramatically, in favor of a parliamentary system, rather than the former absolute monarchy. When von Hinckeldey had formed the Police Union three years later, Richter had quietly doubted the wisdom of such an action. Many felt it was the only means by which to guard against a subsequent uprising, yet it opened the door to an abuse of power that gave Richter pause.

For the first time, though, in light of this new case, he saw the potential wisdom of such a system. From where he sat in Berlin, the present situation undoubtedly called into question the stability of a future united nation. The sort of unity Bismarck sought. And their illustrious minister—a devout Pietist—would, without question, oppose the actions of these regional leaders. Assuming, that is, that he and Jan confirmed all that his source had alleged.

"What is our next course of action?" Jan asked. He stood at the head of the desk, his body coiled as tightly as a spring. Richter suspected that, should he give the word, Jan would bolt out the door in full pursuit.

"We dig," Richter issued the standard answer. "The problem is that much of the information we need is closely protected by local law enforcement."

"Who don't want us *meddling* in their affairs," Jan interrupted.

"Yes, who don't want us anywhere near what they consider to be their business. And this family isn't the local blacksmith, engaged in shoddy business practices. Or a tavern fight that resulted in an accidental death. They won't want us there any more than anyone else will."

"But we have a right to be there."

"We do." Richter replied slowly. "But the quieter we are and the more we accomplish by means of stealth, the better. Besides which, if the full extent of this *tale*, as you referred to it, is true, we're going to need to proceed very carefully. There is far too much at stake.

"Austria was easy—not to discredit your excellent work there, but obtaining information from them was a lot less sensitive than it will be once we're closer to the *nest*."

"The nest of vipers."

"But that is where we must go. And I say we begin with Herr Willenheim, following his movements from day to day. It's only a matter of time before he gives away some association that's less than savory or indicts himself in some way. Who knows? It may be that we'll be there right *when the match is lit*, as my old mentor used to say."

"So we're going to Bavaria?" Jan rushed across the room to grab his coat.

"We are. And soon. But first we need to prepare."

Jan set to work stacking outstanding files in boxes when the door blew open. Outside a heavy, wet wind prophesied a coming storm. Leaves and dust rose in the vacuum and settled just inside the door.

Richter looked up to see his associate, Markus, burst through the doorway, panting as if he'd run far. When he could speak well enough to be understood, he slammed the door behind him and whispered hoarsely, "We've just received word. Edgar Willenheim is dead."

"Dead?" Jan stared at the man, his mouth open. Richter didn't move.

Markus nodded. "Dead. It's been ruled a suicide."

"What do we do now?" Jan looked at Richter in horror.

"We go to Bavaria. Now."

Chapter Three

Bavaria

The bolt scraped as her sitting room door opened. Clara refused to turn her face from the gravel drive beyond her window seat. Outside, a line of carriages approached the house, some bearing family crests on the doors, most noble but indistinct. In her mind she heard the clatter of the horses' hooves and the crunching of the wheels as they churned over the gravel path. Her head throbbed in time with their approach. She closed her eyes and massaged her temples.

"Good day, Fräulein," Jutta said. Clara waited, expecting more, despite the girl's customary quietude. Even her footsteps seemed reluctant, wary. But the girl said nothing more.

When she had awakened, it had been Jutta who had informed her, using small phrases—*your father, terrible accident, my profound sympathy*—her dark eyes wide and full of pity. It had angered Clara to see it, and she had turned away, huddling down in the bed. Most likely Jutta had taken it as sorrow. Now she focused on the leaded glass tracery before her, following the outline of the panes with her finger. Raindrops landed on the glass, clinging to their form then falling away into obscurity.

"How long has it been?" Clara asked.

"Two days."

Two days. She could still feel the rain washing her face, splashing off of the veranda. Could still see the spiring cedars before her and beyond, the forest lit with the energy of the storm, beckoning her. And then his face reflected in the glass. Berend.

He had known somehow. Clara turned and risked a glance in Jutta's direction. As she did, her vision swam and tilted, provoked by the sudden movement. Jutta continued to set out Clara's mourning attire, her gaze averted, her expression undisturbed. Her hair was neat, arranged as usual. Nothing out of the ordinary. But then she rose and winced slightly. Clara smiled, though the satisfaction felt shallow.

She turned back to the line of carriages, crawling forward like carrion beetles drawn to the destruction of others, eager to consume and then pull the ground out from under their victims. Berend had followed her, had watched her. No matter how careful she was, he knew her every move. Even now, he was undoubtedly outside her door, standing guard. Or worse, his scowling henchman, Hagan.

He must have carried her back to her rooms, for that was where she had awakened a few hours ago. She had no memory of anything in the interim. No knowledge of where she had been—if she had lain in her bed for days or had been kept somewhere else. No ability to recall who may have circled her bed, looking down on her as she lay helpless.

A coach had circled the fountain and come to a stop in front of the entry below. The coachman dropped down to hold an umbrella over the emerging guests, blocking them from Clara's view. Behind her, the insular sounds of Jutta filling her bath with water, opening armoires, and closing doors. With them, a faint wisp of air that rustled Clara's dress as the girl returned.

After her bath, her skin still warm, Clara sat at the dressing table and watched Jutta brush and dress her hair. It was too short for many of the sweeping, rolled hairstyles women were wearing. But at fifteen no one expected her to wear the styles of a married woman. Instead, Jutta parted it in the middle then swept each side back, pinning them tightly. She twirled the back sections into curls so that glossy ringlets hung behind her ears.

The mourning dress lay on the bed, a bonnet beside it. Clara looked at the black crepe then away. Black, the color of captivity. She rose and lifted her arms. Clara looked at herself in the mirror. The black dress seemed to overshadow her, diminishing the color of her face and hair, making her appear wan. A shell of herself gazed back at her from within sunken eyes.

Jutta met her eyes in the mirror then looked away. "Your mother was here while you were still sleeping."

Clara's heart surged then faltered. "I don't remember."

"No. But I should think you'll see her. People have been arriving all morning. She's most likely downstairs receiving them. And supporting your grandmother."

"My grandmother has never needed anyone's support."

Clara caught Jutta's reflection in the mirror as she turned away. For a moment she would have sworn that the girl smiled, but then she turned back, her face expressionless.

"Perhaps, but she wants you and your mother with her, especially at this time."

Clara sighed. The thought of the so-called mourners filling up the house, nibbling at food, eyeing possible business and social connections filled her with dread. She didn't care to participate in their game.

"It's only a few days," Jutta added, as if she could hear Clara's thoughts. "And what with so many people in the house, perhaps you won't have to do much more than make an appearance."

She finished buttoning up the back of the dress then fastened a jet bracelet over her kid gloves. But Clara was fixated on her words: *so many people in the house*. A house full of guests, many of them here for days under the pretense of mourning. That had to demand some of Berend's attention. Certainly her grandmother would require more from him than she typically did.

Jutta led her to the door, knocked twice, and waited.

Chapter Four

Berend blocked the door, his heavy brow and high cheekbones fixed in their perpetual state of disapproval. Clara avoided his eyes, instead taking in his uniform: black and severely cut, as her grandmother preferred. She pressed around him. Down the hall and a flight of stairs, he shadowed her—his stiff, rolling movements those of something wolfish, inhuman.

As they passed along the main hall, the house creaked and shifted. The ceiling shuddered, raining plaster in streaks down the red damask wallpaper. Ahead of them, a disorienting fog of hushed voices, smoke, and clinking ice issued from the living room. Clara's pace slowed, her spine stiff against Berend's hand pressing her forward.

As they rounded the doorway, the chandelier swayed lightly, casting uneasy light about the space. Someone had taken her father's portrait from the gallery and hung it above the fireplace. Close by, Clara's grandmother sat on a gold brocade sofa. She wore her silver hair, still streaked with dark strands, pulled back in a low braided knot at the nape of her neck. Clara's mother stood beside her. Clara thought she saw Uncle Horst with them. None of them looked up or seemed to notice her.

Men stood in large groups, holding cut glasses full of amber liquid. Several clutched fat cigars and puffed at them. Women clustered about the room in conspiratorial fashion, their heads close, words uttered behind gloved hands. They shot quick, questioning glances at Clara's mother and grandmother and then, looking back at one another, shook their heads.

From one of the closer groups, Clara's Aunt Lotte—her late Grandfather Conrad's niece— spotted her and hurried over. Behind her, four women watched Clara with beady eyes, like wary fowl scouring the ground for unsuspecting worms.

Lotte gathered her into an embrace. "Oh, Clara, dear, there you are. How horrid. I still can't believe it. Thank you, Berend; I'll take it from here." She steered Clara into the room, back to her circle of women. "And you...I can't imagine what you're feeling."

Around her the other women towered, uttering condolences, their voices compassionate, their eyes dry. *It must be so terrible. And you so young. He was so lovely—didn't we all know it? No one could ever compete with him.* The other ladies murmured words of agreement.

Clara remembered at least one of them from a luncheon her grandmother had held in August, three months prior. Her father had been home, enclosed in his library, focused on business. But after lunch he had emerged onto the veranda, to the exclamations and delight of all of the women. Clara remembered it clearly: him standing straight and tall in a white linen suit, his dark hair gleaming in the sunlight, his brown eyes laughing at their fawning. He had winked at her, a smirk on his face.

You were so close. They peered down at her, their mouths open, waiting.

Clara stumbled for a response. Within her, conflicting and competing feelings warred: relief, grief, and the sense that this was simply the tail end of a loss that had begun years ago. As the words formed in her mind, she saw how wrong they would seem. She flushed with shame. "Yes. So close," she muttered.

They sipped their drinks, nodded in sympathy, and went on talking, politely relieving her of the attention she clearly wanted to avoid. *No one was surprised when he captured the baron's daughter. She is the loveliest creature.* They all turned and peered at Clara's mother across the room.

Even in full mourning, perhaps even more so because of it, Clara had to agree: her mother was the most striking woman she had ever seen. Tall and graceful, with long thin fingers and a delicate slender nose, her pale skin and hair glowed against the black dress. If anything, the dark apparel enhanced her figure as she leaned against the marble fireplace surround.

She must be just devastated. Yes. Yes. Who wouldn't be?

Clara looked back to where her mother lingered, surrounded by a number of guests, primarily men. She bore the sense of weary elegance and aloof intelligence she carried at all times, but nothing that could be characterized as devastation.

Where's his brother? He has a brother? Yes. Although they say he left the family years ago. Asked to leave is more like it.

Clara listened to their murmuring from a distant place, as if she had retreated into a back corner of a cave where she could only hear the faint echoing of their conversation. At the mention of her uncle she started, but by then they had already moved on.

What I can't understand is why? It doesn't make sense? No. No sense at all. Several women shook their heads in dismay.

"What's that?" an elderly woman asked. "What did you say?" She leaned on a black cane, a glass filled with a strange green substance in her other hand. Her over-bustled dress, with its lace neckline, was well out of fashion. It looked more like the eighteenth-century fashion plates Clara had had as a child.

"The suicide," someone whispered.

"Suicide? What suicide?" the elderly woman spat. "Why on earth—"

"Ho! Margareta, what are you up to?" An ample, red-haired man strode to the group, eyeing the elderly woman. He placed his arm possessively around Clara's shoulder, his body radiating moist warmth through his overcoat. "Are you scaring this poor young thing?"

"Werner." The elderly woman nodded.

Werner looked down at Clara. "Hello, sweetheart. Haven't seen you in ages."

Clara smiled back, but on the inside her mind raced, trying to pluck the memory of him out of some hazy, vaporous place she couldn't access. Something about him was vaguely familiar: a smell, or perhaps the sound of his voice. His expression was affable yet her vision narrowed and darkened. She felt the sudden need to flee.

"Liselotte." Lotte stepped up and introduced herself, drawing away his focus. "Edgar's cousin on his father's side."

"Werner Regensbach." He took Lotte's hand and added, laughing, "Edgar's accomplice. We were in school together in Vienna."

"Werner!" Several men overheard them and sauntered over. One gave him a firm hug, slapping him on the back. "Here you are, after all."

"Made it. Business nearly kept me away. But I always have time for the ladies." He grinned at Clara. "I learned that from Edgar."

Clara's heart beat rapidly. Cold tendrils spread throughout her limbs. The other men chuckled and cast furtive glances into their drinks. One of them, an elegant, graying gentleman with a mustache, added, "Edgar always had such a charm with women. They all followed at his heels, waiting for his every word. If I could have bottled it and sold it, we'd all be rich. Well, richer."

The other men laughed.

The mustached man glanced at Clara. His face was sharply defined, his nose aristocratic, and his dress neat, but his eyes were lecherous and his smile pinched. "A hound's a hound as they say."

Lotte started to speak, but Werner cut her off, "Do you remember that girl? What was her name? The baron's daughter. Karla? Or Karlotte? Whatever it was, thank God for Conrad's hefty purse. Whoever said money can't solve every problem has never been to Austria."

"Or Prussia," the mustached man added. "There's no purity among those dogs. Say what you will about their greed, but I'll take Austria or France any day."

A third man, of moderate height, fair and faintly freckled, fidgeted as the conversation took a political turn. "Now wait one moment. Edgar may have been schooled in Austria, but he was a solid Bavarian. Like the rest of us, Herr Schweben notwithstanding. And this *is* still Bavaria. Not Prussia or Austria or France. And it's going to remain Bavaria."

"Alfred…" Werner threw an arm around his shoulder. "Of course. Of course. But you have to admit Bavaria is already divided, whether or not she admits it. One wants the old kingdom; another Austro-Bavaria; and another Franco-Bavaria. And each of them is fighting to claim her. Not to mention Bismarck and those like him who are anxious for a united state. He isn't some toy soldier, playing at territorial disputes. Now hold on a minute. I'm not saying I want to see Bavaria snapped up in the jaws of the minister president. But we can't be so dismissive of the possibility."

Despite Alfred's flustered attempts to speak, Werner continued, "And Edgar understood that as well as we do. He weighed the benefits as you would any matter of business. Independence is an illusion. Change is inevitable. The question is, if we can't be Bavaria" —he held out his hand to stop the other man's protests—"God forbid it should come to that. But if, at some point, we can't be the same Bavaria we've always been, we have to decide where our allegiances lie. We all know what I believe. And what Edgar would have chosen."

"And what would that be?" Her grandmother's voice cut through the tension. She stood just outside of the group's circle. In the midst of the rising tension of the discussion at hand, no one had heard her approach.

"Frau Willenheim, you look as ravishing as ever." Werner caught up her hand and held it to his lips.

Her grandmother struggled not to smile. "Werner, you're the same old devious fox you've always been."

"With honor." He mock bowed to her and laughed. "I was just telling Herr Gottinger that, though we treasure our history and heritage, if we had to choose an ally in the looming conflict, Edgar and I would choose Austria and France as the more pleasurable bedfellows. Clearly you agree."

"Of course."

"You've come to join the discussion then?" Werner asked.

"I'm afraid not. I've come to collect my granddaughter, Clara." She reached out her hand and grasped Clara's. "Given the weight of this occasion, her mother and I would appreciate her presence. I'm sure you understand."

"Lotte," her grandmother addressed her, "would you care to join us as well?"

Lotte mouthed something to the other ladies and followed Lina away from the group.

"Disgraceful bunch of vultures," Lina commented once they were out of earshot.

Her mother drew Clara down beside her on the sofa while her grandmother signaled to one of the servants to bring her a fresh glass of brandy. Glass in hand, she settled herself into a chair beside the fire and leaned back to survey the room.

"They didn't bother you did they, dear?" Helene smoothed down Clara's sleeves as if clearing away the ill intentions of their unwanted houseguests.

Clara thought of Werner's overly eager red face, of the count's leering looks and felt her color rise. "They're arguing that we have to side with either Prussia or Austria."

"Men." Her mother looked relieved. "A time like this and all they can think about is politics."

"No disrespect to Edgar's memory," Horst said, "but Bavaria's future is being decided regardless of our personal circumstances. I have it on good authority that Bismarck has his eye on uniting all of us under the Prussian flag, with himself at the helm of course. For those who prefer Austria"—he nodded in deference to Lina—"there's no time to waste."

"Why do we have to submit to anyone?" Clara asked. "Why can't we control our own future?"

"Because that's how the world works." Horst leaned back, resting his arm across the back of the sofa. "The affairs of the world move by means of alliances and compromises. No one can stand alone even if he wants to. Besides, something always has to die for something greater to be born."

"Bavaria is perfect as it is," Clara said.

"I don't know what any of this has to do with Edgar," her grandmother cut in. She pursed her lips and stared at them with steely eyes.

They sat silently for several minutes, clutching at the drink in their hands, looking around at the guests moving in circles of hushed respect. Clara's shoulders and neck began to ache. At last, Lotte sighed, breaking through the awkwardness. Every eye turned toward her.

"It's so strange. Like it was yesterday when it was decades ago. So many memories in this place." She looked around at the gathering crowd. "He's...was...four years older. I never experienced a time when he wasn't here." She chuckled lightly. "There was this one time. I was, oh, perhaps seven or eight. We were here for the summer. I wanted to play dolls, but Cora wanted to play toy boats on the lake. You know Cora." She faltered for a moment then went on. "You knew Cora. She always wanted to be outside. Always. Running through the woods or swimming or sailing.

"Well, we fought about it for a time. Meanwhile, Edgar was sitting in the window with that knife of his, carving something. Eventually he piped in and suggested we reenact *Die Zertanzten Schuhe*. You remember the story of course, in which the twelve princesses leave their room each night via a secret door. They travel through the hidden passages of a castle and emerge in three successive woods. The trees in the first have silver leaves. The second, gold. And the third, diamonds. From there they come to a lake where twelve princes wait to take them in boats to a castle that stands on the opposite shore. There the princesses dance each night away, ruining their slippers."

Clara looked at her hands in her lap, feeling her pupils dilating, her breath catching—cold and sharp—in her chest.

"It was a splendid idea. We took the dolls and all went well until we got down to the lake. The boats were there, but there were supposed to be princes awaiting our arrival. Well, Cora insisted I be the prince.

Which, I told her, was ridiculous. I was at least a year younger. It only made sense for me to be the princess."

Laughter broke out among several guests.

"That only angered her. The whole afternoon was on the brink of collapse when Edgar, who had followed us, declared he would play both princes. So we set the dolls in their little boats and tied a ribbon to the bow of each one. I thought he would lead them along the shore, but no! He threw himself into the lake. With his clothes on! Even his shoes—those stiff little black ones with the spats Hedy always made him wear. You remember those!

"He threw himself into the water, swam over to the lines, and dragged the boats clear across the lake. Cora and I had to run to meet him on the other side, and he still beat us there. We had our ball. By the time we were done, it was past dinner. Thank God Cora insisted Edgar walk back rather than tossing himself into the water again.

"He would have done it, though. He would have done anything for Cora." She paused, not knowing how to finish. "That's my favorite memory of Edgar."

The guests broke out in light applause. Many were chuckling. Lina was laughing and smiling so hard she had to wipe tears of joy from her cheeks. "Oh, Edgar," she sighed. "I remember that day. Those shoes were ruined."

For a minute or two, everyone was quiet. The fire's flames had diminished to red embers glowing through black forms that were merely a suggestion of logs. Clara shifted in her seat.

"The lake." Werner's booming voice behind her shattered the stillness. "I remember Edgar teaching this little one to swim." He reached forward and squeezed Clara's shoulder from behind the sofa. Clara jumped. "Threw her right in. Edgar was like that. Sink or swim. Isn't that what he'd say?"

He laughed and shook his head. Clara's mind filled with the memory of her limbs flailing as fingers of weeds brushed against her legs; of gagging as her mouth filled with the fetid water. Worse—of something living that wanted to claim her. That had waited there in the black depths intending to reach out and clutch her in its cold embrace. Her lungs tightened, spasmed.

"You want a story? I have a story." Werner's voice demanded attention. "As many of you know—hell, a few of you were there—Edgar and I attended university at roughly the same time. One class apart. So one morning he comes to me with this idea. At the time, I didn't know Cora had just written to him to say she had just gotten a horse. And not just any horse. No. A fine Arabian horse, black as night. I can't recall his name. Sturmisch or Dunkel..."

"She called him 'Dunkel Engel,'" Lina said.

"That's right," Werner continued. "Dark Angel. Anyway, I didn't know this at the time. So he comes to me and says he has a plan to go riding. The university wasn't the most exciting place, if you know what I mean. Naturally I said yes.

"Come midnight, I'm standing outside the headmaster's door. We couldn't go out the lower doors, you see. There was a guard after dark. So we're outside the headmaster's door. I get there and Edgar is already picking the lock. He had to fiddle with it for a few minutes, but he opened it, by God."

Werner chuckled and ran a hand through his hair, sweeping it back. His face was redder with the excitement of his tale. Clara glanced at her grandmother. Lina's face was fixed in stony horror. Lotte and Horst exchanged guarded glances.

"We passed through the headmaster's office and onto his balcony. That was his plan! To climb off the balcony and down the side of the building. He never was right in the head." Beside her, Clara's mother gasped. "Still, we did it. Then we were off. I think it was April—no, the snow was gone; must have been sometime in May. Hell, I don't remember.

"We ran out to the street and down to a neighboring stable. In those days they were that close to the city. Anyway, we ran down to the barn and Edgar 'appropriated,' as he called it, two of their thoroughbreds. Best damn horses I'd ever seen. We must have ridden for hours, through the fields and forests around the area. Mind you, it was dark, but there was a full moon that night.

"And could he ride! I don't know how many fences we jumped, not to mention streams and fallen logs. Daylight was beginning to show when we brought the horses back. Nearly caught us too. Ed hadn't planned on that one—that stable hands are up long before schoolboys.

"They didn't, though. We made it back in time to slip in the servants' entrance as the bakers were arriving. That's still one of the best nights of my life."

"Didn't one of those horses end up lame after that?" Horst asked, his voice flat.

Werner shrugged. "Wouldn't surprise me. Edgar could ride a horse like Phaethon in Helios's chariot."

"It didn't end well for Phaethon," Horst remarked. "Didn't end well for the horse either. They had to put her down."

Clara shot a glance at her grandmother, whose face was drawn and still, and wondered if they were both thinking of another stable on another night.

Horst cleared his throat, drawing everyone's expectant and hopeful attention. "If I may, I have a more recent story. It's a tad different, but I think that when you hear it you'll recognize the Edgar we loved so much."

Lina nodded to him.

"It was perhaps seven or eight years ago. Late September I believe. Lotte and I were here for several weeks, along with a number of others. For several days the weather had turned unseasonably warm. Early one morning, Edgar and I were on the veranda watching the fog lifting over the forests. The sunrise cast the trees in shades of gold and crimson. It was stunning, truly *native soil, fatherland...rich harvesting in every field.*"

Several men and one woman broke into song, and Horst had to wait for the anthem to end, much to the pleasure of all of the guests. Clara breathed deeply. Horst smiled and tucked his hands into his pockets, rocking back and forth on his heels as the spotlight warmed in his favor.

"I suppose it inspired in both of us a sense of renewed love for the fatherland. That desire that men so often have, to feel the soil and taste the wind, to be boundless in a way that connects one to the land

and to those things that can never be fully tamed. Edgar was like that —loyal to the things that kept him wild, the things that challenged him.

"One of those things was the hunt. As I often say, many nations have deer, but only Bavaria has stags. Edgar would have agreed with that. Don't take my word for it; the trophy room is on the second floor—see for yourself!"

"Oh, bother." Lina waved her hand in mock dismissal, but her face shone with pride.

"We rode out shortly after dawn. The air was crisp but not cold. Our horses' hooves crushed the early, fallen leaves as we rode. That smell —of rich decay—filled our senses, mingled with the sound of autumn birdsong and the snuffling of our horses as they snorted and clopped over the packed earth.

"Now…" Horst paused to focus their attention. "It wasn't Edgar who took down the stag. Though he was a fine marksman. No, it was Count Reigelstein who spotted the animal first and took the shot. It was a long shot, but sure enough he hit it. Square in the chest. We rode over to collect the animal.

"I don't know if it was the easy, convivial air of the morning, or the beauty of the autumn day, but none of us were in much of a hurry. The count's groom reached the animal first and dismounted. As the rest of us drew near, we sensed movement. Some sort of shuffling along the ground. At first I think we all assumed that it was the groom, inspecting his master's trophy.

"Until we heard a strange grunting behind the bushes."

Several people exclaimed.

"A wild boar. We must have disturbed its scavenging. Either way, his man was struggling to run from it. The boar squealed and grunted, running this way and that. One moment it was fleeing, and the next it rounded and turned on him. We didn't notice at first the dark stain spreading from the groom's gut, staining his green coat. Another from his thigh.

"The boar had gored him. A number of us jumped down to aid the man but, to his credit, it was Edgar who didn't even hesitate. He sprang from the saddle and dashed to the man's side. The boar turned and rushed at him. Edgar dove out of the way.

"But then he charged—Edgar, that is. He ran after the boar and threw himself on top of the creature. It bucked and squealed but not for long. Edgar unsheathed a long hunting knife from his belt and tore it across the boar's gullet. We managed to ride back with the groom and call a physician in time to save his life. And that's because of Edgar. Because he was always fearless. Brilliant. And heroic."

"Here! Here!" someone shouted.

The stories continued for another hour or two, with many of the guests vying for the opportunity to share their own piece of Edgar's history. Clara listened to all of them with a conflicted sense of curiosity and unease. Few of them knew the true Edgar.

Her mind churned with dark images—memories forced up to the surface, gasping for air. She would have fled from it all if she could have, but her mother sat tightly beside her, her grandmother across from her, and neither would have surrendered her easily.

Eventually the stories fragmented into competing smaller tales. As the conversation drew away from where she sat, Lotte turned to Clara. "I meant to ask if you've been feeling better."

Clara blushed and looked to the side, her mind wheeling, searching for an answer.

"Do you mind my asking? Someone mentioned you were ill."

"Clara." Lina's voice rang out as she rose from her chair. "Lotte, I'm sorry to interrupt, but I'm sure you'll excuse me if I take Clara with me for now. I was just leaving for a time of prayer. I'm sure that would do Clara much good as well. Wouldn't it dear?"

Her grandmother pulled her to her feet, took her arm under her own, and led her briskly out of the room.

Chapter Five

Lina pulled Clara down the main hall, past room after room lying stately and neglected like the carcasses of elegant beasts long picked clean. Outlines in worn rugs marked where furniture had once stood. Chairs that had lined the walls lay toppled in disarray, cast down by some unseen entity. Vases and cigar trays and silver services sat jumbled in a heap on top of console tables and servers.

At the end of the main hall, one wing jutted off at a right angle. There a family portrait hung, overlaid in cobwebs. In it, her grandfather and grandmother sat in carved high-backed chairs; their expressions somber, appraising. Around them, their three children stood. Clara's father, Edgar, bore her grandmother's chiseled features and dark, brooding eyes. Nathaniel and Cora mirrored her grandfather Conrad's fair, open face and red hair. They all managed to appear united in boredom.

Clara would have lingered over the portrait, but her grandmother gripped her arm and strode around the corner and down to the end of the eastern wing of the house. There a studded plank door hung on solid iron hinges. The medieval style was a strict departure from the rest of the house, marking the chapel as something both set apart from and distinctly opposed to the house itself.

Lina pulled a heavy ring of keys from her pocket, inserted one, and pushed open the door. Cold air pressed out from within the stone interior. It smelled lifeless and stale. Rows of wooden pews stood witness to their entrance. The heavy wooden beams overhead and the solid stone walls pressed in on Clara. Someone had lit the candles on the altar and those in metal sconces lining the walls. As several burned down and went out, the cloying scent of smoke filled the air.

Clara followed her grandmother to one of the front pews. Lina lowered herself onto the kneeler and crossed herself, muttering something. Clara mimicked her gestures half-heartedly and knelt beside her on the rounded leather ledge. When she glanced at her grandmother, Clara saw that her eyes were closed in prayer, her lips moving inaudibly. Clara tried to close her eyes, but Werner's red face rose before her face. And the others: the leering mustached count, even Aunt Lotte. They stared at her, hovering around in a circle, questioning, prying.

Shuddering involuntarily, she looked instead at the altar, an intricately carved wooden box draped in a white cloth and covered in silver candelabras, that stood beyond the low, front railing. High above it, the organ loft overlooked the length of the church. For a moment, the shadows in the loft seemed to flicker and shift, as if someone walked there. They stilled then shifted again. The house creaked and groaned around them. She looked up to the roof above, certain it would collapse. Instead, a shrill, discordant cord rang out from the organ, echoing off of the stone walls. Clara gasped.

Her grandmother opened her eyes a crack and shook her head. "It's an old house. Old houses always have stories to tell." She fell back into her contemplation.

Clara turned back to the loft. It rested, its darkness still, but she could feel eyes on her. Something waited there, watching, breathing. Below the loft, an elongated crucifix hung. On it, the Christ figure stared out at her from under accusing eyelids, trapped in perpetual suffering. The hairs on Clara's arm rose. She fought the urge to run. But then Lina sighed deeply, crossed herself and sat back in the pew.

Clara quickly closed her eyes, waited several seconds, and did likewise. She looked around the room. The stained-glass windows were all narrow and deep-set. She didn't have to turn around to know that the double doors in the back of the nave—also wood and iron—were bolted fast. The door back to the house, through which they had come, hung unsecured in its frame. It was, at most, thirty feet from where she sat. She forced her breathing to slow and waited for her grandmother to fall back into prayer. Instead she took Clara's hand and exhaled lightly.

Her grandmother gazed up at the cross, her deep brown eyes misty. "There's such forgiveness here. It may be my age speaking, but the weight of one's sin seems to accrue over time. So many regrets. So much to atone for. And..." Her voice fell off leaving a void in its wake. "And the worst part of it is, it was Edgar who always knew what to say. If he were here..." She faltered briefly then continued, "but now, I fear I'm the reason he's dead."

Clara started. "Why?"

Lina squeezed her hand as if thanking her. "Your father was always a troubled man." Her face seemed to gather for a moment, her eyes unfocused. "No, that's not true. There was a time when he was very strong. When he didn't bear the weight of a conflicted mind. But then, after his sister died, your Aunt Cora...I didn't realize how her death would affect him. And now your mother is saying...suggesting..."

"What?" Clara whispered when her grandmother didn't finish her thought.

"I...I should have understood him better." Lina grimaced, her gaze fixed on something unseen before them. "I should have known what he needed. I should have done more. Instead he grew worse and worse, fighting against the other half of himself, the half that died with Cora. It died, but still it walked. For almost twenty-five years it walked, in Edgar's body. It limped through the halls at night, speaking from a place of torment. Stalking him. Begging to be set free.

"And I never knew how to help him. In the end it was Edgar. Your mother claims it was Edgar who knew how to silence the part of him that couldn't find rest."

A cold hand passed over Clara's body as Lina spoke. She remembered the nights when her father had bolted himself in his room, sobbing and pacing. They clustered in the hallway, Lina and Berend fumbling with the locks only to find the room barricaded. Her mother standing behind them against the opposite wall, nervously chewing on her fingernail, her other hand clutching at her dress. They would hear, from within, the sound, like an animal's low feral growl and fingernails clutching and dragging themselves down the paneled wall.

She remembered the nights when she had awakened to hear him in the hall beyond her door, calling out for Cora in a voice she didn't recognize. She would see the light from his candle pass under the door beyond her sitting room and would hold her breath, trembling and waiting for his steps to recede.

Once, as a child, she had made the mistake of opening the door, stepping out into the hall and responding to him. He had stood motionless, his back to her. Slowly he had turned and what she had seen in his eyes had sucked the breath from her lungs. She had collapsed. But Berend had come, Lina close behind him. They had gripped Edgar fast while Lina held a thick, acrid sponge over his mouth.

A slow creak broke her dark reverie, clutching Clara's heart in its icy grip. Something moved above them. Berend stood in the pulpit, his hazel eyes boring into her. Lina regarded his entrance without comment. After a minute or two, he descended the stairs to the altar then passed in front of the pew where they sat. He stopped beside the doorway and turned to watch them. Clara's shoulders slumped.

"We could all have done more," Lina added. "Whatever his flaws may have been, he was always better than I ever was. Than any of us. We should all pray for his forgiveness."

Clara's head swung toward her grandmother, her eyes wide, her mouth open. But Lina had retreated into prayer again—this time with her eyes open, gazing up at the cross, her lips moving—and didn't notice. Clara felt the heat spreading throughout her body, her hands clenching the edge of the pew. She looked up at the source of her grandmother's gaze and the bile rose in her throat. She edged out of the pew.

"Clara." Her grandmother's voice was sharp, insistent. "I wish you to remain with me and pray a while longer."

"I'm tired. I wish to return to the drawing room."

"If you're so tired, dear, Berend will see you back to your room."

Berend leaned against the wall beside the door, his eyes fixed upon her, his jaw set beneath his salt-and-pepper beard.

"I'd like to see my mother," she mumbled.

Lina sighed. "Your mother is, undoubtedly, engaged in satiating our guests with all the gossip they can possibly consume. The last thing you need is to be drawn into that maelstrom. You will remain here with me or you will return to your rooms."

When Clara stood, impassive, Lina entreated her, "Wouldn't you like to rest here, in the presence of the Lord?"

Clara looked up at the crucifix. In the place of Christ, her father hung, blood dripping from his mouth, his nose, ears; his eyes set on her. She shuddered and stumbled to the door. Berend took her arm, his fingers like a vise, and led her from the chapel.

Chapter Six

The day of the funeral, Clara awoke to a horrible but inscrutable premonition. A shroud of fog clung to the window. Her jaw and neck felt tight, as if she had ground her teeth all night. Sweat covered her body. Clara threw back the heavy coverlet and lay in the chill, drafty room, reaching for the tail end of her dream.

Her father had come to her and had stooped over her bed watching her. His face, at first warm and paternal, had dissolved, leaving the rest of his body leaning over her. When a new face had emerged in its place, she had struggled to move, had fought to cry out. But her mouth had been sealed shut, her body paralyzed. She had awakened with a start to the sound of a thud hitting her window.

She had looked forward to this day as one looks forward to the amputation of a gangrenous limb. She hoped it would purge her body of its diseased memories. She hoped she would finally be able to lay to rest not just her tormented father but also the anxiety and tension that hung in the air. Most of all, she hoped this day would mark a divide between the past and the future.

Yet the premonition grew.

The family and guests who had remained for the graveside ceremony gathered for a somber breakfast. All their prior attempts at jovial reminiscing had ceased. Instead, they sat and stood around the dining room in various states of hushed lethargy. Lamps burned throughout the space, suffusing it with a smoky glow. Outside, the arms of a slender beech tree tapped intermittently at the window.

Aunt Lotte sat in a high-backed chair, a plate of barely eaten fancy bread resting in the windowsill beside her. Horst sat on one side of the table, smoking quietly, a glass of brandy already before him. Her grandmother, at the head of the table, leaned forward in her chair, her shoulders hunched in defeat. Her mother picked at the eggs on her toast, doing more to smear it into a formless mass than actually eat it.

As Clara entered the room, they looked up at her in surprised silence. She took in the lifeless scene and, her appetite extinguished, settled into a chair opposite Lotte. Outside the window, the crooked form of a raven lay on the gravel path, its wing bent back from its body, one beady eye fixed on her.

Eventually the priest arrived, and they arose as one, following the six men carrying the casket. The front door stood open, a laurel wreath tied with a black ribbon, hanging above the knocker. They emerged from the house beneath a dripping, leaden sky. The wind on her face, even the persistent drizzle, should have felt like a relief to Clara who hadn't felt the earth beneath her feet in weeks. Instead the sky hung, oppressive. The rain spat in her face, sparking her skin like small, jagged rocks.

Much of the ceremony went by in a haze. They passed through the iron gates of the family cemetery and stood beneath a large oak tree, its leaves heaped in thick soggy piles on the ground, listening to the funeral rites. Servants held umbrellas over their heads, but the rain drove in sideways, shifting with the wind. Clara's feet and gown were soon drenched below the waist.

Her grandmother cried quietly, a handkerchief clutched in her hand. Her mother's mouth remained fixed, stoic, her dry eyes impressing on Clara the likeness of a tragic Greek heroine. Aunt Lotte sobbed quietly. Uncle Horst held her close under his arm, his long dark mustache dripping water.

At the sight of Lotte, Clara felt tears gather in her eyes, filling her with a deep sense of shame. Part of her mourned the loss of her only father, one who, in his healthy and lucid states had loved her. But the other half of her felt relief as at the silencing of an unassailable foe. She told herself her relief was for his anguish and constant seeking, his restless discontent. Still, guilt warred within her.

When the priest issued the last amen and the pallbearers lifted the coffin, her mother gestured to her and gathered Clara's arm within her own. They followed her grandmother up the wide stairs and into the mausoleum where a hole in the marble wall gaped open, waiting to swallow Edgar in death. Most of the guests remained outside, huddled under their umbrellas.

Rain ran off the coffin and streamed in rivulets on the shining, white-veined floors. Clara focused on her feet as they slid along the slick surface. Ahead of her, a creak. Someone gasped. An instant later, Horst's feet flew out from under him and his side of the casket tipped over. The weight unsettled the group. The corner of the heavy box slammed into the marble floor, cracking the slab. Everyone froze in mute shock.

A sigh issued from the coffin.

Clara backed away until she stood against the wall. Her grandmother clutched her handkerchief to her chest, her face pale, her mouth trembling. Lotte froze, her eyes large. Horst rose on one knee, then the other, his face red with embarrassment. The others stared at the box in horror.

"Edgar!" Her grandmother's voice reverberated against the marble. She rushed forward, her feet nearly flying out from under her. The priest caught her and held her upright.

"No. No Frau Willenheim. I'm sorry. It's..." He lowered his voice. "It's an effect of death. Air may be released after the fact."

But Lina wouldn't listen. She shoved her way between Horst and Werner and clutched at the locks on the coffin.

"Frau Willenheim, I really must entreat you not to..." He looked to be on the verge of pulling her back, then seemed to recall himself.

It was no use. "He's trying to speak to us," she implored, her eyes savagely hopeful. Hagan ran back to the house to retrieve the coffin's keys from the library.

The family and their closest guests waited within the small building, water dripping off their clothes and pooling on the floor. The building filled with a musty smell of bodies and the odor of their breaths. Clara felt lightheaded and weak, her stomach sick despite her morning fast.

When Hagan returned with the keys, Lina tore them from his grip. Her hands shook as she strove to open each lock. Eventually the last one sprang free with a heavy, resounding clang. For a minute she struggled to lift the lid alone, but then a couple of the men stooped beside her and pressed the top back.

There, resting in the interior, lay Edgar in a state different from life, but also apart from death. His mouth had opened just barely, as if he were about to form a word, and for a minute they all hovered, waiting. Clara's heart beat rapidly and her head throbbed.

Lina sank down on the muddy wet floor and grasped Edgar's dry lifeless hand in hers. "Tell me. What is it? I'm listening, love," she begged him over and over. But he remained where he was, caught in limbo.

Eventually the men were able to pry her away and seat her on a bench along the wall. The priest struggled to explain, once more, the phenomena of gas released from a body after death. The men hurriedly worked to secure the coffin then transport it, without ceremony, to its resting place in the far wall. They acted as if the event were nothing more than a dreadful accident rather than a harbinger of impending evil.

By the time the family emerged from the mausoleum, most of the other guests already had returned to the house. Helene and Horst, supporting Lina's weakened body, made their way down the slick steps to the sodden ground.

As they did, Clara caught a sudden movement out of the corner of her eye. Two men approached them. The taller one, in his early forties, was heavyset, with ample sideburns. The shorter one had a round face and wind-reddened cheeks. He bore a small black mustache as if in a desperate attempt to appear older and wiser.

The entire family stopped and turned, watching them draw near. The older man bowed to Lina, his hat in his hand, and cleared his throat.

"Gnädige Frau, perhaps you will recall our recent acquaintance, Chief Inspector Dressler. And my associate, Inspector Metz. I apologize for the unpleasant events that require our presence at such a time. But alas, we have a most urgent matter to discuss with you."

Lina stared at them wordlessly, her eyes glazed in confusion. The man hesitated, reluctant to continue without invitation.

"You see, it has come to our attention that there were extenuating circumstances in the matter of your son's death. Circumstances we simply cannot ignore."

"Circumstances," Lina echoed faintly.

"Yes, circumstances that point to something of a nefarious intent."

When Lina failed to comment, the younger man broke in: "Foul play...Gnädige Frau," he added after the fact, as if to soften his words.

They stood watching her as Lina struggled to understand.

"What are you saying? Foul play?"

Chief Inspector Dressler measured his words. "At first glance, I do admit all the signs pointed to either suicide or an accident. However, I regret to inform you that other, overriding indicators have come to light."

Lina gasped. "What are you saying?"

"Well"—Dressler licked his lips before continuing—"we have every reason to believe your son was murdered."

The sound of the rain dripping onto the bed of decaying oak leaves filled the vacuous silence.

"Murdered?" Lina whispered.

"Yes. I'm terribly sorry. We came as soon as we could."

Horst stepped up and addressed Dressler on Lina's behalf. "I'm afraid your timing is most inconvenient. Would it be possible to return to the house with us to discuss this matter further?"

"Of course." Dressler's hand played with the brim of his hat, turning it in a circle. "We simply meant to convey the extreme urgency of the matter, which is receiving all our attention."

"We've just interred Herr Willenheim," Horst explained.

"I see." Dressler replied. "But as you may have inferred, the matter doesn't end with Herr Willenheim. If he was murdered, we have a murderer on the loose."

For a moment Lina stared at him. Then she began to sway, and had Horst and Inspector Metz not caught her, she would have fallen.

Clara understood her premonition. In one morning's sequence of events—her dream, the voice from beyond the grave, and now this, a charge of murder—her hopes of closure fell to the ground and shattered in irreconcilable pieces.

Chapter Seven

"Murder," Lina murmured through dry lips. She leaned back on a sofa in the morning room, looking peaked and distressed but otherwise alert. Outside the rain had increased. Heavy cloud cover outlined in white light bathed her face in alternating shades of white and black. Her eyes were fixed on Chief Inspector Dressler.

Clara stood as close to the fireplace as she dared. The water ran off her dress, soaking the carpet; still, she shivered violently. Hagan stood against the opposite wall, clutching the smelling salts in his long bone-white fingers, staring at her. His wide lips were drawn down in a scowl, his eyes deep-set beneath heavy brows. The storm, with its white knife, cut his pale face into harsh, angular lines underscored in navy shadows and a sickly, violet hue. Clara looked away from him.

"I'm sure there must be a mistake," Helene suggested. "My husband had no enemies."

"It isn't possible," Lina broke in hoarsely. "Simply isn't possible. I don't know a man alive who didn't want to be him. Or a woman who didn't want to be with him."

"Undoubtedly, Gnädige Frau. Undoubtedly. But you see, we simply cannot ignore the evidence," Dressler reiterated.

"Evidence?" Lotte asked.

"Yes, certain 'indicators' of foul play. We have evidence that Edgar died with a fair amount of poison in his system."

"Poison?" Lotte whispered, her eyes wide.

The floor beneath Clara's feet trembled and quaked. She held onto the mantel's corbel to steady herself. A rumble reverberated through the floor then passed out of the room. As it faded, the walls around her creaked and settled. Jutta slipped into the room and stood to one side, watching the proceedings. Helene glanced up at her and nodded faintly.

Dressler cast a glance at his associate Metz, as if seeking reinforcement. "In a case such as this, when the surgeon examines the—pardon me—the body, he looks for signs of anything out of the ordinary."

"Certainly falling from the roof of a house is out of the ordinary." Lina's tone suggested this was the end of the matter.

"True. Certainly true. And there are, in the case of a fall, particular signs of trauma. However, in this case, the body also displayed indications of poison—dilated pupils, a swollen tongue, and unnaturally red skin, accompanied by a macular rash. And from the looks of it, it was most likely a chronic ingestion, rather than an acute instance."

"Why weren't these signs noticed earlier?" Lotte asked.

Inspector Metz colored deeply and licked his lips. Clara's lip curled as she watched his pointed tongue circle his small, red mouth.

Dressler cleared his throat and nodded several times before responding. "It is unfortunate. Terribly unfortunate. We have only recently discovered a breach within our surgeon's practice. I assure you, we are doing everything to rectify what has come to light."

"What are you saying?" Lina snapped.

"It appears our surgeon was compromised. It seems he accepted substantial payment above and beyond a reasonable salary. Given that and the falsified records, we can only assume someone went to great measures to cover up the nature of the death."

"Who would do such a thing?" Helene asked.

"That's exactly what we intend to determine. If you'll allow me..."

Inspector Metz pulled out and consulted a small notebook from his interior breast pocket. "The poison stems from '*Hyoscyamus niger.*'"

"Never heard of it." Lina scoffed at him, her eyes narrowing to dark slits.

Metz flipped back and forth through the small pages. "Goes by...the name...*henbane.*"

Helene exhaled slowly. "Oh." Everyone turned to look at her. She looked at Lina, whispered, "The sponge." When Lina offered no response, she continued. "Inspector, you may not be aware that my husband was often unwell. His mind troubled him and he was...on occasion, unmanageable. In those states he was a danger. To himself."

Dressler retrieved a notebook and pencil from his own breast pocket and looked at her quizzically. "A danger in what way?"

"He was given to excesses," Lina said, her tone clipped, laced with warning.

"Is that so?" Dressler noted it, his pencil scratching the page in swift strokes. "Such as?"

Clara wondered what they had told him at the time of his death. Undoubtedly nothing. Best to circle the wagons, cut off all external inquiries. She pictured her mother and grandmother, their faces frozen in shock, declaring his death to be the greatest surprise rather than the inevitable. All of them had noticed her father's uncertain steps, his feverish expression, the way his clothes had hung on him rather than clinging to his chest.

Clara recalled a night five years prior. She had been asleep when something had roused her. The sound of running, or perhaps it had been shouts from outside her window. A cry of alarm from the servants had sounded throughout the house. *The stables were in flames; the stable master called for help.* Over the orchards to the west, the glowing incineration mingled with the sunset. Afterward, tales of Edgar, standing in the midst of it all. Laughing. If Berend hadn't arrived in time, he would have burned to death. As it was, several horses, including his most prized black stallion, and the stable master perished. Most of the remaining horses were subsequently sold.

"There was his tendency to walk about the roof," Helene said.

That broke the Chief Inspector from his daze. He flipped back through his notes and rubbed his chin as he read. "Yes. Yes, I recall. You mentioned it was not unprecedented for him to be on the roof, in the middle of the night."

"That is correct. Especially in the central portion where it's flat."

"Hmmm. All right. But how does that relate to the hyo...the henbane?"

"Henbane is just one ingredient in the soporific we administered."

"A soporific?" Dressler asked, notating it in his notebook.

"It's a sponge. An anesthetic. A sedative."

"You administered this 'sponge' to Edgar?" Dressler looked at her, his pencil poised above the page.

"Yes." Helene picked at a loose thread on the arm of the chair. "The mixture is prepared and then soaked into a sponge. When applied to the patient, he loses consciousness. Temporarily. Of course." She appeared flustered to hear the words spoken out loud.

"When Edgar is in one of his states, there's really nothing we can do other than to induce sleep and restrain him until he awakens restored." Lina's voice rose in aggravation.

"I see," Dressler muttered. "And when he awakens, is he restored?"

"Yes." Lina and Helene exchanged a glance but said nothing further.

"Who administers the sponge?"

"I do," Lina said. "Berend helps me. And then Edgar rests until he is himself again."

"Where do you obtain it?" Dressler asked.

"Obtain what?"

"The sponge. This sedative that you use. From whom or from where do you obtain it?"

"I prepare it," Helene said.

"You do?" Dressler paused and scratched his neck where the collar of his shirt pinched at the skin. But then his eyes grew wide. "But of course." He looked at Helene. "Your father. This is all becoming quite clear." He snapped the notebook closed. "If you don't mind, we will need to take a look at your supplies and the sedatives you have on hand. We'll also need a written description of your methods and the various ingredients used. But in the meantime, I believe I only have one final question: did you administer any of this sedative on the day of his death?"

"No. We most certainly did not," Lina said, then softened her words. "If we had, this might have been avoided."

Dressler slipped the notebook and pencil back in his pocket, picked up his hat from a small round table near the sofa, and bowed lightly to Lina and the other family members. "This certainly casts new light on the situation."

He paused as if something still perplexed him; then his face smoothed over and he continued. "I deeply regret this inconvenience. Particularly at such a sensitive time. However, you must understand, given the symptoms and the significance of the person in the matter, there was, regrettably, no way to disregard the findings."

"Of course," Helene said. "Of course. We would hardly expect you to overlook a matter of such importance."

Her face bore every indication of deep concern and relief mingled with submission, but as the inspector turned back to Lina and Lotte, Clara caught a look of understanding pass between her mother and Jutta.

Chapter Eight

By the time Clara returned to her rooms, her skin felt raw and exposed. She stood in front of the bathroom mirror, watching Jutta circle around her. The girl unlaced the bodice and peeled it away along with her skirt, its hem caked in mud. Beneath it, her underclothes, heavy with water and grit, clung to and abraded her skin.

After she had cast them all aside and pulled on a clean, dry day dress, she sighed deeply. It felt like it had been days, rather than hours, since she had awakened with such a sense of impending doom. The terrifying wait, then the funeral. The procession into the mouth of the grave, followed by the breath from the coffin. Then out again, into the hands of the chief inspector, who scrutinized them all with skepticism and suspicion.

The rain struck her windowpanes like hyssop casting an absolution just beyond her reach. She curled up in an armchair and drew her feet up beside her. The flame licked at the underside of a fresh log, sending out wisps of heat.

It should have been soothing, but in the soft firelight, she saw the image of her father's corpse, his mouth partly open. And her grandmother crouched beside him, begging him to speak. The nauseating musty air. The mud streaking the white marble floors. She shivered.

"Are you still cold, Fräulein?" Jutta paused her relentless tidying and waited beside Clara's chair.

"No. No, just tired."

Jutta crossed to the other chair and stood beside it, following Clara's gaze to the rising fire. Her silence didn't fool Clara. She wouldn't have been surprised to hear that all the servants already knew every detail of the funeral. Her grandmother said gossip traveled faster among household staff than cholera in a tribal village.

Clara's focus took in the girl's wary stance and realization struck her. There, not five feet away, lay the stone fireplace surround. She flushed. It had been a waste, but what could she have done? Jutta would have tried to stop her. *Had* tried to stop her.

Instead of Berend, the faces of the two men filled her mind. Dressler with his heavy sideburns and freckled fingers, covered in hair. Metz with his beady eyes and constantly flicking tongue. She looked at Jutta's expectant face. "Do you ever wonder whether someone, if he hadn't died, at least not in the way that he did, whether he would have died anyway?"

"That he was destined to die at that point?"

"Yes."

"I think everything happens for a reason. That it wouldn't have really happened any other way." Jutta eyed her carefully.

"What if the person chooses to do something different? At the last moment?"

"Maybe that's what was meant to be. No one ever has the chance to make two choices at the same time. Does he? And he can't go back. So what he chooses—even if we think he's changing his mind, or going a different way—may be the only thing he ever would have done."

"So my father. Say he hadn't...fallen...would he still have died? Or was he meant to fall?"

Jutta focused intensely on the wood parquet floor edging the fireplace, as if reluctant to meet Clara's eyes. Or answer her question. "Did you know my father died during the revolution?"

The question shook Clara from her present frame of mind. "No."

"He and his brother sympathized with the students' constitutional demands. They knew many of the demonstrators and stood by them. But it cost them their lives. I was an infant at the time, so, unlike you, I never knew him. Everything I know came from my mother's stories about him. After his death, she and I went to live with his parents, my grandparents."

Clara wanted to ask her whether she thought it had been his time to die, but the words sounded horribly insensitive. Clara frowned. "Do they know who killed him?"

"Oh, yes. It was the emperor's men."

"Oh."

"Exactly. There was never anything anyone could do. That's what really affected my grandmother the most. The horrible sense of injustice. Both sons gone in one day."

"What did she do?"

"She became stronger. Her faith grew."

"Why would it?" Clara's body, warm from the fire's heat, filled with a strange discordant chill.

"I think she came to the same conclusion you're suggesting: that when horrible things happen, it's for a reason. That in some way, it had to be. Though we may never understand why in this life."

"But he was murdered."

Jutta just shrugged and smiled sadly. "She always said, '*Liebchen*, we wait for justice.' I don't think she could have said that before she lost them."

"She thinks God will reunite them in heaven?"

Jutta shook her head. "Well, yes. But the justice she waits for is that God will hold his murderers guilty and dole out the punishment they deserve. That there will be a day when they'll answer for their crimes."

"Oh." Clara's nail, torn off at the quick, had begun to bleed. She held it to her mouth, tasting the warm blood. "How do you know?"

"I don't know, in a scientific sense. But I believe it's true."

"That seems silly."

"Is it?"

"She's waiting for a fairy tale. For someone else to pursue justice on her behalf."

"What else can she do?" Jutta countered.

Clara's eyes swept the room. The corners and edges pressed in around her. There was nothing safe she could say. After all, her situation and that of Jutta's mother were terribly different; her mother's justice stood apart from her, separated by an army, a family, a standing. Jutta rose and resumed her work polishing the wooden furniture. At some point she paused and approached the chair again.

"It's like your grandfather."

"Conrad?" Clara asked.

"No. Your mother's father. I've heard he practically detached himself from the entirety of society. He didn't attend balls or summer galas. He didn't hunt or shoot. Instead he spent all his adult years laboring over his studies. Your mother sometimes alludes to his colleagues as being almost exclusively those who could aid him in his work. Instead of socializing with his own class and building up the value of his inheritance, he traveled and spent—from what I've heard—a considerable portion of his estate to uncover ways to treat the suffering and the ill."

Clara's mind spun. She always had pictured her maternal grandfather as a brilliant but misanthropic scientist, but Jutta had described him as something else entirely. Clara had never considered what he *hadn't* done, let alone the idea that perhaps he would have wanted those things.

"He spent many years away from the comforts of home in places that were foreign to his experience, where disease was more prevalent. And it cost him. His wife and his son, your uncle."

"That's true," Clara said softly. Her maternal grandmother and her mother's brother had died of typhoid fever somewhere in India.

"I don't know whether he uncovered any new medicinal sources, or if anyone's life was saved because of his work. Still, your mother describes him as one who was characterized by constant joy. And peace. As if his life, regardless of the suffering, was full of purpose and meaning. He must have believed in his work. He must have had a reason for what he did. Something that made the sacrifice worthwhile. Or gave him hope in some way."

Clara picked at another of her cuticles absentmindedly. She couldn't have said what any of their sacrifices had to do with her. Instead she turned her eyes to the misty, rainswept afternoon beyond the window. She no longer felt certain of her impending freedom. The heat from the fire stifled her. The walls and ceiling of her room gathered in around her, as if the house squeezed her in its selfish clutch.

After Jutta left, Clara settled into the window seat behind the drawn curtain. The ghost of her reflection stared at her from the glass. Beyond lay the southern gardens, the wrong direction.

She intended to go north. Away from all of her family, her history, her father. Months ago she had found a leather traveling bag in one of the house's storage rooms and had sewn a concealed pocket into the bottom of its interior. Within that she had hidden money and jewels that she had taken from the family's collection. Many were her own items. Others were pieces her mother and grandmother never used but were undoubtedly worth a great deal. With these Clara planned to escape.

They owed her that much and more.

Chapter Nine

"How will we escape notice?" Jan fidgeted on the opposite seat of the carriage, his expression lit with excitement.

"By remaining in the foreground. So close to those who are looking that they can't see us."

"Like an elk within a herd?"

"That's right. Or a single fish within a school. By carefully assimilating, hopefully we will blend in so perfectly that our presence is disguised."

"Hmm. In plain sight." Jan sounded delighted with the idea.

"I must remind you these people are extremely dangerous. More so than we had suspected. They will do anything to conceal their activities."

The carriage jolted along the road, the sound of the wheels squelching through the mud and muck as the wind buffeted the small vehicle. For a time both men sat lost in thought.

"It seems like a setback, though. Edgar's death," Jan said.

"Perhaps," Richter conceded. "Perhaps it is."

"He might have provided us with so much. And now...the trail is dead, with him."

"I don't know. If even half of what our source indicated is true, then it's only a matter of time before someone reveals his hand. We'll have to stay close to the situation, see who the players are, what they want most. And what they have to lose."

"All while steering clear of local law enforcement."

"Absolutely. We'll have to appear entirely disinterested in what they're doing for this to work. But..."

"What?"

"It's possible that we can look farther afield, where loyalties aren't quite so certain. But in the meantime, we're going straight into the heart of the matter."

"We are?"

"*I* am. You are going to hang back. I need you to remain inconspicuous for the time being. Until we see how this plays out and what our next course of action is. If there's one thing I've learned it's that everyone distrusts the man lurking in the bushes at night, but few question the one who knocks at midday." *At least that's what I'm counting on.* "If anything, Edgar's death may just be the thing we need. What better time for distant, scarcely remembered acquaintances to appear than after a death? Any other time might be infinitely more suspicious."

"I suppose that's true."

"Besides, who can question my association with the deceased? No one but the deceased."

"And he isn't talking."

"Let's hope not."

Chapter Ten

*S*he displays no signs of guilt, though that hardly means anything. Lina regarded Helene for a moment, her presence still unnoticed. Her daughter-in-law leaned over her crude workbench, a brush in hand, filling in the color of a sickly-looking flower in her notebook. Its petals were a dirty yellow, stained with heavy veining. The room, which had once been a larder that abutted the kitchens, was characteristically dark, with two small windows set so deep in the stone walls that they admitted little light or warmth. Several candles stood about the space, suffusing it with a hazy glow. The interior wall was lined with shelves, the exterior one with a long narrow table, all of which were covered in bottles and jars. At the far end of the room an open hearth, added in recent years, stood dark, scraped clean of ashes. Lina shuddered.

"Hello, Mother." Helene glanced up from her work.

Lina pressed forward and, with a thud, dropped a heavy book of Bavarian legal history on the end of the workbench.

"What's this?"

"Oh, just an old book of Conrad's." Lina glanced down to where the book lay with torn bits of paper protruding from the edge closest to Helene. "I thought it might be wise to know more about our legal system. In light of yesterday's unpleasant proceedings."

"Hmm."

"For example, did you know that even after a person's death is ruled to be an accident, a case can be made against certain parties, indicting them of murder?"

"I suppose that would be the case." Helene bent her head lower over her drawing.

Lina frowned. *She's unflappable. Definitely guilty.*

The sound of a woman's step, the light scraping lilt of her shoes against the stone floors in the kitchen, drew their attention. Jutta appeared around the edge of the doorway. Her eyes took in the two women, and then, seeing Lina, she blanched and seemed about to withdraw.

"Well, what is it?" Lina prodded her.

"Frau Willenheim." Jutta reached into the pocket in her dress and withdrew a recognizable yellow envelope. She stepped forward to pass it to Helene. Instead, Lina snatched it out of her hand and tore into it, extracting the telegram within. It consisted of only one line.

Fortune sends the best she can bear.

Lina turned it over, knowing the back would be blank. She read the note a second time. "I can't make any sense of this." She handed the note to Helene, who scanned it and set it aside with a shrug.

"Most likely someone who heard and means to send his good intentions."

"So oddly put, though." Lina logged a mental note to consider it later. *Oddly put indeed. And she doesn't even flinch. She's clearly up to something.*

"That will be all, Jutta. Thank you." Helene nodded to the girl, who swiveled on her toes and hurried out of the room.

When several minutes had passed and Helene showed no interest in resuming their prior conversation, Lina tried again. "It might be wise to take down your laboratory."

"You think so?" Helene asked. She hardly seemed to register what Lina said.

"Perhaps. You never know. What with the inspectors snooping around and digging into everything."

"I suppose," Helene said. "But they already know. They took samples, verified our methods. At this point it seems a bit late for that. Besides which, wouldn't that appear to be an admission of guilt?"

"Oh. I would never suggest that. We don't have anything to hide."

Helene looked up briefly and smiled. "Of course not. Besides, I think you're right. Edgar's death was an accident."

Lina frowned and narrowed her eyes. "Yes. I've never suggested anything else. It's just that, despite how careful we might be…I'm sure we never considered—I certainly never did—that we were keeping a poison in our home. Regardless of its medicinal purposes."

"No," Helene responded ambiguously.

"It's occurred to me, though, that perhaps it isn't wise to keep such things around where they might become something of a liability. After all, some of the ingredients *are* potentially lethal."

"That's true." Helene paused and regarded Lina. "If it makes you feel better, I'd be happy to dispose of anything toxic, including the sponges I have on hand."

Lina watched her critically. Helene's face was perfectly unemotional —guileless even.

"If we want those ingredients again at some point—for medicinal purposes—we can always reacquire them." Helene seemed to give it additional consideration as if she were humoring Lina, then resumed her painting, adding shading to a long green tubular branch.

Lina's eyes narrowed at Helene's indifference to the subject matter. But then her temperature began to rise. She shifted uncomfortably from foot to foot. Sometimes, in her intense focus on the manner of Edgar's death, she forgot it was her son, her favorite child, who was the silent subject of her investigation. She had just buried her very reason for living. Her need to know why she had lost him was also a need to know how she could, in some way, attempt to cancel out his death.

They had flirted with danger in so many ways; this time was one too many, and Edgar had paid the price for it. But of course, everything she had done had been to protect him: his reputation, his career, his precarious emotional balance. Half of her distrusted her prior assurance of the accident. The other half was resolute. Besides, what motive did Helene have? She always had desired to help Edgar, to care for him; she was infinitely tolerant of his wild mood swings and his erratic habits.

"I think you're right." Helene's voice cut through the silence. Lina tensed. "If this had been a murder...if we did have a poisoner among us —not that either of us would believe that—it's altogether possible the ingredients could be used against someone else. One of us." Helene's blue eyes were round with apprehension.

"Against us?" Lina was taken aback at the idea. "Why, that's ridiculous. Who could possibly hope to get away with the same crime twice?"

Helene leaned forward and dropped her voice as if others were in the room. "I don't know. But now that you mention it, it certainly is a cause for concern. After all, who on earth would have wanted my poor husband dead?" She shook her head, her eyes moist. "If someone had done that to Edgar, just think what he could do to me. Or you!"

Lina's mouth dropped open, speechless. Never had she suspected there was any danger to herself. Yet Helene had spoken truly. Until they knew why someone had wanted to harm Edgar, there was no way to guarantee that such a fate wouldn't befall any of them.

Chapter Eleven

The fox didn't stand a chance. At least that's what the artist had intended to portray. Richter stood, hands in his pockets, gazing at the oil painting. A fox cringed in a small clearing, encircled by snarling hounds, their jaws gaping and dripping blood. In the distance, beyond the trees, hunters approached on horseback. Their expressions bore the entitled satisfaction of those who know they are the hounds in a world of foxes.

"Hmm." Richter grunted to himself. He turned back to survey the ornate room. Above a chair rail of intricate paneling, gilded about the edges, the walls were papered in what appeared to be a light-green floral brocade. As he ran his fingers across the surface, his skin felt rough against the fine, embossed surface. Yes, silk. Chairs and sofas in a similar fabric littered the room. None were used on a regular basis; he was certain of that. It wasn't the presence of dust that indicated as much; in fact, the furniture was impeccably clean. Rather, it was a smell that lingered in the air: one of neglect and cavalier indifference. Like mold unabated.

It was that smell that set the tone for him. There was always something, usually a singular item or impression: a child's toy crushed and lying in a corner; a woman's necklace snagged and hanging from a chair; the acrid scent of rotten meat; a muddy footprint just inside a second-floor bedroom window. That one thing resonated in his mind, like a chord struck, speaking of what had been and laying out before him what he would discover. Invariably the entire truth would cluster around that one central impression.

"Very interesting..." He smoothed his mustache as he considered it.

"*What* is interesting?" A woman's voice, sharp and commanding, preceded her entry into the room. Richter turned toward her approach. Frau Willenheim was striking in the way that defensive and venomous creatures often are. Her light-olive skin was unmarked by wrinkles or spots. She bore a gravitas that gave to her features a natural elegance that defied any single element or particular beauty. Yet her dark eyes called to mind the unblinking gaze of a cobra, coiled in wait.

Richter assumed an expression of refined and formal confidence as he stepped toward her, cutting off her approach. "Karl von Moltstedt."

He had done this for too long. His approach was flawlessly executed —the lazy, affected air of one who could no longer be impressed by anything or anyone; who had no concerns that exceeded his bank account; yet who managed to extend the proper expression and word at each required moment. Immediately Lina seemed to revoke her clipped tone, as if questioning her initial impression.

"Your painting..." He pointed, striking a casual stance. At Lina's silent confusion, he added, "It's terribly interesting. The vantage point. I have a similar one, but it's told from the perspective of the hunter. Whereas this one..." He waited for Lina to take the bait.

"Of course." She smiled a cruel, half grin. "The hounds. The moment before their victory is sealed." When Richter extended his arm, she tucked her hand under it and allowed him to lead her to a sofa. "I've always liked that one as well."

"Yet the fox is so crafty and cunning," Richter suggested.

"He's no match for the hounds, especially when they are unified in purpose."

"Indeed," Richter echoed, smiling. He leaned back on the opposite side of the sofa, extending an arm across the back.

"Jutta mentioned your association with my son."

"Of course. Yes, of course. I was so sorry to receive the news. I came as quickly as I could, but you see, my business often keeps me far from here. And alas, I wasn't able to be here sooner. My deepest regrets."

"Thank you." Smiling, she leaned toward him slightly in a manner that invited further comment.

"You see, your son and I were only occasional acquaintances. I'm sure you know his business often took him to places such as Paris and Berlin." Lina nodded in affirmation. "But he made such an impact on my colleagues and me. He was quite remarkable. As was your late husband, Conrad. I so enjoyed the few occasions we had to meet and dine together. Always such a pleasure."

Lina's face beamed with pride.

"When I heard..." He shook his head. "How devastating. Well, I knew I had to come offer you my condolences, as belated as they may be."

Lina's expression grew warm and inclusive. "What business are you in?"

While Richter explained his cover to her—that he was the head of a Prussian organization concerned with sensitive legal matters for many powerful entities and individuals—he watched her face. The story was close to the truth, close enough to be corroborated, when necessary, but far enough that he was able to distance himself from the suspicion that would have accompanied him as a member of Prussian law enforcement. Nonetheless, as he spoke, Lina's lips pursed, forming small lines that aged her considerably. Her eyes grew darker and guarded. It told him a great deal without the need to ask a single question.

"You must have other close relationships—acquaintances, associates of Edgar's—with whom I may have also done business." He waved a hand in grand gesture as if to indicate the breadth of his influence.

"Oh, I doubt that." Lina raised her eyebrows and looked down into her lap where she fidgeted with the heavy rings that adorned many of her fingers. "Most of Edgar's associates have little use for that side of the world."

"Prussia, you mean." Richter spoke the implied insult for her. "I think you'd be surprised. After all, your husband and son were in Berlin often enough." He went on to list a number of notable persons with whom she would certainly *not* have any connections but whose names she likely would know. As he spoke, casually flaunting his associations as if they were of no significance other than perhaps a shared affiliation, he watched her face.

In the tensing of her eyebrows, the line that formed between them and the clenching of her jaw, he read a reticence to acknowledge any of Prussia's leadership as deserving of her mention. Yet, in the uncertainty and unsteady gaze in her eyes, accompanied by her endless twisting of her rings, he could clearly discern a war in her mind. She was impressed, impressed enough as to be uncertain whether these connections might be of any use to her. And yet wary.

If Richter's source had spoken truthfully, she was weighing the benefits that such alliances might bring her. Yet there was always a risk. As he watched her, Richter was nearly certain his information was true. Lina was inextricably entwined in a web that required a constant balance of incentives and intimidation. To threaten that balance by including new players would greatly increase the already substantial risk. And yet, the potential gain...

He decided to meet her play for play. "It's wise to form alliances before our regions are united. Those preexisting bonds are more likely to leave your interests intact." He left the implication open-ended, knowing she never would suspect he had any true insight into what her "interests" were, yet knowing full well that's where her attention would be.

"Intact? Bismarck is nothing but a fox in the henhouse," Lina scoffed, rising from the sofa. She strode to the window and stood with her back to him, gazing out at the gardens beyond.

He smiled faintly and stroked his mustache before replying. "You know what they say: 'The best defense against a fox in the henhouse is to bring out the hounds.'"

At that she barked a short, tense laugh and turned. Richter rose from the sofa and broke the ice. "Gnädige Frau, I've already taken up far too much of your time. My intention was solely to express my condolences. I'm very sorry for your loss."

"Thank you. I greatly appreciate your devotion to my son's

memory." Her smile was forced, yet she seemed to linger on the brink of further comment.

Best to leave that door open, Richter thought as he took up his hat. He held the hat aloft and glanced around the room. "I must say, your home is impressive. Some of these pieces"—he gestured to the art on the walls—"are the finest I've seen outside of the Altes. And the interior. Truly magnificent. Baroque, I believe. It calls to mind the works of Johann Lukas von Hildebrandt."

Lina's face lit up in admiration. "Astonishing. You know your architects. Of course this house predates him, but we've done much to incorporate his style in the central rooms."

"I confess he is one of my favorites," Richter confided.

"If you have time, I'd be happy to show you some of the highlights."

That's what I'm counting on, he thought as he followed her into the hall.

"Where did you find it?" Jan asked, incredulous.

"In the bushes." Richter whispered, conscious of their precarious location. Several floors below them, he heard the murmur of gathering diners. Outside darkness had fallen and a sporadic breeze whipped the thin curtains on either side of the open window.

They were in the upper room of an inn as far from Waldensee as was practical. If Richter could have, they would have stayed even farther away.

The floors creaked as Jan crossed the modest room, nearly clipping his head on the sloping eave. "Why didn't they find it before?" he asked. On the small table in the center of the room lay the curious find: a torn clump of fabric. It was wrinkled in a pattern that indicated it had been balled up, as if it had been clutched in a hand. Yet it had lain under a bush, coated in muddy rain water to the point of near nonrecognition.

"That's a very good question. Although I admit it was hardly obvious. And what with the weather being what it is...well, it was sheer luck that my visit coincided with some of the few dry hours since the incident."

As if on cue, a low rumble sounded in the distance. Richter strode to the window and pressed the sash down. The curtains fell limp.

Frau Willenheim had warmed to his numerous admirations of the estate as she had shown him about the ground floor. It had been easy to suggest a brief tour about the well-manicured gardens. Though they lay in the clutches of imminent winter, a structural integrity about them had intrigued him. So he had spoken truly when he had praised the combination of elegance and simplicity in their form.

If the sun hadn't struck the backside of a wafting cloud at just the precise angle, casting a faint beam of light on the portion of bushes beside the path, Richter undoubtedly would have missed it. Yet there it was: a shadowy suggestion of something apart from nature, a form that seemed both misplaced and oddly hued. For despite its generally muddy appearance, in places it gave off a subtle sheen of color. Later he had been able to double-back and retrieve the cloth.

Now it lay before them on the table, the subject of intense scrutiny: a mud-speckled swatch of burgundy fabric.

"How do we know it's important?" Jan asked.

"We don't," Richter admitted. "Yet I have a feeling it is." Years ago, at a younger age, he would have been reluctant to say such a thing, aware of how foolish and unreliable the statement seemed to be. But he had learned many things in as many years. One of them was that, though intuition wouldn't stand alone, it was often the carefully honed light that guided his path in the early stages of any investigation, when all paths appeared to be equally dark.

"And," he continued, "the proximity to the crime scene was uncanny."

The fabric had been entangled in the dirt and limbs between a beech hedge and the windows of a formal dining room. Just beyond, the gravel path where Edgar's body had lain still bore the faint signs of disturbance from the accident. The rocks were displaced in an unusual pattern, as if they had been knocked aside and not yet raked back into place. The only thing of which he was certain was that this piece of cloth held a story.

Now that he had it, however, he wasn't sure he wanted to hear the end of the tale.

"It appears to be from a woman's dress." Jan leaned over the table. A small lamp that stood beside him cast a reddish glow onto his face, elongating his features. He pointed to a portion of the encrusted fabric where the mud had dried and chipped away. "See here? It bears a faint pattern. Of a small bird or flower. Maybe both—I can't tell." He stood up straight and looked at Richter.

"Yes," the chief inspector responded reluctantly; he could see that as well.

"If it is associated with the incident, then that person had to have been with Edgar on the roof. Right before the fall."

"Hmmm."

"Perhaps someone tried to stop him from jumping. Or tried to stop someone from throwing him from the roof." Jan shrugged.

"It's possible. But unlikely. Anyone trying to stop him would have certainly said so in the process of the investigation. Yet the report indicates that no one was present when Edgar fell. To your other point, someone who tried to stop the murderer would have likely wound up with a similar fate. No, Jan. I think the truth is far simpler than that."

"Could it have been torn, perhaps after the incident or even beforehand? Then fallen to the ground? Could it be entirely unrelated?"

"It's possible." Richter held two fingers to his lips and studied the fabric as if, in its muddy depths, he would see the true sequence of events.

"Then how do you plan to determine which it is?"

"I don't."

"You don't?" Jan's mouth gaped open.

"No. At least not directly. The murder of one man—even one of such prominence as Herr Willenheim—is not our primary concern. The greatest threat to the emperor is most likely not this man's murderer."

"I see." Jan nodded, regarding the fabric again. "But then what about this?"

"I don't know yet. But something tells me it's significant. In the end, I suspect the truth will come out."

"What if the truth isn't something we want to know?"

Richter understood what Jan meant. There was something unsettling about the entire thing. Edgar's disturbing behavior, the family's potential involvement in darker circles. And now this fabric: it skewed his impression toward further troubled explanations.

"I always want to know the truth," he said, but wondered, for the first time in twenty-eight years of police work, if he truly understood the cost.

Chapter Twelve

Lina could no longer stand still, especially in the cold stale air of the mausoleum, her dress damp in places, drenched in others. Not without her insides shaking or her hands walking up and down her sides. She'd never been the kind of person anyone would call tranquil or content. She wasn't known to recline, her mind settled on some abstract idea, her gaze fixed on the falling snow beyond the window.

She had work to do. A family to run, a household to manage. Before Conrad had died, she had been busy entertaining his business associates and keeping up his connections throughout the region. After his death, she had still had purpose, direction, albeit a different one. But now she could hardly live with herself. Her skin felt claustrophobic. But where could she go? Where?

That morning she had awakened with a start, her head pounding, heart racing. She knew that something was wrong. Something the inspectors had said the day of the burial. Something that she had dreamed, but that had fled once she had awakened. She lay back and fought to remember what it was. Eventually she gave up. But as soon as she had Berend's attention, she asked him to schedule an urgent meeting with the two men. Now the four of them clustered together in the family tomb, discussing her suspicions.

"Feelings are notoriously unreliable, Gnädige Frau," Inspector Dressler said, his deferential tone barely masking his skepticism.

"Yet we suspected as much," Metz suggested.

Dressler shot him a silent warning. "We certainly don't want to discredit or overlook any crime that may have been committed. Or any evidence that may have arisen. But I fail to see what we have to suggest that such is the case. Other than this intense feeling you have."

"I wouldn't expect you to understand. He wasn't your son. But *I*... *I'm* his mother. I know when something isn't what it seems to be. Regardless of whatever evidence there may or may not be. You said it yourself: there were indications of foul play."

"That's true," Dressler admitted.

"And now I'm telling you those indications may not be so easily dismissed."

Lina's set jaw and the hard lines of her mouth and eyes warned the two men against arguing with her. Berend stood to the side, watching the proceedings.

"All right. I will agree with you that the circumstances surrounding Edgar's death raise many questions. Why an elegant, well-to-do man with a young family, no financial troubles, and many admiring associates would take his own life is beyond me. Notwithstanding his somewhat troubled mental state, it still seems questionable.

"And why a man with such a history of appearances on your roof— a roof that is, in that section of the house, entirely flat—would suddenly lose his bearings and tumble off the side, is also problematic. Yes, it's possible, but less likely than we would typically see in the case of an accident.

"And the question of the surgeon who appears to have accepted some sort of payment. A bribe per se. Although that's as of yet undetermined.

"Beyond that, there is the issue of the henbane in his system. That was, by far, the most inexplicable of all our questions. However, you've allayed our fears about that with your explanations of the..." He consulted his notebook briefly before resuming. "Ah yes, the 'soporific,' as you described it."

Lina regarded him with small dark eyes, her jaw working faintly as she clenched and unclenched it.

"I will say that, on examination of Frau Willenheim's *laboratory*, all did seem to be in order. We consulted an independent chemist who confirmed both her methods and the ingredients used. As far as we can tell, she is as you insisted: a very educated, highly competent young woman.

"Which brings us to the only remaining question: who would have wanted your son dead?"

Lina blanched in shock and confusion. The words, uttered so succinctly, sounded cold and callous. Yet wasn't that what she had wanted them to consider? That someone had in fact set out to murder her beloved Edgar?

"I suppose it would have to have been someone large enough to force him from the roof," she intoned, her mind working furiously.

"Never mind that," Dressler shook his head. "Motive first. Who would have had the motive? Who would have gained from Edgar's death?"

Lina sat on one of the stone benches and grew still, thinking intensely. Outside, the rain poured down, harder than it had for days. Inside, the room grew humid from the water evaporating off their wet clothing. Mingled with it, the stone walls of the mausoleum exhaled a cold shroud of death. She felt confused and lost and yet irritated as if a bitter weed grew within her soul, clawing and scratching for a full claim on her mind and affections.

"Remember," Dressler added, "if there was foul play, the murderer very likely would have used the concoctions from Helene's laboratory to dull Edgar's senses. So, if that's the case—and I'm not ready to suggest that it is—we would want to consider who has access to that laboratory."

"Everyone has access. The door has no lock and it's off the kitchens. Any member of the family or the household staff knows it's there. And any outsider would have little difficulty accessing it. The staff come and go by the servants' entrance day and night." Lina seemed dismayed and lost by the idea. "Maybe someone broke into the house for that purpose."

Dressler laid his hand on his sideburn and considered the idea. "It's unlikely. We found no sign of a break-in. All the doors and windows, including their locks, were in place. It's far more likely the foul play originated much closer to home."

"Why would you suggest that?" Lina clipped, glaring at him. "I can't think of a single person who knew Edgar who would have wanted him dead. He was dearly loved. Dearly." Her eyes filled with tears, flooding her with shame. She averted her face, blinked back the tears, and resumed her pacing.

"I'm certain that was the case. However, it stands to reason that someone—assuming there was in fact foul play, as you firmly believe—accessed the house in the dead of the night. A house that was quite thoroughly locked and barred against entry. It's also true that the extent to which Edgar had ingested the soporific—on a regular basis, from what our surgeons can tell—would have rendered him easy to overcome."

Chief Inspect Dressler again pulled the notebook from his pocket and flipped through it. "Yes, as I have recently learned, this mixture that you use, when ingested—particularly on a regular basis—has a dulling effect on the musculature. That means it is likely he had some weakness or paralysis of his limbs. Enough so that he would have been relatively unstable and highly prone to manipulation." Dressler returned the notebook to the interior pocket of his coat.

"Yes, he hadn't been his normal self for some time..." She let the thought die.

"Thus, as you can see, as hard as it is to find someone who might have wished your son ill, it's equally difficult for us to believe an outsider, without disturbing any of the doors or windows, had full knowledge of the medicinal 'sponge,' as you refer to it. And that said individual was able, on a regular basis, to administer it to him in such doses that he would have likely died in the near future, with or without his disastrous fall."

"What?" Lina cried, her hand clutching the chest of her dress.

"Gnädige Frau," Dressler began, unable to conceal some measure of impatience. "What I'm trying to say is that, while the sponge itself was in perfectly good order according to the physicians we consulted, the dosage of henbane Edgar had ingested was far greater than a mere anesthetic would require. It implied a great frequency of use, which concurred with your statements."

"The sponge isn't ingested," Lina insisted. "It's merely moistened and held over the mouth. He breathes it."

For a long span of time, all four parties stood fixed, eyes wide, staring at one another.

"But it was," Dressler whispered. "It most certainly was ingested. To the extent that, if he hadn't fallen, he most likely would have died in the near future."

Berend's deep voice shook the small space when he spoke. "Why didn't you mention this before?"

Dressler shook his head as his color rose. "We certainly did suspect foul play. And for this very reason: the presence of the poison. Yet the explanations of his state of mind...the use of the sponge...the expertise with which it was produced...the confirmations of our experts. Everything seemed to concur with your statements on the day of the funeral: that the signs of poisoning were in fact merely unfortunate side effects of the...the precautions as it were, that you took to preserve Edgar's life. But now..." His voice died off as he sank onto a bench.

Inspector Apprentice Metz stepped in. "It never occurred to us to consider that the soporific was intended to be inhaled, not ingested. It was so subtle. So insidious."

"Yes. 'Insidious' is the word for it." Lina's eyes flashed with anger. "And now I'm certain: my son was murdered."

"It does in fact appear to be the case," Dressler agreed. "Which brings us back to the crucial question: motive. Who would have gained from your son's death?"

For the next half hour, Lina deflected Dressler's questions, maintaining that no one inside the house had any reason to want Edgar dead. Yet all the while her mind raced through every possible scenario. When the chief inspector and his apprentice reluctantly withdrew, having received Lina's promise to inform them at once if any motive or suspicion should arise, she and Berend sat facing each other.

The truth of the matter—one neither one of them would admit out loud—was that Edgar had many enemies, inside and outside of the family. The question wasn't who would want him dead; the question was: who wouldn't? That was a matter that Lina refused to discuss with the police inspector, no matter how loyal he purported to be, or how fervently he assured them their comments would be held in the strictest of confidence.

"Helene had the readiest access to the poison. And the greatest knowledge of it." Berend laid their first card on the table. "She seems to be the most obvious choice."

"Too obvious, perhaps." Lina considered it carefully. "Given her knowledge, she would know that the poison would be detected in his system. And that she would be the most obvious choice. She's too smart for that. Besides which, despite Edgar's constant needs, she adored him." She shook her head.

"Nathaniel?" Berend asked, his eyes averted as if it pained him to even speak the name.

Lina's eyes flew wide in shock, but then her face grew thoughtful and still.

"He most likely believes the estate should have been his," Berend added. When Lina's face flushed and her pupils dilated, he clarified, "Being the oldest son, that is."

"He was also Conrad's favorite." Lina grimaced at the memory. "Conrad never had any taste. It's preposterous. That smug Pharisee, rough and rural, over my brilliant, sophisticated Edgar...ridiculous." She paused as if a thought had come to her.

It's true, though, she thought. *He did always think of himself as too good for us. Following after that French reformer...*

"I don't see how it's possible. He's hasn't been here in decades, what with that Prussian school and now..."

Berend nodded. "You're probably right. Besides, he wouldn't have access to the house. And he almost certainly wouldn't know Helene's laboratory exists." After a pause, he asked, "What about the Aurberg family?"

Lina's eyebrows shot up. "They would have motive, for sure, if they even suspected... No. Now we're back to outsiders—who, as the Inspector said, had no access to the house and likely wouldn't know about Helene's supplies."

"That very likely eliminates all of Edgar's associates as well." Berend said, watching Lina's face closely. She refused to meet his eye and simply muttered as if lost in thought.

"And the servants," she shook her head, perplexed. "The servants had access and knowledge. Some of them. But no motive. Every one of them is loyal to Edgar. *Was* loyal to Edgar," she amended. It didn't escape Lina's notice that Berend didn't reply. She wasn't as blind to the goings-on in her household as she often let on.

The only other person in the house, other than the guests, was Clara. And she was clearly out of the question. A daydreaming artistic sort, she simply wasn't cunning enough to pull off such an audacious crime. Besides which, she was confined to her rooms whenever she wasn't accompanied by a family member or one of the staff.

That left...no one. Lina bit her lip and unfurrowed her brow, willing away a brewing headache. Still it was a productive feeling, like an unslaked thirst that drives one to discover a hidden well. She was determined. This investigation would have to be her own. Regardless of the chief inspector's good intentions, only she, with Berend's help, would be able to ferret out the guilty party.

Chapter Thirteen

The next morning, Lina strode briskly down the central hall of the house until she reached an expansive set of double doors. She entered the home's library and quietly closed the door behind her. The dense cloud cover outside cast the room in shadows.

Most of the furniture lay beneath white sheets. This had been one of her husband's favorite spaces, but she rarely used the room. Her feet clipped across the wood floor, echoing in the cavernous space. She approached the closest set of bookcases and walked her finger along the row of spines. All the books pertained to philosophical matters. Not what she wanted. She moved to the next section and the next.

After the meeting with the two inspectors, everything she and Berend had discussed had left her hopeful yet frustrated. Helene was entirely dispassionate but compliant, as if she were innocent. And everyone else was accounted for as far as Lina could see. Unless one of the servants was a traitor, which seemed unlikely, Lina was entirely dumbfounded. Thus, that evening, she had gone to the last place where she might find answers: the family chapel.

There she had knelt and prayed. She had appealed to God as only a parent can, certain that He would understand the death of a child. That He would see her situation and sympathize with her desperation. That He would see her selfless concern for Edgar's reputation. That He, a

God of justice, a God who had promised vengeance, would grant her the identity of the vile creature who was responsible for Edgar's death.

She had waited in silent meditation for several minutes. She had concentrated on clearing her mind. Before her eyes, she set a black wall that needed only the flickering image of one who deserved her just retaliation. But the wall remained blank. She saw nothing but the red veining of flickering candlelight through her eyelids. A cold envelope settled around her, chilling her hands, slipping its sinuous breath down the back of her dress. After twenty or thirty minutes, when nothing had happened, she tried again.

She reminded God of Edgar—a treasure of His creation. His beauty and brilliance and charm, which had set him apart as one of the finest of all men. Surely God would want to honor his memory, to vindicate his murder, to glorify Edgar as a reflection of Himself. *Give me*, she begged, *the means to do this on Your behalf.*

She reminded God of His love for her. That as one of His most fervent and devoted servants, she was certain of His desire to help her in her hour of need. That what she needed most was to vindicate her beloved son's death—to see justice done, as God would want.

But the silence and the cold deepened. And her frustration grew. She had expected that God's will would align with her own. That He would desire to serve her, to answer her prayers. But as the minutes drew out and became hours, she grew angry and bitter.

She hardly noticed when her mind returned to her own thoughts, no longer waiting for a response from the entity she referred to as God. Her mind grew bright as the darkness gathered around her and the true state of her soul overshadowed the facade. As the chapel's windows had darkened and the candles cast a richer light, she could no longer linger under pretense.

She began to pray silently, without any knowledge or intention. It was, in many ways, the truest form of prayer she had ever offered. Without any attempt to appease or appeal to any being—God or otherwise—she turned inward and worshiped the only one she truly ever had.

Her soul begged for vengeance. Lina poured out her faith and promised to serve the one who would give her what she wanted: her son's killer. As her soul spoke into the void of eternity, Edgar's face filled her heart. Thus it was that, in the midst of her earnest devotion, a dark flame lit within her soul. She recognized it. There in the shadows she saw the answer. She would call on the one who could not fail her. Though he was dead, he was no less so than God. And who would take a greater interest in Edgar's death than Edgar?

Lina's heart had fluttered and skipped a beat. Why hadn't she thought of this before? What had blinded her eyes to the perfect solution? She would have her answer tonight. Edgar's killer couldn't hide from the one who held the truth in his hand: Edgar himself. Lina had laughed softly, her voice echoing off the stone walls. It reverberated as if another had joined her. And where someone else would have cowered in fright, Lina took strength. She would take help where she could find it.

Lowering herself onto the kneeler one last time, she crossed herself again, purely out of habit.

The following morning she entered the library. It took several hours, but she found it: a heavy ancient book. One she had seen on the shelves early in her marriage. A book from her grandparents Conrad hadn't felt free to destroy. Instead it resided in a far corner of the library, hidden in the balcony. She should have known; Conrad would have abhorred such a thing. But then, Conrad had never lost a son.

Chapter Fourteen

As she approached the library doors, thrown wide in anticipation, Clara's legs shook. She half expected to see her father's coffin still lying there, his body white and waxen, but the room had been restored to its former state. All the dust covers had been removed and a fire burned high behind the grate. The reflection of the flames shone in the onyx surround and the gleaming mantel.

One of the servants had set out a round table, surrounded by five high-backed carved chairs. In the center, a heavy silver candelabra stood adorned with flaming white tapers next to a bowl of soup and a loaf of bread. Steam rose from each. The rest of the room lay in shadow. A dark figure shifted in the corner. Berend stood there watching them. The flickering firelight reflected in his eyes.

At the sight of him, a shiver clutched Clara's insides, locking her legs. A wave of acid forced its way into her throat. She coughed, her throat raw, burning. Lotte set a hand on her shoulder and leaned over her.

Horst shook his head, the lines on his face deepening with misgivings. "I'm not sure this is a good idea."

"Are you questioning me?" Lina turned on them. Something dark passed across her eyes, sending a chill through Clara's body. "Because if you are, I'd certainly like to hear it."

Helene eyed Clara. "She isn't well. Perhaps this can wait for another evening."

"She's never well. And no, it cannot wait. Besides, Edgar favored Clara. If he'll speak to anyone other than myself, it'll likely be her. Bring her."

Lina paraded into the room with Horst trailing behind. Her words left Clara's fingers cold, her body weak.

"It'll be okay," Lotte said, her arm around Clara, urging her forward.

"She's very *sensitive*," Helene explained.

Clara shuddered as they helped her into a chair.

The five of them took hands and closed their eyes. Lina instructed them to focus, to meditate on Edgar, and their memories of him, until she called him forth from the grave. Clara had no intention of doing so, but as they fell into silent contemplation, her mind betrayed her.

She tried to concentrate on her favorite memory: of a summer party they had held when she was seven or eight. Instead she remembered him playing croquet for the first time, his dark hair gleaming in the sunlight, his white jacket flapping lightly in the breeze. The way he always smiled on one side, his lip mocking. He had stood with her mother on the lawn, teaching her to swing the mallet, both of them laughing as he chased the ball that careened down the lawn toward the lake.

She tried to picture the lake in spring, the cattails edging its cool depths, the ducks paddling in lazy circles. Instead she remembered him rowing her and her mother across its cold depths, a picnic basket in the bottom of the boat. She had carried bunches of wild water mint into the boat. But when she looked down, his feet had crushed the velvet leaves. The crisp scent of their desecration filled the air. The water around her had darkened, its surface rippled by something other than their boat. A small voice gurgled from its black depths. A pleading sound. She had cried out, desperate for land. He had only laughed, his grip tight around her wrist.

"Edgar," Lina intoned, "we have gathered here to speak with you. We welcome you into our midst."

She fell silent as they all waited. Clara sensed the light shifting beyond her eyelids and opened them briefly. For a fraction of a second, one of the long tapers seemed to burn more brightly, its flame fluttering on an indiscernible breeze. The scent of the soup, its surface oily, turned her stomach. Lotte and her mother were watching the candle. Sensing nothing more, Clara shut her eyes again.

"Edgar," Lina resumed, "we are here to seek justice for your death. We—those who love you most—are here to honor your memory. Bless us with your presence. Help us expose your killer and clear your name. If you love me, show me who harmed you."

For a few minutes they sat in silence. The whooshing exhale of the candles seemed to grow louder in the drafty darkness. Mingled with it, Clara heard her own breathing. But then, something seemed to seep through the air around them, like a cold arm enveloping them. It fingered her hair. And stroked the side of her neck.

Clara's eyes flew open. The others were looking around as well, still clenching one another's hands. The fog of their breaths hovered over the table, mingling with the steam from the food, suffusing the entire table in mist. As the cold descended, a draft passed over them, buffeting the candle flames. They flickered and fought against it.

"Edgar." Lina's voice rose in pitch, a touch of desperation around the edges. "Edgar, are you here?"

For a second Clara thought she heard a high, piercing scream, but then it fell silent and she couldn't have said with any amount of certainty what she had heard. All that remained was a sense of something otherworldly, something unnatural hovering in the air. Her heart trembled in her throat.

The floor beneath them shook. And then the walls around them. A terrible grinding crack, the sound of stone splitting filled the air. Then, beyond the table, over Lina's shoulder, a mist gathered and took shape. Clara heard herself gasp and cry out. Lina's eyes grew wide, fixed on Clara. The others looked from Clara's expression to the point in the middle of the room where the fog took form.

"Clara?" Lotte rose in shock, her eyes unblinking.

"Edgar." Lina's voice cut through hers. She dropped back into her chair and turned, searching the darkness for the identity of the gathering presence.

Clara gripped the edge of the table, her knuckles white and arched. She felt as if her soul were being severed into two jagged pieces. When she looked up, a young woman her own age with long, thick, red hair stood before her. Her eyes glowed like black flame. Her body quivered with a depth of substance, as if she could consume the light and swallow all of them, absorbing their souls into herself.

From somewhere within herself, Clara heard a savage wailing issue forth. Her teeth chattered. She tried to speak but couldn't. Dropping her head, she gasped for air and focused on the table until her jaw loosened. It was tight, the muscles sore.

"She's...she's..."

"What?" Lina cried. "She? She's what?"

Clara shook her head and said the only thing she could think of. "She's dripping." But then she realized it was true. Water ran from the girl's muddy white dress and off the ends of her hair, puddling on the wooden floor.

"Cora!" Lina whispered hoarsely.

Cora. Her aunt. Her father's sister who had died so young.

The girl grinned, her mouth dark, and spoke. "Ah, yes, her worst nightmare. The witch calls and *I* answer." She walked closer and leaned down, her face alongside Lina's cheek, her gaze settled on Clara. "Were you hoping for someone else, Mother dearest? My not-so-long-lost brother, perhaps?" She turned her lips to Lina's ear and lowered her voice to a whisper. "I won't tell you where he is, but I can promise you that you'll see him again. Still, it probably won't be the joyous reunion you're expecting."

Lina seemed to sense something near her. She rose and edged away from it, around the table until she crouched beside Clara, clutching at her sleeve. Her fingernails dug into Clara's arm. "Where's Edgar? Where is he? Where is Edgar? Edgar," she wailed. "Edgar, where are you? Why do you trouble me this way?"

Cora stood, her finger stroking the side of Lina's vacated chair. "Hello, Clara. We finally meet. I had hoped you'd resemble Edgar in some way, rather than his shifty little wife. At least you look nothing like the swamp rat, but perhaps that's more flattering than she deserves." She grinned toward Lina, who still cowered alongside Clara's chair. "Does she still have an obsession with water? A fondness for *baptizing* all things she finds unsavory, unwanted? Didn't you have a cat? I distinctly heard something about a cat. Ah, yes, a small white kitten with gray markings. I'm sure the hag told you she ran off. Never liked cats."

Clara fought the tears that rose to her eyes. "What?"

"What is she saying? What?" Lina hissed, shaking Clara's arm. "Why is she here?"

"Why *am* I here? An excellent question." The house creaked again, a sharp rending noise. Clara ducked. Cora laughed. "That'll hardly do any good. This house is ready to fall, my naive little niece. All that holds it together are secrets and lies. If you aren't out from under it when it goes, it'll take you with it. And you're just fool enough to let it. To let *them*."

Cora edged around the table, sidling up alongside Clara. She turned to whisper in her ear, her breath rancid and smelling of rotten meat lying by the road in the July sun. Clara exhaled, her eyes watering.

"Do you know what lives within this house?" Cora asked. "At its very core? I think you do. I think you've figured it all out. It feeds on what you give it then takes what it wants."

Clara shook her head. "I don't know…"

"Clara?" Her mother started to rise, her face drooping with impatience.

"Ah denial. Yes, stupidity is always so much easier. There's no accountability. No need to deal with all those unpleasant questions. You know the ones I mean. All those niggling voices that keep you up in the middle of the night. The ones that know what hides here in the dark. How have you been sleeping, dear niece?"

"What do you want?" Clara mumbled, her mouth leaden, numb.

Cora stepped away, strode across to the fire, gazed into it for a moment, then turned. The sight of her eyes, the black orbs that pulled Clara into them caught the air in her lungs, leaving her frozen, unable to draw a breath. "I know what *you* want," Cora said. The sound filled her mind with darkness. "And it just so happens I can work with it. Because, you see, there's something I want too. Oh, you look surprised. I forget how young you are. Didn't you know that you'd have to pay? That there's a cost? Always a cost. Always a price.

"You'll have to put away that precious ignorance of yours. Learn to face those things you'd like to forget. The things you've been trying to avoid, refusing to remember. Are you willing to expose all the hidden things: the shame and the guilt and the treachery that have eroded the foundation of this house?

"How badly do you want that? Will you risk it? Will you pay?"

Clara gasped for air, shook her head vigorously. "I don't know. I don't know. Don't ask me."

"What?! What is she saying?" Lina hissed, clenching her arm.

Cora shot her a smug smile of victory. "Your other option is to tell me to leave." She leaned closer, bent over the table. "Say it. *Cora, leave.* That's all you have to say and I'll go.

"But you won't. You'll never leave this house. You'll die here. Not a lingering death. Or an easy, quiet passing. No, your death will be a violent one. Your life will be taken from you before the snow falls."

Clara gasped, her eyes wide.

"But...on the other hand, if I stay...if you ask me to stay...I will show you everything that lies hidden here. You will be exposed. They will be exposed. And you will never be the same again. A part of you will die. A part of you may live. Is it worth it? Would you risk exposure, shame, even your own life? Is that something you can live with? Is it something you would die for?"

"Yes." Clara's voice quavered; she was uncertain whether she meant what she said.

"What is she saying?" Lina demanded, her fingers digging into Clara's arm.

Cora turned away as if that was all that needed to be said. Then she turned back. "Tell her that her days are numbered."

Clara repeated Cora's words. Lina recoiled from Clara as if she had been thrust away. She fell to the floor, her face ashen, stunned. When Clara looked back, Cora was gone. The mist was dissipating, the room growing warmer. They sat in collective silence. Clara laid her throbbing head on the table and listened to her lungs panting for air. She could still see Cora's ghost before her eyes though the room was once more still and empty.

When she looked up, Lotte was leaning back in her chair, her fist pressed to her lips, tears running down her cheeks. Horst knelt beside her, his arm around her, speaking softly to her. Helene watched each of them carefully as if she measured the event solely by each of their responses. When Clara looked up and caught her mother's dry-eyed expression, she recognized a spark of controlled intelligence: as if her mother's carefully submissive stance were simply a facade; as if something much deeper and more complex lurked there.

But then Berend was at Lina's side, lifting her gently from the floor and helping her back to her chair.

"What was that?" Lotte asked, between choking sobs. "What just happened?"

"Cora," Lina whimpered, as if that one word held all the meaning they needed.

It was a long time before they left the room. The library bore no signs of the appearance Clara had just witnessed. The floor was dry where before water had pooled; the candles glowed softly, steadily; the fire filled the space with a pleasant warmth. The soup and bread had cooled.

Yet everything was changed. The air smelled foul. Like death, like change, like a felling blow that, once leveled, can never be recalled. Clara felt weak and unstable, as if she had been torn in two and hadn't yet discovered which limb was missing.

The Silver Wood

"*Antiquity! I like its ruins better than its reconstructions.*"
    —Joseph Joubert

Chapter Fifteen

"It doesn't mean a thing! That's what. I regret ever suggesting it," Lina exclaimed, ostensibly to the rest of the family, although she met no one's gaze.

Clara eyed the breakfast table before her, set out with cold meats and cheeses, and looked away. The room rocked then settled. Then rocked again. After the séance the night before, she had moved from her bed to the window seat to the armchair beside the cold fireplace. If she had dozed at all, she couldn't recall. Her eyes throbbed.

"How do you know?" Lotte asked.

Lina cast a quick, disapproving glance toward Clara, her thin lips pressed together. "What proof is there? What evidence? It's all hearsay. I can't say what happened. Or didn't happen. And neither can you."

"No. No, I'm certain something happened," Horst countered. "The candles. The cold. And Clara's response. I may not understand all of it, but I could have sworn something...or someone was there."

"Pfft." Lina waved her hand at him. For the first time that day, Clara noticed her grandmother's fingers were bare of their usual heavy rings. Their knotted nakedness belied Lina's air of dismissive disregard.

"Ah, false bravado. How characteristic of her!" Cora hovered behind the head of the table, her arm across the back of Lina's chair. "She's so eager to dispense with the entire incident. A little *too* eager for someone who truly believes it was meaningless."

Clara's eyes watered at the sight of her. Something in her aunt's expression had cooled as if her eyes were less piercing or her intentions were less nefarious. Still, she glanced at the girl and quickly looked away. She had no way to take back her assent from the night before and, even if she did, no way to escape her own destruction. If the ghost spoke truly. Something within her warned her that Cora was a risky ally, but her words rang true. Lina's dismissal was clearly contrived. She spoke vehemently yet she was obviously distressed.

"Horst is right," Lotte said. "I can't forget the sense that I had: of someone in our midst. It was...it was too real to be nothing."

"I have to side with Mother on this one," Helene countered. "I neither saw, nor heard, nor felt anything. Isn't it more likely that we're all simply overtaxed? Given the funeral and the incident in the mausoleum..." Her voice tapered off. "It could so easily have been nothing but a figment of our imagination. Through no fault of our own."

"Oh. How magnanimous," Cora said. "She's trying to excuse you from your imposition on all of them."

Clara threw her mother an accusatory look and returned her attention to the plate before her.

"Yet behind her manufactured sympathy and her natural skepticism, she's smugly pleased at dear old Lina's distress."

Clara's gaze darted between her mother and grandmother. Yes, there was something there. Something each of them wanted to conceal.

"You wouldn't know anyway, would you?" Clara said to her mother and grandmother. Four sets of eyes turned on her in shock. She said it again. "I know what I saw and I know what I heard. You can disregard it; you can explain it away. But it won't change the truth."

She turned to her grandmother. "You knew better than to try to call up the dead. Anything can happen and it did. So what? It wasn't Edgar. I can't understand you. Do you really hate your daughter that much?"

Lina's eyes were dark and menacing. "I won't answer that question.

Keep in mind that this is a young woman whom you never met or knew. You have no idea what she was."

"Mother," Helene cautioned, but said nothing more. Neither she nor Horst had ever met Cora, who had died so early.

"I knew her, of course," Lotte stated. "I thought she was lovely. Very accomplished, intelligent, obviously devoted to Edgar. You've said it yourself: the two were inseparable. He practically worshiped her."

Lina's flinched as if she'd been struck. "Accomplished? Yes. Intelligent? Yes. But also capricious, manipulative, and deceptive. And very rebellious."

"Rebellious? She was certainly headstrong and willful. But that's true of many children. I don't remember her being rebellious. If anything, I recall her being very devoted to her studies."

"Yes, and to at least one of her tutors. Don't tell me what I do and do not know about my own daughter. Cora *always* had an agenda. And the only reason Edgar chased after her attention was because she was the only person in the world who didn't adore him. Not because she was particularly virtuous or good.

"No, make no mistake: if it hadn't been for that haughty little tramp, my Edgar would still be alive today. But she set her sights on ruining him, on ruining all of us. Oh, you don't believe me? I see it in your face. Well, ask Berend. Ask any of the older servants who were here at the time.

"Who set fire to my room? The one I used to occupy. You remember it. The blue-and-green one on the second floor, with the primroses in the wall covering; the ones you loved so much. You remember it...when was it? Christmas? Yes, when you all came for Christmas. Conrad showed all of you what she had done. Ask your brother, Theodor. He was there."

From Lotte's startled countenance, Clara suspected her grandmother spoke the truth.

"I wonder what you did to deserve it," Clara responded. Something about her grandmother's past behavior, her current demeanor, and Cora's suggestions had merged into a new picture of the truth.

"*Deserve*? How dare you? I deserved nothing. She was a wicked child —that's what she was."

"Was she?" Clara spoke the words around a piece of ham, her appetite suddenly renewed. Her grandmother certainly was hiding something, but did that negate what she said about Cora? She looked up to see the girl leaning against the wall, laughing, her expression unsettling.

Clara turned her focus back to her plate. Was Cora a malicious, self-seeking entity? Was she deceptive, leading Clara to some unknown, disastrous end? Possibly. Yet she recalled Cora's words: that she was at risk regardless of what she did. If she didn't uncover the truth, she would die in this house. If she *did* uncover it, she risked death as well.

Which was worse?

Beyond that—beyond the risks and her aching head and the spinning room—Clara felt alive. The suggestion that something lurked beneath the surface, something she could uncover, gave her a sense of renewed purpose. Those who held her prisoner had their own vulnerabilities. Things they desperately wanted to remain hidden. Clara smiled to herself.

And her grandmother–the steely bulwark—had been reduced to fear and trembling at Cora's presence. That was an unprecedented phenomenon. Yes, in retrospect, when Clara stood back from the prior night, when she separated herself from her own terror, she knew Cora was right: there was more to this story.

What was the risk? What could she lose? She was already a prisoner. What wouldn't she risk to escape this life? There was no going back. The only option was to move forward, to trust Cora, to put herself in the hands of one who might be manipulative, who might have her own agenda, but who could possibly help her. Besides, Clara had nowhere else to turn. Everyone and everything else already had failed her.

The others were still debating Cora's inherent virtue or lack thereof, but Clara was no longer listening to them. She had made up her mind. She would know the truth, whatever the cost.

Chapter Sixteen

Lina slipped in through the door and cast a furtive glance behind her. The hallway lay as silent as the grave should be. But wasn't. She still couldn't understand what had happened the night before. Why hadn't Edgar appeared? And what did that mean? Where was he? Although she refused to entertain her fears, they lingered there at the edge of her mind, demanding attention.

She turned her thoughts to what *supposedly* had happened and felt the heat of her anger radiate out from her core. Why Cora? What interest did she have in Edgar's death? And Clara's account of the malicious girl...naturally it would be Cora who would haunt them. Lina's fingers twitched.

If that's who actually had appeared. If *anyone* had. Something no one but Clara could confirm. It made no sense whatsoever. In fact it was absurd.

And what Cora had said about her future... Lina clenched her fists to still the trembling in her arms. Why would she say such a thing? It had to be nothing but Clara's imagination. *She's merely bitter and passing her frustrations onto me,* Lina thought. *Attempting to assault me. The girl's a liability, one that will need to be removed if things escalate further.*

Lina scowled and pressed the door closed behind her. During the day, Clara had spent the bulk of her time with her tutor. In her absence, the bedroom fireplace lay dark and cold. And the curtains, hanging open to the foreboding sky, let in very little light. Just inside the sitting room, Lina could faintly make out the painting that hung over the settee. It fit Clara well: a young girl idly resting outside in that Rococo style in which pastels flow into one another with a hazy, indistinct quality. Trivial and frivolous. Even the subject's class was ambiguous, although she had the freedom and luxury of idleness that only wealth tended to afford.

Lina couldn't see the value of such things. Art should bear historical significance. It should be distinctly defined: light versus dark; clear, well-differentiated colors rather than interchangeable ones. Caravaggio. Raphael. Rembrandt. Most important, it should be serious. Whether it pertained to the hunt or the throne, the subject matter should portray lives of purpose and significance—not idle, mindless pursuits.

Resigned to Clara's irredeemable nature, she strode into the bedroom. The drawing table stood near the entrance from the sitting room—the worst place for such a task, far from any natural light. But then, no part of the suite, despite its south-facing windows, had any measurable amount of sunlight even in the best of conditions. Not with the deep-set walls and heavy stone frames bordering the leaded casement windows. Lina opened the drawers beneath the table and carefully displaced the contents. Nothing but watercolor paint, stacks of drawing paper, a strange white paper-wound pencil-like object, chalks and the like.

Lina tried both bedside tables. They contained books borrowed from the library downstairs, spare candles and matches, a pile of ribbons. More books lay on the small tables near the bedroom fireplace. Who could possibly need so many books? Lina stood at the edge of the bed and looked around, perplexed. Where?... Then she froze and crouched beside the bed. Her knees creaked and ached as she sank to the floor.

There, under the bed, lay a moderately sized leather bag. Lina didn't recognize it. Inside, she carefully picked through the contents: clothing, soap, a comb and brush, a drawing of a bird. The bottom felt odd, as if it weren't quite flat, yet there was nothing there. She sighed deeply and sat back against the base of the window seat. That Clara had such a bag was not news. Berend had told her, of course. The girl might as well keep such a thing. She would never make use of it.

That wasn't what Lina was looking for.

After a few minutes, she rose from the floor, pressing down on the wooden edge of the window seat to help her. She slipped the leather bag back under the bed and crossed the bedroom to the dressing room. Opening each of the armoire doors, she shuffled through the contents. But it wasn't there either. Deeply confused, she returned to the bedroom and dropped back onto the window seat.

Clara was an artist and a writer. One who frequently requested journals from their stationer. Journals that couldn't be anywhere else than in her suite. But they weren't. And the fact that she had hidden them...wasn't that a clear sign of guilt? Lina shook her head, perplexed. There must be evidence somewhere. Someone had stolen her son. Had taken him from her. They couldn't have done so without leaving some trace of the crime.

Berend had searched throughout the servants' belongings and had painstakingly listened in on numerous conversations, public and private, but none of them had indicated any guilt. There was discussion, a great deal of discussion, about the family, the odd happenings at the funeral, the timely yet inexplicable appearance of Inspectors Dressler and Metz, and every other bit of family gossip. But nothing that implicated anyone or suggested any knowledge of a reason for Edgar's untimely demise.

Lina was at her wits' end. Helene showed no guilt whatsoever and Clara...well, Clara was an enigma. In the past, Lina had overlooked the girl as incapable of anything of any measurable significance. Yet who else was there? Since Conrad's death, the three women had been the only family members residing there.

She turned and looked out across the rain-washed lawns. It hadn't rained as much in Austria, her childhood home. Or so she recalled. It had been so long since she had been there that she was no longer certain.

And the land rolled in Bavaria, in gently undulating forests and a peak here or there that the locals referred to as mountains. Lina remembered the stark, craggy peaks in her homeland, with tendrils of snow creeping down from their heights. Perhaps it had been her youth, but the Austrian peaks had seemed so much higher, so much starker. Maybe they were alike. Maybe it was simply that Bavaria didn't feel like home.

She felt like a traveler, passing through for a night, as if she were bound for something, or somewhere else. But didn't know where. She couldn't remember if she had felt that way earlier in her marriage to Conrad. Perhaps she had been so busy that she hadn't noticed—busy with their social engagements, her children, Edgar.

Thinking about him drew her attention back to the room. Heavy curtains hung just beyond the window seat. If they were drawn, the seat would be something of a cave: the perfect place for a young girl to sit and read...or write. Lina's eyes narrowed. She ran her hands around the paneled walls on either side of the recessed seat. They felt solid. She sighed.

Even if she did find the journals, she wasn't certain what she expected to find: a gripping tale of intrigue and conspiracy? A plot to bring down her son? For certainly Clara couldn't have killed him alone. She couldn't have killed him at all. She was too small, average height at the most, with a narrow frame. And she didn't have the spirit for it. Lina could see that now. Her shoulders sank; her body suddenly tired, heavy.

The sound of the bolt turning broke the silence. Lina's heart leapt into her throat.

Smoothing down the seat cushion and casting a quick glance around to ensure that nothing bore a trace of her search, she hunkered down once again behind the bed. Someone entered the sitting room and lit the lamp on the table. Then the person passed into the bedroom. The footsteps seemed to pause at the fireplace not more than twenty feet from where Lina hid. She held her breath.

But then they moved on, into the dressing room. From around the side of the bed Lina made out the telltale skirts of one of the servants. And the dark hair and unmistakable form of Jutta. Lina pressed herself upward, feeling the blood rush to her face, hearing her knees pop.

The girl was in the bathroom. Lina slid in long, rushing steps across the bedroom floor. The crinkling of her gown grated in her ears. She reached the sitting room door, clutched the knob and turned it, slowly. Without pausing to look back, she slipped out and gently drew the door closed again with a faint click.

Chapter Seventeen

Behind her, Jutta stood, limned by the storm's rolling shadows, watching her leave. She frowned, her gaze fixed on the door as it closed, as if its solid back would crumple and fall under her scrutiny. Beyond it she heard the faint sound of Lina's dress rustling as she passed away from the rooms. Still, she waited ten minutes before leaving the suite.

When she knocked lightly and heard the familiar greeting, Jutta entered the door to Helene's rooms and closed the door behind her with only the softest click. Her mistress sat at her writing table, as she did most mornings after breakfast, responding to letters from friends and associates.

"Hmm. Jutta." She looked up with a faint smile, held up a lone finger, and quickly returned to the paper before her. Its surface scratched as the pen moved across it, Helen's slanted delicate handwriting filling the surface. She finished the line, signed her name, and held the pen aloft, a satisfied look on her face. "Finished. Well, with that one at least. It's a wonder these women can accomplish anything, what with their constant correspondence."

"Perhaps that's the extent of it."

Helene chuckled and stood, pressing her hands into her lower back.

It cracked. "Oh, good heavens, Jutta. It bores me so. The pretense. But I suppose it must be done."

"Must it?"

"I wouldn't want to alarm my mother-in-law."

Jutta sighed and drew up alongside the desk. "No, certainly not."

"I could set myself afire, parade naked around the town, and grow a beard without her noticing. But to drop the courteous response, the formal engagements, the calls? No. That would send her into fits. Let alone the menu planning. Though she manages that herself. She never could trust me with that one. Thank God. I suppose you aren't here to hear any of this, though."

Jutta glanced back at the door as if her piercing gaze could assess the possibility of an eavesdropper. She lowered her voice to a whisper. "I think we have a problem."

Chapter Eighteen

Two nights later, Clara awoke to the sight of her breath hanging above her, red in the dying glow of the fireplace embers. For several minutes she lay there, watching the shifting red mist, feeling disoriented. But then she realized the room was cold. Much colder than usual. She sat up sharply.

One of the windows beyond the window seat was open.

Both curtains were drawn back, allowing the cold breeze to flow into the room. Clara scanned the room, trying to penetrate the shadowy corners. The room lay dark and still, save for the gusts that rode ahead of the rolling storm clouds.

Slipping from under the cold sheets, she crossed the wooden floor. It was faintly damp, as if the mist had floated in and settled. She knelt onto the window seat and edged over to the open window. It flapped in the wind, nearly slapping her in the face. But then it lost momentum as it swung nearer the house.

She pressed it wide and held out her hand. Moisture gathered in her palm. Below her the yew bushes lined the gravel path. It was a long drop—far too long for her to make safely, but the idea was exhilarating. Her soul soared. In the distance, a flash of lightning purpled the dark sky. It looked like freedom. Not yet, not tonight. But it had to mean something. An open window always meant something.

She sat there in the darkness, her arms out the window, the rain beading and running off her skin until she shivered so much that she reluctantly drew the window closed and secured the latch. Then she tiptoed across the slick wood floor and into the bathroom to retrieve a towel.

It wasn't until she had entered the room that she noticed the dark figure sitting on the edge of the bathtub. Clara yelped and jumped back.

"If you jump at every shadow, people are going to think you're mad."

Clara shuddered to hear her voice: the sound of one without humanity, of unchecked misery and hatred and malice. Cora reached out her long, thin fingers and smiled a sick smile. The nails were dirty and jagged.

Clara's heart was still racing from the shock. She wanted to ask her what she was doing there, but she already knew the answer. The window had been open. She had wanted this. There was no way to turn back now.

"You did invite me. You *do* remember that, don't you?" Cora rose from the bathtub and walked toward Clara. Before Clara could move, Cora passed through her. A violent wave of cold radiated through her body. Clara hunched over, stunned, the wind knocked out of her. By the time she caught her breath and reached for the doorframe to help her stand, Cora was at the panel in the dressing room wall. She flashed Clara a questioning look over her shoulder then slid open the panel and stepped through.

Clara paused for a second then followed after her.

When the panel slid shut behind them, Clara turned to see Cora waiting for her. Her entire body glowed as if she were afire. As Clara drew near, the refulgence seemed to gather strength and fill the space, gathering them into its womb. Cora turned and began to lead the way along the hidden paths.

Eventually they stopped before a narrow doorway. Cora passed through it and disappeared as if she had been swallowed whole. Clara waited, surrounded by utter darkness. Still, there was no sign of Cora. She reached through the entry then stepped through, groping around her. In her hands she clutched a dense mass of fabric. Ahead, she heard Cora laughing.

Clara ducked her head and parted the dresses, for that's what they were. She pushed through and emerged from the door of a slender closet. Her hair and nightgown sizzled with static. They were in a dressing room, quite similar to her own. Clara turned and looked around. The mirrored doors looked back at her, pitying her disheveled appearance. She grimaced and smoothed down her short blond hair.

When she looked back, Cora already had moved into the adjoining bedroom. Several lamps were lit. A fire grew in the fireplace. Clara opened her mouth to ask whether the logs had been there, then recalled the unnatural sphere of light and shook the question from her mind.

She paused then turned in a slow circle. She had never been here.

The room was immense, easily half again as large as her own. It was nothing like her bedroom, with its heavy, ornate red and gold damask. This room was airy and light, with intricate white moldings. A beautiful pale green silk covered the walls in a pattern of white, gold, and soft pink flowers. High above them, a crystal chandelier hung still and blind, cobwebs laced throughout its ornate beadwork and across its long, willowy arms. An ivory-and-rose Aubusson rug covered the wood floors, revealing them only at the edges of the room. A gilded birdcage stood near one wall, the feathered bones of its former occupant lying inside. The room was like an intricate and fragile garden, lying in slumber.

Beyond, out the tall windows hung with thick green curtains lay the estate's lake, its surface dark, like a black eye in the windswept landscape. Clara shuddered. Regardless, she could imagine how spectacular this suite would be in the spring and summer—to wake up to the view of the rushes waving beside the water, the trees whispering in the soft wind, and the lawns sparkling with dew.

"Do you like it?" Cora smiled proudly, glancing around the space as if drinking it all in.

"Yes." Clara choked back the words she wanted to say: that this was what she would have chosen for herself. But she had never had a choice, any choice. Everything in her life had been chosen for her.

Cora laughed, her hazel eyes glowing with a strange fire. Her face shone with aggression and barely controlled rage. "You're no match for my mother."

Clara blushed. She walked to a tall dresser, coated in dust. Still, she could make out the wood roses carved into the edges. She ran her finger across the unfolding petals. Cora was right: Lina was a force she couldn't even mollify, let alone control. She cringed, picturing the two, both of them unyielding, in constant conflict.

Yet she was envious of Cora's strength. Clearly she had been able to prevail over Lina in some ways. Wasn't this room evidence of that?

"Why are we here?" she asked without turning.

"Don't you know?" Clara turned to see Cora sitting in an armchair by the fire. "Don't tell me you don't know your own mind."

Clara glanced around the room. Of course. It had begun with Cora, the one who had appeared in Edgar's stead. The truth had to start somewhere. Why not here?

She frowned and slid open one of the dresser drawers. It held silk stockings and undergarments but nothing else. She pulled open each of the others and rifled through the contents. "Why did you die?" she muttered. Wasn't that the first priority? This girl who had appeared, uninvited and unwanted, who issued provocative statements, and who clearly had some interest or agenda, had died early. At fifteen?

"Yes. A month before I would have been sixteen," Cora said, as if she could hear her thoughts.

At fifteen years old. But why? And how? And, most importantly, what role had she played in the family? In her father's life?

The dresser contained nothing that indicated anything about Cora, or her death, except she had had a large quantity of very fine lace and silk undergarments. Clara spied a large, elaborate white dressing table along another wall. Its surface was grimy with dust and neglect. She sat down in the small upholstered chair. The drawers on one side were held fast, as if they were locked. Yet she didn't see any keyhole. The drawers on the other side opened readily. Several contained stationery and wax. Another was filled with pots of rouge and powders.

Clara had never had any cosmetics. Her grandmother never would have permitted it. And of course there had never been any real reason for such a thing. They hardly entertained any longer. At the thought of the attention it would draw, Clara's fingers curled in and clutched at her dress.

She stretched them out and exhaled slowly. Before her, a bottle of perfume sat on a mirrored tray. She closed the drawers and took up the perfume. The scent was strong and alluring, like night-blooming flowers. She fingered the bottle with its etched form. Then she turned it, to mist the perfume into the air.

The bottle slipped from her fingers, hit the table, and rolled. It fell down the back of the table, smashing on the wood floor. The smell of jasmine filled the air.

"Damn!" Clara exclaimed, bolting up from the seat and pulling the table back from the wall. She gathered up the bottle and the shards that had cracked and laid them back on the mirrored tray. Perfume puddled on the floor. She ran for the adjoining bathroom and returned with a towel.

Stooping, she pressed the towel against the wood. But when she took it up again, she noticed blood mingled with the perfume. She held up her hands. A long cut split the end of her index finger. She sank against the wall and pressed the dry corner of the towel to the wound. It stung.

Across the room, Cora gazed into the fire, seemingly unaware or indifferent. Clara sighed and made as if to rise. But then something caught her eye. Even in the candlelight, she clearly made out faint signs of wear along the panel that backed the drawers of the table. As if something had pried at the panel on multiple occasions.

She rose and pulled open one of the drawers of stationery. There, in the front, lay a long letter opener, its crystal grip etched with the letter *C*. Clara grasped it and crouched behind the desk. The flat, pointed end fit snugly into the edge of the panel. It popped open. She slid it out of the track and set it against the wall, out of the way.

Within the back cavity lay piles of journals and papers. She opened a journal. It was filled from cover to cover in a large, irregular font, so unlike her own. The last entry in that one was dated February 9, 1836, when Cora would have been twelve. Or eleven.

"Eleven. My birthday was in October." Clara jumped, startled to hear Cora's voice. She had forgotten she was still there. She had turned from the fire and was now watching Clara. "Bring them all. There aren't that many. I was never the consistent writer that you are."

Clara stacked all six journals and brought them. She settled into the other armchair and set them beside her. Then she picked up the one with the earliest date but hesitated. Something about it felt like a turning point, as if by reaching for it and reading what it contained, she would be drawn into the force of a violent maelstrom from which she couldn't escape.

Still, she opened the first page and began to read.

Chapter Nineteen

I t took all night, but she read them all. All six of Cora's journals. The earlier entries were largely superficial. Talk of studies, visits to friends' houses, the family's social schedule. But then late in 1836, some of the entries sparked her interest.

October 15, 1836

The ball was nearly ruined this year. Mother said Mary Therese was to be my charge. It was my responsibility to ensure she enjoyed herself. Supposedly this gives Father opportunities in business, but that's a lie. He can find his own opportunities. She's just angry I took her copy of Monsieur de Monbron's infamous novel. Such an eye-opener. And in the hands of my dear, Catholic mother. She really should find better hiding places.

Thus, I was chained to the side of Mary Therese, that insufferable, chopped-faced bore. I knew all the boys would just ignore me entirely. Worse, they would think I'm like her, what with her standing beside me. Worse yet, Friederike was there with her powder-pink gown. Layers and layers of silk. And her blushing cheeks and black hair. All eyes were on her, as usual.

I could hardly stand it any longer, when Rosamund practically ran toward us, her punch glass jostling to and fro. If I hadn't acted quickly...as it was, it's just so clumsy of me. And, handy thing, Rosamund isn't known for grace. Either way, there was Mary Therese, her yellow gown covered in sticky red punch.

Of course, her mother carted her off and that was the last we saw of her.

It couldn't have come soon enough. Georg was sympathetic. So sympathetic! He's so nice. Nice enough that we danced four times! Thank God for punch!

Besides, how did Mother even find the book? Is she snooping? I wouldn't put it past her. Crazy bitch.

Clara cringed on behalf of poor Mary Therese.

"She's married to a Duke. Save your sympathy." Cora's voice broke through the stillness and the sound of the crackling logs. Clara eyed her skeptically and resumed her reading. For nearly two years, there were few entries, none of them of note. Then they took an interesting turn.

June 28, 1838

It rained today. Edgar and I had planned to row all afternoon, but that certainly wasn't going to happen. Not with Mother constantly "sensing" lightning. I think she just wanted Edgar to sit with her all afternoon and review the household accounts. "Here, Edgar. Sit by me. Do you see, Edgar, how all the expenses tally?" I can't imagine why she thinks he gives a damn.

Eventually dear old Berend came along with a message for her. When she left the room, so did we. Of course we couldn't have gone down to the lake anyway. Someone would have seen us crossing the lawn. And Mother would have dispatched her faithful lackey to retrieve us.

The attic it was. With the trunks of old dresses and fur stoles. Besides, no one would think to look there, as long as we weren't too loud. I just adore Edgar. Have I mentioned that he calls me Fanny when we're alone?! It's our private joke.

We didn't make it back until supper, and late at that. You should have seen my Mother's dour expression. It's like she owns Edgar. Or thinks she does.

…

August 5, 1838

There should be a rule that one doesn't have to attend Mass the week of one's birthday. Positively insufferable. And it had to be the woman at the well. So zealous! So repentant! A lesson for us all! I could be ill. Especially with Father Vogel staring down his nose at me, trying to coerce me into feeling guilty. And Edgar all the way at the other end of the pew. This will be my worst birthday ever. I just know it.

Besides, what a sham! As if anyone else can tell me who I am or what I should do. Or not do.

…

May 2, 1839

Spring! Finally! I don't think I could take another day of snow or slush or rain. I might as well be dead for five months every year, stuck inside. There's nothing to do but read—ugh! Or listen to Mother's interminable lectures about household management—ugh! Or attend to my lessons…which I must do to appease Father. But so dull.

Edgar is home on break. We went riding today! All day. We didn't bother asking Mother. She would just have said no anyway. She glares at me practically daily now. I think she's just jealous that Edgar prefers me over her. And that neither of us has any use for her.

I took a hot bath, but still(!) I am so sore. I must be horribly out of shape.

Hedy glared at me when she saw the stains on my riding habit. I don't know when she put on such airs! Looks like someone has forgotten her station.

…

December 13, 1839

Thank God for Christmastime. Mother is so much busier with preparations and oversight that Edgar and I have a reprieve from her constant nagging. (I told Father it's too bad we can't enter her in the Grand National! He laughed hard enough to turn his freckles red!)

Anyway, speaking of Mother, turns out I've uncovered a little secret of hers. Let's just say I now understand her inordinate affection for a certain brother of mine. One whose name begins with "E." And she has the gall to look down her supercilious, self-righteous nose at me!

I wonder what such a secret is worth to her! I know what it's worth to me. And to Edgar.

...

August 11, 1840

I showed Mother the letter. Now she knows that I know. I had debated whether to let her in on my discovery, but as I always say, "Fortune smiles on those who make their own." Besides, it's nearly our last chance. Edgar is due to return to Vienna next month.

Now she's going to have to back off and leave us alone. Or Father will be wiser than she might otherwise wish.

That was the last entry Cora ever made.

Dread spread through Clara's chest as if she were there, twenty-five years ago. As if she knew the doom that awaited her aunt and could do nothing to stop it. A scream muffled by time.

But at the same time, something about the entries troubled her. Something about them was *off*. And the last one, *the letter*, had to be connected to Cora's death. *Did it still exist?* She glanced at Cora, but the girl didn't look up. *What would it contain*, even if the letter could be found? Her stomach clenched. The room around her, so immense before, seemed to close in. The thought of the bird's bones lying on the base of the cage filled her mind. As if the journal entries had opened doors that should have remained closed.

Chapter Twenty

"Aren't you worried we'll be seen?" Jan leaned forward and peered around the side of the dilapidated boathouse.

"If you keep doing that, yes."

Richter and Jan hunched behind the wood building, sheltered from view of the main house. It was an ample structure, two stories, but dwarfed by the looming house that stood up the hill. A light rain was falling, soaking through their clothing, but Richter refused to risk exposure by opening umbrellas and enlarging their presence.

He fumbled with the lock on the door then felt it catch. The interior of the casing was corroded, and his makeshift key turned reluctantly, making a scratching noise as the pins succumbed. They slipped inside. Several windows, coated in brown grime, surrounded the space. He paused, waiting for his eyes to adjust to the veiled interior.

Lines and coiled rope hung on walls and lay in piles on the floor. Small canoes and one- or two-person sailboats sat neglected, covered in spiderwebs. Richter felt a finger run up his neck and jerked reflexively. In his mind, the entire room seemed to crawl.

"What?" Jan turned in time to see him flinch.

"Spiders." Richter shuddered again as he took in the space. It rose two stories in the center, above two boat stalls, with an elevated balcony encircling the perimeter. And it had that smell, the smell all boathouses have: of oiled wood and stagnant water. Coupled with an air of disintegration.

It wasn't a native smell for him. His childhood memories smelled of leather and varnish and of his father, leaning over his bench for hours refining the heel of a lady's shoe. That smell—the smell of an overheated cobbler's shop—smelled like home. This smell was something else entirely. That impression, coupled with the reason for their visit, felt disorienting.

"She died here?" Jan walked around the perimeter, darting quickly past windows, and taking in the surroundings.

"Just outside. The cause of death was drowning." Richter edged around the room then up a rickety set of stairs to the balcony above. He walked slowly, pressing the floor with his foot, testing it for weakness. Jan followed. As they drew near one of the upper windows, Richter stopped and gazed out from around the edge of the window frame. The rain pelted the lake. If he hadn't felt the presence of death so acutely, it would have been mesmerizing.

"How do we know it was murder?"

"We don't," Richer conceded. But he did know; his particular sense told him. The boats crouching upside down, concealing what lay beneath them, the grime on the windows that clouded the truth, the ever-watchful arachnids that hovered in their webs, waiting for their next victim: all of them told him. But more than these, it was the surface of the water below them in the two stalls of the boathouse. It shimmered with a strange sheen in the filtered light: grime, lying on the surface of the water, obscuring its depths. It told him everything.

"It does seem strange. A sixteen-year-old girl."

"Indeed."

"An experienced swimmer and boater," Jan added.

"She was." Richter nodded, his eyebrows arched. He watched the silent hulking structure up the hill. "Sometimes one too many coincidences is just that."

Jan followed his gaze. For days they had lurked, at all hours, watching the activities surrounding the house: the servants' comings and goings, the timing of lights on and off, and all of the entry points.

"Word is Edgar adored his sister and she him," Richter added, leaving the rest unspoken.

"His wife seemed to be devoted to him as well. Quite the charmer, I guess."

Jan was trying to be humorous, to lighten the weight of the situation, but Richter had seen too much for it to ease his mood.

They had finished their inquiry into Helene's past. The beloved daughter of a prominent baron. She had been a young child, too young to travel with her mother and father and brother to India, where he searched for and studied botanical sources.

They had left her behind with a nanny and a household of servants, but when her father had returned he had come alone. His wife and son —Helene's older brother—had contracted typhoid fever and died. They were buried in India, the illness too hazardous to risk transferring abroad. From Jan's research, her father had returned home to gather for a memorial with family, to take comfort in his one remaining daughter, then had returned to India and his research.

Years later she had traveled with him, learning to notate and draw those elements of the local flora they discovered. He doted on her, pouring out on her all the affection he had felt for his lost wife and child. Thus, she grew to be brilliant, exposed to disease and death, but entirely insulated from loneliness, madness and abuse.

In many ways, Helene came to her marriage with Edgar entirely naive to human depravity, despite the suffering of the world, with which she was well-acquainted. Her father died only a year or two into their marriage, when Edgar was his healthiest and his admiration for Helene was apparent to all. He died thinking he had done well by his daughter, marrying her to an aspiring and charming young nobleman.

"It isn't consistent, though." Jan said, breaking Richter's reflection.

"What's that?"

"Her death. Left lying in the lake, drowning in plain sight, while the others...vanished."

"Good observation," Richter agreed. "What does that tell you?"

"I don't know. It seems to indicate a different murderer. Or different motives. Possibly both, assuming they are connected at all."

Richter nodded at his young apprentice. Jan was promising. Overly eager but promising. He had a good head on him, able to pull together disjointed details more quickly than Richter had ever seen in one so young.

Jan was right. Throughout the region, reports documented at least 130 unsolved cases of missing girls within the last ten years, most of them within a convenient radius of the estate. Yet almost every one of them lay *within* the jurisdiction of Bavarian law enforcement. *Just within.*

It didn't necessarily mean anything, but the quantity was striking, as was the regularity of the occurrences. All the girls were blond or red-haired, between the ages of six and twelve—too young to be runaways or delinquents. At that age, girls were at home, helping their mothers around the house, playing with dolls. They were accompanied, watched, kept within a safe proximity of their parents. Yet they had vanished into thin air.

They were all children of working-class families. And they were always taken near inns, public markets, or fairs. One moment, the parents were buying and selling furniture or clocks or apples in a market, with their daughter sitting nearby. The next, she was gone. In some places the public had grown paranoid and fearful, banding together to ensure that at least one adult was on guard while the others rushed to complete whatever business had brought them from the safety of home.

To Richter, it seemed convenient, planned even. The type of girl, the places, the manner in which they had disappeared was all too consistent to be unrelated. Besides which, several witnesses had identified Edgar and another German man—one Richter had recognized when he met Lina: her manservant, Berend—around the time of the disappearances. It was simply too convenient. As he had told Jan, one too many coincidences is frankly one too many.

"...a man that time, though."

Richter turned. Jan had been speaking to him, probably for several minutes, and was now looking at him expectantly. Richter racked his brain for clues as to the most recent subject.

"Aurberg."

"Right," Jan continued. "'The Aurberg Incident' is what I've heard some call it. Word on the street is Herr Aurberg was asking questions."

"What kind of questions?" Richter asked.

"The kind that resulted in his body washed up on the banks of the Lech River. According to his family, he had no business or history there, no reason to be anywhere near the river. They're whispering foul play. Saying he was looking into Edgar's activity. Something seemed off to him and he was determined to uncover the truth.

"Seems to me like he was on to something. And that all these are connected. But where does that leave us?"

Richter sighed. "That's a good question."

The truth was, every bit of the evidence pointed to a circle of monstrous activity, with Edgar at the center. But with his death, where did that leave them? Where were the missing girls? Some twenty-five years ago, Cora had been found, floating in the lake just below them. The Aurberg fellow had been found on a bank of a river. But the girls— they just up and disappeared.

Why? Even if Edgar was a monster, what on earth would he do with 130, or more, young girls? What had Aurberg uncovered that had led to his death? And why on earth had Cora died—the one girl whom everyone said Edgar adored beyond life itself?

It was maddening, yet there, on the hill, the house glowered at them, like a large eye, fashioned in the shape of angular stone pieces, daring them to challenge it. Richter suspected that the trail was far from dead; that it lay sleeping, waiting to resurrect itself. So he would wait too. And when it stumbled out of its cold slumber, he would be watching.

Chapter Twenty-One

"Where are we going?" Clara's voice sounded muffled to her ears, drowned in the deep, blood-red carpet that ran along the length of the long, thin hallway. Her lamp cast flickering shadows that rose and danced onto the low barrel-vaulted ceiling above them.

Cora ignored the question.

Along the hall, doors stood on either side—doors that led to relatively small suites with unimpressive views of the cottage garden and the front of the family chapel. But among those deceptively simple rooms stood only one that could be their destination.

The rooms here were isolated from the body of the house, in an area that should have been secluded and vacant. Yet Clara cringed with each step, glancing around them every few seconds as if someone would hear; as if a door suddenly would fly open, exposing the two girls in a part of the house that carried its own curse. The air sizzled around her, alive with memories that pressed in on her, catching her feet, dimming her sight.

She saw the door drawing near, pulling her, as if through a tunnel. Cora stopped short before it and turned, waiting. "Stand back."

The hallway around Clara constricted. The walls and floor rolled like the deck of a ship. She turned and leaned forward until her forehead rested against the wall. It felt cool against her skin, clean, broken only by the soft raised texture of the brocade.

She felt him long before she saw him.

The smell of him—of cigars and cedar and his musky hair oil—filled the air. Clara held her breath but too late. The scent brushed against her face, crept into her nose and eyes, demanded admittance. She heard his pants rub against his legs as he walked. Heard his jacket, unbuttoned, slap his chest. "Dead," she whispered, her eyes clenched shut. "Held by the soil. Taken by the worms and the ravens and the creatures of the dark. Exposed to the night crawlers. Dead. Held by the soil. Taken..."

Above her prayer, she heard Cora whisper, "Edgar," and in that moment he spoke. "Oh." One word, his voice full of despair and meaning. Clara's eyes flew open. Her head turned. He had stopped, his expression fixed on Cora. But then he broke eye contact with her and looked around as if lost. He plodded on, his steps unsteady, an open candle in his shaking hand, its flame fighting to retain its small life.

He turned and passed as mist through the closed door to his room.

"What are you doing?" Cora hissed beside her ear. "Come on."

"It's locked," Clara rejoined, her mouth dry.

"You need to see this." Cora opened the door and pressed it wide, waiting.

"No," Clara whispered. "No. I don't need to know. I already know. I can't..."

Cora stepped closer. "This is the way. The way out."

Clara let her forehead fall forward against the wall. She closed her mind, silenced the memories. Locked them out. It was too much. *It's the way.* She already knew what she would see. What she held firmly at bay. *But it's the way.* I understand. I already understand everything. Everything I need... *It's the way.*

She took a deep breath and pushed away from the wall. Cora stood near the door staring at her, her eyebrows raised. *No going back.* She swallowed, wiped her palms on her robe, and followed Cora through the door.

It lay there before her, as it always had. His long narrow bedroom, the space heavy with wood paneling and substantial carved furniture. As if their mere weight could ground him, could hold his mind still. Gold curtains hung from the bed's full tester, ropes of cord holding them back at the thick posts that marked each corner.

In the fireplace a fire raged. Before it stood a large table, topped with books and papers and an inkwell. In the center an enormous silver candelabra gleamed. A high-backed chair stood on the opposite side of the table, across from the fire.

A solitary chair.

The room—a den like those that house the wolves that howl in the forest—was unchanged. She couldn't count the number of times she had stood here in the hall, cringing against the wall or cowering behind her mother. Times when he had turned, had become something else, something wild and unhinged. His eyes would darken, the lines of his face would deepen, and he would turn on her, or her mother, laughing hysterically or sobbing in anguish. Or the times that he would bring her here, his fingers clutching, intense, and would drag her into the room, his words incoherent.

She would scream and scream, fighting against the long, bony fingers that bruised her arm. His face, so close to hers, his eyes intense, searching her face, looking for something she couldn't give him. A sympathy that lay beyond her understanding. Sometimes her grandmother and Berend would come to subdue him, would send her away. Sometimes they didn't hear. Or chose not to.

Here, in this, his sanctuary, his mind could roam, unchecked. In this place, he was both physically and emotionally closed off from the rest of the family. Now, in hindsight, hidden from his view, the thought softened Clara's fear, filling her with a sense of sympathy and curious sadness.

As she watched him, he leaned over the table, his hands on its dark surface, a depthless pool in which the fire mirrored his madness. Cora drew near to him, laughing lightly despite his apparent suffering. The dissonance gave her laughter a strident tone.

"Stop," Clara pleaded.

"Poor Edgar." Cora ran a finger down the side of his arm. He didn't move or show any sign of recognition. She laughed again, sending a cold wave through Clara's body. She shuddered, pressed back against the wall inside the door, and watched, frozen, unwilling to venture any closer to either of them. But just then Edgar seemed to shake, as if he cried. He drew the chair back from the table and sank into it. Resting his head on his interlocked fingers, he gazed at the fire.

A few minutes later, he spoke. "Are you here?"

Clara gasped, her eyes jumping between the two. *He knew? How did he know?*

"Is he a...a phantom?" she asked.

Cora looked back at her and grinned. She leaned over Edgar's shoulder and whispered. "Yes, I'm here."

He lifted his head, desperately seeking her in the gloom. "You're here? Where are you?"

"I'm here. I'm here." She rubbed his shoulders, attempting to soothe him. Instead he grew increasingly agitated and distressed.

Throwing back the chair, Edgar rose from the table and paced to and fro. "What did you do? What did you do to me? How could you leave?" His voice was broken. His eyes sunken beneath his brow, their gaze intensely disquieting.

Every moment Clara feared he would see her standing there unbidden, unwanted. Yet his stare, though it ranged the room, desperately peering, failed to take her in. She shook her head. *No. He can't see me. Wouldn't see me, even if his gaze could pierce the shadows of this accursed space.*

Cora wrapped her arms around Edgar. He stopped, seemed to feel her presence, seemed even fearful of losing his awareness of her touch.

"Where did you go?" he whispered.

"Nowhere. I never left you. Never left."

"But you..."

"The lake," she barked a bitter laugh. "My baptism. My mother must have been satisfied in the end. Wasn't it what she always wanted?"

Clara stood transfixed. The sight of them brought to mind something she had heard Aunt Lotte say once to her mother, when Clara was much younger. They had spoken in whispers of Cora's death. Lotte had said Cora had been "the spring to Edgar's winter; the mocking breeze to his flame." At the time it had seemed silly, overly dramatic even. But now, watching them, she could see it. Edgar breathed in Cora's presence; her soul was his oxygen. Clara could see how this relationship had been like a fire, fed of its own will.

As if she sensed Clara's thoughts, Cora looked up and caught her eyes. Cora's gleamed with unspilled tears. "We were inseparable, you know. The same person even. To be with Edgar was to be made whole, dreadfully complete. I gave him my spirit. He lit my darkness, rounded out the shadows, gave it purpose. And he protected me."

Clara caught the last bit and frowned. She struggled to picture Cora, her flaming auburn hair glowing in the firelight, with her vicious fighting spirit, needing any protection. Her face must have given her away, for Cora laughed.

"It's true." But then her voice softened. "There's so much you don't know." Cora shook her head and turned from where she gripped Edgar. "You have so much to learn. So, so much. Don't feel bad, Clara. He couldn't protect you. He wasn't whole. After I left, his mind broke. Always searching, always reaching. And even this"—she looked down at her outstretched arms—"even this is only the faintest relief for him."

Edgar started to pace again. It called to mind the sound of him treading the halls, his voice low, the words almost imperceptible, like a constant moan. Even as a young child, she had understood the words were not important. They were nothing more than the exhalation of a sorrow that words couldn't describe.

She had heard him calling for Cora in the darkness of the night but had attributed it to his delusions; had assumed his madness drew him back to an earlier time when his mind had been whole. She had thought it was youth and health that had kept him that way. Now she understood that it was Cora. That his sorrow, his fractured mind, his constant restless seeking was not a search for *when* he had been whole, but rather a desperate grasping for the one who had made him so.

Cora caught Edgar midstride and dragged him down to where he huddled on the floor. She wrapped him in her tenuous embrace and spoke soothingly into his ear. The words were indistinguishable, but Clara understood it all.

She realized she had ceased to be afraid. Cora was right: she didn't understand. She hadn't. She'd had the perspective of a child, one who expects one thing from a father and, not receiving it, sees only her own disappointment. She had never seen him as Cora did: as a man who had loved more deeply than most ever dreamed and who had lost everything that gave his soul its reason for existing.

How had she missed it? What else had she missed?

A fire grew within her, a driving need to know more, with or without Cora. Something was still missing: some piece still lay unturned. She felt it just beyond her reach.

Chapter Twenty-Two

"The latch is right there. If only..." Jan said, mostly to himself, his fingers itching. He stood behind Richter, struggling not to fidget, watching his mentor manipulate the lock. Periodically they both froze, listening for footsteps in the dark alley. But other than the scurrying of rats and the occasional howl of a cat, the night lay still around them. The moonlight, diffused by high cloud cover, shone silver on the wet stone road. It was a good night for what they needed to do: bright enough to work without lighting a lantern and alerting anyone to their presence.

"Thank God he doesn't have a dog. And be quiet. The doctor is likely asleep above us," Richter cautioned him. He jiggled the lock for the last time, felt the latch rise, and pushed the door open. They stepped down into the building and closed the door behind them.

Most of the first floor appeared to be a good-size square room. Off to one side stood two tidy exam spaces, each outfitted with a cot, a side table covered in instruments, a chair, and a chest of drawers. Curtains that hung from beams in the ceiling stood open, waiting to be drawn to enclose each space in privacy. Above them, a sound like a boot scraped against the floor. They froze, waiting for footsteps on the stair. After a minute, the sound died away into silence.

There was only one thing they needed and only one place it was likely to be. Richter crossed the room to a heavy oak desk and slowly pulled open one of the drawers, which was unlocked. He set the lantern next to him on the chair. Less than five minutes later, they had what they wanted: a pressboard file, tied closed, the subject of its contents written in clear letters across the top.

Clara Willenheim

Richter relatched the door before they retreated down the alley. Once they were far enough away to risk speaking, he turned to Jan. "I have no doubt you know we couldn't just break the window..."

"Yes. Yes. Of course."

"...but just to be clear, there are at least two reasons why we can't. For one, it would potentially alert someone of our presence before we could find what we were looking for. And for another, even if it didn't, it would leave clear evidence of the fact that we had been there. Which would cause the doctor to search about until he discovered what was missing. At that point, alarms would be raised, questions would be asked, and we would lose our advantage.

"No, Jan, the key to what we do is stealth. In everything. Even the smallest thing. The fact that no one knows we were ever there gives us the upper hand."

"Won't he know the file is missing regardless?"

"It's unlikely. And we'll return it soon. Tonight if possible. Within a day or so at the latest. It's highly improbable that he will look for it before then."

They walked on through the shadows until they reached their waiting carriage. They climbed in, feeling the cab rock and creak. Richter pulled the curtains closed, lit his lantern and set it on the seat beside him. He untied the file and rifled through the papers, then carefully set them aside in the same order in which he had found them.

"Well?" Jan asked. "Is it what you thought?"

Several minutes later Richter retied the file. "Yes, unfortunately it is."

Chapter Twenty-Three

For several days, the memory of her father's ghost clung to her like a rash she couldn't scrub away. It filled her sleep with nightmares, woke her countless times, and plagued her memories throughout each day. She couldn't concentrate on her studies. Even her drawings turned dark and haunted: the sketch of an iris, its violet petals speckled with disease; a mountain meadow in spring full of slinking shapes creeping around trees and hiding in the long grass. If she could have, she would have clawed at her skin in order to carve it out of her mind. Her only relief lay in turning her mind back to the mystery of the letter.

A few nights later, Clara slipped through the hidden passages until she reached a jutting side wing on the western side of the estate. There she pushed open a bookcase panel. The smell of her grandfather—of peppermint and cloves, of his pipe tobacco and his beloved wool sweaters—wrapped its arms around her and took her breath away. For a moment she stood, blinking, looking toward his prodigious desk, waiting to see his white hair slicked back, his rheumy eyes gleaming with mischief. But the only movement around her came from piles of papers shoved aside, spinning loose across the floor.

His private study lay tucked up a short flight of stairs from the ground floor. Decorated with model ships, a large ship's wheel and seafaring paintings, it had a pleasant inconsistency with the rest of the house. As if Conrad had wanted to break with all that existed around him.

As if he wanted to be free from this house as much as I do, Clara thought.

She stepped around piles of books and ledgers and files stacked on the floor. Bookcases stuffed with books and papers lined the walls. Stacks of paper filled the large desk.

"Like walls," a voice said behind her. Clara's heart froze. She turned to see Cora standing near the door. "Like insulating walls and barriers."

"Yes," Clara said, willing her pulse to slow. She took a deep breath and looked around. It was true. Towering stacks impeded anyone from moving easily throughout the space, as if the isolated study hadn't been enough to give her grandfather a sense of separation. *We're all looking to escape*, she thought. *What hope is there for me?*

"Ah, philosophy. The endless hole into which bored intellectuals bury themselves from reality. Are we here for a reason?" Cora laughed, as if at a private joke, her caustic tone cutting through Clara's thoughts.

She was right. The letter was the only next step she had. Cora's allusion to it in her journal, in conjunction with the timing of her death, was too coincidental to overlook. *Besides, I can't wait to find out what my grandmother didn't want my grandfather to know*, Clara thought.

She already had searched her aunt's rooms again on the off chance that she had kept the letter, but it wasn't there. Which left only two places where it might be, only one of which was relatively safe: her grandfather's study. She sat at the desk and perched her lantern on the edge of a lofty stack of paper. The flickering flame gave her pause. She looked around at the countless pieces of dry paper—an entire room of kindling. But outside the window, the gloom lay heavy and dark. It couldn't be avoided. There wasn't enough moonlight.

She turned back to the desk and picked through each of the piles before her. Then she opened the drawers and thumbed through the contents. She checked the desk for secret compartments, but found none. And no sign of a personal letter. Clara sighed and moved to the bookcases.

There were books on agriculture, on animal husbandry, on history. One on the architecture of the estate. Several related to ships and sailing. And ledgers. Ledgers going back hundreds of years. The ones that were shelved in order by date predated her grandfather or were from his childhood days. Clara flipped through each and set them back on the shelves. None of them contained a letter.

As she stepped back, she heard a sigh. Behind her, in the shadows, a shape sat hunched in his armchair.

"Opa?" She rushed over and knelt beside him, clutching his hand. His skin was warm and dry and paper thin, as she had remembered it. "How are you here?"

"Clara dear." He patted her hand. "Shouldn't you be in bed?"

"I'm looking for something. A letter. It was something Cora would have written to you. She and my father—"

"Your father isn't well. Hasn't been since Cora died. Perhaps even before that. There was always something about him that didn't fit."

"Yes, yes. But there was a letter. Did Cora write you a letter? The night she...the lake."

"Ah, yes, the lake. The lake. The egress of egrets. She was a bird that could never be held, would never be content with our little lake. She had to fly free. In her own way." He sighed deeply and reached up under his glasses to rub his eyes. "Clara, dear, I'll tell you something that took me a long time to learn. If I had known it earlier, perhaps I would have made very different choices. No, no, I'm sure I would have. It would have been impossible not to. Not that you should repeat that to your grandmother.

"Sometimes the greatest evil is the one that's closest to you. That can make it the hardest to see. But you have to see it. You have to. It's the only way to ever be free from it."

"Yes, of course. That's what I'm trying to do."

He smiled at her, his wrinkles crinkling around his eyes. "Well, you're farther ahead than I was at your age."

"Evil must be destroyed," Cora interjected. "Rooted out and cut down." Clara jumped. Once again, she had forgotten she was there.

Her grandfather looked at her as if he also could see her. "Yes, it does. Or it will always own you. You'll never escape it so long as it lives."

"What are you saying?" Clara faltered, her hand falling away from his. "That I should…?"

"You have to dig deep until you reach the very inmost point. That's where you'll find what's holding you. That very thing. That's your enemy. Look for it. Don't stop until you find it."

She looked down through blurry eyes. "I don't know how to do that." When she looked up, he was gone.

She bit her lip and ignored the rising sense of panic in her chest as she waited for her eyes to dry. At the memory of her grandfather, she smiled sadly. She felt like a mouse trapped in a maze of paper. Most likely her grandmother never came into this room. She wouldn't have been able to stand Conrad's idea of organization.

"Maybe that was his idea all along," Cora said.

At that Clara smiled. Then something struck her. She kneed through the piles picking up a ledger here, a pile of papers there. Of course. They were all organized by date. All of them from her grandfather's lifetime. Each stack represented a year of accounting, business documents, and other correspondence. She sat on the floor and took up the most recent ledger.

So many payments. She had had no idea they had incurred so many costs. Some of the names she recognized—household and grounds staff, her tutor and drawing instructor—others she didn't.

She set it aside and picked up another. And another. The contents were all similar. Yet something about them felt important. She rushed from stack to stack, flipping through the papers. Nothing. None of them seemed to contain a letter or any reference to one, but perhaps they would tell her something. She stacked several to take with her.

If Cora had died because of the letter, she almost certainly hadn't shown it to Conrad. Lina would have it, assuming she had retained it. It was exactly what Clara had known in the back of her mind. It was exactly what she had feared. If the letter still existed, it would be in her grandmother's rooms.

Chapter Twenty-Four

"Why now?" Clara asked. She lingered at the bend in the passage, clutching the stack of ledgers under one arm, her lamp in the other. Ahead of her, Cora approached a break in the wall. A panel Clara had hoped to avoid.

"There's no time like the present," Cora joked half-heartedly. "Set those down and get over here."

Clara stood fast. "Yes, but why tonight?"

Cora didn't respond.

"Why tonight?" Clara repeated, the words trailing off in a whisper. Cora had disappeared through the panel.

Clara set the ledgers down, raising a cloud of dust. *Why do I listen to her? Why? When she's clearly half mad.* She shook her head at her own cowardice. *Because she promised a way out, that's why. Though there's no sign of one. Nothing but one riddle after another. Ah...but is that really it? Is it only about a way out? Or is it something more?*

She sighed, resigned. Though her legs trembled, Clara tiptoed to the panel and peeked through. The bedroom lay in a lush state of velvet blackness. She stepped through the panel, her feet sinking into the plush carpet, and looked toward the bed—an immense carved behemoth, capped in a tester edged in long bullion fringe. Clara heard her grandmother snoring lightly beneath the bedcovers that rose and fell with the sound.

Across the room, Cora lingered beside a heavy black desk. Clara had seen it before on several occasions—an impressive piece, replete with an inlaid ivory floral pattern—but its hulking form and long legs gave it the air of a prowling cat, seeking to ensnare an unsuspecting victim.

"Well, are you coming?" Cora leaned back against the wall, her dress and hair squelching against the plaster.

"Shh!"

"She can't hear me. Even if she were awake."

Clara stepped across the thick carpets, glancing back once at the bed. She slid open a drawer. In it lay various stacks of stationery—paper, cards, and envelopes—embossed with her grandmother's monogram.

AWM

She closed the drawer.

The snoring ceased in a sharp inhalation. They froze. The bedcovers shifted as if her grandmother meant to cast them off and rise. She mumbled something indistinct. Then she shifted, turning onto her side, facing them. A minute later, the sound of her regular, steady breathing resumed.

Clara exhaled, deafened by the pounding of her racing heart. She turned back to the desk, opened another drawer, and sorted through the contents. Beside her, Cora still stood, her arms crossed, her thin fingers drumming against her arms. They flashed like white bone in the darkness.

"Where is it?!" Clara exclaimed under her breath. She stood and gazed off in thought, her jaw clenched, her fingers gripping the edge of the desk. But then she remembered Cora's desk. Her eyes lit up. "Help me with this," she whispered.

They slid the chair out, its legs shushing across the carpet, cutting across its pile in two dark slash marks. The desk resisted, its solid mass anchored in friction. Clara wrenched it until she pulled it far enough from the wall to see behind it. A letter opener lay in the topmost drawer, beside the stationery. With it she crouched down behind the desk, her hand poised. She bit her lip and looked over to the bed where her grandmother lay. In the gloom, Clara could picture her eyes peering through her transparent, paper-thin lids. Watching her. She couldn't tell whether she really slept. Whether or not her eyes were closed.

"If she can see you, it's too late," Cora chided with a smirk.

Clara shot her a patronizing glance and slid the letter opener into the gap in the back panel of the desk. As she rocked it gently, holding her breath tightly in the oppressive silence, she looked at the preexisting gouges along the edge of the panel. Seeing them gave her courage. She pressed harder and felt the panel pop away from the desk's frame. The sound seemed like an explosion. For a moment Clara sat, stilling her body, watching her grandmother sleeping no more than twenty feet away. Waiting.

"She learned this from me!" Cora chuckled, looking into the desk's back compartment. "Nosy witch."

Clara jumped and glared at the girl.

"She's watching youuuu," Cora whispered, laughing under her breath.

Lina lay still. Clara could no longer tell if her breathing rose and fell in a steady, deep rhythm. Looking at her, she felt a pressure rise in her chest. A heat that ran across her shoulders and down her back. Filling her arms with a sense of strength, invincibility.

Clara rose and crept toward the bed. The smell of her grandmother's rose-perfumed ointment hung like a cloud around her. Beneath the smell, she detected the bitter, citric scent of feverfew mixed with chamomile. It reminded her of a deathbed surrounded in flowers. Her grandfather, Conrad, had lingered for years in his makeshift bed in the library. It had had a similar smell minus the roses but had filled her with a desperate sadness. Somehow, in her grandmother's case, the addition of the floral scent gave her bed a morbid incoherency.

"That's the smell of hypocrisy," Cora leaned over the elderly woman, her nose within inches of her sleeping face. "Falsehood."

"Yes," Clara whispered.

"There's a faster way." Cora turned her head, her hair swinging precariously close to Lina's face. "A faster way out." She glanced at the letter opener that Clara still clutched in her hand.

Clara grasped it and stepped back a foot.

"It can all end tonight. The doors flung wide open. Who's to keep them any longer? Berend won't. Hagan won't. Your sycophantic mother surely won't."

"No," Clara said, but her mind spun. The spiring cedar. The door to her room locked at all hours. Days unaccounted for. The last several years during which her father had gradually cut off her visits to friends and relatives. And their visits to the house. Over time she had noticed a trend. Everywhere she went they were there. Watching. Her father. Berend. Hagan. Monitoring her sessions with her tutor. Reading every letter she received or sent until she eventually ceased to send any.

"You thought it was him," Cora stood, gazing down at her mother. "While she hid in the background." She bent forward again, her hair brushing along Lina's cheek, their dead strands caressing the curve of her brow. "It's always you, isn't it, Mother?" she whispered.

Clara gripped the letter opener more tightly, feeling the waves, hot and cold, course along her legs, filling her belly with desire. Her fingers trembled. The heat of her skin seemed to rise and mingle with the oppressive smells around her. As if they drew her in. Invited her. Her shoulders quivered. But then she looked at Cora's face, her eyes black, knowing. She gasped and stepped back another foot, feeling the cold room envelop her once more. A barrier seemed to rise, delineating her from Cora. "I...I can't."

Her neck ached with tension, but she strode back to the desk as if she could shake off what she had seen reflected there. Crouching behind the edge of the desk, she lifted the panel and set it aside. She knew what she would find. The gouges had spoken of it. There in the dark space lay three lone folded pages. She clutched them up and tucked them into the pocket of her robe.

Across the room, Lina shifted again in her sleep, flopping onto her back. Her eyes were still shut, but her breathing was still. Panic rose in Clara's chest. She grasped the desk panel and quickly slid it into place. The two girls shoved the desk back against the wall, replaced the chair in its former position, and dashed for the passage.

They slipped through the panel in the bedroom wall, latched it behind them, then scurried for the bend. Cora clutched the lamp; Clara scooped up the ledgers; and they ran. Twice she tripped and nearly fell. Once her foot rolled over a dead rat lying in the shadows, her ankle twinging in protest; another time she stumbled on a steep staircase where she misjudged the distance to the next tread. The thought crossed her mind that she needn't run, but her muscles were wound too tightly to stop. So they ran, burning off the tension and anticipation and sense of injustice that had gripped them for too long.

At long last they arrived outside Clara's dressing room. Cora burst headlong into the space, laughing heartily. Clara stumbled through the opening, panting, her chest heaving with the exertion. Her vision swam. She dropped the ledgers and doubled over, breathing deeply, waiting for her dizziness to subside. When it did, she looked at Cora and shook with silent laughter. Tears streamed from her eyes. It was several minutes before they grew quiet and huddled together on the ottoman in the center of the small mirrored space.

Clara turned to her aunt and handed her the folded pages. "What is it that we risked death to extract? And why couldn't we have done this during the day, when she's gone?"

At Clara's words, Cora's face settled into grim resignation as she unfolded the papers and stared at them. She handed one to Clara. "Read this first."

Clara scanned the page. It was a letter to Cora, signed from Edgar.

Cora,

My love! Tonight the moon will be full. I can't help thinking of you every time I see it: your pale skin shining in its light. Haven't we delayed long enough? Tell me you'll come with me and be done with this heartless womb, this prison of secrets and lies. Meet me at the boathouse at midnight.

Forever Yours,
    Edgar

Clara read it several times. The light from her lamp, set on the carpet at her feet, shone up through the paper, imbuing it with an energy that seemed to come from within the words themselves.

"You were going to run away?" She turned to Cora, her eyes wide, her mouth open.

Cora nodded.

"But then how were you drowned?" Clara looked about her, her gaze absent, her mind racing ahead. "Was that...was that when?"

"Yes." Cora's voice sounded far away.

"How?!" Clara asked to no one in particular.

Cora just handed her a second piece of paper. Clara took it and unfolded it slowly, reluctant to read any more.

Cora,

    My love! Tonight the moon will be full. I can't help thinking of you every time I see it: your pale skin shining in its light. Haven't we delayed long enough? Tell me you'll come with me and be done with this heartless womb, this prison of secrets and lies. Meet me at the boathouse at ten o'clock.

Forever yours,
    Edgar

. . .

She looked from one to the other. "But they're the same...no...no...wait. Ten o'clock. Midnight." Her mind spun. And then she knew. Everything she had suspected before that moment collided into one comprehensive image.

Lina. It was her grandmother who adored Edgar, worshiped him even, and had jealously guarded his attention and affection. But it was Cora whom Edgar treasured. Not Lina. *Cora*.

"How did she know?"

"Edgar entrusted the letter to one of the servants to pass to me after my music lesson." Cora shook her head. "We had no idea how deeply the treachery runs in this house. No idea that young girl would inform Hagan. Who would pass the note to Berend? Who would open it and give it to Lina?"

"Then it was Berend? At the lake?"

"Both. It was both of them."

Clara's cheeks flushed with anger. "Where was Edgar? How could they do this?"

"You already know."

"Oh." Her heart grew very still. "Of course. He came later. At midnight."

"It was already too late."

The images in Clara's mind were overpowering: of the sturdy German servant overtaking Cora and dragging her out of the boathouse and into the lake; of her grandmother watching from the water's edge as he drowned the young girl; of the two of them, brushing off the weight of the incident, casually discarding it in the darkness as something that had to be done; of eighteen-year-old Edgar, blissfully ignorant, rushing down the lawns, searching through the boathouse for a girl who no longer existed; of his headlong dash into the lake, gathering Cora into his arms, the water streaming from her hair, his mouth open in a howl of agony and despair.

That last one never left her: Edgar caught mid-wail, eyes wide, Cora's lifeless body lying in his arms. Instead it replayed over and over, leaving an indelible imprint on her soul. When she finally looked up, Cora was watching her.

Now Clara understood her aunt's bitterness and the cynicism that so frequently colored her words. There was nothing she could say. The letter said it all. Except *why*. Did she really die simply because they intended to run away together? When she finally voiced the question, Cora handed her another letter. She recognized the font with its irregular looping style.

Chapter Twenty-Five

He arrived early in the morning, in an old carriage—a one-horse gig without ornamentation—that belied his true standing. Berend caught a glimpse of a black Homburg before it was eclipsed by the driver's outstretched umbrella. Then the man's face lifted and the air collapsed in Berend's lungs. His heart cinched in panic. His mind spiraled back through the years to the white house in Austria.

The house of Lina's childhood. And his own.

She eventually had acquired a brother, but as he was eleven years her junior, she was practically an only child. By then, Berend, the youngest son of her father's manservant, was already her closest friend and companion. In late summer, they climbed into the hills to pick wild bilberries, returning with their lips and hands stained purple. When the snow fell, they fastened sleds and raced down the slopes, competing for the crown. Then returned to the house at dusk to light candles in the attic windows and reenact *Macbeth* and *Medea*.

Until one day, *he* came.

Every so often, Lina's father had had a reason to entertain a prominent Bavarian duke at his house. On one of these occasions, when Lina and Berend were twelve or thirteen, the duke had arrived accompanied by his son, Heinrich. The boy was exquisite, several years older than Lina and insufferably arrogant. He attempted to cloak it, but his calculated words and scarcely concealed appraisal of her and her home gave away his poor view of her station. Berend hated him immediately.

But not Lina.

His indifference only drove her to try harder, disappearing then reappearing in her best gown and newest rings; taking the boy to the stable to see her new pony, unaware of his own three imported Arabian horses. The more she tried, the more Heinrich's face bore a gaze of contempt and boredom.

The first time he and his father left, Berend breathed a sigh of relief, his face flushed with shame and embarrassment. But Lina glowed. She saw in Heinrich the ideal man, the epitome of class and grace and, not knowing anything about his society, could only imagine herself at his side one day. She articulated as much—to Heinrich, to the other servants and to her parents, both of whom merely smiled benevolently, refusing to adjust her expectations or dampen her pride.

Thus it was that, when the duke began to frequent the house, often accompanied by his son, Berend felt the first of many premonitions. His position often allowed him to watch while remaining largely unobserved. What he saw did nothing to allay his fears. Rather than discouraging Lina or politely deflecting her attention, Heinrich grew conniving.

Over the years he deferred to her wishes, building up her trust, and then, once she had reason to hope in his favor, he'd dash those desires. As a result, Lina grew increasingly cynical and bitter. Yet, rather than acknowledge him as the source of her anguish, she pushed that anger and distrust onto others. Meanwhile, she maintained a desperate and unassailable defense of Heinrich's character.

She was eighteen when they received word of Heinrich's engagement to the daughter of a prominent family. Lina's family cowered, awaiting an explosion of rage and emotion. When instead Lina grew quiet and withdrawn, her parents marked it as maturity and looked on her with the sense of pride and awe that one looks on a wild horse that is newly broken.

Everyone except Berend.

He knew better. He understood that while silence is, for many, a place of reflection and gathering strength, it wasn't for Lina. For her, prolonged stillness was a place where poison is slowly leeched out into the water and knives are sharpened.

She grew collected and shrewd. Her actions were graceful, her words appropriate, yet her eyes seemed to recess and darken. Part of Berend feared her, yet another part—the part that had always loved her— trembled, awaiting the outcome of whatever grew within her.

Less than a year later, her father managed to arrange a marriage between Lina and Conrad. Conrad's father, Leopold, a man who prided himself on astute observations and egalitarian opportunities, esteemed Lina's father, despite their somewhat different social standing. Of course, she put her best foot forward, showing herself to be both clever and socially adept.

Berend breathed easily, thinking the matter solved. As the son of her father's manservant and her lifelong companion, Berend was gifted to Lina as her personal servant in her new husband's home.

For several years, the currents around him fell still. Lina gave birth to her first child, Nathaniel, a boy who, from birth, was a mirror image of his father, Conrad. The servants would look out to the lawns where Conrad walked with his business associates, one hand holding his ubiquitous pipe, the other tucked into his pants pocket, only to see the young Nathaniel, no older than three, trailing the older men, a stick in his mouth, his hands buried in the pockets of his smart little shorts.

For all Berend could tell, Lina seemed happy. She bore the contented and cheerfully occupied air of any young mother. Her son, a lanky but strong boy, did nothing to tax her patience and instead, with his easygoing and thoughtful personality, required little attention or discipline.

Thus it was that, when the child was three or four, she socialized more frequently, throwing large gatherings at the estate and often leaving the house to stay with friends and associates. Berend generally accompanied her, acting as an aide and a personal bodyguard while they traveled to and from estates throughout Bavaria.

It wasn't long before she secretly befriended a woman by the name of Madame Aurberg, a French lady who had married a Bavarian count. Conrad disliked the Aurberg family immensely. In the past, Herr Aurberg had passed along false business advice that had resulted in a great loss for Conrad and several of his associates. Behind closed doors, it was widely whispered that Aurberg had gained much of his money in a similar, distasteful fashion.

Further, Madame Aurberg was spirited. Her irreverent and opinionated nature and her vaguely off-color stories found a welcome recipient in Lina. Berend couldn't decide whether Lina's affection for her stemmed from the relief she felt in temporarily abandoning the enforced propriety of Conrad's world or whether the woman's controversial nature awakened the dormant fire that Lina had left smoldering all those years ago.

Whatever it was, the two were fast friends and Berend found himself shuttling Lina between her own home and that of the countess on a regular basis.

In fact, it became such a typical occurrence that he was taken completely unawares when, on one such occasion, while he sat in the countess's garden awaiting Lina's emergence, he witnessed a familiar face and a haughty step slip out the side door and into a waiting carriage. Even he, given to observation, with a fine memory and careful reliance on the facts, questioned what he had seen. It wasn't until he had witnessed a subsequent incident that he trusted his eyes.

It was Heinrich.

He was five or six years older, a significant enough timespan for a young man that it rendered him substantially changed. Yet it was clearly him. There was no mistaking that bearing and the set line of the young man's jaw.

Berend never learned how the duke, well married and expecting his third child, had come by Madame Aurberg or why one who had dismissed Lina with such contempt, had grown to seek her company in a strange woman's home. Perhaps marriage and fatherhood had sobered his perspective of his own importance. Perhaps they had contributed to his spirit of fatigue and boredom. Whatever the case, Lina was indeed the reason for his visits.

The one thing Berend did gather was how much Lina had learned from her childhood mistakes. She no longer catered to Heinrich or sought his approval; if anything, her conduct was entirely the opposite. She treated him as her inferior: one who was fortunate to receive her attention when and if she should grant it. And she held out information and interest, always projecting an enigmatic air. Simultaneously she teased him, vacillating between vixen and ingenue.

It had the exact effect that she had planned. She mesmerized him.

That was the spring and summer of 1822. By fall, her situation was obvious. That December she gave birth to a second son—this one tempestuous and greedy, with black hair and a stocky build. They named him Edgar.

Berend quietly considered Conrad's appraisal of the boy and often caught the man staring quizzically at the child who was so unlike himself. He may have attributed the boy's coloring and high spirit to his mother. But whether or not he ever discerned the truth, Berend couldn't say. Conrad never gave voice to his thoughts within his earshot, and Lina said nothing to that effect.

With the boy's arrival, her frequent visits to the Aurberg house dwindled then ceased altogether. Heinrich's wife had given birth to their third child, and Berend suspected he had tired of Lina's games. Perhaps he had grown wise to it and felt himself manipulated.

Berend suspected Lina's ultimate desire had been not the duke's impression of her but a constant claim on his attention. Thus, he had no doubt she had, at some point, managed to convey to the man that her second son was his. Nevertheless, as Lina's activities were barren of any indication of subterfuge, Berend suspected her attempts to ensnare him had failed. Instead Lina redirected all her obsession for Heinrich's attention onto his child.

It wasn't until those many years later, when Edgar's mental state had come unhinged, that she had found the leverage she needed with Heinrich. And he knew it.

Now, as he stood before them once more, Berend watched the man with carefully disguised distaste. His salt-and-pepper hair was full and slicked back. He was tall and broad with a strong, aristocratic bearing; a medium-toned, rectangular face; a strong jaw; and the slightly bored, insolent gaze of one whose standing is a foregone conclusion. Aside from the heavy amount of white mixed in with his dark hair, he looked much like Edgar. Enough that, had they ever been in close proximity, people would have begun to question.

He regarded Lina with a patronizing expression, while she chastised him. "...you would have attended. It was irresponsible and insulting."

"Don't berate me, Adalinda. You know as well as I do that it wouldn't do. And further, I won't be herded about like cattle because of some whim."

"Whim!" Lina scoffed. "The death of—"

"Besides"—he cut her off—"if there is, in fact, an unsavory character about, the less he knows about our *shared interests*, the better. Coming here at all is unwise. What were you thinking? Think what this could do to my reputation."

"How can you say that at a time like this? Didn't his death mean anything to you?" Lina's face radiated rage, but underneath, Berend spotted disappointment. Through her careful mask of anger and indifference shone a suffering like that of a child whose favorite parent has pushed her aside. It was astonishing to witness. Heinrich was the only person who'd ever had the power to reduce Lina to a desperate youth. Berend cringed, embarrassed on her behalf.

She paused then changed tactics. "I need your help. I can't do this alone, Heinrich."

"I don't see how I can possibly do anything that the proper authorities aren't already doing."

"Would you like me to remind them of the Aurberg incident? Or of those whose interests might have been threatened by Edgar's *activities*? Should we bring *those* to their attention?"

"They already know." Heinrich shook his head then seemed to reconsider. "You might be right. Undue attention begets trouble. What do you want from me?"

"Look into them. The Aurbergs. And the others. Anyone who had reason to gain from his death—either as revenge or self-preservation. Maybe someone has been talking, wanting out of the circle."

"That's a long list."

"*Someone* wanted him dead. That's a problem for both of us. Anyone who hated Edgar enough to kill him may have reasons to come after us."

"Hmm." Heinrich smoothed his mustache then ran his thumb and forefinger down the edges of his mouth. "I see your point. I'll put someone on it. Someone discreet. And the poisoner that you mentioned?"

"I'm taking care of that." Lina waved it off curtly.

"You've neglected several things, though." Heinrich's eyebrows rose and his gray eyes surveyed Lina. "In fact, you've disregarded the most obvious person of all."

Lina gaped at him, surprised. Her mouth turned down into a scowl. "Ridiculous. Absolutely preposterous."

"It isn't." Heinrich took a step toward her, his substantial frame dwarfing hers.

"Of course it is!" Lina said. "He's over three thousand miles away. And has been for more than twenty years. He didn't even make it back for the funeral."

"You underestimate him. You've made an enemy of him. Did so long ago with your fawning over Edgar. He has every reason to resent him...and you. And he takes after Conrad. Very much so, in fact, if I remember correctly. The boy is wise and careful. Something you should be."

Lina paused to consider his words. "I suppose you have a point. But even if he did resent Edgar, he's not here. He has no access to the house and no knowledge of anything that happens here. He's been gone for too long."

"Possibly," he said, without agreeing.

Lina fingered her rings absentmindedly. Meanwhile, Heinrich stood lost in thought, a finger to his lips as he reflected on the situation.

"Heinrich," Lina began, waiting for a response.

"Hmm."

She approached him slowly, as if fearful of upsetting the moment yet driven to do or say something. As she drew near him, she reached out a hand and set it on his arm. "With Edgar gone, you're all I have left."

Heinrich didn't look up, but only lifted a hand to rub the side of his face. Lina moved in closer and encircled him with one arm. As he registered her proximity, he flinched and grunted.

"Don't cling to me, Adalinda! And don't play with my emotions. Just because you've succeeded in manipulating everyone else doesn't mean you can manipulate me."

At his words, she shrank back, wearing a wounded expression. She quickly replaced it with a hard grimace of anger and determination.

"There's something else you haven't addressed," he continued. "Have you left anything incriminating?"

"Meaning?" Lina asked, her face mocking and full of false innocence.

He cast her an irritated look of long-suffering. "Don't play dumb with me."

"Of course not! Do you think I'm a fool?"

"I certainly hope not. That's a risk you can't afford."

Chapter Twenty-Six

Clara fled. The gallery, an interior, windowless alley of sorts, stood in a rarely traversed portion of the second floor. It was the sort of space one passed through from one place to another, or a conversation piece for new and curious visitors. A space through which none of the existing family or servants had much need, or desire, to travel.

Earlier, she had been in her window seat, journaling, when out of the corner of her eye she caught movement and turned to see an anonymous vehicle ambling up the lane. Since her father's funeral, visitors were rare. Visitors arriving in the predawn mist were unheard of.

She'd seen Berend rush down the steps and quietly usher the stranger into the house. By the time Clara had realized where they were headed, and by the time she had reached her grandmother's room and lifted the peephole, she had missed the bulk of their conversation.

The visitor's back had been to the panel, his head lowered, his hat in his hands as if lost in thought. He had taken a step or two away then turned around. She had gasped and dropped the latch, listening to it creak in the darkness.

Now, as she looked around the gallery, her dead ancestors, the guardians of history, stared down at her from their framed canvasses hung against arsenic green walls. She shuddered beneath their gaze. In many ways, the gallery was a graveyard: a memorial to those who had come before them. With the exception of her mother's, grandmother's and Uncle Nathaniel's portraits, Clara's own likeness, painted the prior year, was the only one representing the living. It felt strange to gaze upon herself, seated on a stone bench in the conservatory, a background of ferns and vases brimming with white tulips and hyssop framing her expression. An expression that was far too wise for her years.

Her grandmother had insisted on the historical consistency of their portraiture, a tradition that had begun several hundred years ago when Conrad's ancestors had built Waldensee. Most were more traditional in nature, capturing the subject in a staged setting within one of the drawing rooms: heavy velvet curtains, or topiaries, or a high-backed chair, draped with yards of heavy fabric symbolizing wealth and nobility; or simply a portrait, floating suspended within a background of gold foil. Her own painting bore the more casual setting and color that, as her grandmother had determined, befitted a young lady. At some point in the future, it would be set into storage, to be replaced with an adult version that complied with the historical trends of her ancestors.

Most people who visited the house and viewed the gallery commented on the fine workmanship of the art or the striking lineage of such a notable family. They said it with pride, sometimes with a hint of envy mixed with admiration. Yet, as Clara circled the rectangular perimeter of the narrow space, her lamp cast long shadows up on the visages of her family history. As she met their eyes, she saw them as captives imprisoned in pretense—birds trapped in a narrow cage, repeatedly singing an aimless tune. Regardless of her grandmother's assertions, her own portrait, so disparate from the others, clearly did not belong.

But her father's did.

As she studied that portrait, her hands grew clammy; her lamp shook. There was no way to doubt what she had seen. The man Berend had ushered into Lina's private rooms was an older likeness of her father. Tears smarted in her eyes. Then a creak sounded at one end of the gallery, coming from the panel she had only lightly closed.

Her heart lurched. She glanced about frantically. There was nowhere to go. Then she caught a glimpse of auburn. And heard water dripping.

"I wonder how long it took my father to discover the truth," Cora said, her gaze dark, full of fury. "Perhaps he never did."

Clara groaned inwardly at the sight of her otherworldly aunt. Yet, at the girl's words, she glanced back at Edgar's portrait. His eyes bored through her. She looked away.

"My dear mother, on the other hand... You read the letter," Cora said.

Clara knew what she meant. The third letter. Not the one Edgar had written, begging Cora to come away with him. Or the forgery that had sealed her doom. But the other one. She reached into the pocket of her skirt and withdrew it. The paper was soft, worn, more so since she had retrieved it from Lina's desk. The folded edges furled lightly beneath her fingers.

She held it up at an angle, her lamp faintly illuminating the faded ink, written in Cora's distinctive looping style.

Dear Father,

I have discovered something of utmost importance to you. You know of my deep affection for my brother, Edgar. You also know of my mother's obsession with him. She holds, for him, an unnatural and disproportionate devotion, something, I'm sure, pains you, given your ardent faith. All this you already know.

But I doubt you have any knowledge of the roots of this affection. I've only recently learned of it. If you were to ask yourself, what do my brother Edgar and the Duke Heinrich von Ehrenschau have in common, you would be wise. For they are of the same blood. And my mother's fawning over the duke has transplanted itself as the worship of his son.

I'm sorry to tell you this. It gives me no joy to cause you pain. Yet I feel compelled to inform you of her adultery and persistent idolatry.

Do what you will with this information. I merely seek to do right by you.

. . .

Your faithful daughter,
  Cordelia Margarete Willenheim

Clara read it through and then again, a second time. Flecks of light played before her eyes. She felt as if she had fallen and had the wind knocked from her lungs. It all made sense—horrifyingly clear sense. She let the letter fall to the floor. Beside her Cora was still. She stood beside the bench, gazing down at the fallen letter, long desensitized to the truth.

So many details, so many things Clara had heard, and thought she understood, now fell into place. She understood why Lina had trembled in fear when Cora had appeared at the séance. To be confronted with the spirit of the one whom she had killed; to know that any moment she might be exposed must have shaken her to the core.

Most important, Clara now saw in startling clarity that the real monster was her grandmother. The one who would kill for Edgar's undivided attention.

She also understood why Cora had insisted they acquire the letter in the night, when Lina lay merely feet from them. She had known that this knowledge could cripple Clara, that it could shut down her will to go on. But they had walked into the heart of the lion's den and had taken one of its teeth. Doing so had fortified her. Had given her the strength to take more.

Clara gritted her teeth. It definitely wouldn't shut her down. She wouldn't allow Lina to win, to hold her captive in this prison. Her father was right: it was a "heartless womb," a "prison of secrets and lies."

Clara picked up the letter and reread it. Of course Edgar was Heinrich's son. Why had she never seen it before? Because Heinrich had never come to the house and never would have done so, for one obvious reason: the striking resemblance between the two was uncanny. If they had stood side by side, there would have been no question in anyone's mind. Although, perhaps when Edgar was young, the association would have been overlooked.

She looked at Cora, whose hair shone ruddy against the green walls. Above her, a portrait of Clara's uncle, Nathaniel, mirrored Cora's visage. Both were of moderate height, with strong but lean limbs, fair freckled skin, red hair, and striking hazel eyes. Similar to those of her grandfather, Conrad.

But Edgar, with his waving dark hair, olive skin, and muscular body was nothing like either of them. In the back of her mind, Clara always had assumed, without giving it any conscious thought, that he took after her grandmother.

She looked back at the letter in her hand. Though it was meant to shock the reader, its false sincerity grated at Clara. It was unlikely her grandfather would have failed to see through Cora's intention: to thwart Lina's attempts to keep her and Edgar apart. He must not, however, have understood the nature of their relationship. If he had, he would have done everything in his power to separate the two. He would have been Lina's greatest ally in that, something Cora never would have encouraged.

"Did my grandfather ever see this?" *He's not even my grandfather.* Clara felt a sudden pang of sadness and loss.

Cora shook her head. "I never intended to give it to him. My father was a good man. We didn't agree, but that letter would have devastated him. That's something I never would have done to him. Unless I had to.

"Call me a fool if you will, but I was ignorant of how evil my mother truly is. She wouldn't stop. Wouldn't leave us alone. So I showed it to her. Told her the cost of her continued meddling might be higher than she would be willing to pay. Clearly she agreed."

It made sense. Edgar had been consumed with Cora and oblivious to his jealous mother. In a desperate, unwise attempt to stop her from her persistent interference, Cora had tried to blackmail her mother. But it had had an effect she hadn't foreseen. It had threatened Lina in a way she couldn't ignore.

Clearly her grandmother hadn't been willing to risk Conrad's knowledge of her indiscretions. And Edgar's undivided attention was worth any price, even the price of her daughter's life. Clara thought back to the conversation she had barely overheard and Lina's nervous clinging to this man she had never known.

"She must have loved him," Clara thought out loud.

Cora turned, her eyebrows arched in disbelief. "*Love*? Love had nothing to do with it. Not for her marriage to my father—your grandfather—or her relationship with Heinrich. Didn't you know? Conrad married down when he married my mother. She was the daughter of an Austrian burgher. He wasn't a tradesman or a peasant farmer, but he wasn't in Conrad's circle. Not by a long shot." She laughed lightly, brushing her fingers along the gilded frames as she walked back and forth.

"But she was *ambitious*. Oh, yes. You don't believe me? I suppose you'll have to take my word for it since you can't ask him. She went after Conrad and she won him over. Conrad's father approved at first and then, on closer inspection, changed his mind. Thought his son's sights were set a bit too low. That he was shopping in the stables.

"Of course, the problem with ambition is it always looks beyond one's current situation. My grandfather used to say that as a warning. *Ambition in life is a precarious thing: a healthy amount wins the race, but an excess will dismount you.* He was a man of many sayings. But of course, most of the time he was right.

"In Lina's case, he most assuredly was. Once she won Conrad, she set her sights higher. She used him then Heinrich to establish her own reputation. Their glory—and subsequently Edgar's—became her own sense of self-worth. Therein lies the danger: her identity was, in her mind, linked to theirs. Any rejection or loss of esteem from that other person wasn't simply a matter of a disappointment. No. It became, for Lina, a fatal wound to her life's purpose and meaning. That's the sort of mentality that perpetually teeters on the brink of destruction."

Clara listened to her in horror. She couldn't imagine having so tenuous a grasp of who she was. To not know her own mind, to have no firmer convictions or character than what someone else might ascribe to her, was a frightening idea. Like a boat, tossed about on the sea, never coming into view of land. She shuddered at the image.

"So she needs Heinrich's attention to validate her, especially now that she no longer has my father," Clara summarized.

"At the very least."

"I'm surprised he doesn't just ignore her."

"Why is that?"

"I would guess he finds her frustrating. Someone so emotionally demanding."

"I'm sure."

"But then why was he here? How is she able to summon him so easily? What could he possibly want from her?"

"Silence, of course." Cora brushed a long strand of soggy hair behind her ear and gazed at Clara thoughtfully.

"But Edgar is gone? And she would hardly speak ill of him."

"No. No, she wouldn't. But Heinrich's involvement with Lina goes well beyond Edgar. That's what he can't risk."

"Then they're *still* having an affair?" Clara turned up her lip at the thought.

"Not at all. That ended nearly as soon as it began." Cora smiled grimly.

"Then..."

"Perhaps my mother has something more. Something she can hold over him."

Clara recalled the tail end of the conversation she had overheard and Heinrich's allusion to something incriminating. *Evidence.* He had asked Lina whether she had removed all of the evidence. In that instant, before she responded, her grandmother had turned away so Clara had seen her face clearly. It bore a reticence that told Clara everything: she most assuredly had *not* eliminated whatever it was that he feared. Any more than she had eliminated the very letter that had threatened her so dearly. Which meant that somewhere—most likely within the walls of the estate—lay some evidence that would implicate Lina in some way.

Clara felt a thrill run through her, along with a sense of danger. "I have to find that evidence," she whispered to herself, lost in thought.

"You know she's a murderer. What more could you need?"

"Don't you want to know?" Clara's arms tingled. She jumped up from the bench. "Oh, I suppose you already do. You could just tell me.

But you won't, will you?"

"I don't see how whatever evidence there might be—assuming there really is any—could help you."

"Why wouldn't it? You said I needed to uncover the secrets hidden in this house. Secrets about my family. *Our* family."

"You have enough already. Enough to get out."

"I see. You don't want me to find it...whatever it is. You and my grandmother aren't so very different, you know."

Cora's eyes darkened in her ashen face. "What do you want, Clara? I thought you wanted to get out of here. I thought you understood that staying here would be the death of you."

Clara's breath caught in her throat. "But you said..." Then she understood. She saw Cora's duplicity as if it slithered across the floor in front of her. Saw her drawing her to Lina's bedside, the letter opener in her hand, her lip turned up, her eyes aflame, waiting for Clara to strike. Saw her leading Clara on this goose chase, not so that she'd understand why Cora had died, but so she'd know what Lina deserved. "You deceptive, manipulative witch."

She turned and ran for the panel, leaving Cora standing in the graveyard of her ancestors. Where she belonged.

<h1 style="text-align:center">Chapter Twenty-Seven</h1>

Berend watched Lina as she hunched over her lap, paging through a stack of paper. Beneath them, the carriage lurched over the rough terrain. In the distance, a village approached, its ominously familiar road snaking through the valley. A night, not many years past, flashed through his mind. He quaked. Dread, burning like acid, roiled in the pit of his stomach.

"We shouldn't be here," he muttered. Lina seemed not to hear him. He cracked his knuckles and took a deep breath, willing his back muscles to relax.

"I'm losing him." She glanced out the window and shoved the stack aside, its contents disappointing. Several of the top sheets bounced and fluttered to the muddy floor, joining others from her frantic search. Stacks of paper, the sheaves casting at all angles, perched precariously beside her on her side of the carriage.

Berend watched them, his mind unsettled. "No, Lina. You're not."

"But I am. I have. It's all fading. So soon." Her voice cracked, her eyes welling with tears. She hurriedly brushed them with the back of her hand. "Sometimes I can't even picture his face."

Thus far today, his deep voice, which usually soothed her so easily, had had no impact on her. He inhaled, weighing his next words carefully. "No. It has nothing to do with Edgar. None of this does.

You're pushing yourself too hard. Trying to be what they want you to be. Forgetting you don't need them. Any of them.

"What you need is rest. And time to mourn. Not the endless witch hunt or this...this...what is this now? An obsession? Without Edgar, none of this makes an ounce of sense."

If she heard him, or considered his words, she gave no indication.

"And then *he* came." Lina paused for a moment, her eyes fixed on the floor. "And *he* could hardly be bothered. Wasn't the least bit concerned about the death of his son. His *own son*. Or for me. Is that too much to ask? Is it?" Her voice rose in pitch as she queried him, her eyes finally meeting his.

Andreas, an elderly stable master they'd employed since the night of the fire, clucked over the steady clopping of the horses' hooves. The carriage jolted to a stop. Lina's eyes bore the desperate look of her youth, the look that always had the power to grip his heart. Her hand clutched a single sheet of paper lined with names.

"Ah. Your search was successful," he surmised, cringing inwardly. She folded the paper carefully and tucked it into a deep pocket.

They alighted in fog and light rain, before an inn—The Woodsman's Daughter—a half-timber structure packed with crumbling wattle. The city streets looked much like they had the last time they had been there: strewn with offal and waste—some animal, some human—broken bottles, and a single crushed baby bootie, caked with mud and filth. The air smelled foul, as if the fog were laced with disease and degradation.

Andreas drove off in search of the stable. Berend followed Lina as she turned away from the inn. She stepped quickly across the cobblestone road and turned down a narrow alley.

"Lina," Berend tried again, speaking to her back. "We shouldn't be here. You know that. It's early. Come. Let's go home to a warm hearth. I'll make your favorite mulled wine. You can rest. Then you'll remember. Trust me—it'll all come back. All the best things do. It's this weather that's coloring your thoughts, darkening your mood."

She strode on before him, deaf to his pleas.

The balconies of the buildings on either side of the narrow alley overhung the lane, their timber frames leaning at haphazard angles. Berend ducked in several places to avoid clipping his head on the rough edges. Beneath the overhangs, the path lay in stygian darkness. Yet there was movement: the quick scurrying movement of rats and furtive, flitting creatures, but also the wary, slinking movements of those who wish to remain unseen. Berend flinched at the thought of hands reaching out to grip his boots as they passed by.

Ahead of him, Lina trod, her back straight and stiff, resolute. He opened his mouth to remind her that this wasn't the only way. That there were other streets—wider, more trafficked ones. Knowing full well that she would declare them to be too conspicuous...as she had last time. That she would prefer this way of sickness and death for the security she believed it afforded her.

She gasped and came to a sudden stop. He nearly collided with her. Something shifted in the shadows beyond them. A figure crouched there, its head covered in a black veil. It shuffled low to the ground. Berend heard a guttural noise, something between human words and a feral growl. And a voice so low and raspy that he couldn't make out what it asked of them.

He reached into his coat to withdraw their purse. But then the creature laughed—low and harsh, then rising to a point that was high and shrill. A cold wave passed through Berend's body.

"Money? No, no. Money is of no use to me," she said, her voice like a reptile slithering over stone.

Berend took hold of Lina's shoulders, trying to move her around the creature, but she stood frozen.

"Adalinda. I remember you," the creature hissed. "Have you come to take from us again? How needy you must be—so full and yet never satisfied."

"Wait!" the woman shrieked. Lina jumped then leaned back, her shoulder blades tight. The woman's sibilant voice dropped to a harsh whisper. "I hear a voice. *Voices*. They call out from an unmarked grave. Do you hear them? Can you? They grow louder." The creature pressed in close to Lina as if she would take hold of her.

"Lina, come. Let's go." Berend took hold of her arms, trying to pull her back the way they'd come, but she stood fixed.

Lina quivered under Berend's hand. "Who are you?" she croaked.

"Why, you don't know? You don't remember?" The veiled figure shifted where she crouched, sending up a noxious odor of decay mixed with blood and rotting meat. "One who, like you, filled up the full measure of her wrath." Lina finally moved and tried to press around the crone, but a bony hand shot out and gripped her wrist, arresting her retreat. Lina struggled against the woman as she drew her down. "Take a sniff, dearie. That's right. Breathe in the death that clings to you. Inhale the death that awaits you at the end of your road. For it is already a part of you."

"That's absurd." Lina gasped as if she couldn't breathe. "I'm as alive as any woman."

"Are you? What kind of life gains strength from the dead? Or wastes youth on the sickness of the aged? Or clings to the tomb, having cast off the light? No, Adalinda, you walk in death and lie down in death and rise again to live among the dead."

"What do you know of me? Who are you to question me?" Lina whined, fighting to tear her wrist away. "I have no memory of you."

"What is memory? Where is it to be found?" the veiled figure hissed at her. "Heeee...he ate away at your life. Now, in death, he'll claim the rest of your soul."

"Leave me alone, you foul creature." Lina jerked away from her.

The woman cackled and lifted her veil. Beneath it, her mouth was disfigured, torn; her face covered in raw, bloody skin and bulbous growths. One eye gaped open, its surface clouded over. Where her nose had once been, two chasms stood. Her face was that of one who is neither living nor dead. Lina trembled then shot forward toward the end of the alley. Berend followed on her heels, glancing back to see the woman throw off her veil, stumbling toward them.

"Run!" the hag shrieked. "Run from me. But know this. This is your face. This is who you really are. This is what you can't outrun."

As they rounded the corner of the alley and emerged into the village, the woman's laughter floated on the mist and fog, filling their mouths and clinging to their skin.

Hours later they sat at a small table in the corner of a public room on the opposite side of town. They sat in silence, plates of stew long cooled before them, the congealed fat covering the largely uneaten food in gray clumps. The echo of the creature's words still rang in Berend's mind, above the sounds of the crowded room and the crisp melodic notes of a zither.

He glanced at Lina. Her face was blanched and drawn, her eyes distant. He reached across and took her hand in his. She met his eyes, her own despairing and blank.

"We could leave here, now," he urged. "We wouldn't even have to wait for morning. Let's get Andreas. He could have the horses ready in less than an hour." When she didn't respond or show any sign of comprehension, he whispered, his words barely audible, "This is a bad place, Lina. We don't need to be here. You don't need this."

Her eyes blinked rapidly, registering his words. "But I do."

"No, Lina." He squeezed her hand. "You have so much. A graceful home. A family and friends."

She pulled her hand away and cut him off. "Those things never meant anything to me."

"You never *allowed* them to," he contradicted. "This is unhealthy. Haven't I loved you like a brother since we were children? I can't bear to see you languishing when you have so much to live for."

It was the wrong thing to say. He knew it as soon as the words left his mouth. Her disoriented, needful gaze melted into a cold, steely resolve. Yet she smiled faintly, acknowledging his constant care for her.

"Oh, Berend. No. My reason to live died weeks ago."

"Even if that were true, this wouldn't be the answer. You don't need them. You think you do, but you don't. And that *woman*..." He refused to consider that creature who lurked in the dark and smelled of the grave.

"She knows nothing. She certainly doesn't know me," Lina's clipped tone marked the end of her emotional languor. "No, Berend. We came here for a reason."

"No…"

"Yes, Berend."

He tried one last tactic. "Lina, the favor of others rises and falls with the wind, based on nothing more than their own shifting, selfish desires. That can't be the measure by which you know yourself. It isn't stable. Or true."

It was the most pointed comment he had ever made, and he desperately hoped it would cut through her desperate plan and take root. For an instant, her face fell in shock and confusion. When she spoke again, her voice quavered.

"We cannot know our own countenance without a mirror."

Berend cast aside the memory of the creature. *This is your face. This is who you really are. This is what you can't outrun.* "But this. This taking. This using of others can never cover your loss. It can never give you what you want."

"But it already has! It has given me *exactly* what I want. And it will continue to do so for as long as I choose." Her voice rose in a feverish whisper. For a moment, Berend saw Edgar in her histrionic madness. "What are they, but cattle, ambling through life? Directionless. Hopeless. Bound to repeat the worthless history of their ancestors, ad nauseam."

He wasn't sure whether she spoke out of anger or a place of desperate fear; most likely it was both. She no longer was watching him. Instead she leaned back in the obscurity of their corner, quietly watching the other patrons in the long, crowded space.

The door opened and a man and woman entered. From their clothing it was obvious they were rural farmers, here to sell their goods in the market square. Behind them, two young girls lurked, shrinking from the noise and commotion. One—a girl of five or six—clung to her mother's skirts. The other, a few years older, held on to her father's hand, her long blond hair plaited down her back, her face ruddy and chapped from the cool, wet weather.

Lina turned to Berend, a faint smile twisting her face, her eyes dark points in the candlelight.

Chapter Twenty-Eight

"I don't like it." Richter shook his head as he stood at the edge of the window, peering out at the lingering dusk. They already had lit the candles in their attic room. He could hardly make out anything but the room's reflection in the glass panes.

"Yes, but I'm out of other ideas. Unless you have one." Jan paused, waiting for a rebuttal and then, his comment confirmed by the prevailing silence, continued. "We're at a standstill. Frankly you said it yourself: there's not much more we'll be able to uncover from the outside. And now, two more are missing."

Richter winced at the sound of his own words repeated. He racked his brain in vain for an alternative. They had uncovered so much, but all of it whispers and hearsay. There was talk of an illicit relationship between Adalinda and another man, a powerful and well-known duke. Richter had seen the man once or twice, although they had never met. And it was true: Edgar bore a striking similarity to him.

But there were also other rumors, particularly among the townspeople closest to the estate. They spoke of prominent individuals coming to and from the house at all hours of the night when, as one elderly seamstress commented, "no honorable Christian business could be inferred."

Richter suspected she was right. They had found further evidence in the doctor's office. Edgar's daughter had been pregnant less than a year prior and had suffered a miscarriage. It gave credence to all that their source had said. If that was true, the rest was likely true. As they drew closer to unearthing what was likely to be the largest web of crime he had ever uncovered, Richter felt an irresistible desire to back down.

As a boy, he had spent summers with his aunt and uncle not far from here, at the edge of a large forest. He and his cousin, who were only one year apart, and a group of their friends often ventured into the woods, where they enacted all manner of games and explorations, usually forgetting to return home until after dark.

That day in particular, they had engaged in a spirited game of sheriff and robbers. Richter had fought for the part of sheriff, a role he had coveted from an early age, and had won it, partly because most of the boys wanted to be robbers and partly because he had been a particularly tenacious child.

They had refined the rules of the game over the summer, establishing a standard protocol. Early in the day, the sheriff would stash loot in tree hollows, between large boulders in the shallow river and under bushes. Then all the robbers would disperse throughout the woods. Their objective was to find and steal as many of the items as possible.

The sheriff of the game was required to foil their attempts, lock up any captured offenders, then stash the confiscated loot in his own stronghold. Alliances among robbers were allowed but often resulted in betrayal. Finding and then restealing the loot from the sheriff's stronghold was highly respected. The game ended when the sheriff had successfully apprehended all the robbers, or the robbers had captured all the goods. Even then, success was often contended.

The variations of the game made it one of their favorites, and they often spent every day fording rivers, running among the trees, and lying in sunny meadows. Therefore, on that August day, when Richter heard one of the boys shout, he thought nothing of it. He assumed a singular triumph had occurred and one of the others was busy hiding his newfound treasure.

But then, minutes later, he heard another shout. And then one that resembled a scream. And then a confused, distant clamor. He ran, leaving his loot behind him, his few *captured* robbers trailing him into the forest. They rushed toward the sound of the voices, stumbling across tree roots, their feet catching on low-lying vines and fallen branches.

As they hopped from rock to rock across a narrow creek, Richter slid on the moss and slipped into the cool water, soaking his shoe and twisting his ankle. When they reached the clearing, they nearly fell over the other boys who were huddled around one—Klaus—who lay on the ground, his eyes wide, his lips pale, his face beaded with sweat.

"Bit him." "Came out of nowhere." "Hidden there." "Did it bite him a second time?" All the boys were talking at once. Finally Richter heard the word "snake" and understood. Then he shouted, "Stay here" and ran. He ran back the way he had come, trudging through the river, leaping over ferns and beds of leaves, always looking for the most visible, the most open patch of ground on which to land.

By the time he reached his uncle's farm, he was shaking and limping, his ankle aching from the trauma of running after his slip into the river. He found him in the fields, with several other men and panted out the story.

Though the men ran and though they knew from his description exactly where Klaus had fallen, by the time they reached him, the boy was unconscious. They rushed back with him and ran for the town physician. The next day Klaus died.

Shortly afterward, the men of the town, led by Richter's uncle and Klaus's father, headed back into the forest bent on finding the viper's nest and destroying it.

Richter sat in a chair in the cottage, his foot bandaged and propped up on a stool, and watched their backs grow smaller as they crossed the field then disappeared into the woods. In that moment, it wasn't the end of innocence, as he felt the weight of tragedy and his own mortality, that troubled him most. It was the sense that his uncle's and the other men's safety was jeopardized by his actions.

Yes, he knew there was a viper's nest. Yes, it was a threat that probably should be eradicated. Though he was merely a boy—no more than fourteen that summer—and though the men chose to go, partly driven by fear and partly by anger, Richter bore, for the first time in his life, a deep understanding of his responsibility for others. It wasn't until each of them returned, their expressions rigid, their bags full of the snakes' mutilated corpses that he felt the weight of foreboding lift from his chest.

He had never questioned his uncle at that time; had never asked him why the hunting party was so summarily dispatched without any mention of alternatives. It wasn't until many years later that he even considered that the men could have forbidden them from the forest, could have warned them of danger, using Klaus as the unwilling example of their admonitions.

Instead they had acted as one, as if the presence of any malicious force, regardless of the likelihood of personal harm merited action in and of itself. If he had thought to question it as a boy, he would have struggled to understand the risk. But now, years later, he understood. He understood why destructive creatures had to be found and destroyed, regardless of the risk. Because evil grows when left unchecked. And because there are always others who might venture near that nest.

Yet the idea of his words endangering an innocent person still filled him with that same sense of foreboding. For several long minutes he looked at Jan's expression—full of righteous fervor —and saw instead, the backs of those men heading across the field.

"They know who you are," Jan prompted, waiting for a response. "Or at least, Frau Willenheim thinks she does."

Richter sighed and tucked both hands in his pockets. "That is true."

"But they have no idea who I am."

"Also true." Richter walked toward the young man then stopped and assessed him carefully. "But you know what you'll be walking into. Or what we suspect you'll be walking into."

"Yes." Jan's answer came quickly. Too quickly. Richter flinched to hear it and to see his open, eager expression.

"We've agreed," Jan continued. "If your source is correct, there's no way we can disregard what's happening in that house."

"Definitely not."

"And there's no real way to confirm any of our source's claims, without being party to them."

"No. Unfortunately." Richter saw the inevitable rising up before him. Lina and this duke, who was likely Edgar's father, and the others who were involved—it was impossible to say how *many* of them there were, and *who* they were—played their cards very close to the chest. Which only made him more suspicious. Something so widely whispered to be true had to have at least some degree of validity.

And now two more girls were missing. Taken from an inn several towns away. He had never liked the word coincidence. As his old mentor used to say, *Too many coincidences are evidence of one coinciding incident.* There was no other explanation other than that something was happening in that house. Something was occurring that should not be occurring. Richter was sure of that. And they were running out of time.

"So this is really our only possible solution." Jan rocked back and forth on the balls of his feet. When Richter said nothing, he added, a grin on his face, "I'd wrestle you for the honor, but unfortunately they'd recognize you."

Jan meant it as a joke, and Richter tried to smile at the poor attempt at humor, but his apprehension wouldn't allow it. The young man was right, of course. Richter had planned on a longer timeline. One in which he could finagle his way into Lina's inner circle. But with additional young girls missing, he could no longer afford to do things as he had hoped. He had racked his mind, desperately grasping for any other viable option, but unfortunately Jan was right. They really had no other choices.

"Well?" Jan squinted, his sandy eyebrows drawn together, watching Richter's reticence with confusion.

Richter's chest sank. Though he knew the risk of this viper's nest, a danger far greater than the one of his childhood, he desperately prayed the end would be the same as it had been for his uncle: that Jan would emerge from the woods wiser than when he had gone in but otherwise unbitten.

Chapter Twenty-Nine

Clara hesitated, torn between her fear and hope. Above her, the narrow stairway rose from the third floor to a single door. Behind her, Berend huffed, his knees creaking. He held a lamp in one hand, its flame flickering and swinging with his exertion. If she went back down, she'd be left with what she had: Cora and Cora's not-so-disguised agenda. But if she went up, the risk of disappointment could crush her. She rubbed her palms together, locked her fingers, and willed them to be still. When Berend looked up at her in question, she exhaled and continued up the stairs.

The door stood unlocked as it always did. Heavy and swollen in its frame, it resisted entry and only creaked open when Clara shoved against it. Swirling, blowing rain pressed into her, whipping her dress around her legs, and forcing her breath back down her throat. She turn her head to gasp for air.

The day was changeable, deceptive. It had begun dry, with a hint of sunshine sifting through the cloud cover. By late morning, however, the sky turned dark as night, with pouring rain crashing in waves against the morning room windows. Now a shifting mist blew around the rooftop, assailing her from all angles. In the distance, golden light limned the edges of the low cloud cover.

Clara glanced out beyond the roof and recalled the significance of this place. Panic rose in her chest like a large bird beating its wings against her, forcing her toward the edge, demanding that she look down to where the gravel had broken his fall. She blinked back the images that rose in her mind and ran across the slick surface. Standing water puddled in low points, slopping into her shoes and splashing onto the skirt of her dress. At the far end stood the rooftop conservatory, a late addition to the estate that everyone except her mother had since neglected.

From outside its glass walls, Clara saw her mother bending over one of the potting beds, oblivious to their approach. Berend pulled open the door so Clara could enter. It slammed behind them. Her mother rose with a start.

Seeing her guarded expression, Clara flushed, ashamed. Her heart sank. She had pictured something else. She wasn't even sure what exactly. That her mother would welcome and embrace her? That she would be eager to hear what had troubled her so much lately? Maybe, though those were so inconsistent with Helene's careful, calculating nature. At the least, she had hoped for an ally. Or just an alternative to Cora.

But then Helene relaxed and smiled gently. "Clara! What is it?"

Clara smoothed a sodden strand of hair behind her ear and wiped the mist from her face. Her black dress was speckled with dark spots. She stepped down the opposite aisle, a raised bed of decaying plants between them. Her mother appraised her, a journal and pencil in one hand, her eyebrows raised as if she expected a valid reason for the intrusion.

Clara faltered. "Herr Wiegmann had to leave early today. His mother is bedridden," she began. "He hoped I could spend time with you this afternoon. Studying botany."

"Ah, yes," her mother responded, as if she had expected as much. She returned to the subject of her scrutiny. "What did you study today?"

Her tutor, Helmut Wiegmann, a small rotund man with an ample measure of good humor and regional gossip, had delivered a lengthy monologue on the Ottoman Empire and its current relationship to the Germanic states. Usually, after her history lesson, they would break for lunch, after which she would return for her literature and mathematics lessons.

As she provided Herr Wiegmann with rote answers about Sultan Selim I's creation of a navy on the Red Sea, she pondered her predicament. She felt like a puppet led about by Cora and her grandmother. Did she even have free agency? And if she did, why hadn't she found the way out? Was her imprisonment a result of her own determination? How could that be when she would never choose it? Would she?

Her head began to hurt.

"Fraulein?" Herr Wiegmann looked at her, expecting an answer.

Clara racked her brain to recall the recent train of the conversation. Yes, Suleiman the Magnificent. "He failed to take Vienna," she said.

"That's right. When was that?"

"Both times. In 1529 and again in 1532."

He nodded, smiling to himself as if he were greatly pleased and proud, presumably of her. But all Clara could think about was the navy of an empire that, at the height of its power, couldn't take Vienna. What did that mean for her?

Her mother looked at her, perplexed. Clara just shrugged. "The same as every morning: French, philosophy, and history." But then something crept into her mind and she added, "We discussed Suleiman the Magnificent and his efforts to take Vienna."

A nervous look passed over her mother's face, and she glanced past her to where Berend stood near the door. Clara turned away until the smirk faded from her face. When she looked back, she could no longer find the words she had wanted to say. Instead she picked at the wilting leaves in front of Helene. A thick smell of organic decay filled the room. "Aren't they all dead?" The space was cold and dim despite the glass shell, lit only with a couple of lamps her mother had carried with her, and the one Berend held.

"I don't think this one is." Helene felt around the base of the plant, looked at the underside of its leaves, and jotted a note in her notebook.

"It looks dead to me." Clara leaned over it. But on closer inspection, she noted the stem was green despite the browning leaves.

"Sometimes what looks dead just needs some nurturing to rebound." Helene shot her a furtive look then moved down to the next plant in the row.

Clara slid down the opposite side. "Wouldn't they be better off outside?"

"No. Most of these would never survive if they were. That's why they're in here." Helene scanned the room then bent to examine large floppy leaves that lay in the dirt. Her head tilted to the side as she considered it.

Clara felt her frustration grow and bloom into something just shy of anger. "They look pretty neglected to me. I'm not sure they're any better off." She fought back her tears and bit her lower lip to avoid saying any more.

"It probably looks that way," Helene concurred. For several minutes she walked, examined, and made notes in her journal. Clara thought the conversation was over. But then her mother sighed and looked at Clara with regret in her eyes. "Winter is always the hardest season for any plant."

"It isn't winter yet," Clara whispered.

"For these plants, it's been winter for quite some time," Helene countered. "But you see, plants have an innate sense that spring will come again. That if they hold on, if they rest where they're planted, the sun will return."

"They give up."

"Far from it. If they gave up, they would all be dead. But many of these are not. They're sleeping. They're waiting for what comes next."

"But couldn't you have helped them? Isn't that the point of a conservatory?"

"It is." Helene exhaled slowly, not meeting Clara's heated gaze. "But even the best conservatory can't make it summer when it's not. And it *is* partly my fault. I didn't know what to do about them for a long time."

"But now you do."

"Yes. I do. That's why I'm here. There's a lot that I can do now that I see the true state of things."

Clara frowned, confused. She didn't understand what they were talking about, and she didn't dare ask. She had been wrong to come here. Wrong to suggest it to Herr Wiegmann. Her mother had no intention of helping her leave this house. And she wouldn't believe any part of what Clara had discovered about her grandmother.

Chapter Thirty

Jan groaned, his head in his hands. He slumped over on the edge of the bed in their attic room. The inn below them was still relatively quiet as the late afternoon faded. Soon patrons would arrive and take up places in the public room, where they could dry off in the overheated space, listen to folk music, and drink.

"I'm not sure you're right." Richter stood watching him. "This may be just what we need."

"How can you say that?" Jan's muffled voice was tinged with despair.

"You met this other gentleman? This Werner Regensbach?"

"Yes, but he's so far below the duke. It doesn't help us. We need the duke. How else can we get into that house and verify what they're doing?

"It was that comment about leadership." Jan stood and paced before kicking the wall in frustration. "So stupid. So, so stupid. That was what did it." Jan couldn't erase the memory of his meeting with Heinrich. It played over and over in his mind. Though he had tried to assume the part of a nobleman's child, the duke must have suspected him.

. . .

"You come highly recommended. I've heard much about your business acumen. And at such a young age." His tone carried a strong element of incredulity, but Jan waved it off, thanking him instead.

"It's easy to succeed with the mentors I've had the privilege of having. If anything, I've done nothing but follow their example."

"Very wisely said." Heinrich nodded and twisted one end of his mustache into a point.

"It's something my grandfather always told me: the best thing for any young man is that he allies himself with and learns from strong leadership."

"Is that so?"

Jan merely nodded.

"But what is 'strong leadership?'"

"What do you mean?" Jan colored, searching his mind for any possible misstep he may have made.

"Some might claim that Prussia is just that."

"Oh, well..."

"In fact, many would say that Bavaria would be wise to place itself under Prussia's 'strong leadership.' You see, Diedrich, sometimes..."

Richter shook his head thoughtfully. "He probably was just testing you."

"But he turned the entire conversation into a political debate. I didn't even know what to say."

"Exactly."

Jan sighed deeply and leaned against the wall. "I'm not following you."

"You were up front with him. He knows you're not Bavarian. So he pulled out the one trigger that would anger a Prussian loyalist the most. And you didn't know how to respond."

"Yes..."

"Think about it, Jan. You—or *Diedrich*, as it were—came with a very high commendation. And you were able to speak to it well enough to be convincing. Heinrich is a staunch supporter of Bavarian independence. Someone like him is likely to question what game you're playing. He would want to feel you out, see which side you're on. If you were in with the chancellor's forces, you would have either defended Prussia, tried to negotiate with him about the advantages of a united central state, or pretended to secretly sympathize with Bavaria.

"You did none of those. Someone clever, with malicious designs will rarely falter in such a case."

"So I'm not clever."

"He likely sees you as a neutral party. Worst-case scenario, he has no idea what to make of you. But he has almost certainly dismissed you as a threat."

"All right. I see where you're going, but I don't know how that helps us. He still sent me off to this other person. Werner." He walked back to the bed and sank down.

"And you'll take the job."

"What?!"

"What would it look like if you didn't?"

"Like I was lying, playing him."

"Absolutely. Besides, I think you've overlooked one crucial factor: you have presented yourself as someone who is related to those who are very high in Prussian society. And he can't be sure you aren't who you say you are. Which means Heinrich can't brush you off without risking social disgrace. He has to know you'll communicate with your supposed grandfather, who will in turn communicate with his friends and colleagues, some of whom may be essential to Heinrich's network of allies."

"But Werner..."

"Who is he? I don't know. But he has to be close enough to Heinrich's network that being close to him will keep you very close to the duke. Close enough that your *purported* grandfather will be satisfied that his name was honored. And close enough that you'll likely be able to ingratiate yourself further with Heinrich and win his confidence."

"Then why didn't the duke take me on himself?"

"Simple. He doesn't trust you."

"Okay. That makes no sense at all." Jan shook his head. "One minute I'm not a threat and the next he doesn't trust me."

Richter smiled, pleased with himself. "Actually it makes all the sense in the world. You're not a threat politically. But he doesn't trust you personally. Look at it this way: who trusts people most easily?"

"Children. Simple people, I suppose."

"Right. People who have no malicious designs. People who have no thought of evil, let alone a history of evil they carry. They assume no ill intentions on the part of others because they have none themselves. And they likely have had no experience with such people.

"But Heinrich is neither a child nor a simple person nor an innocent one." Richter watched as Jan's eyes lit up with understanding. "He expects evil from others because that's what he is."

"So he couldn't possibly trust me...or anyone else," Jan added.

"No, not at first glance. He'd almost certainly assume that you, like himself, are duplicitous. He'll want to keep you close enough to save himself any social embarrassment, but far enough that he'll be shielded from your nefarious intentions–whatever he might suppose those to be."

"But then where does that leave us? We don't have years to win his trust. And as you've said, he isn't likely to trust anyone he doesn't know well enough."

Richter held his finger up and waited, lost in thought for a moment. "Actually I didn't say exactly that. I didn't say he wouldn't trust anyone." He strode confidently toward Jan then stopped, a sly grin on his face. "Who would an evil person trust most? For that matter, who would anyone trust most?"

"I...I don't know." Jan righted his spectacles, which were sliding down his nose. "People who come referred to them, perhaps. People who are associated with a group or organization they respect. Particularly those groups of which they themselves are members. People who belong to the same congregation." His eyes assumed a far-off look then fastened onto Richter, who was waiting for him to come to the conclusion. "People who are the most like themselves."

"Aha!" Richter tapped his finger in the air and beamed at him.

"That's right. We trust those who are most like ourselves. Those who have the same tendencies. Especially those whose vulnerabilities match our own. Because we understand them, we sympathize with them.

"It's the wife engaged in a secret tryst who's most likely to sympathize with the woman who kills her husband out of a desperate desire to be free from his oversight. It's the man who's swindling money from the bank where he works who secretly envies the jewelry thief. It's the man who's mired in a web of depravity who has compassion for the young man who's a slave to passion."

Jan stared at him for a second before the implication set in. "Wait a minute. A slave to...what?"

Richter grasped him by the shoulders and looked down into his face. "What better way to get into their confidence quickly than to prove you're one of them? That you're a young version of themselves? You must be a mirror of Heinrich's own dark nature."

"What are you suggesting?! That I..." He couldn't even voice the idea; it was so distasteful.

"Yes, exactly!" When Jan still stared at him, his mouth open, Richter backpedaled, "We wouldn't have to go too far. The key is the appearance of the thing. It needs to appear to be a credible attempt to engage in illicit activity. The right form of illicit activity."

"Won't that just get me booted to the curb?"

"No. No! It definitely won't. Trust me. Best-case scenario, you'll really be a promising young man—the kind they will include in their *activities*. And if they're involved in the sorts of things my source has indicated, the worse you appear, the better."

"And worst-case scenario?" Jan asked, incredulous. "Even before I win over said individuals, there's a matter of the local law enforcement."

"No, there isn't." Richter smiled and walked to the window to peer out into the fading daylight.

"Why is that?"

Richter turned and sent him a knowing glance. "Because they're in on it."

Chapter Thirty-One

If the curtains had been drawn as tightly as they usually were, if Clara had been sleeping as soundly as she normally did, if she had latched the window properly, and if the clouds hadn't parted at just the right time, letting in the piercing moonlight, she might never have discovered the truth.

But as it was, she did.

She had been sleeping fitfully, her vertigo refusing to settle, a mild but persistent nausea filling her chest. Every time she moved—rolling onto her back, over on her side, stretching her legs out diagonally, or curling up in a ball—she felt increasingly uncomfortable. Finally she threw off the heavy covers, thinking she was too hot, only to shiver as a draft wafted over her nightgown.

Through the break in the curtains, a bright stream of moonlight shone into the room, drawing her attention and rendering further sleep impossible. She arose, padded across the rug to the cold wood floor, and then, gripping the curtains to pull them tight, realized the window was ajar.

As she knelt across the window seat and leaned forward to pull the window closed, movement caught her eye. There, at the far end of the gravel drive, beneath the skeletal forms of the denuded trees, a dark shape drew near: a vehicle of sorts. Attached to it, a lantern hung, swinging lightly as it advanced. The swaying light gave it the jaunty air of a man strolling confidently up the drive. Clara sat back on her heels, her hand still gripping the window latch and stared in surprise.

When it came closer, she made out the unmistakable form of a fully enclosed Landau carriage. Its curtains were drawn unnecessarily, for even with the brief interlude of moonlight, there was no way to make out the person or persons within. It looked vaguely familiar, as if it might have been among those at her father's memorial, but in the dark she couldn't make out the crest on the side of the cab.

As it circled the fountain, a tall figure dashed from the front of the house, his hands extended. *Berend?* He rushed toward the carriage and spoke quickly with the driver, pointing toward the far drive that looped around the chapel. The driver tipped his hat in understanding and continued on around the fountain, doubling back to the adjoining drive around the side of the house.

Clara leaned out the window and watched as the figure turned and marched toward the house. It *was* Berend. At any other time, the rain and cloud cover might have obstructed Clara's view. But at that precise moment, the pale, cold light illuminated his face and form. Just then he looked upward. She gasped and sat back with a start, leaving the window gaping open.

Her heart racing, she backed through the curtains then pulled them tight. The clock on the mantel read 1:49. Just then, a figure stepped out from behind the bed curtains.

"Now why on earth would anyone arrive at such an hour?" Cora shook her head as if perplexed. She still wore the same white dress, and her sopping hair still dripped incessantly, but her face had changed. Her eyes were sunken and bloodshot. Her face had grown gaunt.

When she lifted a bony hand to clutch the bedpost, Clara gasped and fell back, collapsing into the curtains. As she fell, her back struck the edge of the window seat. She hunched over on the floor and moaned, reaching around to rub her bruised flesh.

"What are *you* doing here?" she groaned.

"You're here."

"I *don't* need you." Clara said.

"Of course you do."

"No. I don't."

"How would you know? You've done nothing without me. And you'll accomplish nothing else without me."

"You sound like your mother," Clara muttered.

Cora's face grew darker, her expression vicious and calculating. She looked ready to issue a sharp retort, but then she glanced toward the fireplace. The clock read 1:52. "Fine then. Where are we going? Why don't you lead the way, since you're so capable?"

Clara looked around, uncertain. Her back hurt when she twisted. She looked back out the window. The driveway lay still and dark, Berend and the carriage long gone. A graveyard of secrets she couldn't hope to resurrect. "I suppose I'll head for the chapel and see for myself."

"They aren't in the chapel."

"How would you know?"

"Because I know where they're going. And what they're doing. And why they're here at this hour. All the things you also know but refuse to see." Cora's teeth had grown menacing in some way. Her gums were darker. "Besides, you'd just get yourself caught."

"By whom? If they aren't there, there's hardly any risk."

"Hagan is there. The guests aren't."

"Why wouldn't he be with them? Or in bed for that matter?" Clara asked.

"Because their guests already have what they came for," Cora stated without emotion. "Do you want to know the truth or do you want to sit here questioning me all night?"

Clara bit her lip. *I could have sworn they were one and the same.*

"By all means, Clara, proceed."

The girl wasn't going to tell her. There was nothing to be done but to pick up where she had left off.

"Fine. Come with me. Or don't." She crossed to the dressing room, refusing to look behind her, and took a robe from her armoire. A minute later, she heard Cora follow her through the passages.

Chapter Thirty-Two

"My list is missing," Lina hissed. She pulled the door shut behind her so she and Berend stood alone in the hallway of the east wing. Ensconced gas lamps cast heavy amber pools of light bordered by pockets of deep shadow.

"I can't understand how…"

"It was in my desk. You saw it in my hand merely days ago. I found it and put it back in my desk." Her voice rose to a whispered scream, her face pulled tight. "This is her doing; I know it." Lina watched his face. He hardly seemed concerned. A door opened farther down the hall. Someone peered out then disappeared again, slamming the door. She winced. "They need to be quieter."

"There's no one to hear." Nevertheless, his voice dropped. "She isn't well; that's certain. But how would she manage it. I just don't see…"

Lina felt her frustration grow. "No. No. No. That's not the point and you know it. She's been following me. She knows something or is looking for something. God only knows what she thinks she's discovered. Or what she understands. Or what she might do with what she had found."

"Okay. I believe you."

Lina knew he didn't, but there was nothing she could say. She had explained it to him clearly. Several times. And he had to know. They couldn't afford to have that girl—anyone for that matter but *especially* her—snooping around. If Clara had gone through her personal papers, what more had she discovered?

"If she can get into my room, she could just as easily be here. Tonight." She glared at Berend.

"Lina, I can't possibly..." Another door opened near them and a man emerged, only partially clothed. Berend set a hand on her shoulder and looked down at her with that expression of perfect confidence she had always trusted. "Look, we'll get to the bottom of this. We'll watch her more closely. We'll do whatever we have to do to uncover what's going on. But right now we have to deal with the business at hand. I'm telling you she isn't well. Whatever she might or might not know."

Lina watched the count approach them expectantly. Berend was right: Clara wasn't well. In fact, she was clearly ill, had been since her father died. Maybe even prior to that. A head sickness that showed up in odd ways. In her illusion at the botched séance. In her eccentric, artistic flights of fancy. She smiled at the thought, her mind turning to new possibilities, one in particular that would solve everything so easily.

But in one thing Berend was right. There was nothing they could do in the middle of the night, with a house full of guests and potential complications. Tomorrow—tomorrow they would revisit this problem. If the girl couldn't be contained, they would have to take more drastic action. They couldn't afford to have her snooping around. Or getting out, God forbid. If she did, especially with that list in hand, the downfall would be catastrophic.

Chapter Thirty-Three

In retrospect, Clara's skin had crawled from the moment they had entered the attic. But it had been easy to shut it out. To ignore it. At first. To look away from the heavy trunks against the wall beneath the grimy windows. To turn away from the moonlight that filtered through the panes in greasy, yellow strands, and to forget that night so many years ago and what she had seen. Or at least, to press it behind something else—a convenient and more current focus.

The ledgers she had taken from her grandfather's study never would have fit in the base of her window seat, a space already more than half filled with her journals. So she had hidden them in the attic—far from where Jutta or her grandmother might discover them. Here, over the last few days, she had been able to lay them out and scrutinize the contents. She had hoped they would tell her something.

She needn't have bothered.

In less than an hour, Clara let the last ledger's sturdy cover with its triangular leather corners fall shut. Nothing. She stood and looked around in frustration. The attic was littered with furniture, heavy mirrors, wardrobes brimming with old clothes, and trunks. But nothing that suggested any incriminating evidence.

Cora sat in a chair in the shadows watching her, an impish smile playing on her lips. "Find the answer to the riddle yet?"

Clara crossed to a similar chair and curled up in its worn velvet, the warp and woof showing through in places. She pulled her legs up, hugging her knees. From where she sat, she couldn't escape seeing the window set high in the attic wall. And beyond, the moonlight scuttling out from behind the cloud cover. And beneath them, a trunk coated in gray dust. An icy ball settled into her stomach and sent tendrils skittering along the lengths of her arms. She hugged them against her chest, rubbing at them beneath the sleeves of her robe, willing her skin to warm and banish the feeling of something foreign and invasive creeping along her flesh.

She blinked and focused on Cora. And the ledgers.

They contained the same payments to the same people, with small differences, month after month and year after year. She'd accidentally picked up several older ledgers, notated in a crisper version of her grandfather's handwriting, before his hands had begun to tremble. Even they, dating from twenty or more years ago, contained much of the same.

Of course the family income fluctuated, but the expenses remained relatively constant. One outlier—a one-time payment to a Baron Hildebrand—stood out in an early journal. Otherwise, the payments were fairly standard. A monthly allotment notated for Berend that, given its size, surely included the wages to be doled out to the servants. Separate payments for carpenters, music instructors, her tutor, and her art instructor. And in the last ten or fifteen years, payments to someone named Emil.

Either way, Clara had found nothing that helped her, and she had no idea where to look next. In an estate of this size, evidence could be anywhere. Even if she knew what she was looking for.

A strange sound—like a mewling kitten—whispered in the stillness.

Clara froze, silencing her thoughts. "Did you hear that?"

"Hear what?" Cora narrowed her eyes at her, her expression mocking.

There it was again. Not a mewling, but a small, strangled sound, as if something, or someone were crying in the distance. A child. It grew louder, muffled but louder. The room around her seemed to expand.

The walls pressed outward; the ceiling rose to twice its height; the furniture swelled. But rather than sensing this as if the world around her had grown, Clara felt suddenly small, exposed, certain of something she couldn't articulate.

"You've heard that sound before," Cora said.

Outside, a flash of light cut through the night. Then she remembered.

She had been six, maybe seven, the first time her parents had taken her to Tänzelfest in Kaufbeuren. Beforehand, they had tried to excite her with the idea, her mother with a detailed discussion of the program of events, her father with erratic exclamations of her impending joy. But still, she had been unprepared.

If they had told her about the fireworks and the flaming torches; about the actors and musicians; about the brilliant splashes of color in the pageantry and costumes and flags; about the music that threaded its way into her soul and carried her along, she would have soared with anticipation. They went at least three or four years in a row. Then they had stopped.

She hadn't recalled it since then. Until now. Had forgotten it entirely. Strange.

"It's right there, if you'd just take hold of it. What did you see in the trunk?" Cora gestured to the one beneath the window.

Clara shivered as her aunt's words echoed in her mind.

"Who..." she began. Then stopped. The trunk across from her seemed to shudder. She stared at it, the cold ball uncurling its long bony fingers from her stomach, crawling up her chest, gripping her spine. Her back felt locked, paralyzed. Dust seemed to rise from the trunk's soiled and filthy surface. It trembled again. Then jerked. As if something lay hidden within it.

Clara yelped and jumped from the chair. She ran behind a heavy chest of drawers, where she crouched, her fingers gripping the side of the wood. She peered around it. The trunk trembled again.

She looked up at the moonlight, and just then, the gleam of light cut out from behind a cloud and fell onto the wood floor before her. The shape of the clouds, the particular coloring of the stained beam of light, and the trunk all coincided in her mind.

Tänzelfest.

Something she wasn't supposed to have seen. Something she had fought hard not to remember. Bored of her mother's and grandmother's conversation, she had left her mother's side. Had gone to find her father. They had brought two carriages. Behind the second a thud sounded. Then that same small strangled sound. Her father and Berend had cursed.

She had stepped lightly toward the back of the carriages, her black boots crunching on the rocky path. They hadn't seen her until it was too late. By then she had seen Berend bending over the trunk, righting it from where it had fallen, its lid flopped open. She had seen the small white shoes, a buckle broken and hanging loose. And a slender, pale arm, marred by four dark bruise marks. Then the trunk closed and was secured roughly onto the back of the carriage.

Clara looked back to the attic trunk. It seemed to lie still, but a shudder had gripped her and wouldn't let go. She stood, her legs trembling and wobbly, and stumbled to a wardrobe. After flinging open the doors, her hands tore at the clothes, pulling them from the hangers then discarding them on the floor.

Finally. She held one of her mother's summer dresses from years ago: a pale-green one covered in tiny sprigs of white flowers. Clutching it in her sweaty grip, she fell to the floor, knotted the dress into a ball, and scrubbed the surface of the trunk, rubbing it with both hands. Still, the dust gathered in the crevices and clung. It smeared in arcing patterns, willfully resting her attempts to expel it.

She ground the dress against the surface until it tore and her arms ached. Then threw the ruined dress to the side. She fell back on the floor, her breath heaving, her sight blurred. Around her the room spun. Fast. Then slower. And slower. It grew still as her heart rate leveled off. She started to rise when a crash sounded, catching her off balance. This time the trunk lay still and mute, having said what it had to say.

The crash shook the floor again.

It was a door. Just a door closed too hard. Then another. Below her.

Clara breathed out slowly and stood, brushing her dusty hands down the front of her night robe. Then she paused. *Below her?* The only rooms beneath this section of the attic were the third-floor ones near Cora's rooms. Rooms that were consistently unoccupied, unused.

She tiptoed across the floor then stopped. The sound of scurrying and movement filled the silence. Yes, there was definitely someone there. At an hour and in a portion of the house where no one had any legitimate reason to be.

"We don't have time for this." Cora's voice cut through the tension.

Clara jumped. Cora stood next to the chair, watching her, waiting.

"What's going on?"

"Oh, I don't know, Clara. Maybe they've just come to pray. In the bedrooms below us. At three in the morning."

"I'm tired of your games, Cora. Either tell me what's going on or leave."

"I thought that you don't need me. That you've been fine without me. So why don't you tell me how you're going to discover the answer to this little riddle. Pray tell."

Clara turned and ran lightly and swiftly for the way back into the hidden passages.

When they drew near the rooms in Cora's wing of the house, she heard faint voices, sounds of movement and someone crying. A woman. No, a girl. A young girl's pleading voice. Clara stood within the wall, her hand shaking as she grasped the cover to the peephole. The air vibrated in her ears as she held it in her hands.

It slid to the side with a soft, grating noise—the sound of tiny shoed heels dragged across a hardwood floor. The sound of a trunk being loaded onto a carriage. She dropped the cover and stepped back.

"No. I don't want to see this." Her whisper was hoarse, her breath ragged.

"Oh, no. No, you don't. This is going to end." Cora gripped her arm and yanked her toward the wall, shoving her face up to the opening.

She held the cover open. Clara tried to shut her eyes. But found she couldn't. Not anymore.

Candlelight licked at the cold shadows. The sound of heavy breathing and whimpering expanded to fill the darkness. A slender arm, gleaming white, lay pinned to the mattress—the sheet bunched, clenched in a tiny fist.

Clara's breath caught in her throat. Eventually she moved down the dark passage to another shielded glimpse of another room. Then another.

Beside her, Cora whispered, "Don't you remember the bird?"

Her mind filled with the image of dappled sunlight through the boughs of the apple trees. She had been nine or ten. That spring her father had hosted a business associate and his family. Their son—a boy with a round head, a tiny nose, and gleaming caramel eyes—had been her constant playmate. He was the one who found it.

A bird, lying in the soft grass of the orchard. One of its wings was broken, the long line of feathers turned in a sharp angle. They had knelt beside it, their eyes wide, watching its small beak open and close in a silent plaintive cry. He had pressed on the bird's abdomen, heard its small squeak of protest. Then, when Clara had looked at him, his eyes had narrowed.

He reached down and clutched the other wing, the healthy one, in his hand. And twisted. A brittle snap. Clara gasped as the bird's eyes widened, its mouth wide. When she looked back, he held a small pocketknife in his hand.

"No." She clutched at his arm.

Around them, a cold, damp breeze gathered. The leaves shivered on the boughs above them, raising Clara's hair. A tremor ran through her. He looked at her again. She nodded.

He clutched the pocketknife and drove it into the breast of the bird. Suddenly she tasted rain on the air. Felt the trembling of the earth beneath her. Heard the distant lapping of the lake and the thrumming of a flock of geese taking flight. Felt her heart lifting, fluttering, as if she would rise with them.

Clara stepped away from the wall, into the shadows of the dark passage, her heart pounding, her eyes bright.

Leaves of Gold

"It is not until we have passed through the furnace that we are made to know how much dross there is in our composition."
—Charles Caleb Colton

Chapter Thirty-Four

"Him! Him! That...that vile creature! That disgusting disgrace to humanity!" Richter shook his finger toward Jan then turned back to shout at Inspector Metz.

Jan had followed Richter's instructions carefully, and it had worked exactly as planned. Perhaps too well. Jan glanced around the stark, cold cell and felt a flush of shame. He felt his color rise, flooding his skinny neck.

He had never been on this side of a jail cell. It felt remarkably different. The powerlessness, the knowledge that he was at the mercy of others cast a startlingly different light on the space.

Outside of the cell, he heard Richter still shouting. Twice he had peered around the police inspector's desk to yell insults and threats at him. Even though he knew it was a sham, Jan struggled not to cower. For some reason, his mother's face rose into his mind whenever Richter's voice rose. Her eyes were downcast, unable to meet his. And he couldn't blame her.

But Richter had been very specific. Jan was not to display any shame other than a thinly veiled attempt to appear remorseful. The more contrived, the better. According to Richter, anything else was likely to have an adverse outcome.

Above all, he was not to deviate from the plan in any way.

Their associate, Markus, had found her, an orphan, in some larger city—Ingolstadt or Regensburg; Jan was too flustered to recall. He had explained to her what she would do. And gain. Of course she had agreed. She had had no reason not to.

It had gone exactly as planned. Jan had taken her to an inn where Richter—the girl's "father"—and the local police had found them. But now he felt dirty, as if he had violated some sacred commandment he hadn't known existed.

Richter's constant shouting—his features contorted and purple with rage—didn't help.

"He's clearly, *clearly* the abductor you've been looking for. Why, you saw it with your own eyes. Isn't that just what you need: to stop this horrific criminal before any more girls go missing? The police are lucky...damn lucky, if I say so myself...to have me here. To have such a concerned citizen when the very criminal you had failed to apprehend simply fell right into my hands. He should be shot! Tortured! Castrated! I'm damn sure you aren't going to miss your one opportunity to see justice done. Damn sure! If I have to do it myself..."

Jan heard Inspector Metz trying to explain to Richter that yes, a crime appeared to have been committed. Of course, he wasn't able to speak to whether that was certainly the case until he had reviewed the evidence. But he could confirm Jan most likely wasn't the one responsible for the missing girls. He was simply too young. And his technique was—proven by his current state—ineffective. The man— and they did in fact believe it was *one* man—who was responsible for such a vile crime as the one to which the girl's father alluded, would have had more refined methods of capture. He almost certainly would be very hard to catch.

Eventually Richter, coaxed by Metz, relinquished his attempt to oversee what he insisted should be a nearly immediate execution. He wasn't persuaded. But he recognized his inability to effect any solution. Thus he left.

When, less than an hour later, Jan heard the door open, he assumed

Richter had returned. He didn't even bother looking up from his cot where he was resigned to spending the night. But then footsteps approached his cell, and he found himself staring into the faces of Chief Inspector Dressler and Jan's new master, Herr Werner Regensbach.

"Ah. So this is the young man. Most unfortunate." Dressler stood looking at Jan, his expression inscrutable.

Jan stared at Werner, his eyes wide, waiting for his response. Then, an instant later, he recalled Richter's admonitions and fought to assume a sheepish, roguish look that could only be interpreted as a lack of remorse.

"Diedrich," Werner began, "this is quite the predicament. Indeed it appears you've had quite a night."

Jan shrugged and launched into a poor defense of his actions. "It isn't what it seems. The things they're accusing me of..."

"Vile accusations," Dressler stated. "Frankly, young man, your behavior does indeed appear to be quite reprehensible."

He continued to speak, outlining the implications of Jan's conduct. Jan was only faintly listening. Instead he reminded himself to assume Richter's perspective and watch for what the two men *weren't* saying.

Dressler wore a guarded expression that was neither condemnation nor condonation. He spoke of consequences, yet his face showed no sign of anger or censure. Rather he seemed almost unsettled, as if he was out of his element. If Richter was right—and Richter was usually right —Dressler not only knew of the activities at the estate but also was involved in them. It wasn't surprising then that the incident at hand, crossing over between his professional obligations and his personal proclivities, was perplexing. Yet the inspector wore a troubled, questioning gaze as he assessed him. Jan had the sense that something about the situation—something other than Jan's supposed intentions— troubled him greatly.

His master, in contrast, was clearly unable to hide his thoughts. The man looped his thumbs into his vest and thrust his chest out as he watched Jan. On the surface, he listened to Dressler's assessment, nodding his head and fixing his lips in a hard line. But his eyes betrayed him. They glinted, clearly amused at the boy's attempts. He bore the look a proud parent has when a child has just said or done something particularly admirable.

A tremor of disgust washed over Jan. It was all he could do to maintain his flippant, impenitent air.

They were staring at him, waiting. Jan dug through his memory but could find no thread from the conversation. Instead he picked up the easiest resource: an excuse. "I didn't mean anything by it. It might have been the beer. It hit me harder than usual."

Dressler notated his comment in a small journal.

Werner nodded, his expression reaching for a way to justify his sympathy. "It'll do that sometimes. Especially in a lad as young as yourself. I wouldn't be surprised at all."

"Werner, with all due respect, this is hardly an excuse. If a little beer rendered a man a reprobate, Bavaria would be full of criminals. You yourself have been known to enjoy the darker varieties as often as not."

They cast a glance at each other, laden with meaning. Clearly they knew one another, were even on intimate social standing. Jan made a note of it to confirm to Richter.

"I'm not a kidnapper!" Jan protested.

Two sets of eyebrows rose as they considered his words. Dressler's pencil hovered above the page of his notebook. "What were you planning to do with Fräulein Maier?"

"Do?" Jan felt his color rising.

"Do. Yes." When Jan didn't respond, Dressler added, "You were with the young girl. Alone. In a private inn. You must have had some end in mind."

"Come now, Dressler, old boy. Leave the kid alone. I think it's obvious there's an innocent explanation. Isn't that the case?" Werner nodded to Jan then proceeded without waiting for a reply. "Can we even say a crime has been committed? They were alone, but did you witness anything more compromising?"

"I don't know what I was thinking," Jan echoed, following his lead. "I liked her. We were just talking."

"Hmm." Dressler made another notation then rubbed his bushy sideburn thoughtfully. "Most people wouldn't consider such behavior to be to be innocent, young man. You'd best think twice in the future or you'll find yourself in much hotter water than you're in now."

"Emil, has he even committed a crime?"

Dressler ignored the question as he studied Jan. A ray of dark suspicion flooded his eyes. "Tell me: your accent is distinctly northern. Have you ever attempted such a thing closer to home?"

Jan racked his brain. To say no would undermine his "in" in Werner's world. To say "yes" could open him up to investigation.

"Girls in the north are more amenable."

For a moment, both men stared at him, their mouths open in puzzled shock. Then Werner rocked back on his heels and roared in laughter, tears streaming from his eyes. Even Inspector Dressler turned away, rubbing at his lip as if to conceal his inability to maintain a straight face.

Eventually the two men walked away. His master winked at him; the inspector shook his head and chuckled under his breath. Jan heard them faintly talking with Metz in the front room. Sometime later they returned. Dressler held a set of keys in one hand. When they reached Jan's cell, Dressler inserted the key and turned.

"Come on, boy," Werner said. "You're coming with me."

Jan glanced at Dressler, whose expression was both conspiratorial and suspicious. He didn't ask questions or wait for the inspector to change his mind. Rather, Jan plucked up his wool overcoat and rushed out of the cage. He didn't breathe more easily until they were several blocks away.

Werner placed his arm over Jan's shoulder and winked at him. "I think we understand each other, young man. I think we do."

Jan struggled not to tremble with rage.

Afterwards, Dressler sat on the edge of Metz's desk and eyed him skeptically. Metz leaned back in his chair. Silence hung in the air like shards of glass.

"What do you make of it?" Metz finally asked.

"Honestly I haven't the slightest idea. The entire incident is absurd, juvenile even. Any practiced criminal would have made a better go at it."

"Maybe he *isn't* practiced. Maybe he's just getting started."

"Do you think so?"

"Me?!" Metz asked, confused, then paused to consider the question. "Well, now that you ask, I suppose not."

"Why?"

"I don't know. It just doesn't feel right."

Dressler nodded, his face lined with concern. "That's exactly it. Everything about the incident points to intent. Even from the boy. Werner tells me he hails from a notable family in Prussia. Was referred to him by Heinrich von Ehrenschau. To do such a thing..." He shook his head. "There's something incohesive about it. Discordant."

Metz raised his eyebrows. When he did, they mirrored the black line of his mustache. With his mouth open, he appeared comical, like a caricature one would see in the local papers. Dressler suppressed a smile.

"Herr Regensbach seems taken with him."

"Herr Regensbach sees what he wants to see."

"You think he's familiar with..." Metz trailed off, leaving the unmentionable unspoken.

"I have no idea. It may be that he is. And this far from home, he's looking for what he's accustomed to having. Yet...he feels green."

"He is young."

"Yes. But there's young. And then there's *young*. His eyes are just a bit too wide for the situation."

"I see." Metz twirled the ends of his mustache and leaned forward. The front of his chair jolted as the legs hit the wood floor. "Perhaps he's looking for something that might age him a bit."

"That's just the problem." Dressler muttered the words, mostly to himself. "That is *exactly* the problem. He's looking for something. My gut tells me that he's up to more than appearances would indicate. The boy is a potential liability. We need to know what he's looking for. And why." His eyes were set on Metz but were unfocused, lost in contemplation. "And that begins with who."

"Who?"

"Yes. Look into him. His purported family. His history. His connections. Anything you can find. I want to know who he is, where he's from and what he's doing here."

Chapter Thirty-Five

Back in their attic room in the inn, Richter watched the frustrated young man pace, his face averted from him. "Are you saying that you'd like to back out?" he asked.

"No. No, it's just. I don't know what I'm saying." Jan was blushing again, his face a rich crimson. "It's just that you didn't see his face."

"Werner's?"

"Yes. It was...it was like staring into the eyes of a dragon."

"I can imagine."

"Can you?"

"I think I can." And Richter could. He had stared down many dragons over the last nearly three decades of his career. Of course many didn't have that same degree of remorselessness. But he knew what Jan was referring to. There was a kind of man who held a gleam of vicious delight in his eyes. Who longed to destroy, to take, to ruin. Who delighted in his own power over others. Who would do anything—lie, steal, kill, rape, devour—if it satisfied even his most temporary appetite. Men who were the soulless embodiment of evil.

"He seemed to rejoice in me. In what he thinks I meant to do. And to a child." Jan's face vacillated between disgust and disbelief.

"He is why we do this job. Men like him."

"Yes..." Jan couldn't disagree with him but didn't know how to articulate what bothered him most.

"It should trouble you. If it didn't, that would concern me more."

"It's not just that he's evil. It's..." Jan felt like he held the answer but couldn't quite focus his thoughts on it. "He thinks I'm like him," he finally said, though that didn't quite encapsulate what he really meant.

"Are you concerned people will believe you're something you're not?"

"Partly." Jan rose and stepped over to the window to peer around the curtain and onto the morning street where vendors hurried by with carts full of merchandise to sell in the market. For a moment he wished he lived such a simple, straightforward life. The kind of life in which a man could disregard the vile and heinous ways of the world, could live a simple life of growing, or mending, or blacksmithing. A life untainted.

He tried voicing it out loud. "There's something to be said for being blind to evil. Untouched by it."

"Ah." Richter rubbed his chin. "I see."

"Do you?"

Richter leaned against the wall and watched his apprentice. The diffused light through the curtain cast a soft glow on one half of Jan's face and left the other half in shadow. Richter noted the young man's step had dulled since his arrest. The spring he had had in Berlin was dampened, weighed down even. It was more than just the appearance of nefarious intent. Rather, Richter likened it to an awakening of sorts. An enlightenment.

To care about justice, to long to exterminate all of the evil in the world was one thing. To stand in the dragon's lair was another. And to pose as a dragon oneself was yet another. It was a hard balance to strike without losing one's self.

"Your contention, if I'm understanding you correctly, is with yourself in the midst of all this. With the fact that you don't know how to wear a dragon's mask without becoming one yourself."

"Yes. Yes, that's exactly it." Jan felt shame just hearing Richter articulate the idea. He tried to explain. To articulate how his notion of himself correlated with Richter's explanation.

He had felt a certain thrill in their anticipation of this undertaking. Had wanted to vanquish evil. Had hardly felt more than the smallest notion of fear as they set out to act on it. But when he had entered the room with the girl, his body had begun to shake; he had almost faltered. Then, when he had clutched her to himself, he had felt something come over him: a shifting of his identity had changed in that instant, as if he had awakened something within him. Something repulsive. Worse, when he had looked into Werner's narrow, predatorial eyes and had seen his approval and that conspiratorial grin, Jan had seen himself as one of them.

"I don't know how to go on," Jan concluded.

Richter watched him silently, allowing the moment to settle before speaking. Jan was like a son to him. "I don't want to risk you in any way. If anything, I hesitated to suggest this course of action in the first place."

"I know. I know."

"If you don't want to go on, we'll find another way."

Jan flinched as if pained by the thought of backing down. "No. That's why I was so eager in the first place. We don't have another way. Not one that's as expedient or hopefully as effective. And if we wait..."

He hesitated to finish the sentence. Richter paused, reluctant to push him, knowing the risks were too high. He would have to carry the weight of that if their plan turned foul.

"But..." Jan crossed his arms and leaned against a wall, his eyes focused on a spot on the floor. "It must affect you. Doesn't it? I understand this is different from anything you've seen to date. But you've still seen some grim things. You've played the part of the dragon before. Doesn't it change you in some way? When do you reach that point? The point of no return."

"I think you've already crossed it."

"Oh." Jan's face fell.

"Jan, everything we do, everything you see will change you. To drive a sword through any amount of evil in the world, one must be within arm's length of it. To some extent you've already seen more than you've ever seen before now. You had heard of it. But looking the dragon in the eyes is different from just knowing he's out there.

"But I think you're overlooking something crucial. You're forgetting these things change us in positive ways as well." Richter stepped to the wooden chair that stood beside the small table in their room. After pulling it out, he turned it and sat on it backward. "Jan, no one becomes a monster overnight. It takes many small choices—both to choose evil and to shun what is right."

"Oh."

Richter continued, "The opposite is also true: continually facing down evil and *not* giving in changes us as well. It changes us for the better.

"We acquire a knowledge of evil. A much greater knowledge than we might otherwise want. But stepping out in the field every day with the right heart builds in us a strength we wouldn't otherwise have."

"I'm not seeing—"

"Character. Strength of character. Because remember, we aren't just standing against something. Anyone who stands against anything inherently stands *for* something else. And vice versa. So yes, the peddler you watched from the window, the one who will never truly know most of the evil that exists around him, has a simple life. And there is beauty in that."

Jan blushed that Richter had understood his thoughts so easily.

"But that man will never have to build in himself the heart of a warrior. The man who battles injustice and darkness and remains steadfast. The one who remembers who he is and what he stands for. That man grows in patience and perseverance and hope. He, sometimes more than the man who never has to stand for anything, knows the value of beauty and the simple pleasures in this life. He goes home to his family and his hearth with a heart of gratitude. He knows how much there is to lose so he takes nothing for granted.

"That's why I do this job. Because it's right. And I want to see justice done. But also because it gives me a profound respect for all that is good."

Jan's eyes had lit up as Richter spoke. His face bore a cautious look of hope.

"As much as I hate the risk to you. As much as I would take your place if I could, I cannot. You are the only one who can enter into that household and possibly change the future for all the young girls we have every reason to believe are there. Held for some dark end."

"Yes," Jan declared with a weak smile. "I'll do it. I want to. I couldn't live with myself if I left them there for a day longer than was absolutely necessary. No matter the cost."

They left the words that hung between them unspoken: that there was always a cost; that even if he returned unscathed, some part of him would never be the same.

Chapter Thirty-Six

Although Clara had known Cora's wing of the house would be empty, the evidence of the festivities wiped clean, she hadn't expected it to look so abandoned. She slipped into first one room then the next. None of them bore any sign of what she had witnessed only two nights ago. The tables were bare of glasses. The ashtrays empty of ashes. The floors were free of clothes and scattered personal items. And the beds smooth and made up as if no one had been here in years.

"Perhaps your mind is coming unhinged." Clara only partly turned to see Cora standing next to a bedside table, fingering the long silk curtains that brushed its edge.

No. There was no way she had imagined it. There was no dust anywhere. Not a speck of dust in a part of the house that likely received only infrequent cleaning. Even more than that, there was a smell in the air. She lifted an ashtray. It smelled of cigars. And the air smelled of men. It filled each space with the shadows of life. Living breathing people moving throughout the rooms, leaving an indelible mark.

That was enough for her mind but not enough to declare the crisply tucked bedcovers and polished tables liars. Until, in one small room, beneath the edge of a bed, trapped between the bed frame and the wall, she spotted a glimpse of red. The only trace of evidence. She bent down and pulled the strand. A ribbon. A young girl's ribbon, the color of a soot-filled dawn, filthy and old, but out of place nonetheless.

Clara rose, the ribbon clutched in her hand. Cora stood watching her, her face twisted into a smirk. Clara turned away and squeezed the thin thread of her sanity. As she did, the ghost of a memory drifted past her. Two men, their shirts hanging down over bare legs, sauntered across the floor toward the opposite wall. Each held a glass of caramel-colored liquor. Their faces, laughing and relaxed while a young girl lay whimpering on the bed.

Her rage rose, expanding within her. Until it burst and disappeared with the vision.

She ran to the wall where they had been and were no longer. She reached up and ran her hand over the faded wall covering. Behind her, on the opposite side of the room, the door to the passage stood open where she had left it. The door through which she had entered.

Yet the vision had to mean something.

She ran her hand along the fireplace mantel. The wood was smooth, gleaming even, as if recently it had been polished. And underneath the mantle: nothing. Slowly she exhaled and leaned against the smooth edge.

"What did you think you'd find?" Cora was still smirking.

Clara rolled her eyes. "If you have something to say, feel free to say it." In the ensuing silence, she sighed and pushed off the corbel. A grating sound rumbled from the wall beside her. She turned and fell back several steps, her eyes wide.

There before her gaped a dark passage. She rushed to the table in the center of the suite, retrieved her lantern and dashed back to the opening.

"Are you coming?" Clara called over her shoulder.

"I thought you wanted to get rid of me."

"That's right. Don't come." The passage branched off in opposite directions. Clara looked both ways; then, seeing the well-worn sign of footsteps in one direction, chose that one. As she pressed on through the corridor, she saw no signs of other entry points into the house. No peepholes into adjacent rooms. Nothing that gave the passage any possible interpretation other than the obvious one. It was meant strictly as a conduit to the third floor's east wing.

Behind her she sensed Cora's presence. As they approached the tunnel's dead end, Clara spotted a strange lever lying against the wall. She pulled it up and a door swung open.

Beyond it stood a landing and a stone staircase that fell away into darkness. Above her the steps circled to a door that led to the roof. She knew exactly where she was.

The tower.

She felt the moist night air emanate from the stone. She turned back to see Cora close the door behind them. Her eyes seemed to glow from their sunken sockets. Her body seemed to have withered within her clothes, as if something ate away at her ghostly life. Around them, the wind whistled and howled as it sought entry into the tower. She turned and ascended the worn stone stairs to the roof.

"Clara." When she turned, her eyes wide in question, Cora stood on the landing, shaking her head. "We're going down."

Clara looked past her, to where the steps fell away. The black depths pulsated with a dangerous comprehension. In that moment, a memory of wailing despairing cries rose up to her, filling her with a dark premonition. She had known, hadn't she, that more than just the wind echoed here.

Shivering, she clutched at the cold wall. Cora watched her, waiting, but Clara's eyes were locked on the darkness below. Something wet trickled between her fingers. She recoiled in disgust. Just then, a cry rose in the gloom. The sound of it filled her ears and flowed through her limbs, building in her a steely resolve.

She swallowed hard and took a step down. Three more and she reached the landing where Cora still stood transfixed. Clara nodded lightly, her tongue dry. Slowly they descended into the unknown.

The darkness seemed to swallow the light from Clara's lantern so that she could barely see more than two steps ahead. Thirty steps. Forty. Forty-two. Then the floor leveled out and a heavy wall rose before them. Something scurried past: two tiny orbs glinting in the lantern's glow and then nothing.

The air hung cold and torpid in the depths of the house. The cloying scent of disuse and decay washed over Clara, filling her mouth with rising bile. Her throat stung as she swallowed it back down. She looked to the left and right. Both ways lay in darkness.

"Toward the chapel," Cora whispered, pointing to their right. Clara picked her way down the dark hall.

When they rounded a corner, a faint glow of light greeted them from a distant point high in the wall. Clara's heart leapt in her chest. "That must be it. Hurry." She ran toward it, her lantern swinging before her, casting high shadows on the walls to either side of her.

The first thing she sensed was a faint movement. The air above her hummed with energy. Then the ceiling seemed to detach, as if a dark form separated from the shadows. It shattered into moving shards. The distant light quivered. A cacophony of squeaking, squealing cries arose, mixed with the sound of claws scratching at the walls. A faint breeze ruffled her hair before a wing clipped her face.

She spun out of its way and into the path of an oncoming bat. It caught in her hair, its screams filling her ears. Clara struck at it, tearing at her hair and casting it away from her. Disgust sent shivers through her body. She heard her own screams mingled with those of the creature. The lantern fell from her hand, its wrought iron frame clanging against the ground. The candle whooshed out, filling the air with the acrid smell of smoke.

"Shhh!" Cora's harsh whisper washed over her as she shook with horror.

In the distance, the sound of voices approached. She fell back against the wall just as a distant door swung open. What had been a small square opened into a probing wash of golden light. Beyond it, the two girls huddled in the shadows.

The silhouette of a man stepped into the doorway, He stood, unmoving, staring into the darkness. Behind him, another voice spoke, the words indiscernible.

It was Hagan's voice that answered. "No. Nothing. Probably those damn bats again."

In the silence, Clara imagined that her heartbeat echoed against the stone. And that he heard her. Hagan stood for what seemed like minutes, his face concealed in darkness, staring down the tunnel. Clara looked down to where her lamp lay, its flame extinguished, its ox horn panes unbroken but glinting faintly in the shadow of his feet. Then his shadow shifted, as if he had seen it and would advance toward them. Instead he reached out, gripped the edge of the door, and pulled it closed.

Clara sank to the dirt, her legs trembling, her breath fast and quick. Flashes of crimson light pulsed before her eyes, blinding her. She sat, waiting for her vision to focus and her heart to slow. The sounds beyond the door grew fainter and infrequent.

Several minutes later, they rose and Clara reclaimed her lamp. Faint candlelight still glowed through the small window in the door. They crept toward it.

When they reached out and touched the solid door, Clara took a deep breath. Whatever the outcome, she would confirm what lay beyond it. And why it awakened only at the darkest hour of the night. She gripped the handle, a heavy iron circle, and turned.

The door held fast, bolted from within.

<h1 style="text-align:center">Chapter Thirty-Seven</h1>

"Nothing? How could there be nothing?" Dressler was growing irritated with the entire situation. It didn't help that his associate was continuously moving something about in his mouth. As he did, his eyes assumed the vacuous gaze of a cow. "What are you chewing?"

"Ma-th-tic," Metz attempted through his heavy congestion. Dressler saw the bright white lump of mastic rolling around in his mouth. A filthy handkerchief lay wadded on the corner of the desk.

Dressler took a step back and reiterated his question. "How could you have found nothing?"

"I dunno." Metz shrugged. "No one seem-th to have heard of him."

"Hmm." Dressler turned and crossed the room. He was fully repulsed by his associate's chewing, not to mention his nose, which was now dripping into his oiled mustache. Instead he gazed out into the street. It was late in the afternoon. After 4:00 p.m. He never had to consult his timepiece. With the narrow streets positioned the way they were, he could read the slant of the shadows in the alley beyond their door in any season and know the time.

At this point the corridor lay deep in shadow. The fading sunlight cast a long wedge across the upper floor of the building across the alley. It was fitting. Though it had only been a few days since the boy's arrest and subsequent release, he had hoped to unearth something regarding his past. It was too early to have heard back from Dressler's connections in Prussia. But Metz had gone to work looking for any sign of the boy's activities or whereabouts in recent days.

Still, they had found little.

"He might be simple," Metz suggested in between bouts of coughing and blowing his nose. Dressler kept his distance.

"Hmm." Dressler shook his head and watched as the cabinetmaker across the alley swept out his shop. Wood shavings settled on the cobblestone path and grew dark as they absorbed the muddy puddles of water that stood in low places where the ground had settled.

Metz sighed. "Then who i-th he?"

The more Dressler considered the strange case of young Diedrich, the more perplexed he became. And the more convinced he was that Diedrich wasn't what he appeared to be. His initial instincts—that the boy was looking for something—hadn't diminished. If anything they had grown. He now believed the boy had been playing a part. There simply wasn't any other option. His actions were inept. And inconsistent with his nature. His eyes radiated a youthful naivete. Neither his attempts at insolence nor his flippant disregard rang true.

Dressler knew too much. Had seen too much. Had eaten of the darkest of fruit. This boy, for all his play acting, most certainly had not. But as to his intentions, neither of them could fathom what they might be.

Dressler turned back to meet his associate's watery stare. "Didn't you say you discovered where Herr Regensbach has him working?"

"Of course. He-th hi-th clerk. He-th with him in hi-th offi-th nearly every day."

Nodding, Dressler strode back to his desk. "Excellent. From now on, you will follow him. Day and night. I want to know where he's going and what he's doing. He has to sleep somewhere. I want to know where that is. And every person with whom he associates. Everything and anything you can find."

"But..." Metz was breathing heavily through his mouth and staring at Dressler in disbelief.

"Get going. And round up Körbl. It's high time he made himself useful. Have him bring in the girl for questioning."

"But th-e..."

"Just do it. I want to hear her story again. Something about this doesn't make sense, and I want answers. Sooner rather than later."

Chapter Thirty-Eight

Clara gripped the edge of the window, set high in the wooden door, raised herself up on her toes, and peered through the opening. The voices had moved on and sounded merely as faint echoes in the depths of a cave. Beyond the tunnel door, the hall turned to the left. She could see nothing other than the stone wall that loomed ahead of her, its surface dancing with flickering light. After several minutes, she and Cora made their way back to her rooms.

"I knew there were catacombs..."

"But?" Cora prodded.

Clara shook her head, uncertain. None of the family should be down there. *Ever.* All the recent generations were buried in the cemetery on the grounds. Or in the mausoleum where her father had been recently interred. The catacombs were a thing not just of past generations but of past centuries.

She couldn't recall having ever thought of them. At least overtly. Now she realized she'd always had a certain image of the tombs in the back of her mind. One of earth-carved tunnels, like wormholes or the winding labyrinth a rat might carve through the soil. And filthy, spiderweb-laced passages. Not the sort of place anyone this side of the last century would ever frequent. And definitely not the kind of place where voices echoed with an air of familiarity.

"Do you think they're there?" Clara asked.

"Who?"

Clara shot her a dirty look. "Who do you think?"

"Why do you think they're here somewhere?"

"Where else would my grandmother keep them?"

Cora just smiled at her and leaned back in the chair. "So where do we go next?"

"Well, I can't find any evidence anywhere else. And we know someone is down there. I have to know …to confirm…" She let the rest go. Didn't they already know what they would find? Perhaps, but it had to be seen, known, before she could do anything.

"But the door is barred." The way Cora said it grated on Clara's nerves. Her tone patronizing, leading.

"Clearly," Clara snapped. Then it came to her and she flew up out of the chair.

"Where are you going?"

Clara ignored her. *Don't you already know? Since you apparently know so much.* She entered the passages and took off at a brisk pace.

They emerged in Conrad's study. This time it was empty of her memories, devoid of even the scent of pipe tobacco.

"I know you're here," Clara muttered to herself as she stood before the bookshelves. "Ah, there we are." She pulled a volume down from the shelf and set it on top of a stack of ledgers.

"The architectural plans," Cora said.

The pages were discolored, of mismatched shapes, sewn together or shoved together, and held together simply by the weight of the leather covers. As she flipped from one page to the next, the sheets of paper took flight, scraping against one another like the sound of dead leaves.

She froze, her finger poised over a page in front of her. She bent over it, her lantern's flickering light distorting the image. Then her eyes adjusted and the image took form.

She gasped.

"What is it?" Cora asked.

"I found it. The way in."

Chapter Thirty-Nine

A housemaid answered the door and ushered Richter into the same green receiving room where he had met Lina on his prior visit. The fox still cowered under the foaming stare of the hounds. The room still bore the same insouciance. Yet now a large crack in the outside wall ran from floor to ceiling. Furniture had been moved away from the wall. The floor and paneling near the crack bore signs of water damage.

"Herr von Moltstedt. We meet again." Lina strode into the room, her expression laced with irritation. She glanced at the cracked wall then quickly looked away.

Regardless, he stepped forward and greeted her warmly. "I regret that I can't stay long."

"Oh. What a shame. I hope all is well."

"Yes, yes. Merely business. However, I happened to come across something that reminded me of you. And I recalled our former conversation."

"Really."

"Yes." He stepped away to a side table, against which he had propped a large parcel, still wrapped in brown paper. "A certain artwork came into my possession, and as much as I admire it, it doesn't fit in my collection. That said, I recalled your lovely home, and if I may be so presumptuous, it seemed like something that would accentuate your collection beautifully."

"Mine? Why, I'm not in the habit..." Lina faltered.

"Oh, it's no bother at all. These sorts of things come to me on occasion." He tore the paper from the painting and held it up to her.

Lina pressed her hand to her chest, her mouth wide. "It's magnificent. Just magnificent." She stepped closer and stood, appraising the work.

She'd never guess it was a forgery—so brilliantly executed that only the most discerning of eyes, under very close inspection, would know the difference. It was one of the interesting benefits of his line of work. He and his colleagues often had knowledge of and access to the most accomplished criminals in the region.

Lina's face registered nothing but overwhelmed shock and glee. "Is this..."

"Oudry? Yes. *The Wolf and the Lamb*."

"His use of light and shadow...and the expression on the lamb's face."

"Yes." He waited.

"So submissive. Resigned even."

"Hmm." Richter nodded though that wasn't what he saw. If anything, he saw irony painted there. The lamb registered courage, anger even. It leaned forward into the wolf, threatening it to advance. The wolf, on the other hand, arched its back in defense—its eyes wide, uncertain. But he had known how she would view it. And why.

"It's spectacular," she whispered.

"If you can find a place where it will complement your other works. Where it will fit—"

"Of course it fits," she said. "It fits perfectly. But really, I couldn't."

"No, no. Never mind that. As I said, I have a habit of acquiring certain things—art, conveyances, historical items, and the like—and I simply can't find a place for all of them. It's my pleasure to find the ideal home for each one."

Lina was no longer listening to him. She had taken the painting from him and set it against the back of a sofa, where it leaned back, catching the light from several angles. Her eyes were dark, greedy. Her fingers hung in the air, twitching as she studied it.

"You came all this way to bring a painting?"

He chuckled. "No, alas I would be a liar if I said that. I happen to have business in Munich and thought a side trip would be manageable. That said, I must reiterate that I can't stay long."

"How kind." Lina smiled a wolfish smile.

"I hope it isn't an imposition. I thought of you first. That with such a sizable estate you'd have the ideal place for this piece."

"Right here! Yes, right here of course." She looked around and noted several vacant spaces where the piece would fit with her existing collection.

He smiled to himself. *Yes, that's what I was hoping as well.*

Chapter Forty

"That's absurd." Lina shot Berend a patronizing gaze. "Anything can be tamed. Controlled." She hesitated in the doorway to Conrad's private study, reluctant to enter. Her lip curled as she looked from one pile to the next. Cobwebs hung from the edges of the ceiling, catching the wall, the tops of paintings, and the curtain rods in their net. There was no way to avoid it. She wove around stacks of papers and books, narrowly missing a globe stand. Conrad's private study had always been just that—private. A jungle of organized chaos.

Behind her, she felt Berend watching her, waiting. He stood in stark contrast to the room—his heavily starched collar and pressed coat impeccably neat, as usual; his bearing steadfast and constant, as always. She valued his efficiency and his strong, logical mind, unhampered by fickle emotions or that irritating tendency to appeal to the public consensus before making what could only be the best possible decision. She usually accepted, even respected, his willingness to challenge her at times.

Today, however, was a different matter.

She picked up a worn ledger from a stack of bound leather volumes and blew the dust off the top of it. "Disgusting," she muttered. It proved to be one of the family accounts, an older one, dated from 1843.

None of the ledgers that lay below it dated from any time in the last five years. "Conrad never could maintain order." She slapped the book shut, sending up a cloud of dust. "Remind me to have Sophie straighten this room. It's revolting. I want everything off the floor. If we have to store some of these, or put up new shelving."

"Of course." Berend's face remained impassive.

"I don't know why I've left this for so long. You'll need to oversee her. She won't know what to do with some of these papers. And have her see to it sooner rather than later. I need that ledger."

He waited until she had exhausted her train of thought. "Lina, you're not listening to me. Don't you feel it? We're poised on the edge of disaster. This can't continue."

She refused to look his way. "I've been listening to you. But what would you have me do?" Her hands shot up in the air, flinging away the futility of his suggestion. "Bow to those who would try to control me? Cower in fear? No, no. I absolutely will not."

"Clara isn't the issue."

"Of course she is. Not anymore of course. That's dealt with. Summarily and permanently. This time next month she'll be out of the way, out of our affairs forever."

"Yes, yes, but that's not what I'm trying to say."

"But it *is* the principle issue. Exactly what we need most—to have that meddling girl gone from this house. We can't leave her. You know it. And I know it. How does she manage it? Don't you lock her in yourself?"

"Every day."

"Then there it is. You see. She can't be trusted. She has some means of access, some in with the staff. Some way of extricating herself from her room. She might even have found..." Her voice trailed off as she distracted herself with another stack of ledgers.

Berend didn't answer. He knew she understood what he was saying. Yet was trying so hard to avoid.

Eventually she glanced up at him and moved to the desk. "And I've said it before: where does it end?" she demanded.

"That!" He swept forward. "Yes. That's my point. Where does it end? I don't want to find out. And you can't afford to. This will ruin us."

"Berend, don't..." Her tone, which began as a vitriolic rebuttal, trailed off into a silence that said everything. They both knew what the cost of exposure would be.

"Okay. Then what about the others? We won't be so lucky the next time another Aurberg comes along."

Her burst of laughter came out as a mocking indictment. "Why would you even suspect such a thing?"

"It's happened before, Lina. It can happen again."

Lina's skirt brushed against a stack of loose papers, sending them careening across the floor. She grimaced at the mess and stepped over it, leaving the floor littered with old receipts and invoices.

"Once. It happened once. You still haven't suggested why such a thing would ever recur. Besides, even if it did, who would he tell? Come on, Berend. Be realistic. I have the entire situation under control. And Aurberg is proof of that. He was never a real threat. Merely an inconvenience."

"He went to the authorities! Told people who were in a position to do something, Lina. That's the definition of a *real threat*. There could just as soon be another like him.'"

"Dressler would never cross me."

"You don't know that. And what about this green associate of his. Messner. Or Moser..."

"Metz."

"You have no idea when one of them—him, or someone else for that matter—will decide they've had enough. All you need is for one of them to develop a case of guilt. Or for someone to suspect something is afoot and pressure them to expose you. The fallout would be fatal. It's time to shut this down."

"All the more reason *not* to shut it down. Turning them loose would remove every incentive they have to remain loyal to us. No, Berend. You're wrong. We need them involved, close at hand. That's our security."

Berend scowled. It irritated Lina to see it: his subtle disapproval of her. It reeked of distrust. As if she couldn't maintain control. As if she hadn't done so for many years, long before Conrad's illness.

"When does it end?"

"Why would it have to?"

"Oh, Lina! What do you gain by all this? You don't need the business connections any longer. And with Edgar gone…"

She inhaled sharply and glowered at him before turning away. "I can't wait for Sophie. It's unacceptable. Who lives like this?" She crouched near the floor and gathered the pages she had previously unsettled. Berend joined her, stacking them in neat piles on the edge of Conrad's already cluttered desk.

When she stood and brushed her hands down the sides of her dress, she left chalky dust marks smeared across the black stuff. Her self-assured expression had fallen away, leaving a fearfully bitter one. Berend waited for a long while before she responded. When she spoke, her voice was a disparate blend of mournfulness and arrogance.

"You're wrong. We have to hold onto traditions. To the past. They're important. If we lose sight of them, we forget who we are. We're responsible to preserve history so others will value the things that came before them. Otherwise, what is history but a painting? Or dust in a cemetery?"

"No, Lina. He'll never be that. Not to you. Not to us. This has nothing to do with him. Don't you see how much you're risking? What the cost will be?"

"This has *everything* to do with Edgar," she hissed, her eyes black.

He fixed her in a gaze of studied incredulity.

"He's there every time, Berend. And afterward. Walking the halls for days. The other night I woke to find him standing at the foot of my bed, watching me." Her eyes had grown wide, frantic even.

"Oh, Lina, let's let Edgar rest in peace."

She shook her head, vehemently opposing him. "He doesn't want that."

"Yes…"

"No, Berend. You're wrong. And you underestimate me. Why are you worried? There's no one I can't control. Especially that neurotic child, lurking around with some scheme or lolling about in idleness, with her head in the clouds. No. She's as unstable as her father was. I managed his condition for twenty-five years, and she's far more submissive than he was. No. She's no threat whatsoever.

"I appreciate your concern for me, but you have to trust me. I can manage this situation just as well as I've managed every other one."

Berend opened his mouth to respond, but a sharp rap sounded at the door. He stepped around the misshapen piles and opened the door. Hagan stood just beyond. His pale face, with its hard lines, cleft chin, and high forehead, capped in a mass of waving black hair, seemed to float against the backdrop of the dark hallway. For an instant, it was like seeing a ghost, a nameless face, hovering in the dark. Lina's heart froze.

"I'm sorry to interrupt, Gnädige Frau. But you have a visitor."

"Who is it?" Berend asked.

"He wouldn't give his name," Hagan shook his head. "I've never seen him before. He's in the drawing room."

"The drawing room? Why ever for?" Lina gathered her dress and pressed toward him.

"Frau Willenheim insisted."

"Helene? What on earth does she have to do with him?" Lina shoved around him and into the mezzanine's narrow, low-ceilinged hall. She strode along the deep blue runner, past walls lined with gilded maps, a nautical barometer, and a painting of a ship besieged by insurmountable waves.

Hagan trotted after her and Berend. "She's with him. As is Fräulein Clara."

"What the devil is going on?" Lina's voice rose in pitch. Her pace accelerated as she passed out of the hall and down a short flight of stairs.

In the distance, she heard laughter and the sound of voices mingled. She could nearly make out that of Helene. And something else... A shiver of premonition rose up her spine. Her hands quaked lightly as she walked. A quiver shook her chest.

When they drew closer and stepped through the doorway, she saw Clara and Helene, seated on a sofa facing the fireplace. Jutta stood behind them, watching. Their faces were relaxed, joyful even. Helene was twittering about something. The words were lost to Lina as she stood staring at the third figure in the room.

He stood with his back to the door, one hand resting on the fireplace mantel, the other tucked behind his waistcoat. At that moment, with his gaze down, into the fire, his face was shielded from her view. Yet there was something about him that shook her, that clenched her belly in fear.

Lina's color rose. Her eyes narrowed as she watched the three of them, as of yet unaware of her presence. How dare Helene assume control of the guests in this house? And to welcome a man in the drawing room, of all places. She cleared her throat sharply and strode forward. "Whatever is the meaning of this?"

But then the figure turned from the fireplace. She saw it as if an hour of her life passed slowly in frozen segments. The ear that was so familiar. Then the profile. The thick wave of auburn hair. Finally he had turned and stood facing her. Clara and Helene swiveled and stared at her, watching for her response.

Lina heard her own intake of breath. The sharp gasp for air that punctured the silence before he spoke.

"Hello, Mother."

Chapter Forty-One

"He grabbed it! With his bare hands. And cut off its head," Uncle Nathaniel said, his hands resting casually on the table on either side of his empty plate.

"Good heavens! How long did you say?" Clara's mother laughed and shifted in her seat as if she couldn't contain her excitement.

"Five feet. Maybe six. And him, only twelve years old."

Clara's grandmother no longer bore the horrified expression it had the prior day, when she had come face-to-face with the son she had forsaken. Instead the muscles seemed to contort as if some unseen presence wound its way beneath the surface. It began in her eyes, dragging them deeper into their sockets. Made them darker. Menacing. From there it twitched across her left cheekbone and down to her jawline like a burrowing parasite. Her mouth moved as if she ground her teeth.

"Isn't that astonishing, Mother?" Helene asked. No one waited for Lina to reply.

Her mother and uncle went back to talking, but Clara heard the words from a tinny, hollow place. As if she stood outside of herself and struggled to filter the conversation through her expectations. She had heard countless offhand, usually deprecating comments about this man from her grandmother. Though she had never met him, she hadn't realized how vivid a picture she had formed of him in her mind. Now, as he spoke of his plantation in India, her mind reeled with the inconsistencies.

Her grandmother had consistently dismissed him as a simple, rural do-gooder. Yet he was elegant, easily as much as her father had been. But strong in a way he *hadn't* been. And fearless in a way no arrogant person can understand.

Likewise, she had read about India—the dry, barren landscape plagued by torrential rains and sweltering heat. But he spoke of rolling green hills, forests of towering Hollong trees twenty or even twenty-five times the height of a man, and paths lined with colossal flowering rhododendrons. And of the rich fertile soil that yielded tea in prodigious quantities.

He described the people, hospitable and hardworking, who were like a family to him. Of the joyful children of the land, so content, innovative and courageous. Like the one in his story, who had, without hesitation, captured and destroyed a deadly snake before it could close in on his younger brother. From his description of them, Clara would have thought they were his own children. She looked around the room at the servants standing ready along the wall, at the heavy dark furniture and the cold breakfast resting on the side buffet, and blinked back tears.

Last night she had sat in her window seat for hours, questioning the significance of his appearance. And the timing of it. Why was Nathaniel here? Why return to the home from which he had been so overtly excluded? Why now, long after her father's funeral?

She had felt his gaze on her more than once throughout the prior evening and had struggled to decide what her response should be. Shouldn't it be warm and welcoming? Wasn't he simply the absent but concerned man he claimed to be? A man who had returned home as soon as he heard the news? Or was he something else? She couldn't decide whether his sudden appearance portended a turning of the tide. Or if it was a harbinger of greater destruction.

"Twenty years, isn't it?" Helene asked, her face beaming for a man she had met only once or twice in her life and that nearly a generation prior.

"Nearly. Your wedding."

"That's right. That's right. I don't know how I could have forgotten! You've stayed away far too long." Helene extended her arm across the table, patting the wood. "I hope you're here to stay."

Clara continued to chew the same piece of ham, her eyes squinting, looking from one of them to the other.

"Don't be presumptuous, Helene." Lina's eyes were dark, her expression grim. "Nathaniel is a very busy man. What with his farm. And his *people*. I'm sure he'll want to get back to them as soon as possible."

Nathaniel chuckled without responding. When Lina dropped her gaze to the plate before her, he shot Helene an inscrutable glance. A knowing glance, laden with unspoken meaning. Clara furrowed her eyebrows. They almost seemed to be on familiar terms with each other, though her uncle hadn't lived in Bavaria in decades.

Even if he had, her grandmother never would have allowed such an association. No one, not even Clara's strong but cautious grandfather, had been able to overrule Lina's dislike for the ruddy-haired youth. As the thought struck her, Clara saw the resemblance. Nathaniel appeared very much like his father. As much like him as Edgar was Heinrich. The thought felt buoyant, hopeful, but she tethered it, pulling it in securely. It might be that he was something else entirely, she reminded herself. Unlike either her father or grandfather.

Her uncle's face—guileless, open—told her nothing. Did he know what lay beneath the house? Did he know that his mother frequented the halls of the dead in the darkest hours of the night? Was he complicit? Was the timing of his visit merely a coincidence?

Her thoughts returned to the architectural plans she had uncovered. She shifted in her chair and looked to the clock above the door. Around her, the family lingered, in no hurry to end this farce of a breakfast.

Her uncle seemed removed from the doings of her father and grandmother. Yet there was something in his gaze. Something piercing that made her feel unmasked and vulnerable. And something in the set of his shoulders. A flash of knowledge passed through her mind like lightning—there and then gone—leaving an unsettled impression that she had missed something crucial. As the thought entered her mind, he turned his attention to her.

"I can't stay away indefinitely. But now that I'm here, I won't leave until I've gotten to know my niece. Why is it that you've never mentioned her, Mother?" His gaze was calm, unflinching as he turned to stare at Lina. *It's his self-assurance*, Clara realized. Her uncle was perfectly collected and confident. Her grandmother couldn't hope to unnerve or dominate him. And she knew it.

Lina colored. Her eyes grew wide and moist as if she had been called to account for some hidden guilt. "We've rarely had an opportunity to correspond. It must have slipped my mind. And if you'll recall, Clara isn't the one who abandoned her family for those who are boorish and uncultured."

Her uncle's face darkened considerably. He stared at Lina with an intense, unblinking fierceness that caught Clara's breath in her throat. Her grandmother seemed suddenly bent and pressed back in her chair, her chin lowered, her neck covered, as if she were a cornered dog cringing at the end of a rifle. Her uncle made as if he would say something. But then he turned away from his mother and met Clara's gaze.

"Clara. Tell me about yourself. Do you have any hobbies? Are you a scientist, like your mother?"

Clara blinked several times, blinded by the sudden attention, her mind blank.

"She draws." Helene shot her a smile of approval and encouragement.

"Ah! An artist. That *is* something. I love art as well. You have the desire to create?"

"Yes." Clara's cheeks warmed.

"Any particular subject matter?"

"Birds....recently I've been drawing birds. I used to draw flowers or just landscapes."

"Then you must create 'en plein air'?"

"Um—" Clara faltered and glanced at her grandmother.

Lina cut her off. "As you well know, Nathaniel, no bird remains still long enough to be utilized by the artist. Not unless it's caged. No, Clara works primarily from books and her prolific imagination. She's gifted enough not to need to sit outside for art's sake. As you also know, our climate hardly favors such pursuits much of the year." She leaned forward, her elbows on the table, her hands steepled before her. It made her appear imposing. Yet Clara wondered if she wasn't using her hands as something of a shield.

"Come now, Mother. The subject itself is hardly the crux of the matter." He turned back to Clara. "Have you heard of John Constable?" Clara shook her head "He made a career out of resisting such illogical practices. Art, like much of life, can only flourish in the light of truth.

"Therein lay two of his tenets. First, that art must have at its core a desire to reflect not just nature but the truth behind nature. To do this, one must study truth. In your case, not another artist's rendition of the world but your own observations of the environment.

"Second, that in doing so, one must consider the role of light on the subject matter. For the quality of light dictates how we understand the subject of our art. A bird in a cage, or in a sketch in a book, is caught in stilted, unnatural light. She cannot understand herself or the world anymore than an observer can truly understand her. But to see her in the pale shimmering glow of a sunrise, to see her turn her face to the dawn, to see the confident trust she exudes when she opens her wings and glides across the dew-covered ground—that is to understand her.

"The artist must know the truth. To do so, he must be exposed to the light. He must observe. He must be free."

Lina's expression had turned sour. Clara noted it, yet she was captivated by her uncle's speech. His words echoed in her heart and stirred a long-buried desire to be, to experience, to know and be known. The desire to say something about the world. About her life. Something true.

"She doesn't just draw nature." Lina's smile turned smug. "She drew a self-portrait once. Didn't you, Clara? Why don't you tell him about that?"

At the memory, Clara blanched. They all seemed to be staring at her, waiting. A darkness, like a weighted cloud, pressed down on her, extinguishing all the light her uncle had just brought into the room. Harsh lines on a page; the eyes obscured; hatch marks across the face; no mouth. It flashed in bursts of violent pain across her memory.

She had drawn it four years prior, shortly after her grandfather's funeral. One morning, after they had laid the gentle, confident man to rest in the family mausoleum, she had crossed her bedroom to find her door locked. From then on, Berend or Hagan stood sentinel at all hours. Her father raved in the halls in the dead of night, walked the edge of the roof, and tore his room apart. And she had become a prisoner.

"Really, Mother," Helene said.

Nathaniel leaned back and ran a hand through his hair. "I've been away for so long. Regrettably. I have so much to catch up on." He turned to Helene. "And you, my dear. I haven't seen you in ages. I'm looking forward to hearing all that I've missed."

Helene clapped her hands together; Clara jolted upward, startled. "That's it. That's just the thing. We should host a homecoming party for Nathaniel."

"I don't..." Lina started.

"Oh, it won't be any trouble at all. In fact, I would do all the planning. What do you think, Nathaniel? Oh, I don't know why I'm even asking. Of course you'll love it. Think of all the people you haven't seen in years. And Lotte and Horst. You just missed seeing them. And everyone else. They'll be thrilled to hear that you're here. They'll all want to see you."

"I would be honored."

"Helene," Lina cautioned. "As kind as your suggestion is, it's entirely inappropriate. To appear to be celebrating during a time of mourning..."

"What better time, Mother? It's a way to remember and honor the son you still have."

Clara watched her grandmother's face. If possible, her coloring appeared to turn green. Simultaneously she seemed to be trying hard to bite her tongue. And failing miserably.

"Helene. You've failed to consider the guests themselves. How will they view such a thing? It's entirely improper. These are very powerful people. They can hardly be expected to drop everything and rush over here. Besides which, many of them mightn't even remember Nathaniel. He's been gone for so very long. The idea is...frankly, it's—"

"Mother, don't be so modest. Of course they'd come. Consider how many people have dropped everything to be here before. To support you when we lost Edgar. I'm sure they'd want to be here now, to honor your son. Most of them would certainly try. Even if it's just for a night..."

Helene continued talking about her plans for the event. She and Nathaniel discussed family friends and acquaintances he hadn't seen since he was a young man or even a youth. But Clara only faintly listened. Her grandmother's eyes had lit up at something her mother had said. Then she had clearly retreated from the conversation, lost in thought. From her expression, Clara knew her grandmother was conspiring, formulating a plan.

"Helene," Lina interrupted. Her eyes flashed black. "On second thought, I think your idea is a brilliant one! Let's throw him a party. The largest, most elaborate party we've ever hosted. I'll manage the guest list. It'll be just the thing."

Helene smiled and laughed. The fervent, celebratory tone of their conversation picked up. But Clara watched the twisted smile on her grandmother's face and felt nothing but unease in the depth of her stomach.

Chapter Forty-Two

Throughout the day, Clara watched the clock, her body restless, fidgeting. Everything centered on Nathaniel. Her mother and grandmother hovered about him, listening to his stories of his life abroad, suggesting he revisit this or that memory in the house. Clara felt tethered, dragged about. She spoke little and instead assessed the responses and interactions of each of her family members. What she had seen in Lina's eyes hadn't diminished. If anything, she had grown quiet, still, like a snake in the grass. In contrast, her mother seemed almost giddy. So much so that Clara caught her grandmother eyeing Helene more than once, her expression laced with suspicion.

When Berend finally locked Clara into her rooms that evening, she ran for the dressing room panel. "She's up to something," she muttered, her teeth clenched.

"I assume you mean my mother. Shocking you'd even think such a thing." Clara started and turned to see Cora behind her. "I'm joking. Carry on."

They made their way through the hidden passages to the tower stairs and began the long trudge to the roof.

"Where are we going?" Cora asked.

Clara didn't bother responding. In her mind, her grandmother's smug, twisted grin hung before her face. Each time Clara had caught her sideways glance, she had seen in her expression some dark agenda. Since the memory of the trunks had resurfaced, she understood her grandmother's apprehension. Berend had surely informed Lina of Clara's discovery, making Clara a liability. As she uncovered more and more of the truth, she realized her grandmother must know, must sense that as Clara grew, she became more of a risk. They would do something. Something terribly irrevocable. The only question was what.

There was no time to waste. In order to escape she had to stop them. And to do that, she had to find that evidence.

Through the stone tower, the wind moaned and wailed. They stepped out the door and into a lashing rain. Clara tucked her chin into her chest, turned away from the wind, and pushed her way across the roof. Her skirts whipped about her legs, her feet kicking up puddles. Water flooded her lamp, extinguishing her light.

She sighed. "Damn."

They dashed into the rooftop conservatory and slammed the door behind them. Clara wiped the rain from her eyes and peered around her. One of the glass panes in the ceiling on the south side had cracked. Water poured through in a steady stream, splattering on the edge of one of the raised beds and running off onto the floor. Toward the back of the conservatory, shelves stood full of watering cans, pots, and shovels. She set the lamp near the door.

"This way," she said. When they reached the far wall, she looked out the filmy windows to where the roofline marked the eastern edge of the house. Below that, the steep roofline of the chapel fell away, blurred by the gray obscurity of the tempest and the encroaching night.

Clara pushed aside a small table of clay pots, their forms clattering against one another as they jostled. There, flush with the floor, lay a rectangular panel.

She crouched, grasped a ring set flush in its surface, and pulled it up. "Help me," she grunted as the panel moaned against its hinges.

Cora bent down beside her, gripped the edge of the heavy steel plate, and lifted. It was painted to match the floor, the ring set into it virtually seamless. Even without the table above it, if she hadn't known where to look for it, hadn't seen the detailed plans, Clara doubted she would have noticed so small a detail.

The plate rotated back on its hinges and fell open with a reverberating clang. Below them a staircase opened. Clara groaned, her body shuddering from the memory of bats, their fluttering skeletal wings and toothy squeaking mixed with distant, wailing cries of distress.

"It's a strange entrance. Who would have ever used it?" Cora stood, gazing into the abyss below them.

Clara shook her head. "There must be others. Better ones. But they aren't on the plans."

Carefully they lowered themselves into the darkness. The stairs were precariously steep, doubling back on themselves only a few times. After a few minutes, Clara felt as if she were wading down into the humid air near the earth. Still they descended. The walls grew moist and slippery, the stone covered with the pungent odor of mold. She gritted her teeth and closed her mind as she leaned against the slick surface.

Without her lamp, her eyes strained in the darkness but made out little. Only a glimmer of moonlight reached them. And a strange light, sickly yellow, that seemed to emanate from Cora's eyes. At one point something ran across her hand as she clung to the surface of the wall. Her stomach lurched, but she didn't dare lose her grip. The steps were steep and uneven, falling away into a black void.

Finally she stepped down onto what felt like a smooth floor. Water trickled between the stone walls and ran along the edges of the ground. One slender stream cut away from the wall and carved a narrow inlet across the hard-packed earth to the center where it pooled. It smelled stagnant. Clara edged around it.

"There's nothing here." She squinted in disbelief, her hands groping about the walls. "The plans showed... It should lead to...or did at one point..."

"You should know better than that, Clara. They're all practically the same." Cora traced her hands across the stone until she found a telltale seam. Following it up to a higher point, her hand found something and pushed. A lever shot out from between the stones and hung quivering. She gripped it and pulled.

The wall groaned as a narrow doorway of stone swung open a few inches then stopped.

"It's stuck," Cora said. "Come. Help me."

The two girls pressed their weight against the stone and shoved. Clara winced as her hands slid across the wet, slimy surface. But as they pushed, the door caught then broke free, swinging into a dark tunnel.

Ahead of them stood a solid wall, but to the right and left, a corridor stretched out into the darkness.

"Bats," Clara whispered.

"No. Not here. Bats would be an improvement."

Clara trembled. She looked to the left then the right. *Which way?* The switchbacks in the stairs had thrown off her sense of direction. She paused, struggling to recollect the number of turns they had taken.

"I think it's to the right."

They moved down the hall to a point where the tunnel took a left turn, jogged for a short distance, then curved around to the right. There they stopped again.

"Let your eyes adjust," Cora said.

Clara's breath seemed to echo against the stone that surrounded them. A strange smell filled the air—a stale, cold decay that reminded her where they were. Eventually her eyes caught a glimpse of a shadowy form of light in the distance, but rather than comforting her, the light cast shadows along the wall, revealing lurking forms around them. Only the smooth, uncluttered ground beneath her felt solid and unthreatening.

They crept down the long tunnel. As one of the strange forms grew closer, Clara realized what it was: an arched stone recess in the wall. Centered on the floor in the recess stood a heavy stone box, within which was surely the remains of one of her ancestors. She faintly made out spiraling stone pillars on either side of the recess, but all that lay within was shrouded in darkness.

Every fifteen feet or so, they passed another recess. Similar spaces lined both sides of the corridor. Eventually Clara's curiosity overcame her fear, and she began to pick out details around her. Heavy iron sconces hung between each recess, awaiting flaming torches. The packed earth beneath their feet had given way to smooth stone: a geometric tile floor. And above, the barrel-vaulted ceiling was inlaid with a tile mosaic that ran the length of the space.

Clara could imagine the beauty of it. She could almost feel the centuries of history; of a torchlit assembly of her ancestors solemnly following the coffin of their father or grandmother or son into the tombs; of the tile shining in colorful scenes of knights in battle, of wounded warriors returning home, of feasts and marriages and death watches; of the intonation of the priest and the responses of the mourners.

In some ways she preferred this to the mausoleum where her father lay. It held more history and was more personal than the cold, characterless marble structure. Yet here she sensed the gaze of the dead. Everywhere she walked, she felt their eyes on her and their rotting breath on the back of her neck. Her hair stood up as she glanced left and right. There was no sign of anyone. Nothing but stone. Still, she knew they weren't alone.

She was so preoccupied that she didn't notice when Cora stopped. Clara almost collided with her.

"Shh!!" Cora glared at her.

Just then they heard voices. They were drawing closer. Cora gripped her wrist and pulled her into the nearest recess. As they edged around the tomb, Clara pictured slithering creatures and beds of rats, but when they sank to the ground behind the stone, she found it surprisingly dry and clean.

The voices drew even closer. Berend and someone else. It wasn't Hagan, but the voice was familiar: a man's. Definitely not one of the servants. A voice she recognized, but couldn't identify.

"...new stock. I'll admit I didn't expect it after Edgar died," the familiar voice said.

"Lina will be pleased," said Berend.

As they approached, the swinging light of a small lantern preceded them. Then they stopped. Light shone around the edges of the tomb, like fingers reaching back to catch at them and drag them into the open. Clara's hands and feet trembled; she was certain they had been found.

"I almost expected Edgar to appear. Everything's just as he would want it."

"Hmm. Yes, I believe that was her intention."

Clara heard the disdain in Berend's voice.

Cold radiated from her back where it pressed against the stone. She willed her breathing to slow. Her heart pounded in her ears, nearly drowning out the two men, but then she heard them moving on.

Something clanged loudly. She heard stone on stone as something slid then caught. It sounded close, possibly from the next recess. And then steps receding. Finally a heavy sound—of air and stone and earth—exhaled like a deep sigh of regret. The shadowy gloom settled around them once more.

"Let's go," Cora whispered.

They slid out from behind the tomb and hurried softly toward the source of light at the end of the tunnel. Clara's feet shook, her jaw weary from clenching her teeth. At the corner, Cora reached back an arm indicating they should stop. While she peered around the corner, Clara looked back. If there was anyone, or anything following them, she couldn't make them out in the darkness.

Cora nodded to her, waving an arm for her to follow. They stepped into a wide space lined with broad doors made of thick steel bars. The tile floors were gone, replaced by nothing but packed earth. As they passed the first door, Clara gasped. There, huddled against the wall beside a filthy pile of bedding, sat a young girl. She was no more than seven or eight years old, her blond hair hanging in a thick braid. Her eyes were wide, filled with fear and something else, something Clara recognized but wouldn't name.

At the sight of them, the girl started and cried out. Then she was up and rushing forward to grip the bars.

Clara heard footsteps nearby.

"Shh. She must be quiet," Cora said.

Clara held a finger to her lips as Cora pulled her away. They ran past several cells, each filled with at least one young girl, the youngest perhaps five, the oldest no older than thirteen. Finally they drew near a room, this one without bars, its door wide open. Cora pushed her into it and up against the wall behind the door.

"Where have you been?" Lina's sharp voice rang out in the hallway just beyond them. Clara covered her mouth to keep from crying out. Her eyes watered. Just when she thought her grandmother would reach in and pull them out, Berend's voice answered.

"I was seeing Emil out."

"Why would he leave so soon?" Lina's voice was incredulous, bordering on irritated. "Everything is exactly as it used to be. If anything, better. They're certainly younger. It can hardly be that—"

"No, no. Just the opposite. He has to catch a train in a few hours. He was extremely complimentary."

"Oh. Then he wasn't displeased?"

"Hardly. He said he could nearly feel Edgar's spirit here with us."

"Well, then."

Their voices moved away down the hall. Clara felt the blood flooding the veins in her eyes. She practically saw red in the darkness where they stood.

When Lina and Berend had been gone for several minutes, they risked a glance around the door. The hall was empty. Cora started out the door.

"No," Clara hissed, pulling her back into the room. "No. We're not going anywhere until you tell me what's going on. Who are these girls? What does my grandmother want with them?"

"Don't you already know? It was about Edgar at first. And then Lina, who found something that benefited her. Ask yourself...what does she want with them? You tell me. What does Lina want more than anything?"

Clara shivered, her eyes wide in the darkness. Suddenly the air in the room seemed oppressive, pressing in on her. She wanted to ask what she meant, how it could be. But she already knew the answer. It stood out in front of her, where she held it apart, away. Instead she stumbled out into the flickering light of the hall. A shadow moved in one of the cells. Clara dashed over and gripped the bars, her eyes searching the depths for a face that would meet her own.

"Hello?" she called out.

No one responded, but she made out the faint sound of someone breathing.

"Hello?" she repeated. "Are you there? Somebody?"

She waited. It seemed like minutes before she heard rustling and then a soft voice. A child's voice.

"Hello?" The girl spoke it as a question but not an optimistic one.

Clara's heart lifted. "Who are you? What's your name?"

"Meike."

"How old are you, Meike?"

The girl didn't respond. Just stood, silently waiting as if confused.

"She looks like she's eight or so," Cora interjected. "And that she's been here for some time."

The shadows moved. A small form approached the barred door. Cora's eyes cast a strange light over the girl's face. Still, Clara could hardly make out her features.

"Don't you want to go home?" Clara pleaded.

"Home." The girl uttered the word from a place of deep emptiness. Hollow, hopeless. Clara understood that sound. She wanted to run, wanted to flee from it, from this place and never return. To live forever and never hear such a sound again.

"Yes, of course. Home. I'm going to get you out of here."

"She's so optimistic," Cora opined. They both ignored her.

"I am home." The girl drew back several steps, into the shadows.

"No. Don't you want to be free?"

"No." Her voice rose, echoing in the tunnel.

"I'm going to save you," Clara said. She felt the heat rising in her face.

"No! No! No!" The girl fidgeted and shook, her hands flailing about in the darkness.

"They aren't here, Meike. It's just us. You're safe."

"No!" The girl rushed forward and slammed her fists against the bars. Clara gasped and stepped back. Meike was young, but her eyes were not. They were sunken and dark, full of horror—the eyes of someone with a premature knowledge of evil. She moaned and gripped the bars, shaking them as hard as she could. They scarcely moved. Instead her small body swung back and forth.

Clara swallowed hard. "Stop. Stop it! I said we're going to get you out of here."

From deep within the girl's throat, she growled then hissed at them.

"Don't you want to go home?"

She stopped swinging and stared at Clara. Then, in an altered voice like gravel skittering across broken glass she whispered, "It's better alone. Better in the dark. Where they can't see. Where they can't take."

Clara took a step back and stared at the cage in shock.

"She's broken," Cora stated flatly.

"No. She'll be fine. When she goes home."

"No. She'll never be fine. Can't you see, Clara? She'd rather remain in the cage she knows than risk the one she doesn't. There is no home for her."

"Yes, there is. What is wrong with you? What is wrong with both of you?" She glared at Meike. "You're leaving here. I'm going to save you. Why don't you want that?"

Cora raised both eyebrows. "So what's your plan?"

"What is wrong with her?"

"I already told you."

"Your answer is ridiculous. Nonsensical."

"Now who sounds like her grandmother? Maybe you're not so different after all."

Clara clenched her teeth.

"What's your plan?" Cora repeated.

"What are you talking about?"

"To get her out? And the others?"

Clara stared at her for a moment. Anger filled her body, rushing with hot adrenaline from her chest down her legs and arms. "I need a key. Obviously there must be a key. There are only two people in the house who would have it."

"So you intend to storm Lina's room, demand the key, then return here to unlock all these cells and ferret..." Cora looked around, taking in the scene with her unnatural eyes. "...ten or twelve girls up to your room? To do what?"

"I'm not going to *storm* her room, you fool." Clara glared at her. "I'll sneak in and find it when she isn't there."

"You don't think she'd keep the keys on her person at all times?"

A vision of Lina rose in Clara's mind, a heavy ring of keys in one hand as she deftly unlocked the chapel door. She had pulled them from her pocket. Undoubtedly the keys to these cages were on that ring as well. She swallowed hard, suppressing her urge to scream.

"Meike?"

Her small shape had receded into the black corners of the cell, away from Clara's rage.

"I have to go and find a way to get you out. All of you. To take you home. To your parents. Okay? But don't say anything. I don't want anyone to know what we're doing. They would try to keep us in cages forever."

The shadow didn't move. A faint dripping echoed in the distance. And then a heavy thud. And another. The sound of a man's footsteps.

Clara shot a look behind her. There, beyond the cells stood a door. She ran to it, rose up on her toes, and gripped the bars of a small window. Beyond lay a corridor she recognized. Bats. She gritted her teeth and gripped the latch, but it was locked. No matter how she shook it and pulled, the door held fast.

The footsteps grew closer.

Cora grabbed her hand and pulled her back into the small room where they'd hidden before. "He might pass by," she whispered. "All we have is the element of surprise."

Clara took in the dark space. A dirty, bare mattress lay on the floor. Otherwise the room was bare. She felt her vision closing in, her sense of balance tilting. The footsteps grew closer then stopped. She smelled him in the shadows just beyond the door.

Then he was there in front of her. Hagan.

"You! What are you doing here, you worthless bitch?" He grabbed her arm and dragged her out into the vaulted corridor. "Didn't your father teach you where you belong? On a leash?" He grinned down into her face, his teeth crooked, his face ghostly white.

For several seconds Clara's breath caught in her chest until she thought that she might suffocate. But then she gasped for air, kicked him as hard as she could, and wrenched herself free.

"Run!" Cora screamed.

Clara dodged around his lanky, lurching form and took off for the tiled hall of tombs. Behind her, she heard his ponderous tread. She threw herself forward. Faster. Harder. Until she collided with the wall at the end of the hall. Grasped the rough-hewn surface and remembered: left. She jogged left. Came to the end of the turn then took a right.

Then she came to the door still propped open. She and Cora threw themselves through the opening. They grasped the lever and pressed it up. The door swung shut. Then they were running, taking the stairs two at a time. They burst into the conservatory as a flash of lightning crossed the sky.

Clara didn't stop. She ran through the conservatory. Across the roof then into the tower, pulling the heavy door closed behind them.

Chapter Forty-Three

They escaped to the only place Clara could imagine being at that moment, the only place that felt safe: her grandfather's study. A place her grandmother hated. A place no one would think to look for her.

For hours Clara paced, her thoughts racing, her body tingling with adrenaline. Despite her anger and the horror of it all, she felt strong. Not invincible. No. She looked around the study, reminding herself that it was, for her in that moment, nothing but a hiding place. But still, she had discovered the way in. She had found the evidence her grandmother needed so desperately to hide. That gave Clara some amount of power. But what should she do with it? What could she?

Even when she tired and collapsed into one of the armchairs, she shifted and fidgeted. There she stared into the cold, lifeless fireplace, rehashing all that she now knew while Cora listened.

"I can never go back to my room," Clara said, though she knew even then that she would.

"No."

"Now that I know everything."

For once, Cora refused to meet her eyes. Eventually she responded. "You have what you need."

"She's exposed now. It's only a matter of time."

"You don't have time," Cora countered.

Clara dismissed the comment. She had enough time. She had to. Why else would she find all of this? For a moment she wished that Jutta were there instead of Cora. What would she say? Wouldn't she say that everything happened for a reason? Yes. Yes, Clara knew she would. Didn't that mean that anything Clara uncovered would contribute to her grandmother's downfall and Clara's salvation? She frowned, suddenly confused, uncertain.

She shook the thought from her mind, returning instead to the present victory. "They know that I know."

"Yes," Cora conceded with a note of warning in her voice.

Eventually Clara grew tired, so tired that she felt nothing but confidence and triumph. Her heart felt light, exhilarated even. She forgot to be afraid. Thus she headed back through the walls to her rooms. She pushed the panel to her dressing room open and listened. Silence.

"Jutta?" she called. "Are you there?"

For the first time, she sought the quiet, gentle presence of her maidservant. She wanted someone to know she no longer felt powerless, but there was no response.

She glanced into the bedroom. The fire had burned down low, leaving only the glow of the embers crackling and bathing the room in a red haze. The bed curtains were drawn. There was no sign of Jutta. She retraced her steps to the bathroom, where she caught her image in the mirror. Her face was filthy. Strings of cobwebs hung from her hair. Black streaks coated her hands. Her dress was smudged with gray marks. From one side hung a webbed sack containing some shriveled creature. She gasped shuddered and flicked it away.

Sticky tendrils of the cobweb clung to her hand. Shaking it and rubbing her hands together did nothing. Instead she ripped off the dress and her underclothes until she stood naked in the pale light. It was too late to draw a bath, but Jutta had left a pitcher filled with water. Clara poured some of it into the basin and used a cloth to wipe down her body. Then she leaned over the bathtub and poured the water through her hair.

Finally, she stood, shaking with cold but clean. So clean. She pictured herself placing another log on the fire, sitting in its warm glow, and brushing her hair dry. As she gripped her hair with the towel, her head turned slightly to one side. A tall shadowy form moved beyond the doorway. Followed by a soft thud. Clara seized a robe and wrapped it around her.

"Hello? Jutta?" she called, knowing it hadn't been Jutta. She peered around the doorway. The dressing room lay in shadow as it had before. She pulled on the robe, and crept out of the bathroom.

One of the armoire doors stood ajar. Clara's stomach clenched. Her hands trembled. She stepped toward it, lifted her hand, and paused. Then she grasped the door and flung it open. And then the other.

Nothing.

Clara exhaled, her heart still quaking in her throat. *Quickly*, she told herself. *Don't give them any power.* She went from armoire to armoire, flinging open the doors. Though her body shook, she ignored her fear.

They were all empty. The panel to the hidden passage rested securely. As she had left it.

And then she knew.

Slowly she turned and stood, staring into the otherworldly light in the bedroom. Nothing moved but the shadows cast by the dying fire. She placed one foot forward. Then another. She didn't look to the left or the right. She didn't need to.

Finally she approached the side of the bed and reached up to grasp the heavy curtains. Her breath came in quick, shallow bursts. Steeling her nerves, she flung the curtain aside.

There on the bed lay the sodden body of Meike. Her eyes were open, the pupils beginning to cloud over. Her skin was an unnatural shade of white mixed with violet bruises. One hand stood crooked and outstretched, frozen in the clutches of death. Her fingernails were coated in mud and silt and blood, as if she had attempted to claw her way to freedom.

Pinned to the front of Meike's dress was a note, the paper translucent in spots as the moisture from the dress soaked through. The smeared letters read:

. . .

Someone saw
too much.

Clara heard her blood pounding in her ears. And above that, a high-pitched wailing shriek. A frenzied madness rose through her, filling her chest. Her legs loosened and she ran. Ran through the bedroom. Through the sitting room. And threw herself against the door to the hallway.

She pounded with both fists. And screamed. But no one came. She ran back to the bathroom. To the hidden passage. Where could she go? What could she do? Her body felt weak. As if she were dissolving. Separating into pieces. A faint click sounded from her sitting room. She ran back to the door and pounded again, screaming until she felt hoarse.

Eventually she heard footsteps running down the length of the thick, carpeted hallway. A key turned in the lock, and she fell into the stiff, inhospitable arms of her grandmother. Behind Lina, her mother and uncle pressed into the room.

"Clara. Clara, what?" Her mother took her from Lina and held her close. As Helene smoothed back her wet hair, Clara gulped back sobs and struggled to speak. It was useless. Her voice came out as nothing more than an inarticulate whimper.

"There. There," Helene said. "Help me lead her to the fire."

They sat her in one of the armchairs while her uncle laid two fresh logs on the embers. He stoked them until several sparks sent up flames that licked at the dry wood, charring its surface.

When she could suppress her wailing cries, Clara pointed to the bed and attempted to draw their attention to the body that lay there.

"A what?" Helene, who had been kneeling before Clara, gripping her hands in her own, shot up.

"There's nothing there," Lina declared, her lips pursed in displeasure.

Clara twisted in the chair and stared in horror as Nathaniel pulled back the bed curtains.

The bed was empty. He ran one hand along the bedcover then rubbed his fingers together. "It's wet. Someone lay here." He indicated the depression in the pillow.

Lina huffed. "This is ridiculous! And in the middle of the night." She turned on Clara. "What do you think to gain? Is it attention? Is that what you want?"

"Mother!" Helene stepped in the middle.

"Well, just look at her. She's soaking wet. Her hair is practically flooding the chair. And the floor. Of course the bed is wet! Why wouldn't it be?"

A burning heat spread through Clara's body. She clenched her fists.

"You. You witch!" she screamed. "You evil, wicked bitch. There was a body. A young girl. Meike. Lying there!" Clara's finger jabbed toward the bed.

"Meike?" Helene started to ask.

"Really? Then where is she now?" Lina strode to Jutta's small room. "Where are you? Come out, come out, wherever you are!" She crossed the bedroom and ripped aside the curtains covering the window seat. "Oh, look! She must be in here. No? Perhaps not." She tromped into the dressing room. Clara heard the armoire doors opening and slamming in succession. "Oh, young girl? Wherever can you be?"

"Stop!" Clara shouted, holding her hands over her ears. "Stop!" Hot tears flowed down her face. Her mother rose and wrapped her arms around her, murmuring something lightly, but Clara didn't hear it.

"Enough!" Nathaniel roared. Clara choked off her sob. Helene froze and stared at him wide-eyed. Even Lina paused, midstride, her mouth open but silent. "That is just about enough! I don't know what is going on here, but it is going to stop."

"Jutta," he gestured to the doorway where Jutta stood. Her breath came short and fast, as if she had run far. "You locked up the house?" When she nodded he continued, "See to her. Make sure she changes. And sleeps. Don't leave her under any circumstances. We'll discuss this in the morning."

Jutta nodded, curtseyed politely, and rushed to Clara's side.

"And you, Mother. I think we've had far too much excitement for one night. We will leave Clara to rest. And then we'll get to the bottom of this. Later."

Lina moved to say something, but just then the bedroom door opened. Berend, followed by Hagan, stepped through the doorway and quietly took in the scene. Berend shot Lina a look, to which she closed her mouth and moved to follow him back out the door.

As he turned to go, the fire sent a ray of light across him. His hair, though it was slicked back carefully, was very wet. And across his wrist, four jagged lines marked where the skin had recently been torn.

Clara narrowed her eyes and stared after the three of them as they withdrew.

"Devils," she muttered. But then she remembered her mother sitting beside her. For a fraction of a second, Helene's cheeks rose. Then her face quickly assumed a careful appearance of concern. It was long enough though. Long enough for Clara to confirm that her mother played at some game. A carefully constructed game. One in which her every word and action and expression were controlled. But to what end? And why would she need to deceive Lina?

Nathaniel set Jutta to work changing the bedding. Helene retrieved Clara's brush and sat beside her, gently gliding the bristles through her hair. As Clara watched the flames' soft light and listened to them crackle, her nerves settled and gave way to exhaustion.

And then they left.

In the end, the image of Meike still vivid in her mind, Clara refused to sleep in the bed. Instead, Jutta helped Clara gather several pillows and blankets and arrange them in the window seat. The maidservant drew an armchair up beside it and settled herself into it with a blanket. It gave Clara a sense of separation, as if Jutta had used herself to divide Clara from the room and the house beyond. She fell fast asleep, enveloped in the sense that she was floating out into the stormy night. And leaving it all behind.

Chapter Forty-Four

The next night, Clara crept into her grandmother's room, pausing at every creak and whisper from the walls. It grew late, the sky an undulating iron gray and black like smoke billowing from some great locomotive bearing down on her. Yet the room lay empty. Lina must still be in the drawing room, she reasoned, sitting in her armchair beside the fire, Clara's mother across from her.

Clara opened each of her grandmother's desk drawers and those in the bedside tables. None held the key. Nor did the armoires and the pockets of their contents. She glided toward the window, her shoulders hunched. In the waning moonlight, she pulled a piece of paper from her pocket and turned it this way and that. It held a tiny list of names organized in rows, filling its front and back. Some were familiar—business associates of her father and grandfather. Most were not.

"It's an odd sort of address book," a voice behind her said.

Clara started, but didn't turn. By now that voice was unmistakable, expected even, despite her wishes.

"I don't need you here."

"Ah, but you do. How will you ever find the way out of this hellhole without me?"

"I'll take my chances."

"Hmm. I suppose you will." Cora laughed and plucked the list from Clara's fingers. "I wonder what Lina is up to." She laughed again, her tone one of mocking incredulity, as if she could be deriding Clara, Lina, or the situation itself. Perhaps all of them.

Clara sighed. "You said you'd leave me alone if I asked."

"It's too late for that. Too late by far. You're stuck with me."

"That might be—"

Footsteps approached just outside the door. Clara ripped the paper from Cora's hand and stuffed it into her pocket. She turned toward the bathroom. Too exposed. The dressing room too far. As the lock turned, she slipped behind the curtains. The toes of her slippers rested on its pooled hem. Around her the room fell still. Her own breath seemed to fill the silence, to billow the curtains. She held it in.

"...just a moment," her grandmother said.

From the edge of the curtains, Clara saw her grandmother's back as she strode into her dressing room. A door opened then closed again. She walked back into the bedroom, a coat over her arm, her gaze distant and detached. Clara pressed against the wall, holding her body frozen, but Lina passed by without glancing in her direction.

Clara heard her footsteps retreating toward her sitting room. The door opened again.

"Here they are." It was Berend's voice, low and firm.

Then the door shut, the room falling into a hollow void that was somehow worse than her fear of being discovered.

"Let's get out of here," Clara exhaled.

Cora said nothing, only grinned and followed her to the panel in the wall.

"Ah, you know where they're going," Cora said when they emerged in the library. She said it as if it amused her.

Clara strode to the windows. The sky had brightened, the moon peering around the heavy cloud cover. Beyond the drive, two shadows moved. They strode purposefully, without cause for alarm, as if their actions were beyond scrutiny. Something within Clara twisted and flared. She turned and ran for the library door.

The ground floor's axial hallway lay still and dark. She dashed for the front door, forgetting she was a prisoner. She had lost all consideration for the past or her dreams for the future. In fact, she held no regard for herself at all. It wasn't until she had gripped the front door's handle, flung it open, and stepped outside that she remembered.

"Where are you going?" Cora jumped in front of her, gripping her arms, holding her fast.

Clara shoved her aside and ran toward the gardens. Seconds later, a whoosh shoved her from behind. She tripped, sliding as she landed on her forearms. Gravel tore the sleeves of her dress, scraping her arms. Her chin skidded along the ground. A flash of black and red bolted across her sight.

"Get back in the house!" Cora screamed in her ear.

Clutching at the front of her dress, Clara stumbled to her feet. She stood with her back to the drive that bent around toward the chapel. And looked in the opposite direction from where her grandmother and Berend had disappeared. Beyond the gardens and down the hill to where the treeline beckoned. "Why? Are you afraid I'll leave? I don't know why I didn't see it before. Maybe because I was always alone. Waiting to be alone when I could have waited and followed them. There had to have been opportunities. Times like this. Even now. By dawn I could be miles from here, lost in the forest. Gone from them."

"That won't fix anything."

Clara laughed. She turned and pressed up toward her aunt. "No. No, it won't. Which is why I'm not leaving. But I'm not playing your game either. I know what you want."

She looked back toward the house. In the distance she saw the curved flower beds, long dead, and beyond them the jutting edge of the servants' wing. Many of the lights were still on, their work only recently finished. She strode toward the corner of the wing. There she paused for a moment. She knew where they were going. Cora had been wrong before. She hadn't known. She hadn't known anything beyond the fact that Lina's coat and gloves would lead her outside. The library had simply been the first thought she'd had. Then she had seen them heading around the side of the chapel. Even then she hadn't known.

But now she did.

"Get back inside." Cora's face appeared ghoulish in the shifting shadows of the ashen sky. "This is pointless. You have what you need."

"No." Clara shook her head, not looking back at Cora.

She turned to head off around the chapel, toward the family graveyard. But a hand shot out, gripped the side of her head, and slammed it into the wall of the house. Waves of searing pain radiated down her neck, across her shoulders, down her arms and legs. She clenched her teeth to keep from crying out as a spasm shook her back.

"They'll catch you." Cora paced in tight circles, hedging Clara in against the house. "What are you doing? Why? Why are you doing this?"

"Since when do you care?"

Cora huffed. When Clara tried to dodge her, she shoved her back against the wall. "There are things you have to do. You'll never be free if you don't. They can't catch you. They can't."

"Why would you care?"

"What do you gain? Here." Cora gestured around them.

"I…I don't know." She looked toward the woods again, far from the house. What *had* she thought when she had seen her grandmother leaving? She couldn't say. There had only been the urge, the need to follow her, to uncover what she did under the cover of darkness. But that wasn't exactly true, was it? In the deepest part of her soul, she had known all that mattered was that she try to free the other girls. The ones who never saw Meike return. Who probably had witnessed her death and knew their own would follow.

Clara shook her head. "I have to free them. It's all of us or none of us." A bolt of pain shot through her head from one temple to the other. Her ears rang. She clutched the front of her dress and leaned forward, breathing deeply. Then she took as deep a breath as she could, drew strength into herself, and wrested away from Cora.

Cora grabbed the back of her dress, tearing it, and slammed her back against the house. Waves of pain shot down Clara's arms and legs. She felt sweat run down the back of her dress despite the cold. Cora pressed her back against the stone, her face filled with hate, her breath rancid.

"No. You listen to me. If you die, she gets away with it. With all of it. There will be no one to stop them. Everything your father did. Your grandmother. Get up. Get back in the house."

Clara felt her mind rise from the midst of the pain and press it down. Behind. She looked fully in Cora's face and knew she was right. And wrong. She had to live. But she also had to uncover the truth.

She turned away and pushed at the corner of the house, propelling herself forward. She ran, half stumbling, half tripping toward the family cemetery. As she fell through the open iron gate, she crumpled to the ground. Another wave of pain shook her body, this time filling her with nausea. She crawled off the path, toward a grassy swath marked by a tombstone. In the distance she saw movement near the mausoleum. A figure emerging from beneath the covered steps.

"So very positive. Is this what you came to see?" Cora bent over her and read the tombstone aloud.

Dorothye Frena Willenheim
1412–1469

No epithet. No description of her as mother, daughter, friend. Just:

Verily, verily, I say unto you,
"Except a corn of wheat fall into the ground and die, it abideth alone;
but if it die, it bringeth forth much fruit."

Clara moaned and curled around herself in agony. Her stomach clenched. She had seconds to raise herself up on shaking arms before she vomited. Even in the veiled moonlight, she made out clots of thick crimson lying in the dormant grass.

"Who is that?" Lina's voice snaked through the darkness and misting fog. "Berend, come here."

Clara lay her head on the frozen ground and turned to see the water dripping from the edge of Cora's dress. The night swam before her eyes, mingling with the soft breeze. She closed her eyes.

Chapter Forty-Five

Clara leaned back against the pillows watching her mother and Jutta bustle around her, even seeming to listen to them. In reality, though, she focused intently on the hushed conversation on the other side of the bedroom between her grandmother, Berend, and the doctor.

"It is troubling," the doctor said. "Particularly given all that you've told me. Her nerves are at a fever pitch. One more excitable moment and she's likely to break down entirely."

"So you agree with me?" Lina leaned toward him, her expectations clear.

"Oh, most assuredly. Most assuredly. If she doesn't improve soon, I'm sorry to say I could recommend no other course of action. It can't continue. To remain in this environment, in which her mental state is so deeply affected, would be detrimental. Exceedingly detrimental."

Clara narrowed her eyes. *Exceedingly detrimental?* Was he even a doctor or did her grandmother simply coerce the latest traveling salesman to play the part?

"How soon?" Lina asked.

They shot a conspiratorial glance in her direction, their eyebrows arched in suspicion.

"No more than a few days, a week at most. It can't linger. Not if you care for her well-being. Not at all."

"I don't need to be in bed," Clara cut in. "I'm perfectly fine." She didn't tell them, but she felt tired, as if the night before had cost her something she couldn't yet determine. She had needed to see what her grandmother planned to do. And she had succeeded. Some deep part of her knew what Lina had accomplished—not in a tangible sense but in essence. She couldn't say exactly what Lina had taken, but she had obtained something from her father's coffin. And for some dark end.

Clara understood what she had given up. They never would have found her. No one in the house—master or servant—could have tracked her effectively. They weren't skilled in the ways of the forest. If she had made it out, if the forest hadn't claimed her for itself, she could have been far from here by now. But she had chosen this. She had something to do. In that, Cora was right.

She needed to be free from this bed. And they needed to leave. All of them. Her grandmother and the doctor shook their heads then turned away to whisper something she couldn't catch. Berend glanced back at her.

"Clara, no," her mother whispered. "It's best not to say anything."

Clara winced as if she'd been slapped. Tears filled her eyes. "Why not? I'm not ill. Definitely not *psychologically unstable*. Why can't you see that? You don't believe them, do you?"

"I do... I mean, I don't." Helene leaned over her, her voice low. "Oh, Clara dear, you can't see. You don't understand. It's best to be quiet, to keep your peace. For now."

"For now? For now? Until what? Until they ship me off to an asylum? Is that what you want? To be rid of me?" Tears flowed down her face, her voice trembling in anguish.

"No. No. Of course not. I would never..."

"No, you would never. That's right. You would never. What about... about... Did you even know who he was?"

At that Lina spun around and fixed her in a dark grimace.

"There, there," Jutta cut in between the two of them and pressed a cool, moist cloth to her forehead. The girl's hands, so small and slender, were both strong and tender. "Let's lie back, fräulein. There's no need to do or say anything more right now."

Clara turned her head away, her eyes stinging, her face hot. She heard her mother move off to question the doctor.

"Let me put a cool cloth under your neck."

As she rose up, Clara heard the faintest sound as of a whisper barely breathed. "Wait. Be still and wait. It's not too late." She turned and looked at Jutta, but the girl refused to meet her eyes.

"There you go, fräulein. I'm sure that's much more comfortable." She raised her voice. "You could probably do with some rest now. This is all so very trying." She shot a glance toward the huddled three. A few minutes later they left. Clara heard the door lock turn. Shortly afterward she fell into a deep sleep.

At some point later, she awoke to the sibilant sound of whispering. Her mother had returned. She and Jutta sat by the fireplace, their chairs pulled close together. Clara closed her eyes and breathed slowly, deeply, her ears straining to catch their words.

"... after effects?"

"No. No bleeding or other pain that he could tell. The doctor didn't seem to believe there was any physical explanation."

"Hmm. I thought she was well. As well as we could expect."

Jutta didn't respond.

"Wasn't she?"

Jutta's shoulders curled forward. "Yes, if you mean functioning. Eating, drinking, moving about. But what is that? Animals do as much."

"Then what?"

Jutta paused as if searching for the right answer. "It's as if she believes she's scrutinizing another woman through a dusty window. But there will come a day when she realizes the window is just a mirror. Part of her might already sense as much. And that much reality can be overwhelming. I think she's forestalling the realization."

"Hmm. You don't think she can bear it?"

"No. It's weighing her down in a way she can't carry. She doesn't have the strength, the foundation for it."

"I see your point. I'll have to ask him. He'll know what to do."

"He won't hide anything from her."

"No. No he won't. But it's too early. It isn't safe. I don't know...I don't know..." Her mother's voice trailed off in a whisper. "Still, he could reach her."

"Yes."

Clara's heart beat faster—her body tense, poised, waiting for what would come next. But the two women slipped into thoughtful silence. Jutta rose to place another log on the fire. At some point the soft firelight, the warmth in the room and the emotional exhaustion caught up with her. She fell into a fitful sleep.

She sat in a shallow boat, the winged dragon on its prow swaying lightly as it cut through the water. In one hand she gripped a long oar, its blade dripping and poised over the river. The water snaking beneath her gleamed black as obsidian, its surface speckled with starlight. Towering aspens, their branches coated with snow, lined the woods on either side. Around her the forest was still. Snow lay evenly on the ground, its surface undisturbed by wind or wayfarer. No sound echoed in the darkness. No night bird swooped. No prey scurried. All lay frozen, unchanging.

For some time she rowed, her mind still, empty as she watched the endlessly repeating landscape: white ground, white-and-gray spotted columns, and the black ribbon of water carrying her farther from her home. Deep into the forest. A forest unlike any she had ever seen. One that lived at the edges of her consciousness, beyond the tangible world. She gave herself up to it, slicing through the water with her oar, feeling the still, cold air envelop her in its pure embrace. Relishing the freedom and joy of solitude.

Until she sensed something. A presence. A faint awareness grew in her mind. The knowledge that she wasn't alone. That something drew near, sought her out. Whether the other one had always been there or had just appeared, she couldn't have said. But she no longer felt the ease of the quiet, dark river and its solitude.

She twisted to study the shore as it sailed past. The erect forms of the trees took on a new aspect, as if they stood at attention awaiting an order. The moon hung low, immense above her, her boat reflected in its lucent eye. The snow covering the ground swallowed its light, reflecting a dull ashen surface coated in grime.

Movement caught her eyes.

A long red ribbon writhed through the water. First on one side of the boat. Then the other. It kept pace with her, slithering in a long bloody streak across the black surface of the river. Something swooped low overhead. A shriek cut through the silence. Clara clenched her paddles and dug them into the water. Faster and faster. But its surface merely parted then pulled together again, the red and the black unassuaged.

Her panting breath filled the cold, dry air. The muscles of her arms ached with the exertion. Her shoulders quaked and locked. Something tore at the paddle, wrenching it from her grasp. It sank into the inky depths. She fell to the side and clutched the edge of the rocking boat. Short blond hair reflected in the water. But through it a face rose, its features unmistakable, unavoidable, its mouth caught wide, screaming in agony and accusation.

When Clara jerked awake, the room was empty, the bed overly hot. She drew herself up to sit against the back of the tester. Outside she heard the steady sound of falling rain. She concentrated on that, letting the sense of it washing down the house still her mind and soothe something within her.

Chapter Forty-Six

Helene bit her lip and peered through the grimy window of the rooftop conservatory. It was sullen outside, the sky full of frozen spitting mist that sparked off her skin like tiny arrows. An oppressive, violent weather that mirrored the state of her spirit. When she turned around, Nathaniel was leaning against the edge of a potting table, ostensibly watching her. His eyes were unfocused, though, as if he were lost in thought, weighing his words. The first thing she had noticed about him was that he possessed a self-control that registered as something otherworldly. His measured responses and the succeeding events and comments—even from the others in the family—always seemed to fit together in perfect harmony. It both awed and unnerved her.

From under the table, a rat—sleek fur the color of ash with shining black eyes—darted out and ran to a back corner. She shivered in disgust. During much of the year, the conservatory was one of her favorite parts of the house. She often spent hours each day moving up and down the rows of plants, watering them, talking to them, fussing over their leaves, and propping up drooping branches. But today the space just felt dirty. It reminded her of disease and death, the very things that her father had worked so hard to eradicate.

As if he had heard her thoughts, Nathaniel fixed his eyes on her, waiting.

"You don't seem to understand what we're dealing with." She breathed slowly, checking the impatience that rose into her chest. "My father spent his entire life fighting disease. And for all his efforts, and progress, he hardly made an impact. This...this is unlike any known disease. It's a contagious malignancy. One that creeps into the minds of men and changes them so they rot from the inside out. Then they spread it to everyone around them."

"Yes..."

"Not to mention the victims themselves. Your own sister. How many others have to suffer before we eliminate this disease?"

"Helene."

"And what about Clara? You know what he did to her!" Helene wrung her hands, her voice rising. She stopped for a moment and clenched her teeth, struggling not to scream. "If I had known—"

Nathaniel took her hands and held them fast. When he spoke, his voice was low, soothing, little more than a whisper. "Look at me. You *didn't* know. You couldn't have known. And as soon as you did, you did something about it."

As soon as his grip loosened, she flung his hands away. "That monster. She...she was carrying..." Her voice choked back the words. "Even now, she practically begs for help. And I can't say anything. Do you know what that's like—to have to hold back the very thing your child needs and watch her suffer?"

"She's safe for now. Nothing you do or say at this point would help her in the long run."

Helene remembered that fateful night. The one on which she had first seen Edgar emerging from Clara's room. The horror that she had felt had only been rivaled by her confusion. Surely she was wrong. Surely what appeared to be true wasn't. But then she had followed him. And confirmed her worst fears.

No. That's not true. She'd confirmed her worst fears later. Fears she hadn't even anticipated until she had followed her mother-in-law and had learned of her network of evil.

"They're monsters. All of them." She crossed one arm over her body and chewed at her thumbnail. "The whole world is filled with monsters. It makes me sick. Isn't there any justice? Any way to right all of it?"

"They aren't all monsters."

"They are."

"No. Most of the Bavarian people would never participate in something like this, let alone support it. But they're ignorant of the evil that surrounds them. Others want justice but have no power to seek it. And still others are currently working to do something. You know that. Of all people, you know that. You can't lose hope. Your own husband—"

"My husband was a monster. I don't want to hear it." Helene stepped back and exhaled the frustration that filled her body, tightening her muscles, filling her with the desire to fight. He wouldn't help her. She had thought he would, but he wouldn't. Now she felt as if the only salvation she had threatened to slide out from between her fingers, leaving her stranded at sea.

Fortune sends the best she can bear.

He had sent that message, of course. The one that had perplexed her mother-in-law. Nathaniel's contact from his childhood days in Prussia, a region with the "bear" as its mascot, Otto von Bernuth, whose name meant "fortune," had sent someone. Someone who aimed to help her in uncovering and uprooting Lina's ring of associates. She had yet to meet this person, but she had hoped for as much. Had pictured it even—a violent end to the evil around her. Only to discover his intentions lay in arrests and prosecutions.

She should have known. They would never result in anything. The sorts of people involved, the degree of power and influence in Lina's circle, would never suffer any true justice. They would go free. They would return to the sorts of evil she had witnessed and it would all recommence, left to grow unchecked.

"This event is the opportunity we've been waiting for," Helene reiterated, her face flushed with frustration.

"Yes, but not for what you're planning."

"It's the best chance we have. Everyone in one place. You know Lina will invite them all. All of them in one place, at one time. This might be the only chance we'll have to destroy this...this...cancer. You're the one who's opposed to me."

"I have never opposed you. Everything I'm doing is for your benefit. And Clara's. And all the other faceless, nameless victims. Everything I'm doing—we're doing—goes against those who exploit and use others. You know that."

"But this plan. Your plan. It won't accomplish anything."

"Of course it will. I think you mean it won't accomplish what you want it to accomplish. Helene, this vengeance of yours is like an inferno. It can't be controlled. It will backfire, like your attempt to silence the medical examiner. But this time there will be consequences."

She bit back her anger. "I only want justice."

"Do you?"

"Yes. Yes..." She turned away from him again to stand by the window.

"The path you're advocating leads only to destruction and death."

"I know."

"*Your* death, Helene. If you take this path, it will destroy you."

Was that true? Was that the cost of justice? She wanted to ask him what he saw as the alternative, but she already knew the answer. She had written to him because Nathaniel was the only person she suspected would have no connection with any of this. The only person Lina would never involve. Who lived so far from her network of connections that he might have the capacity to do something. To find some way of fixing what was so horribly wrong.

And now that he stood here, she knew hoping in him had been in vain. She had known the answer all along—if there was to be any satisfactory end to this, she would have to be the one to bring it about. Some crimes could only be atoned for through the most violent and torturous end.

Chapter Forty-Seven

"Here?" Lina exclaimed. "But that's impossible! He was thousands of miles away."

Inspector Dressler rubbed his sideburn and shot her a wary glance. "I'm sorry to say he *was* here. My sources are rarely incorrect, particularly in a matter of such importance."

Lina stared at him then turned to look at Berend. His look would have been inscrutable to anyone else. But she knew he was as surprised by this news as she was. They had thought that Nathaniel was in India. That he had only just arrived a week ago. Yet the inspectors had confirmed that Nathaniel had been near the estate shortly before Edgar had died. Her mind spun with images, memories from his childhood. None of them were useful or applicable, yet she couldn't dam the racing stream.

"It's just not possible," she repeated. "Besides, I thought you were investigating the Aurbergs."

"We were. Gnädige Frau," Metz piped up, his boyish face round and pink above his ridiculous mustache. "All the Aurbergs have alibis for the night of Edgar's death."

"And preceding it," Dressler added. "Not to mention that we can find no evidence of any correspondence, association, or financial exchange that would suggest foul play."

"So they're innocent," Lina surmised.

"We have no reason to believe otherwise."

"And Nathaniel?"

"To be perfectly honest, Frau Willenheim, we have no idea why he was here. His presence is a fact. But the nature of it is entirely unknown."

"He would have motive." Lina gazed around her into the dark recesses of the library, as if there she would uncover the answer.

"It's certainly possible." Dressler wagged his head from side to side. "Although...everything we've discovered indicates he was entirely settled and satisfied with his life abroad."

"What are you suggesting?" Lina snapped.

"Just that he doesn't seem to have desired his brother's death. We don't see any indication that he wanted the house, the estate's other holdings, or anything that would come with his title. Or lifestyle. From all indications, he wanted just the opposite."

"Humph." Although Lina found such a claim absurd, she held her tongue.

"There is...uh...one other matter of relative importance. It concerns a young man who goes by the name Diedrich."

"Never heard of him."

"He's recently taken up study under one Werner Regensbach."

Lina's gaze shot up, her eyes flashing recognition. She turned to Berend. "Is he the..."

Berend's face fell. "I believe so."

"He was here. Recently."

"It pains me to inform you that he has come to our attention lately. Under somewhat suspicious circumstances. We took it upon ourselves to look into his past. It appears he is actually someone other than whom he appears to be. But what, or rather who, is another matter. He's associated with a man who seems to go by many names. The one we uncovered is a..." Dressler drew his small notebook out of his pocket and flipped forward until he found the page. "...ah, yes, Siegmund Mahler."

"Mahler." Lina stared at him, puzzled. "I've never met a Mahler."

"No, I don't suppose you would have, Gnädige Frau. To put it quite succinctly...though we can't confirm anything yet...we suspect he's a member of the secret police. Headquartered in Berlin."

Lina paled instantly. Her pupils grew wide. She paced, one arm clutched protectively across her waist. Dressler cleared his throat but hesitated to speak until she was ready. Finally she stopped and addressed him. "What do you suppose his motive could be?"

"It would be wise to assume the worst."

"They know," she whispered.

"It is possible."

"How?!"

"I truly could not say. But I would be remiss if I didn't advise you to take the utmost precaution at this point."

"Can't you arrest him?"

"Well, that does present its problems. Technically there is some question as to whether the young man actually committed any crime we can prosecute. He was captured in the company of a young girl. But there was never any actual evidence of criminal activity. Any activity whatsoever." He shot Metz a grim look. "When we tracked her down later to substantiate her former statement, we discovered that she's an orphan earning her living in a local tavern. That her supposed *father* in the entire charade—Herr Mahler himself—had paid her to play the part of a victim.

"In addition, Herr Regensbach is quite fond of the boy. Has practically taken him under his wing as the son he never had."

"That doesn't surprise me," Lina said.

"Lastly, if this Mahler's motives are what we estimate them to be, any *disappearance* of the boy..." He left the implication unspoken. "Well, it would arouse interest sooner than we are prepared to address it."

"I see." And Lina could see. The cells of young girls stood as a testimony against them, should unwelcome guests suddenly alight on the scene. Normally she would trust to the secrecy of the house itself to hide such evidence. But if they were determined, it was only a matter of time before they would find the access points.

By the time Inspectors Metz and Dressler took their leave, Lina could taste the bile rising in her throat. She and Berend hurried down the lawn to the family mausoleum. The one place she knew they wouldn't be overheard. At least, not by the living. She hadn't expected Dressler to bring her news that hit so close to home. As it now stood, even whispered conversations in the library, at the far end of the ground floor, left her feeling exposed and vulnerable.

The morning's light sleeting mist had dissipated. The wind carried the crystalline bite of snow, as if to warn her of a coming storm.

"We have to shut it down." Berend didn't wait for her opinion or lead in the conversation.

"Yes," she readily agreed. "I didn't think it would come to this."

Berend refrained from additional comment. They both knew this was exactly what he had feared most. And had predicted.

"After the party," she added."

"Lina..."

"No, Berend. It's only days away. There's nothing that will stop me from this last memorial."

"That isn't wise."

Lina glared at him. It had to end. She knew it now. Berend had been right. It was only a matter of time before the entire system imploded, bringing them all down with it. She had done what she could to shield her son. More so, even. Still, it wasn't enough.

She couldn't have predicted this foreign element. Damn them. Their constant meddling. It was that fox, Bismarck. Wasn't that what she had told that gentleman—what had his name been? *He's nothing more than a fox in a henhouse, tearing everything apart.*

"But how?" she asked, shaking her head. They both knew what she asked: how could anyone outside of Bavaria know of their doings?

"Someone talked," Berend said.

"Clearly, but it's not in anyone's interest to do so. That's the point. To say anything is to expose oneself."

"Unless someone grew a conscience. Wanted out. Wanted to shut you down without publicizing his change of heart. He could have brokered a deal: immunity for exposure. You have to admit it's highly plausible. One man's innocence for countless leaders' exposure and removal. It's entirely in line with Bismarck's agenda. A region free from any obstacles to unity. No one to resist his ascension."

"I see your point. But how does that help us?"

"I don't know."

They stood for several minutes in the mausoleum's icy clutch, lost in thought, before something occurred to Lina.

"There is another possibility. It could have been someone inside the house. A rat."

"Who? Only Hagan knows anything, and he would never speak of it." *And possibly Clara*, he thought, *but she has no access to the outside world other than her tutors. Whom we monitor.*

"Who do we know who has Prussian roots? Who's always been a little too perfect to trust?"

"But Helene has no knowledge of any of this."

"Possibly. In either case, I want this Diedrich removed." Lina recoiled at the thought of all that he knew.

"Of course. But—"

"No buts. He's a liability. I don't want him anywhere near this house, or this family, ever again. I can't afford for him to talk, to say any more than he already has."

"Lina. Wait a minute. Hear me out. Given what Inspector Dressler told us, we can trust that he *is* a rat. But he's a baby rat..."

"A rat's a rat," Lina interrupted. "I know how to deal with a pest."

"Hold on. What do you know about rats?" When Lina stopped and waited, finally willing to listen, Berend continued. "Where there are babies, there are adults. Yes, Diedrich is a liability we can't afford. But if we kill the baby rat, we'll never know where the others are."

"And *who* they are."

"Exactly. The best way to uncover a rat's nest is to feed the baby and wait. It'll only be a matter of time before it wanders back to its nest."

Lina's eyes shone black with gleeful malice. "Ah! How wise! Yes, that's the way to do it. To eliminate the entire bunch of them."

Chapter Forty-Eight

Jan paced alongside the carriage, pausing to listen for the sound of anyone approaching. The horses shifted nervously, their hooves squelching in the mud and detritus. A heavy fog hung around them, obscuring the road in both directions. Richter bent over the open side of the Thurn und Taxis carriage, his lantern perched on the seat, his hand rapidly sorting through a bag that rested on the floor. On the other side of the wagon, the courier stood gazing into the denuded forest across the road. His hand shook as he raised a cigarette to his lips.

Jan strode back to the door and looked over Richter's shoulder. "We have to go."

Richter paused, a letter gripped in one hand. Then he shook his head and bent over his notebook where he was jotting down names in long rows. "I don't hear a thing."

Jan leaned back and looked off into the murky night.

"Relax," Richter added. "It's highly unlikely anyone would be out at this hour."

Jan turned and looked off into the woods. *Why are we out at this hour?* he wanted to ask, except he already knew. Jan was in too deep. And Richter's attempts to insert himself into the equation had been unsuccessful. At this point they needed names. Specific people they could pursue and hopefully incriminate. People who might prove to be the liability to Lina's enterprise. Who might reveal an entry point into the system.

Word had reached them that Lina was planning a homecoming ball for Nathaniel. A homecoming ball meant invitations, presumably to those who were Lina's favored acquaintances.

It hadn't taken much for Richter to bribe the local mail courier so that when he picked up a large shipment from Waldensee, they were informed. The mail was *detained* long enough for them to meet the wary man on a deserted stretch of road in the middle of the night. A quiet place where Richter could rifle through the envelopes and jot down the list of potentially guilty persons.

The resonant cry of an owl broke the stillness of the night. Something shuffled in the undergrowth to the side of the road. Jan's skin crawled. He strode up to Richter and peered over his shoulder.

"Are you almost done?"

His mentor was scribbling rapidly and muttering. "Nearly. Very nearly," Jan heard him say.

Jan froze. From a distance, the distinct rumbling of horses hooves pounded in the darkness. The faint glow of a carriage lantern shone.

"You!" Jan signaled to the courier, who was already gazing down the road, his eyes wide. "Come. Here. Up here. Now."

The man stumbled over, gripped the handhold, and pulled himself up onto the bench of the carriage. The vehicle rocked as he settled into place. "Now?" he hissed.

"Wait." Jan looked from him to Richter's hands. Richter was scribbling furiously and shuffling through one last handful of mail.

In the distance the light grew closer, the sound of the horses distinct.

"Okay. Okay." Richter shoved the rest of the mail back in the bag, pulled the cinch closed and gripped his lantern.

"Go," Jan said.

The carriage jolted forward just as they stepped back. Richter blew out the lantern and handed it to Jan. The two men dashed into the barren wood, their feet catching on tree roots and fallen twigs. They made it to a group of large pines where they crouched and turned to watch the road. Seconds later the other carriage rolled past, its wheels squeaking in resigned protest.

$$Chapter\ Forty\text{-}Nine$$

In the small laboratory off the kitchens, a flame licked at the underside of a log. The blackening surface began to glow. Helene stood before it, a poker in her hand. She stared at the fire as it grew, captivated by its power. The power to destroy. And to give life. New life.

Behind her, on the workbench, stood the glass jars and beakers she kept cleaned and lined in rows along the wall of the narrow room. Beside them lay a small bundle—a hessian sack, cinched closed. She turned and carefully untied the leather cords. It was true she had broken down her laboratory, as she had told her mother-in-law she would. However, there was much she had kept, secreted away in places throughout the house. She had known that she would need them. That this moment would arrive.

She pulled out the leaves and berries of a wild plant. Her father always had said she had an uncanny knack for observation. The sort of awareness that bordered on prescience. It amused him to say so. She had never corrected him, though it wasn't exactly true. If anything, her skill lay in ferreting out the truth in the past, knowing it would repeat. The mouse who remembers the prior winter is the one who prepares for the upcoming one.

What he had never understood was that the stories of her mother's and brother's unexpected deaths had planted a root of fear in her. A fear of uncertainty, of being unprepared for what was to come. Of the deep loss that ensues when the future pulls your world away from you, a world you had relied on to remain constant and stable. She didn't just lose her beloved family. After all, she had been too young to remember them. No, her primary loss had been that of security. She had been left with the knowledge that everything could change in the blink of the eye. For the worse. And that you could be left stranded, alone. That was the crippling thought. The one that colored everything else in life.

It had given her a dogmatic need for preparation. Coupled with a keen ability to read meaning into history. This gave her a strong ability to guard against the future.

And still it had failed her. With her own daughter. What had happened to Clara was unthinkable. She should have known. Should have seen the signs in her husband—his cold indifference to her body, his shifting gaze and inability to meet her eyes. Helene's vision blurred. She brushed away tears with the back of her hand. How had she missed the one thing that mattered most, the very thing that threatened to destroy them all?

She exhaled a deep, trembling sigh. Her heart was heavy, weighed down by all that had happened. And all that she had not done.

And by Nathaniel.

She hadn't realized how far their paths had diverged until he had arrived. Now he threatened to undo everything she had hoped for. She paused, a jar in her hand. Is this what she had hoped for? She couldn't remember. Maybe it hadn't been. Early on she had felt nothing but a frantic desperation—the sort of despairing fury that drives a bird to hurtle itself into the door of its cage, breaking its wings in the process.

He had been her last hope, the lifeline she had looked for in the midst of a perilous storm. When the waves had raged around her and she hadn't seen a way to save herself. And her daughter. But now that he was here, now that Edgar was dead, now that events had unfolded as they had, she no longer needed him. Oh, she would have welcomed the alliance, if it had been possible. But it wasn't.

His plan left a sour taste in her mouth. It reeked of disease left to flourish. No, she didn't need that. Or want it. Now that the cards were all laid out on the table, she knew exactly what needed to be done. She would have to be the one to do it.

The fire was hot. Hot enough to do what she needed it to do. She filled a jar with dried berries and water and set it over the flame. It would heat slowly, reconstituting the black fruit. Then the berries would burst, infusing the water with their deceptively sweet juice. In the end she would strain out the skins and pulp and bury them in the garden. She didn't need them.

From the back of her mind, one of her father's old sayings rose to mind: *When you walk in the Devil's garden, be prepared to eat at his table.* Her father. She smiled a sad smile. What would he say now? What would he think of her? *He'd understand,* she told herself, but her hand trembled. She clutched at the front of her dress to still her nerves. He knew what it was to give everything he had to eradicate a plague. At least to try to.

But simultaneously she couldn't help remembering Nathaniel's words, his certainty that her path led only to destruction.

The water was boiling in the jar. The berries were expanding, filling with a monstrous form of life. It wasn't too late. Her hand hovered. She looked back at the sack, filled with bags of similar fruit. It would take no more than a few minutes to turn the entire sack onto the fire, to empty the jar of its contents and be done with it. To walk away.

But then a series of images rose in her mind: of Edgar slipping out of Clara's room in the dark of the night; of her daughter hunched over and gasping, her body hemorrhaging violently; of Lina's smug, self-satisfied face. She stayed her hand and left the jar where it sat. She watched the juice ooze out, infecting the water. She had ransacked the Devil's garden —the one place where true justice could be had. And she was ready to eat with him.

She emptied another handful of dried berries into a second jar, added water, and set it over the flame.

<h1 style="text-align:center">Chapter Fifty</h1>

Was it the fourth cell? On the right? Clara approached the door and lifted her lantern. "Hello?" Someone shifted in the darkness but didn't respond. "Hello?" she called again. In her left hand she clutched two heavy brass keys. The only keys she had been able to find. The ones she prayed would work.

Each of the last three nights, she had dreamed she crept through the walls within the servants' wing, looking for an access point to Berend's room. Anything other than the main door into the wing. And each time she had awakened in terror, her heart racing, her body covered in sweat, as if something monstrous had pursued her. Something incalculable from which she couldn't escape. She had crossed the idea of Berend's set of keys, assuming he possessed one, off the list.

But in its wake, she remembered something. Two lone keys she had seen in her grandmother's desk drawer. They had been under a stack of blank invitations, cards that were no longer there. The two keys now dug into her palm as she peered into the dark cells.

"Leave us alone."

The voice came from a cell across the aisle. Clara turned to see a young girl, no more than nine or ten, with long red hair, gripping the bars. Her gaze was openly hostile, confrontational.

"I'm here to help you," Clara offered

"I don't know why," Cora said. She leaned against the bars, her arms crossed.

"Go away," responded the redhead.

"I can get you out of here. I can free you."

"How can you?" another voice exclaimed.

"A very good question," Cora added. "We're all *dying* to know."

For a second, the memory of Meike's body—her blue hand raised, frozen in death, reaching out to her—flooded her mind. Clara's face grew hot. She looked away from Cora to see a leggy girl standing just inside the adjoining cell. She was exceptionally tall for her age, with hair that hung in stringy curls. "You'll just get us all killed. Like Meike."

"I didn't—" Clara started to say.

"You're the reason she's dead! If not for you, they would have left her alone."

A heavy clanking sounded in the distance.

"Shh," Clara said, struggling against a catch in her throat. The girls froze. When no one emerged, she turned back to the cells, fumbling with the keys in her hand. She inserted one and then the other into the closest door. The lock held fast, refusing to turn.

Cora nodded toward the girl. "Why are we even here? Now that you know what Lina is doing, you have the justification you need."

"Stop. You'll just kill us all. We don't need you," the tall girl repeated.

"That's enough, Gitta." A girl who looked to be close to Clara's age stepped up to the door of another cell. She had wide-set gray eyes and an angular face that managed to be both unusual and captivating. And unforgettable. The night of her grandmother's clandestine party in the third-floor wing, Clara had seen Werner with this girl. Clara swallowed down her memory of the girl's expression of resigned shame.

"You shut your mouth, Elise!" Gitta said. "Or it'll be you next."

"It'll be me next anyway. I'll take the risk. Now go back to sleep and let me handle this."

The younger girls—for others had risen to witness this abnormal exchange—stared from Elise to Gitta to Clara before ducking back into the shadows of their cells. Clara heard them shifting on their mats. Gitta remained at the door of her cell, watching them.

"Ignore her," Elise said. "She's just frightened. The thing with Meike...they...they made quite a show of it. She has nightmares."

"Who made a show of it?"

"The tall man. The one who's always here. Watching."

"Berend?"

"I don't know his name. He comes with the older woman sometimes. The one with the dark eyes."

Lina. Clara recoiled inside then remembered her intention. "Does one of them carry a set of keys? To the cells?"

Elise shrugged. "I think they both do. He's the only one I've seen unlocking the doors, though. She lets him do it. She seems to be in charge."

"She *is* in charge," Clara said softly. *So Berend holds the keys I need.* That wasn't what she wanted to hear. To get them from him would be far more difficult than it would be if her grandmother held them. But it still meant she had discovered something. She sighed. "Well, I know where to go next."

"You should. My mother's room," Cora said. "When she's out, she's out. It's the perfect moment." She paused and gestured around them. "Isn't this enough? What more do you need?"

A heavy shadow passed over Clara. She spun around, her lantern raised as she peered into the darkness. "Who's there?"

Minutes passed in silence as she waited.

"Do you think you can?" Elise's voice broke Clara's concentration.

"What?"

"Get us out. Help us." The girl's voice had fallen so low that Clara had to lean forward to hear her.

"I want to. I'm trying." Clara stared into the girl's eyes. They were flat, like empty clouds in the midst of a drought.

"Oh, I get it!" Cora leaned in close to her, her voice a harsh whisper. "You think you have to earn your freedom. Is that it? You don't deserve it? You aren't good enough? Look, Clara, you've been captive to my mother's whims for far too long. Freedom doesn't work that way. You either take it at any cost or you don't."

Clara turned away from her. As she did, a chill passed over her body. She felt someone watching her. She backed against the cell, sweeping her lantern in a circle that showed little. The shadows were nuanced, impenetrable, full of varying shades of darkness. When nothing emerged, she chided herself and turned back to Elise. "What you said. Why would you be the next?" she asked.

"I'm the oldest. That's how it works. The big man likes me. For now. But most of the others want the younger girls. Besides, I think they saw me talking to that young guy."

"Young guy? What young guy?" Clara's mind was reeling.

Elise shrugged. "Brown hair. Glasses. Defined chin."

"Who is he?"

"I don't know. He hasn't been here before. Not until recently."

"He comes down here?"

"Yes. Most of them do, if they're regulars. The others wait for the special events, when they haul us out to the rooms." She glanced at the ceiling as if to indicate Cora's wing far above them.

"But he can't be a regular, can he?"

"He comes with the big guy."

Elise didn't even blush. Clara looked away, her eyes pooling in shame.

"What did he want?"

"Who knows? He asked all kinds of questions. About the other girls. How long we had been here. How the whole thing works. About the men. All kinds of questions."

"But he..." Clara raised her eyebrows.

"No. No. It's not like that. The tall man lets him in and then we talk. We have to...pretend sometimes. The big guy thinks he's letting him *borrow* me. It doesn't matter. I think they already suspect something. But no. He's not like the others. He just wants to talk."

"Talk," Clara repeated, but her mind was already somewhere else. She turned and walked away from the cells.

Who was he? What man would come to an underground prison, full of young girls, in the dead of night to *talk*? It made no sense.

Behind her, deep in the shadows, something moved.

"You're no savior," Cora said over her shoulder as they reentered the passages.

Clara ignored her. She had uncovered Cora's murder and her grandmother's clandestine activities. She had penetrated the depths of the house, had risked discovery, had even thwarted Hagan, and she had learned at least two useful things. Now she knew Berend held the keys she needed. She also knew some strange young man was poking around the house, asking all kinds of questions. Whatever he wanted could only work against Lina's schemes, which meant he most likely was some kind of ally. An ally she would happily welcome.

"There's no way in," Cora insisted.

"Of course there is. Otherwise how would they—" Clara pushed ahead.

Cora grabbed her arm, silencing her deception. "You know what I mean."

"I have to. It's the only thing left."

"Not the *only* thing." Cora's eyes flashed with malice.

Clara pulled her arm away and turned back to the passage before her. It was true: there probably wasn't any entry to the servants' rooms via the tunnels. But what choice did she have? She had to know. Had to try.

The wing stood in close proximity to the family chapel, abutting it at an odd angle. Via the arteries of the house, however, the route was long. They made the trek through the subterranean tunnels, then up the steep climb to the rooftop conservatory, back down the tower to the third floor, and through the walls. From there, they snaked their way around the eastern rooms until they neared the back of the house. Then they turned down a narrow artery that cut away from the main rooms toward the servants' rooms.

"There's another option," Cora said.

"I'm pretty sure my grandmother sleeps with the keys around her neck. That's not an option."

"It could be."

Clara pressed her lips together and ignored the suggestion. She knew what Cora wanted like a fawn knows what a stalking wolf is after.

"Did you hear that?" Cora asked. Clara turned to see the girl glancing behind them as if something lurked there, slinking quietly through the narrow space.

"Since when are you..." A low sound spread around them. Like a growl but deeper, more penetrating. It seemed to resonate through the walls, pulsating the air around her like the flapping of enormous wings. "What is that?" She'd never encountered anything but small scurrying things—mice, spiders, beetles—within the walls. They stopped for a minute. Waited. The air hung heavy and dank around them. Musty. But now silent. "It's nothing. Let's go."

"I can help you. My mother—" Cora started.

"Wait. You're afraid!" Clara stared at the ghost of a girl, momentarily speechless, then looked around her.

"Of course not." Cora's voice sounded muffled in the tight passages. The walls around them once again seemed to throb.

"What is that noise?"

"The sound of your own futility." Cora's attempt at sarcasm came out flat.

"Shh." The tunnels suddenly felt darker, claustrophobic. As if the light from her lantern grew dim and the darkness pressed in around them. Her breath lay like lead in her chest. A clanking sound banged against the wooden floor. And then shuffling like the sound of someone or something that dragged its feet in heavy plodding strides.

Cold tendrils of fear ran up and down her spine and down her arms and legs. Her feet felt frozen, stiff. "What's that?" she repeated.

Cora shook her head.

Just beyond where they had stopped lay a choked byway crossed with beams and littered with debris. Clara stepped over the detritus. In the distance she faintly made out the break in the wall where the servants' wing should begin. "Almost there," she whispered. "Nothing to it." Nonetheless she picked up the pace.

A guttural noise sounded behind her. She stopped short, clutching at a beam that arced just above her head. Her blood turned to ice. Slowly she turned. Behind her, the shadows gathered into a strange form, as if something absorbed the light from her lantern but reflected nothing.

"Run," Cora screamed.

She turned and ran, stumbling over joists and uneven boards in the floor, heedless of the noise. She ducked under support beams, clipping one with her forehead. The blood ran hot from the wound. Above her, hanging forms of wings and webs appeared in her path. She careened around and under them, blocking out her disgust.

Behind her the darkness came, its breathing raw, like an animal's. A deep growl rolled from it. She smelled her own fear. She heard herself whimper. She ran. So fast that she missed the darkened turn to the servants' wing. When she realized it and turned to go back, it was too late. The beast drew close, closer.

She sprinted onward. And collided with the end of the passage.

"No. No." Her fingernails clawed at the rough walls. Her lantern banged against the surface, extinguishing her candle. In the darkness, she smelled it coming. Like sweat and fear and lies.

Then her fingers, desperately circling the wall, caught a familiar shape. A lever. With all her might, she tore at it and threw her body against the wall. The door sprang easily, swinging open. She flew out, onto the wooden floor of a balcony.

She half crawled, half ran from the open door until she reached a railing. She looked around, confused. Below her lay the family chapel. Moonlight glowed through the stained-glass windows, giving them an unholy aspect. In the center of the loft, the organ stood silent, its keys gleaming like teeth in the darkness.

She turned and looked back. A shadow gathered at the door to the passage then stumbled through. Clara screamed and turned away.

"I told you not to come here." Cora crouched beside her. "Look who's found you. All the years amassed. All the running, fighting, lost in a moment."

Clara clutched at her throat, gasping in fear.

"Did you think he wouldn't find you? That you could lie to yourself forever? No Clara. There are some things you can never outrun."

A heavy, stumbling footstep crashed down, shaking the floor of the loft. Then another.

"No, no, no," Clara whispered, her jaw tight.

Then the lurching stopped, and the sound of a laugh, like a shrieking howl, shook the balcony. The organ bench groaned. For a second, Clara held her breath and waited in terrified silence. A shrill, discordant note echoed off the stone walls. Then another. And another. Flowing together. They became something of a requiem Mass. The sound of it sent burning pain throughout Clara's body.

With it, all her memories came back to her. The sound of her door turning in the middle of the night; a dark silhouette beside her bed in the moonlight; the heavy musk of a man; the wailing agony of him who sought another; the sight of his eyes, bottomless, soulless; her body clenching and releasing, hemorrhaging on the bathroom tile; the sight of the tiny form lying cold and still; her hands covered in blood; the heavy thud and sharp scrape of gravel displaced; the cold tendrils that filled her body with horror; and the feel of the wind curling around her, witness to the truth. In them she saw her judge, jury, and executioner.

She curled into a ball, covered her ears, and screamed until her throat was raw. Until she had exhausted all her capacity to resist. Then she collapsed, unconscious.

Nathaniel stood for a moment, taking in the sight of Clara lying senseless and alone in the loft. He stooped and brushed a hair back from her face. His fingers rested on the side of her forehead. His thumb traced the gash at her hairline, now crusted over.

"Oh, Clara," he whispered. Then he leaned forward and lifted her into his arms. Carrying her, he passed back through the door into the hidden corridor.

Chapter Fifty-One

"Can you see anyone?" Jan asked, fastening his neck tie. He slid a finger between his neck and the heavily starched collar that bound it. "Ugh! Why is it that the more money one has, the more uncomfortably he dresses? It doesn't make any sense."

Richter tried to force a smile but couldn't. "You're advocating for nightshirts and robes in every ballroom?"

"Yes. With Belgian lace, of course. As a differentiating element. These people have it all backward. Privilege should give one room to breathe, not prevent it. As it is, I could hardly manage poor posture if I wanted to." Jan had pulled on his waistcoat and jacket. He managed a mock bow, manufacturing a stiff, frozen posture.

"With or without the Dundreary whiskers?"

"Without! Ghastly."

"They're quite the fashion. You might change your mind in ten or twenty years."

"Hopefully they'll no longer *be* in fashion in ten or twenty years."

Both men were aware of Jan's superfluous speech. But they also knew the reasons for it and therefore held it close, as a bridegroom clings to his bride on the eve of battle.

"Is there anyone out there?" Jan repeated.

Lately Richter had grown suspicious of a certain gentleman he'd observed on more than one occasion. Even in the most sizable towns, one might pass a familiar face on occasion. But there were faces that belonged in a given setting and faces that didn't. He knew the difference. This one most certainly didn't.

The manner of his walk differed from that of market vendors, store clerks, or any other local businessman. Yet he was dressed as one. He never carried merchandise, never walked with a fellow associate, and never seemed to turn into any doorway with an air of true purpose. But more than these, his face bore the marks of one who is aware of those around him in a way that typical passersby are not. The marks of one who is watching for the sole purpose of watching.

Richter had become aware of him within the last week. His face appeared and disappeared in disparate locations—in a local bar, outside a bakery, on the steps of the theater. In every instance, he felt the man's gaze on him, yet, upon turning, his focus was elsewhere. It was far too coincidental for them to safely ignore.

Thus Jan remained far from their attic window, at an angle that prevented him from being seen by anyone passing on the street. Richter peered around the edge of the curtains, scanning the doorways and edges of the street. Someone had been there. The same man he previously had seen. But now he wasn't.

"No," he grumbled. "But we're being followed. I'm sure of it." He had a bad feeling. The sense that disaster loomed around the corner. He backed away from the curtain and grimaced at his young apprentice. "You shouldn't go. It isn't safe."

"Are you ordering me?" Jan asked. Richter's face twisted in a visible display of his conflicted opinion on the matter. When he didn't answer, Jan added, "If I don't go, they'll suspect something."

"They already suspect something. There's no getting around that. I don't want to risk your safety."

"But the investigation..."

"We have some information. Possibly enough," Richter said. "This is foolish. You'd be walking into a wolf's den."

"It's the main event." Jan's face grew simultaneously sheepish and fearful. "Werner knows I'm available. If I don't attend, we'll risk exposure. And our only chance to end this."

And if you do? Richter thought. They both knew it was too soon. If he backed out now, Lina would almost certainly remove any trace of the evidence. Every chance they had to catch her and her associates would be gone.

"I chose this," Jan said. "I have to see it through. It won't be much longer."

No, thought Richter, *it can't be*. For he already had sent his report to Berlin detailing the situation. After Jan's latest visit in which he had spoken with a young girl, Elise, they had been able to substantiate all their contact's claims. It wouldn't be long before reinforcements arrived, but how long did they really have until Jan's alias was discovered? If it wasn't already. For clearly they had already garnered some amount of attention.

"Besides, this is our best opportunity to furnish the ministry with names. That's the one thing we don't have."

"We have some. More than enough," Richter countered. Their evening stopover with the mail courier had given them a healthy list. Not as many names as he had wanted. But more than he had dared to hope for.

"Not enough, though. Not the ones we really need."

Jan was right: the most powerful men were the ones whose activities they could infer but not prove. Those were the ones who hid carefully in the shadows, circumventing the law. They were, by definition, the greatest threat to a unified Germany. An alliance of rebellious, perverse leaders was the last thing the chancellor wanted. Their defeat would remove, in one fell stroke, those whom Bismarck would never abide.

"My contact can obtain them."

"Not quickly enough."

Richter sighed. There was no real alternative and they both knew it. Just days ago they'd had this same conversation in much greater depth. At that point it had been an ambiguous one of ideals and theoretical outcomes. But then, on the tail end of their argument, when he had been close to drawing Jan out of the dragon's lair, Markus had burst through the door bearing the fatal blow: an invitation on heavy white card stock.

At that point everything had shifted. To decline such a momentous opportunity, particularly for one so young as Jan, would be more than suspicious. It would be a death stroke to the investigation. And to that they both held. Yet Richter knew time was running out. For Jan to mingle in such conspicuous company was to invite scrutiny where they could afford none.

As he watched the young man tie his shoes and adjust his hair, Richter knew any further argument was futile. The question wasn't whether Jan would attend the ball. It was, whether, should the need arise, Richter was prepared to make his countermove—the move he had hoped never to employ.

Chapter Fifty-Two

Clara stilled her breath and edged open the cover to the peephole. A serving girl slipped into the receiving room and approached two gentlemen with a tray of glasses. After she curtseyed and left the room, Clara watched the men quietly take in their surroundings and sip at their drinks.

She let the cover slide closed for a moment so she could rest her head against the wall. With the terrifying vision in the organ loft, her vertigo had redoubled. Every step was an unstable one, accompanied by a constant sense of nausea.

Somehow she had returned to her rooms. The fact that she could remember nothing after collapsing struck her with fear. Someone had taken her back to her rooms and had placed her in her bed, but she couldn't understand how. No one should know of the tunnels, let alone have access to them. No one in the family but herself. She shivered, her vision rocking. She had been completely helpless, vulnerable.

But that wasn't what scared her the most.

Something had pursued her through the walls. Something unassailable and hostile. With it came the harsh, strident music that had filled the air; had pressed into her ears, her eyes, her mind. Suffocating. Inescapable. In its unforgiving face she had seen something in herself, something she couldn't ignore.

"I told you everything would be exposed. That was the price..." Cora said.

"...of freedom," Clara finished.

"Yes, but first you have a role to play."

Clara closed her eyes and concentrated on the feel of the wood wall —rough, unfinished—against her forehead. It stilled her head, settling the rising nausea.

A door opened.

"I'm so happy you could join us."

Clara slid aside the cover in time to see her grandmother cross the floor and greet both men. She was dressed in a burgundy gown covered in scrolling black beadwork. It was startling to see her in anything other than black.

Dressler took Lina's gloved hand and held it to his lips. "We were so pleased you thought to include us."

Clara watched their faces carefully, their deferential gazes. She wondered what they would think if they knew who she really was. And Edgar, her esteemed father. What would their flattery look like if they knew the truth? Would Inspector Dressler kiss her grandmother's hand with that subservient expression? What about Inspector Metz? Would he flush with color as he did now?

A rush of hatred rose within her. Not for the men themselves but for the lie, for her grandmother's hypocrisy. A wave of dizziness washed over her. She stilled her thoughts and focused.

"Emil, will our young friend be joining us tonight?" Lina asked.

"Almost certainly, Gnädige Frau. Almost certainly." Dressler tucked one hand in his coat jacket in a show of ease. But the stance set his elbow out at an elongated angle, enlarging his overall bearing.

"He looks like a caged animal rising up and expanding to ward off a potential predator," Cora said.

"And he can be *secured*, should that prove necessary," Metz added. He stood between Lina and Dressler, measuring the words of each.

"And that one," Cora clucked. "So desperate. He must know how easily he's overlooked. Constantly trying to interject himself into places where he's unwanted."

"Hmm." Lina pursed her lips and looked away as if in distaste. But then she rearranged her face into one of appealing interest. "That reminds me. I had hoped to see you gentlemen ahead of schedule. We have a certain matter to discuss." She took Inspector Dressler's arm and began to lead him toward the door. "After tonight I will require your help. Both of yours." She shot Inspector Metz a grateful look. He beamed back at her, all teeth beneath his black mustache. "It's a most delicate matter."

"Of course. Isn't it always?" Dressler chuckled as they passed out of the room into the hallway.

Clara let the cover slide shut and moved around the nearest bend in the passages, to where her lantern sat. So her grandmother coddled up to law enforcement.

"It's wise of her. Keeping them close," Cora said. "It's always hardest to see the truth in the things that are the closest. That way they can easily overlook—or ignore—what they don't want to see."

"Yes, but two can play at that game." Clara took up her lantern; stood slowly, waiting for her head to settle; then hurried through the walls.

Chapter Fifty-Three

The wailing of the stringed instruments drowned out any conversations Clara might have overheard, but she could still see most of the guests. Somewhere between 150 and 200 people mingled throughout the northern ballroom. Many of whom she recognized. Men who had been to the estate on occasion, passing in the halls in deep conversation with her father or her grandfather. And of course, many had come to her father's memorial.

She paused and leaned in flat against the peephole, peering from side to side. And then sat back perplexed. It had taken a minute for the truth to hit her: the only women there, other than her grandmother, were servants. Her mouth felt dry, her eyes wide.

She swallowed and leaned forward again.

The French doors that lined the ballroom stood open to the balconies where men huddled. Smoke drifted back in on the wind, entwining with the snaking candlelight and the shadows of the clouds scudding past the glass ceiling high above.

The two police inspectors stood at the far end of the room—Dressler deep in conversation with a count whose name she could not recall; Metz besieged by two elderly men who spoke in great animated gestures while he patiently nodded in response. She shifted to leave her hiding place.

"Wait." Cora clutched her arm. "Look at that one."

A young man crossed the ballroom floor close to where Clara hid. He was easily fifteen years younger than any of the other men. But it wasn't his age that drew her focus. It was his furtive manner. He circled the room once, twice, without speaking to anyone; sampled a glass of wine; made as if to gaze out the window for a few minutes; then circled once more before slipping out of the ballroom. *Brown hair. Glasses. Defined chin,* Elise had said.

No one else seemed to pay him any attention. Clara narrowed her eyes.

"Now who could he be? And where's he going?" Cora asked.

Clara dropped the cover to the peephole.

The northern ballroom stood alone at the top of two flights of stairs. It was an end in and of itself, with no means for guests to access the rest of the house. The only way out was down the stairs.

She stumbled through the hidden passages, clinging to the wall to keep her bearings, until she stepped through a dark paneled wall into a small smoking room. As a child, she had loved this room, burying her face in the long forest-green curtains thick with the smell of cigar smoke. Now the room smelled stale and cold. She strode across the floor and pulled open one tall, thin door, her jaw tense against the expected squeak.

Beyond the door lay the ground floor's central hall. Clara caught a view of the young man's back as he moved toward its junction with the house's main axial hall. Beyond him stood the front entrance. Two of Berend's guards waited rigid, facing away from her, engaged in some private conversation—on guard from trouble without rather than trouble within.

There was no way to call to the young man without their notice. Clara held her breath and watched. As he neared the main artery of the house, rather than crossing it and continuing out the front door, he swung a hard left. Clara furrowed her eyebrows and waited to see if he doubled back. He didn't. After a few seconds, she shut the door.

As soon as he turned out of view, she knew the answer. There was only one place he was likely to go. Only one that made any sense. She recalled her conversation with Elise.

"He comes down here? To these cages?"

"Yes. Most of them do, if they're regulars. The others wait for the special events, when they haul us out to the rooms."

He wouldn't be in Cora's wing. Not for what he wanted.

Less than twenty minutes later, Clara rounded the corner in the catacombs. There, no more than a hundred feet away, Hagan's hulking form lurched toward her. Her blood ran cold. She froze, a scream caught in her throat, waiting for him to sound the alarm or rush forward. Instead he plodded on, his heavy flat footsteps the only sound in the cavernous space. From his distracted gaze, he appeared to be following someone. A pool of light flowed from one of the recesses. He turned into it and disappeared.

Clara's mouth fell open in shock. But several minutes later, when nothing but an oppressive silence pounded in her ears, she edged toward the light. There, at the back of the recess, a door stood open to reveal a staircase leading up into the house. A staircase she had never seen before.

She stood staring up into the unknown, then crept closer to peer behind the stone box in the recessed space. There, on the floor, protruded a single lever, its small shape casting a long shadow up the back of the coffin. A memory took form—of when she and Cora had huddled in a neighboring recess, listening to Berend and another voice retreat into some unknown space. A clanging noise, like a metal bar shifting. The sound of stone scraping against stone. And the heavy gasp of air cut off.

Clara understood. It was this space. This lever and this door. Berend had escorted someone out of the tombs via this route. *But where does it go?* she wondered. She leaned into the stairwell and looked up to where several lamps lit the edges of the stairs.

A thin finger tapped her shoulder.

"You know, Hagan could return at any moment."

Clara yelped and turned to see Cora inches behind her. She swallowed hard, catching her breath. As it was, when she rounded the turn into the hall of cells, no one paid any attention to her. With Hagan away, the central space stood empty. The dampened sound of several men laughing and grunting, the noise of mats shifting on the floor in the dim light reverberated from the cells.

"The regulars," Cora voiced. "They must prefer the wild cage to the tame bedroom."

The girls seemed to hide in the shadows. Those who hadn't yet been taken to the third floor. Or recently had returned from there. She needed to find Elise. She had spoken with the mysterious young man before. *Brown hair. Spectacles. Defined chin.* And Werner had still been in the ballroom when Clara had left. *The big man likes me. For now. But most of the others want the younger girls.* They had to be here.

Elise's cell stood at the end on the right.

There was no way to avoid being seen, so Clara strode into the hall, past the gaze of several men. One of them stood leaning against the wall of the cell, his face flushed, his chest coated in sweat, rising and falling. He eyed her curiously but said nothing.

"Where's the brooding fellow?" another called out. "I'm about done with this one." He winked at her and laughed in a deep, satisfied way.

Clara trembled and turned away. The distance seemed so much farther under their scrutiny. *The last cell on the right. The last cell on the right. The last cell...*

There it was.

As she gripped the bars and pulled open the door, Elise and the young man turned and gazed at her in open shock.

"It's unlocked," she exclaimed. For a minute they just stared at her, waiting, as if her appearance was the inexplicable element.

"They're too deeply imprisoned to need locks." Cora leaned against the bars. "They couldn't open the doors anyway."

"Only when someone is with us," Elise said at last. "They agree to stay until one of the guards returns to lock the door."

"What are you doing here?" the young man asked.

Clara faltered, her words lost. In her mind she had pictured herself as a gallant figure, eloquent and prepared, but in the reflection of their eyes, she saw herself as nothing but a small girl, foolish to even attempt what she meant to do. But it was too late to go back. She swallowed hard and mumbled. "We don't have much time. We have to go."

"Go where?" they both replied. Their faces were wary, lined with distrust.

Clara stared at them, flustered, heat rising into her face.

"Don't tell him," Cora warned. "Not everything. And nothing until they go with you."

Clara shook her head; Cora was right. Their inertia rose before her, threatening to undermine everything. Giving them the full plan would only give their resistance strength and breadth, transforming it into a steel prison. And they had to accompany her for the plan to work.

"Otherwise they'll just think you're insane." Cora smirked. "My mother will have the doctor back here tomorrow morning."

Clara blanched. "Out. Free," she whispered, and turned to Elise. "I can get you out of here. And the others too."

The young man looked her up and down while she spoke, and then understanding shone in his eyes. "You're her. His daughter."

His daughter. Clara's breath caught in her throat. "We're running out of time. Hagan will be back any minute."

Elise looked from one to the other. Confused? Hopeful? Clara couldn't tell.

"You'll get us all killed," the young man said.

"She'll kill me anyway," Clara countered. "It's simply a matter of time."

"Yes, but someone might be able to help you."

"What do you think I'm doing? Getting you."

He looked aside as if he were ashamed. Or hiding something. "It's too risky."

"Risky? It's *too risky*?"

"What does he think we're doing here?" Cora asked. "Planning an adventure abroad? Organizing a bank heist?"

"We're talking about people's lives," Clara pleaded. "These girls' lives. Elise's." *Mine.*

"Yes...but...well, it's too soon."

"For what? That's absurd. This is our best chance. I thought you'd want..." Her voice trembled, trailing off into a choked silence. "Elise said..."

"What did she say?" His expression darkened.

"She said you weren't like other men."

"What does that mean?!"

"That you...well, you know...you don't..." She hesitated, reluctant to voice what should be so obvious. How could he not know what she meant?

"I'm not *unlike* other men."

Clara arched one eyebrow. "Elise said you ask a lot of questions. Why do you think I followed you?"

"You followed—"

"Are you coming or not?"

"Coming where?" he started to say. But just then footsteps echoed in the distance.

"We're running out of time," Clara repeated, her whispered words echoing in her ears. She held open the cell door and waited.

Elise took several steps out of the cell and paused, looking down the corridor of steel bars. "What about the others? We can't. Not without them."

Clara shook her head. "They're locked. Or there are men with them. They'd try to stop us." The steps grew louder. "Please. You have to hurry. We'll come back for them. *All* of them. I promise. With you I can get the help we need. Come. Please."

Elise took another step, her eyes haunted and wary. It was like coaxing an injured animal out of a cage. But then a dark shadow rounded the corner of the corridor. Hagan. He slowed to a stop, his mouth open. Then he roared.

"You!" One long white finger pointed at Clara. His forehead thrust forward as he fell into an awkward stumbling gait toward them.

"Run! Run!" someone yelled.

Clara turned to see the young man—his face red, his mouth wide—gesturing them to go. Then he was running. He rushed forward, straight for Hagan, his arms flailing. The two men collided, Hagan's body dwarfing the younger man's. Hagan clutched at him, struggling to grasp the writhing, dodging smaller form.

Clara grabbed Elise's hand and pulled. "Come!"

Something in her voice propelled the girl forward. They ran. As they did, the young man blocked Hagan, kept him from reaching them. But when they rounded the corner, Clara hesitated and looked back. Hagan's hands gripped the man's neck. Blood ran from a gash beside his eye. He turned and gazed at her, his eyes sad and resigned.

"What is he doing?!" Elise cried.

"Come on." Clara shook her head at her. "He would have tried to stop us." But her heart caught in her throat as she said it.

"But—"

"Do you want to die?" Clara yelled. She took the girl's hand and pulled her toward the exit tunnel. "We'll send people back for him. For them. Trust me. They'll be here shortly."

Elise nodded mutely. Together they ran.

Chapter Fifty-Four

Clara and Elise ran toward the tiled hall of the dead. There, in the near distance, the lamplit stairway stood, beckoning them. Clara veered around the edge of the stone coffin and raced headlong up the stairs. She heard Elise's ragged breath as she scrambled behind her.

They hardly took in the small room—a spartan workspace—at the top of the stairs. Instead they dashed through it and out the opposite door that stood open, skidding to a stop at the top of a circular wooden staircase. Clara paused, her hands gripping the rails, her eyes stunned by the sight.

There, just to her right, hung the pulpit. Below them lay the family chapel. Above her stood the organ loft. Candlelight flickered throughout the space. Behind her, she heard Elise's heaving breath. Clara recalled the day of the memorial, when she and her grandmother had huddled in the pews below her. Berend's glowering presence had appeared here in the pulpit, seemingly out of thin air. *Here again*, she thought.

"This way. Quiet."

She led the way, down the spiral staircase, around the railing, and over to the door. It stood open. Wide open. The hall beyond was empty. She looked back. Elise shook her head, her eyes wet.

"No. I don't...I don't..." she stammered.

Clara grasped her hand. "There are two policemen here. Right now. All we have to do is get to them. This can end tonight."

Elise paused then nodded. They ran.

The two men at the front door hardly glanced in their direction when they rounded the corner and made for the wide staircase to the ballroom. Nor was there anyone in the halls. The house, for all of its visitors and the dark undercurrent of their activities, seemed deserted.

Clara needn't have feared undue attention. As it was, few people actually saw them enter the ballroom. Those who did considered them curiously then turned back to their drinks and their fellow associates. The two girls pressed through the throngs of guests, in a tortuous path toward where the two police inspectors stood. Neither of the men had seen their approach yet. However, several others had.

The first was Helene. In the back of her mind, some niggling voice alerted her to her daughter's presence long before anyone else had noted it. Slowly she turned, her face puzzled, and realized in horror that Clara rushed headlong toward the two police inspectors. And understood, with a violent suddenness, her daughter's tragically misplaced intentions. And that there was no way she could reach her in time to stop her.

The second was Nathaniel, who caught both Clara's frantic advance and Helene's startled face in nearly the same instant. He took off after Clara, reaching her right when she drew up in front of Inspector Dressler with a triumphant expression of supreme righteousness.

Lina, who had been deeply entrenched in a group discussion, caught Clara's dissonant movement and Nathaniel's flustered pursuit of her. She stopped midsentence and gasped audibly. Her eyes grew wide and dark. Her expression paled considerably. Later, she wouldn't recall thrusting her drink toward the count. Her only real cognizance was on what felt like a painstakingly slow advance toward them. To those who witnessed her sudden shift, she appeared as a hound in full pursuit.

"Inspectors!" Clara practically shouted. "This girl is evidence. Evidence of illegal activities. She's a prisoner. I can show you the others if you follow me. They're kept in cages. Behind bars. These men..." She thrust her finger out and scanned the crowd. "These men are here for—"

"Clara!" her mother cut her off, running over to intercept her. "Clara dear. Come with me."

"No! It's important. He must know."

"Clara." This time it was Nathaniel who drew up behind her, followed by Lina. "Clara, what is this about?"

"Kidnapped! That's what. She was kidnapped. Kept behind bars. And they. They're—"

"Okay. Okay. Hold on a minute," Inspector Dressler said. He still had his punch in his hand. The edges of his lips were tinged magenta. At the sight of Clara and the girl, at the words she uttered, his face transformed into a bemused one. "This is quite a story you have."

"I can prove it," she spat, leaning forward, her eyes sharpened.

Lina looked around, flustered. Clara's exclamations, though largely swallowed by the prevailing din, were beginning to draw attention. Several close groups of people had turned and eyed them curiously. She caught Werner's pointed stare. He looked from Lina to Elise and back to Lina again with a look that demanded immediate action.

"Perhaps this isn't the best place for this conversation…"

"Oh no you don't!" Clara snapped at her. "I'm going to tell these men what you've been doing. And nothing is going to stop me."

"Okay. Okay." Dressler repeated. "How about this? I promise to hear everything you have to say. To take it most seriously. But we'll remove ourselves to—"

"The library." Lina suggested.

"The library, yes."

"But…" Clara cast a concerned look about the ballroom. She had pictured herself cutting off the party with one shout. Drawing Elise, her evidence, into the center of the room and presenting the full, sordid details to all who gathered there. She had envisioned the inspectors' shocked, indignant expressions. Their certainty of her credibility. Their subsequent arrest of Lina. And Berend. And all their guests. She had pictured her leading them to the cells, where she would wait with satisfaction as they shook their heads in disgust. And freed every one of the imprisoned girls.

Thus far, few had even turned to notice her fervent appeal.

"No buts. We'll discuss this elsewhere. All of us. Inspector Metz and I, your mother and grandmother and uncle. And this girl..."

"Elise," Clara's voice came out soft and dismayed.

"Elise. Lovely name. All right. Frau Willenheim, please lead the way."

That was how Clara found herself steered away from the public eye, down to the ground floor, and closeted in the cavernous library with nothing but a small audience.

Berend had followed them. As they proceeded into the room, he shut the door and stood against it, blockading the exit. Once they had all gathered, Clara launched into the full account of her grandmother's activities—from her murder of Cora, to her cover-up of Edgar's crimes, to her escalation and involvement of much of the local leadership. Everyone stood listening, unspeaking, throughout the duration of her tale.

However, as Clara progressed through the story, her courage faltered. Something was off. The police inspectors occasionally shot each other a knowing look, but rather than horror, or dismay, they seemed almost...entertained. And Dressler, though he gazed at the floor in concentration as she spoke, bore a faint smile on his lips. She looked from him to her grandmother, confused.

As she finished and waited for them to speak, he rubbed his mustache thoughtfully. "Interesting tale."

Clara gaped at him. "I can prove it!"

"This is preposterous!" Lina exclaimed.

"What about her?" Clara pointed to Elise. "How do you explain her?"

"She's been in our employ for years. Local farm girl. Helps in the kitchens." Lina shook her head and shot Clara a sympathetic look.

"I can show you the others! There are more." Tears of frustration gathered in her eyes. "Why won't you believe me?"

"Oh, Clara." Helene sighed, turning to the inspectors. "She hasn't been well lately. I'm sure you can understand. Since the death of her father. The two were so close. His death has given her such a shock. And what with all the speculation regarding the manner of his death. Why, it isn't that surprising."

"No, no. Of course not. Quite the burden for such a young one," Dressler agreed.

"Mother!" Clara stared at her, crying freely. "Why?" She turned and looked at Nathaniel, who stood back from the others. He leaned against the bookcases, watching the proceedings with intense and inscrutable concentration.

"She probably should rest," Dressler suggested.

Lina motioned to Berend, who strode toward Clara, his intention clear.

"No!" Clara screamed and backed away. But there was nowhere to go. The hidden door stood past them, on the other side of the room. She'd never reach it. Even if she did, where would she go?

"Do you have..." Berend started to ask. Lina shot Helene a questioning look. She merely shrugged.

"You asked me to dispose of them."

In the end, the inspectors held her down while Berend applied pressure to her neck. Clara's last thoughts were of her mother, who gazed at her in sad acquiescence. But did nothing to stop them.

Chapter Fifty-Five

Helene peered around the corner of her laboratory. The kitchens were bustling with people. One of the cooks—a tall man with bushy hair all askance—shouted orders to several others. She didn't recognize any of them. The family rarely required such an abundant kitchen staff. It was unlikely any of them would notice, let alone comment, on her presence. Still, she couldn't risk exposure.

Not now. Not at the eleventh hour, when all the pieces stood poised on the edge of a precipice. And now, with Clara's declaration, the timeline had escalated. Who knew what Lina would do in response? There was no time to lose.

Oh, Clara. What have you done? A stab of pain radiated through her chest. She should have done more. Should have found a way to reassure Clara that all would be well if she would only wait. And trust. But why should she? Hadn't Clara tried to reach out to her? And hadn't she tried to respond? She had been too careful, too circumspect. After all that Clara had suffered, Helene understood why she needed something to hold on to. Or someone.

But it had been too dangerous. Everywhere she went, Lina or Berend lurked. And Clara *was* still a child. One misstep or misplaced word and everything could fall apart.

I'm too cold, she thought. *Too wary.* Raised without a mother and with a doting but unemotional father, she had developed an independence others most likely read as aloof or unfeeling. Uncaring. But it wasn't true. *Oh, Clara. I'm sorry. What more could I have done? What more should I have done?*

A flash of red swept into the room. Helene caught her breath and ducked out of sight. Lina's voice, clipped and commanding, cut through the smoke and clamor. Helene heard her move throughout the kitchens, asking questions, sampling the food, reminding the workers of her every requirement.

Helene sighed and waited. She looked around her laboratory. Even in the dim lighting, she knew where everything was. Or used to be. All her jars of tinctures and oils and ointments. The empty spaces where her dried herbs and seeds once sat. Decades of work and knowledge meant to heal.

Footsteps drew near the open door to the laboratory. Helene pressed up against the interior wall and waited. But a moment later a voice called out from across the kitchen. She heard the steps retreat. Followed by others. After several minutes, Helene risked a glimpse around the doorway. Only a few cooks remained in the preparation kitchen. This was her window of opportunity. If she delayed any longer, it would be too late.

She waited until the remaining cooks were turned away, focused on the workstands before them. Then she slipped out. Near the end of the kitchen stood a narrow archway. She strode for it and rounded the corner. Risking a look back, she assured herself everyone was still oblivious to her.

The cellars lay down a stone staircase that ran along one of the kitchen's outer walls. Normally they were dark, cold places, but on such a night they were kept lit by necessity. Helene made her way down the steps, quickly confirmed that the space was vacant, and crossed to a large adjoining chamber. Here the family's vast storage of wine lay stoppered.

She paused and looked around the immense space, taking in what could easily be several thousand bottles. Maybe more. It always impressed her. But on that night she paused, suddenly struck by the looming change. Where would so much wine go? Who would enjoy it? It wouldn't be any of the family. Whatever happened tonight would establish a dividing line from which none of them would ever return. If all went as planned, they would be far from here by dawn.

Shaking the thought away, she assessed her surroundings. Someone had pulled numerous bottles of wine from their resting places and had placed them on a table in the center of the room. She lay her bag down beside them and picked up one bottle. So these were the ones Lina had chosen for tonight. Now that she knew, she could begin.

Reaching around in her bag, she grasped the cool, smooth striations of the piece of antler. A spiraling piece of steel protruded from the end. She stabbed it into the bottle's cork and turned until the cork came loose. Loose enough to wiggle it free. After opening her bag again, she retrieved one of several small jars of dark plum-colored liquid. She poured a moderate amount into the bottle, gently swished the contents, and set it aside. She took another bottle underhand, drove the corkscrew into its cork, and turned. Several bottles later she paused to rub her hand. The flesh of her palm was already red and sore.

When she turned to grasp another bottle, she froze. And swore to herself. She hadn't noticed before how few bottles stood on the table. Too few for an event of this size. Around them on the table, circles in the dust marked where others had stood earlier in the evening. Wine that the guests already had been consuming. Not the wine she meant to use.

Damn! She slapped her sore hand down on the table. Her face was warm from her exertion, despite the cool cellar air. She looked around the space again. At the end of the table, lying on its side, was a barrel. She hadn't paid it any attention earlier. Now she wiped her hands on her skirts again and stepped over to it. It bore a mark: "Strasbourg, France. 1472." Surely this was it.

She placed her hands on her hips and leaned back, stretching her spine. A thick plug marked the bunghole on the side of the barrel. A spigot hung off of the head, waiting for the waitstaff to siphon it into glasses for the guests. She pulled herself up onto the table and knelt beside the barrel.

I'm too old for this.

The cork plugging the hole in the barrel's side was close to two inches thick. She exhaled and climbed down again to retrieve the corkscrew. There was nothing else to do, though. It had to be done. Or give up. So she sat astride the barrel and plunged the corkscrew into the plug. It hardly seemed to impact the sturdy cork. But she was able to work it in and turn.

Slowly. Slowly, her hands rubbing raw, she twisted the screw until it rested snugly in the cork. Then she pulled. And twisted. And rocked against the corkscrew. The cork stuck fast for a minute then creaked against the oak. Several minutes more and it came free with a pop and the rich scent of dark wine.

Helene climbed down from the table, retrieved her bag from the floor, and removed each of the jars. She unstoppered them and poured all the contents into the hole in the barrel. As she did, she bit her lip, unsure of herself. She hadn't counted on an entire barrel of wine. And she didn't have time to measure out the contents and calculate how potent it would be. She shook her head and emptied jar after jar. It would either work as planned or it wouldn't.

Grimacing, she pressed the plug back into the hole. *No, that won't do*, she reconsidered. It was too obvious that someone already had opened the cork. She had brought replacement corks for the bottles. She had planned for that. But not for this. But then, perhaps it was fine as it was. *After all*, she reasoned, *they would have had to open it anyway. The pressure wouldn't allow the wine to flow out of the spigot. Better to leave it open as if one of the kitchen staff had done so earlier than planned.*

Gently she rocked the barrel to distribute the contents. Wine splashed out of the top onto her hands and arms. Just then she heard a faint twitter and the sound of light steps. Helene swore again and looked around. In the far corner, at the end of the wine racks, stood several other barrels.

She jumped down and slipped her bag, full of the empty jars, behind the barrels. Then, pressing up between the stone wall and the barrels, she shoved herself back where she could crouch, hidden from view.

Two young people, covering their mouths to conceal their laughter, dashed into the room. Helene recognized the young man. He worked on the grounds in some capacity. Most likely as an assistant gardener. Which rendered his presence there inexplicable. The young girl seemed familiar, but Helene couldn't have said where she had seen her.

They peered back in the direction from which they had come and waited silently. When a minute passed without sound, they looked at each other and giggled.

"Well, Herr Baumann, it seems you've made it to the party after all," the girl teased him, her expression a mixture of coquettish allure and mocking invitation.

The young man looked her up and down, his eyes hungry and insistent. "Hmm. I could eat you up. Every inch of you."

He leaned down and caught her mouth in a possessive kiss. The girl leaned in and moaned against him. His hands were on the laces of her bodice, tearing them open. Helene looked away, embarrassed.

The sight and sound of them awoke in her contradictory feelings. It had been months since she and Edgar had made love. And even then it had been tainted by her knowledge of who he really was. What he had done—was still doing—to their daughter. By that point it had been nothing more than a survival tactic, keeping Edgar ignorant of how much she knew. He had been so volatile and mentally ill that she had felt like a boat lost far out at sea. They hadn't touched each other with true love and desire in perhaps ten years, when Clara had still been very young.

A part of her listened to the young couple with envy and a rekindling of desire. Desire for all she had thought she had at one point. When she had been blissfully ignorant and in love with her elegant, accomplished husband. And in love with an ideal that she had never truly had. That he had taken from her with his sickness.

The other part of her felt nothing but rage. Hearing them reminded her of everything that had been stolen from her. It made her feel akin to Edgar, as if seeing this caused her to share in his darkness. As if it cast an ugly stain across her character and made her into a monster like him. She clenched her teeth and tightened her fists, driving her nails into the meat of her palms.

The sounds from beyond the barrel had quieted. She heard their voices, satisfied and then silent, and risked a look. They were seated on the floor, their backs to the wall. Between them, the girl held a bottle by the neck. For a fraction of a second Helene watched them without understanding. But then she noted the girl's stained lips. And his. Helene's heart fluttered against her ribs in a cold and violent frenzy. She raised herself up enough to see the table.

It was one of the bottles. The bottles she had opened. And into which she had poured the contents of her jar. She looked back at the couple. Their eyes were only fractionally open. They wore the contented expressions of those who have taken what they wanted and found it truly and utterly satisfying.

She pushed the barrel out of the way. The bag nestled beside her jostled, the glass jars clinking loudly. She froze, but their faces showed no recognition of her. Or of anything. Slipping out from her hiding place, she rushed to their side and knelt beside them. The smell of sex hung in the air around them. And the rich earthy scent of wine. And something else. A berry she would know anywhere.

The young man's head rested back against the wall. The young girl's —for that's what she was: a girl, no older than Clara—had slumped forward. Her chin lay against her chest. Helene lifted it and pulled back her eyelids. Her eyes were glazed over, the pupils characteristically dilated. His were the same. Both of their faces and necks were flushed. Helene felt for a pulse but found none.

She sat back and stared at them in horror.

Diamond Light

"The real voyage of discovery consists not in seeking new landscapes but in having new eyes."
—Marcel Proust

Chapter Fifty-Six

Clara awoke to the rough texture of cold stone pressed against her face. A swampy, rotten smell filled the air. And the sound of dripping. Water. She was near water. As she raised herself up on one arm, a bolt of light shot through her head and, with it, jarring pain. She clenched her teeth, bent over, and pressed her palms to her temples.

When the pain settled into a throbbing ache, she opened her eyes. The young man sat near her, his back against a wall of earth. He watched her with a conflicted expression of disappointment and vindication.

"Are you..." she started to say. But his focus shifted from her to a point beyond her. She twisted until she could look behind her. There Berend and Lina waited in the shadowy depths. With Hagan, whose face bore a wicked grimace.

"You should have listened to me! Now it's too late," Cora hissed beside her. "You've let the bitch win."

Several lanterns stood around the perimeter, casting shadows about the strangely formed space. Uneven rock walls glistened with moisture. A floor of packed earth, in some places so smooth that it shone like polished stone. It was some sort of subterranean cavern. Clara could only guess that it linked to the tunnels beneath the house. No more than fifteen feet away from her lay a dark shimmering pool that abutted a wall of stone. A sheen of moisture ran down the side of the wall. From above, water dripped though the rock ceiling, sending faint ripples across the inky surface.

Clara trembled at the sight of it. Something about its murky depths embodied everything that was wrong in the house. As if its black water were the lifeblood of all of the evil the family had ever committed. The air smelled foul, as if it hung in a state of perpetual decay. It was so heavy she could taste it.

Lina glared at them. "How long have you two been conspiring?"

"We haven't—" Jan protested.

"Don't bother." Clara interrupted. "Snakes don't know the truth from a lie."

Lina cackled, her voice sharp and brittle. She turned and grinned at Berend. "They're nothing but two *blind* baby rats. Their teeth haven't even come in. It's insulting. Two whelps conspiring against something they can't even understand." She looked back at the two young people. "What did you really hope to accomplish?"

Meanwhile, Berend watched Clara, his brow furrowed. The candlelight reflected off the white in his hair and beard. To Clara, he seemed lit from within as if a storm surged through him. He knelt near Clara, his face all shadows and hard edges. "How did you do it?"

Clara leaned forward, her face close to his. "Is this the life you wanted? When you were a child, did you say to yourself, *I hope that when I grow up I can be a slave? A pathetic henchman with no will of my own?*"

Berend ignored her comments. Instead he shook his head and addressed Lina. "She didn't. How could she have? Locked in her room day and night. No access to the outside world. No associates."

"Really? Then how is it she walked into *my* ballroom, across the floor amid *my* guests, and confronted *my* police inspectors without *my* knowledge? Or yours? If she's so carefully monitored, what is she doing here?" Lina's voice rose and became shrill, echoing off the walls of the cave.

They stood watching Clara for a moment. Berend shook his head, confounded. "I don't know. One thing I do, though: there are certainly bigger rats lurking elsewhere in these walls. His associate had to have had inside help. One of them knows who that is."

Jan and Clara remained silent.

"I don't have time for this. I have guests. Someone has to make them talk," Lina exclaimed. "Now!"

Berend rubbed his beard and continued to gaze into their faces. He turned to Jan. "We know something about you. That you're not who you say you are, Diedrich. That you've been lurking around places where you don't belong. Playing games. Tell us: who are you really?"

A thin sheen of sweat covered Jan's face. It made his face look like a death mask in the gloom. Still, he said nothing. Clara gaped at him. *What are they talking about?*

"We know you have an associate," Berend continued. "An older man. In fact, he's staying with you at an inn not far from here. Where is he right now? I'd wager a guess that he knows all about your little ruse this evening. That whatever game you're playing was his idea. Is that right?"

Berend knelt at Jan's eye level. "That is right, isn't it? You didn't come here of your own doing, did you? No. You were sent. So right now your associate is off somewhere else. Somewhere comfortable and dry. And you're..." He gestured around them. "...here."

Jan stared from Berend to the floor, his lips pressed together.

"That doesn't seem particularly fair, does it? That you should take the fall for him. No. I don't think it does. Your associate had to know that if you were caught, if we uncovered your plan, you would bear the retribution for his decision. That's right. He knew you would take the blow for him. That's doesn't seem fair to me.

"So I'll give you a way out. You tell us who he is and where we can find him, and we'll go easy on you. After all, this wasn't really your doing, was it? You're just his messenger. You shouldn't be punished for his decision."

Jan opened his mouth as if he would say something, then cast a glance at Clara and turned his gaze back to the floor.

"He has to know something," Lina urged. "Who have they been talking to?"

Berend stared into Jan's face then stood, brushing his hands off on his pants. "He isn't going to talk. Not without encouragement."

Lina waved Hagan toward Clara. "Grab her."

The gangly servant crossed the cave and gripped Clara by one arm. "I'm going to enjoy this, you little witch."

"Fight him!" Cora hissed. She clung to Clara's arm, her gaze wild, imploring. Clara barely had time to consider the fact that the ghost was still with her before Hagan grabbed her.

"No!" Clara screamed. She spun around and kicked at him, her free arm flailing. It accomplished nothing. He was easily a foot taller. And vastly stronger. She hadn't anticipated that one so lean would be so much stronger than she was.

He turned her, gripping the other arm, and held them both behind her back. She tried to kick backward but managed only to slip and slide, scraping her foot against the floor of the cavern. If he hadn't been holding her up, she would have fallen.

Meanwhile, Berend stood, reached down, and pulled Jan to his feet. Unlike Clara, his hands were already tightly bound. A long length of rope trailed behind him. He hardly resisted.

"Fight him!" Clara yelled. "Fight him!" She twisted in Hagan's arms, but he held her more firmly, her shoulders strained. Her wrist ached. She jerked her body to the side just enough, turned her head, and bit down on Hagan's arm as hard as she could. She tasted blood. He screamed and dropped her. Seconds later he kicked her in the head.

Flashes of light shot across her eyes. She crouched on the floor, her breath coming hard. But then she was up, dangling limply under Hagan's arm, searing pain coursing through her body. He kicked off his shoes and staggered down the rocky slope into the pool of water. The water was cold. Clara's muscles tensed with shock; her heart raced. She held her hands out to ward it off. Just beyond the ledge of waist-deep water, the pool dropped off to an unknown depth. Clara quivered in horror, pulling her legs up close to the surface.

Without warning, Hagan plunged her under the surface and held her there.

It tasted of minerals and something else. Something heavy. As her heart lurched, something beneath her moved. The water shifted like a waking beast, sluggish and deliberate. She writhed in Hagan's grip, clawing at his arms, struggling to escape what lay hidden there.

But then she was torn out of the water. Hagan held her close while she gasped for air until she gagged and heaved. The taste in her mouth and the horror within the water filled her with terror.

Water ran into her eyes, blurring the room into shifting shades of light and dark. As she listened to her hiccuping breath and waited for her sight to adjust, she heard Berend's voice.

"...lose her. Unless you tell us. Who is it?" His voice was firm but low.

The light gathered, leaving her a clear picture of him standing there, where he had before, his fingers digging into Jan's arms. The boy was looking away from her. In the soft light, his face gleamed with moisture.

Understanding filled Clara. Jan and an associate. And some unknown person within the household. They threatened Lina in some way. Stood against all she was and did. Someone other than herself or Cora. Hope rose into her throat and flooded her eyes.

"Don't tell them," Clara shouted, her voice hoarse. "No matter what they—"

Hagan shoved her back under the water. This time with her mouth open. She choked and spun in his grasp. Her eyes bulged in the darkness. Silver forms gathered in the gloom, wraiths shaped like women. They reached out, clutching at her face and neck. She realized what she tasted: blood. The pool was full of blood. Their blood—the blood of the ghosts that gathered around her.

"All the girls." Cora floated beneath the water, her long hair fanned out around her. "The ones that are too old, no longer wanted. Meike."

When Hagan pulled Clara from the pool again, she coughed so hard she threw up a frothy mixture of water and stomach acid. Her throat burned. She breathed deeply, gasping for air. The blood pulsed in her ears and temples.

She twisted to see Jan. He was on the ground, his lips pressed tightly. Berend crouched over him. Blood ran from one of Jan's eyes and from a deep gash in his lip. His face was swollen and bruised.

Clara didn't try to yell out or tell him not to worry about her safety. He wouldn't speak. She understood that now. It was as it should be. Silent before those who would only twist and use his words against him. And others.

When Hagan grasped her again, Clara was ready. She dove down beyond the ledge where they stood, into the cold depths. Shocked, he released his grasp on her and fell forward, flailing his arms, fighting to remain above the surface.

Clara clawed the water, despising the suffocating fear in her chest, until she felt the forms envelop her. The weight of her family's history, the trauma of her own past, frozen there in the dark, presented itself as something buoyant, something that could be released.

Cora gestured to her. "The rocks. Tear the rocks away from the wall. Use them. They won't expect it. Crush his skull. And then hers."

Clara paused, thinking, then moved toward the rough rock wall of the pool. It was jagged, hard enough to cut. She tore her sleeve away. Then she dug the soft underside of her arm into a jutting point of rock. And tore. Hard. Hard enough to feel the skin give way. Her blood swirled around her, mingling with the tang that already lay in the depths.

"No. What are you doing?" Cora swam toward her, her eyes black in the depths.

A form gathered before Clara's face. It was a girl, still young, her face round, her eyes too large. She drew Clara into an embrace then drifted away, her body dissolving into the darkness. Another drew near and embraced her, kissed her forehead tenderly, then slipped away. And then another. And another. Clara lost count as she felt herself gathered into the cold darkness.

Then she was rising, rapidly, pulled upward by the back of her dress, and dragged out of the water. Hagan threw her to the side of the pool, where she lay exhausted and spent. Water ran from her mouth, but she no longer felt it. Instead, a weightless hope filled her, as if she had transcended her body and no harm could touch her. Not the truth of her. That part of her was unassailable, indemnified.

From the side she saw Berend drag Jan down into the pool of water. He was barely struggling, his hands twisting and pushing at Berend's body. His half-hearted attempt to free himself filled her with grief. Then he grew still, resigned. She met his gaze.

"I'm sorry," she whispered.

Jan's mouth formed words that never reached her ears, but she heard them still. *I forgive you.*

At some point Berend had removed his jacket. Through his shirt, Clara saw heavily muscled arms flexed against the boy's last struggle. He was experienced at this. He knew what he was doing. And how to go about it. Cora had been right. She had seen it all. Her own death. And the deaths of all the girls who had been imprisoned here for so many years. Anyone who threatened their will.

Berend drew a knife from his waist and, in one quick motion, cut Jan's throat.

Clara turned away, struggling to breathe, her shoulders shaking with her sobs. Her voice rose in the chamber. When she looked back, Jan's body floated facedown on the surface of the dark pool.

Movement caught her eye. She turned to see her grandmother standing just beyond the end of the pool. Lina watched the scene with dark eyes devoid of emotion.

"How can you?" Clara sobbed. "How can you?"

Slowly her grandmother took in Clara's face, her lips turned up slightly as if in delight. "It's easy. I just remember there's only one person I ever loved. Everyone else? Nothing. A tool at best. Otherwise, worthless."

Lina strode to a steel door set in the wall across from the pool, pulled out her ring of keys, and unlocked the door. An overwhelming stench filled the chamber. She nodded to Hagan. "Put her in here."

Hagan half pulled, half dragged Clara across the floor and threw her into the dark space. The door slammed shut. A key turned in the lock.

Their voices resumed, muffled but still audible through the door.

"Who else is there?" Lina picked up where they had left off, as if nothing had happened.

Clara gasped for breath, struggling for clean air in the suffocating space. She crawled to the corner and vomited up stomach acid and what little she had eaten that day. When her stomach stopped convulsing, she tore a wide strip off of the hem of her dress and wrapped it twice around her nose and mouth. Although her eyes still watered, the noxious odor was fainter.

She began to cry again. She still heard their voices, arguing as if they hadn't just murdered someone in front of her. Someone young, with his whole life ahead of him.

"It's her fault," Cora spat. Clara sensed her pacing in the darkness nearby. "She's a murderer by nature. This is her doing."

"It's my fault. My fault. I killed him," Clara said. She lay in the darkness, her voice a distant whisper. "I'm sorry. I'm sorry. I'm sorry."

"Her tutor," Berend responded to Lina. "But I supervise them too closely. I would have noticed if she had said anything."

"Did she slip him a note?"

Berend shook his head. "That would have been impossible. Besides, we watch him. We would have known if he had had any part in this."

"Then who?"

Berend's eyes lit up. "There is one other." His mind filled with images of the one person he always overlooked. The most obvious one of all.

The sound of running steps echoed in the distance. And then Hagan's voice. "Come quickly. Something's happened."

Chapter Fifty-Seven

From within the boathouse, Richter waited. And watched. He could just barely see the eastern edge of the ballroom where Jan undoubtedly was. He pulled his timepiece out of his vest pocket and twisted it until the moonlight illuminated its face: 2:00 a.m. Around him the night seemed unnaturally still, as if all the night birds and insects waited with him.

He glanced back at the behemoth where it stood up the hill. Lights flickered in many windows. The house was still alive and well, even at this hour. Earlier in the night, a light had flashed thrice from the eastern balcony. It was the signal they had arranged: the veiling and unveiling of a lit candle. The ballroom should have been full of them. Enough for Jan to light his one taper, slip onto the terrace, and alert Richter to his presence. Since that first signal, though, nothing.

A shadow of a doubt grew in Richter's mind. Something wasn't right. Beyond and below him, a ripple appeared and spread across the water. He stepped out of the boathouse and stood on the edge of the deck that ran along the front of the building on either side of the two boat slips. He leaned forward in the moonlight.

There it was again: a shudder across the surface of the lake. And bubbles. As if something far below exhaled. It came from the edge of the shore closest to the house. It could have been nothing more than a frog that had alighted from its resting place to dive into the water. Yet something about it felt abnormal. He watched for several minutes then slipped back inside.

He looked at his timepiece again, this time without doubt. Something was wrong.

Chapter Fifty-Eight

The voices moved away, abandoning Clara to her earthbound prison. Although she waited for some time, no light seeped in around the door. Instead she felt as if she floated in a black womb, detached from every part of the world. Rather than shadows or a sense of her surroundings, the young man's body—Berend had called him *Diedrich*—floating facedown on the surface of the underground lake swam before her mind. She had been a fool to trust Inspectors Dressler and Metz. Wrong to trust anyone Lina called a friend or invited into her home. It was so clear now. Why hadn't she understood that before?

In a flash of understanding, she connected the dots. The man she had heard in the hall of tombs when she and Cora had hidden in the recess—Berend had called him *Emil*. His voice, so familiar, yet impossible to place at the time, was now obvious. Inspector Dressler. That's what Lina had called him when they met prior to the party. *Emil*.

"Oh, Diedrich. I'm sorry. It's my fault."

"I don't know why you keep saying that. This is my mother's fault," Cora said. She sounded as if she stood no more than an arm's length away.

Hot tears flowed down, soaking the fabric she had wrapped around her nose and mouth. She longed for a glimpse of him. She wanted to see him alive and well. And to remember that, at least for that brief moment, she'd had an ally. That someone out there could be trusted. Even if the pain of seeing him renewed her sense of shame. But of course there had to be others she could trust. She refused to believe everyone in the world could be so easily swayed to evil.

Berend had mentioned an associate. Someone working with the young man. Someone Lina desperately wanted to stop. He had to be trustworthy.

And there was at least one other.

Her heart paused in shock. Of course. One person Lina hated more than anyone. Someone she had cast from her house. Someone she never would have invited back. Who came of his own accord. Her uncle, Nathaniel. Her memories gathered and took form around her. He wasn't against her. He was against his mother. Did he know what kind of person she really was?

"Yes. He knows exactly who she is. But his methods won't help you," Cora said.

The ghost's words sounded desperate, as if she struggled to seem nonchalant. As if what she really meant was that Nathaniel's methods stood in the way of her own agenda. He could be an ally, a help to her.

But there was nothing Clara could do until she escaped from the underground room. Besides which, she grew increasingly uncomfortable. Where she stood, still leaning against the solid steel door, the cold radiated through her wet skin. *Why would they install a door with no window or pass-through in it?* she thought. *No way to see in and monitor a prisoner. But then why have a room at all in such an obscure place? And why secure it in such an impenetrable way?*

A room, she thought. *A room for what?* She looked around, her eyes perceiving nothing but a humid, inscrutable abyss. A foul-smelling one. The scent of decay was stronger here even through her makeshift gag. Where was she? She had been unconscious when they had carried her down to the underground pool. The lake she hadn't known existed.

She looked up, her mind suddenly reeling. Though she'd never seen this underground labyrinth, she suddenly knew exactly where she was. There was only one reason someone would have dug this tunnel and created this underground lake. A lake that probably hadn't existed before Edgar. And there was only one reason someone would place a locked room next to an underground lake that shouldn't exist.

"There's only one person who believes in drowning as the purest form of death, something of a spiritual baptism. Haven't I been telling you that all along?" Cora sighed beside her.

Clara knew what lay around her. She knew the source of that penetrating, rancid odor. This room held all the evidence her grandmother couldn't afford to lose. The evidence Heinrich had asked her to eliminate. He'd been a fool to ask it. Clara was certain of that. Only a fool would think Lina could ever do so. It would be like setting fire to her memories of Edgar. Like desecrating a piece of his body.

Clara turned to face the interior of the room. She took a step. Then another. And a third and fourth. Her foot rolled across something. Then she tripped. Tripped and fell headlong into a mound of arms and legs and protruding bones. She pushed herself off what felt like a nose or an ear and trembled audibly. Something slick coated her hand.

They were in various stages of decomposition. She couldn't see them yet she could. Her mind filled in the faces of young girls in cells, their hair in flaxen braids. Teenage girls, their bodies rounded and leggy. Whether due to sickness or age, they had all been discarded as useless. Meike was surely there somewhere, lying exposed in the cold darkness, wet and bruised, her body rigid in death.

Who knew how many were in this room? Or even how large the room was. Given her father's history, there could be bodies here from ten years ago. Maybe even some that predated his marriage. His childhood friends had alluded to his sordid doings much earlier in life. She figured some of the girls' bodies could have been there twenty or twenty-five years.

Long enough for some of them to be nothing but bones.

Clara moved back near the door then walked her hands past it, feeling the wall. It was made of hard earth and rock, like the room beyond. She ran her fingernail across it, feeling the dirt fill her fingernails. Then she froze, wondering how many times, as a child, she had walked down the sloping lawns to the lake, not knowing a tomb lay beneath there. And beside it, Lina's signature weapon: water.

For that was certainly why the wall beside the subterranean lake had been dripping. It was connected to the one above ground. Fed by it.

Which means the walls are wet. And soft, she thought. Clara walked her hands along the wall beside the door until it made an awkward bend and headed back toward the mound of bodies. Water ran softly down its surface. Water, the great sculptor of history. It was only a matter of time before the entire thing caved in.

Only a matter of time.

She knew exactly what to do. Gritting her teeth and steeling her mind, Clara climbed over the decaying flesh and rooted around in it until she found what she needed. A sharp bone. A femur or humerus broken and jagged. She closed her eyes, despite the darkness and tore it away from the rest of the skeleton.

Ugh! Her body shivered in horror and disgust.

Then, bracing herself for the task, she returned to the wall beside the door. It was drier than the one alongside the lake but still soft. She set the bone to it and went to work. It came away as it had under her fingernail. In soft streaks of soil. Easily.

She paused, her head turned toward the outside wall. It could be vastly thicker, but it led to the outdoors. She was sure of it. Either the lawns or the lake. For a moment she waited, considering, then turned back to the wall alongside the steel door.

"No. You won't get off that easily," she said, digging the bone into the soft dirt. Beside her, Cora laughed.

Of course Lina had never meant this room as a prison. Not for the living. It was nothing but a tomb. No need for windows on the door. No need for solid walls. Nothing but a lock to keep out the devastating aftermath of prying eyes.

In her mind she could see them as she carved, the girls lying there in the dark. Their spirits haunting the depths of the underground lake. She had embraced them, mingled her blood with theirs. She felt them watching her. Hundreds of clouded, lifeless eyes.

We're going home. Tonight. Every one of us.

As she worked, she recalled her history lessons and laughed to herself. The best way to overthrow a city isn't from without but within. Though Suleiman had failed to take Vienna, she wouldn't. She worked faster and faster, the bone puncturing the soft spongy wall and tearing soil and rocks loose. It grew blunter, yet still she drove it into the wall and pulled.

<h1 style="text-align:center">Chapter Fifty-Nine</h1>

"I don't know. I found them like that." The young cook-servant took a step back.

Berend watched him for a moment then waved him away. The boy practically ran around the corner. Berend heard his stumbling race up the cellar stairs. It didn't matter; the boy didn't know a thing. He'd asked more from irritation than from any expectation.

He was annoyed with all of it. Too many things were going wrong. He had told Lina this would happen, but she hadn't listened. He had known she wouldn't, yet he had still hoped. Hoped to live out the rest of his days in quiet predictability.

Above him he heard rustling in the kitchens—the frantic choreography that was a professional cook staff in the midst of a large event. But here, below it all, the air lay still and quiet, permeated by the scent of sawdust-filled barrels packed with apples and baskets of onions and turnips. And the cool, humid air of the earth. It was a moist, homey smell of good meals and hearty goodwill. Things that reminded him of his youth.

Until he resumed his focus on the two bodies lying before him.

They had been hidden—poorly at that—behind several large baskets of pumpkins, mushrooms, and rutabaga. Whoever had done so had known they would be seen before long. Any servant sent to retrieve vegetables or fruit from the cellar would have been likely to notice something amiss.

Berend had pulled the bodies from their hiding place to the center of the floor where they now lay in conspicuous disarray. The manner of their activities was obvious. Someone had attempted to redress the two, but their clothes were clearly out of order—the buttons on her bodice buttoned in the wrong holes, his shirt tucked in crooked.

Who would bother? Berend rubbed his beard and considered the two youths. A stablehand and a girl who, if his memory served him, they had brought on two years ago to serve the female guests at a ball Edgar and Lina had held over the winter. The guests had stayed for a week or more, skating on the lake, playing cards well into the night. Fräulein Clara had played the harpsichord.

He shook himself. It didn't matter who they were. They were dead. Their eyes were open, partly clouded, staring at the ceiling, their pupils enlarged. He knew the signs now, signs that had alerted the inspectors to foul play in Edgar's death. And of course their lips were stained—blood red against the mottled, flushed tone of their skin. The color of wine.

Berend crossed the small room to the central hub of the cellar spaces, then strode into the room where they kept the bottles of wine. Several stood open on the table. Wine that the servants were airing but hadn't yet taken to the ballroom above. He lifted one and sniffed it. It bore the usual heavy smell of berries and oak, but beneath that was a strange odor, earthy and dark. The rest of the wine bottles in the cellar were intact, the family's signature corks tightly embedded in their necks.

The conclusion was obvious—and only furthered his suspicions. He took the stairs two at a time, his long frame still strong and agile. If he hurried, she'd be just where he wanted her. And she'd never see him coming.

Chapter Sixty

Richter stood in the boathouse, one hand leaning against the weathered wall, lost in thought. Some part of him whispered that something was off, terribly wrong even. It wasn't just the span of time. There were so many reasons Jan might not have signaled. He had considered them all. Any number of legitimate obstacles could have kept him from the balcony.

Rather, it was his sixth sense. Something about the movement of the water bothered him. The strange rippling had recurred intermittently from the same location, marking it as something other than natural. He had moved beyond the boathouse, risking discovery, on multiple occasions within the last hour, just to watch the strange occurrence.

Now, as he watched the house on the hill, it seemed to shift, as if it struggled to break free of its foundation. As if it fought against its constraints and could at any moment throw off its shell and...and what? He didn't know. What was a house without its framing? If houses could have a soul, that's what it would be. A soul set loose from what bound it. Nothing but memories and consciousness.

Now that he thought of it, he wasn't sure if that was true. If a soul *was* really nothing but memories and consciousness. He'd never considered such a thing. His delight had never been in the supernatural and spiritualism, the great hobbies of his time.

But that's what he saw and knew when he watched the house on the hill. It loomed in the darkness, as if breathing deeply, gathering strength. For what, he didn't know.

Either way, it didn't answer his own question: how certain was he that something was wrong? He could attempt to gain entry into the house. He could put his backup plan into action. But if he did and something malevolent wasn't in play, he would jeopardize or even sabotage everything they had done to date. Worse, he would put Jan's life at risk.

Or he could wait until dawn. At some point Jan would reemerge, along with the other guests. Unless he didn't. If something really was wrong, such caution could be deadly for his assistant.

A strange noise drew him out of introspection. The sort of noise that had slowly and increasingly taken up residence in the back of his awareness. He peered through the filmy window but saw nothing abnormal. No figure tracked across the lawn. No great bird harassed the surface of the lake. Even the house, imbued with life as it seemed to be, still stood on its foundation at the top of the hill.

Richter strode to the door for the last time that night. Once he was outside, everything appeared unchanged. At first. But then the ripples grew stronger and more erratic. He walked out onto the lawn and around the edge of the lake. The smell of water mint, crisp and clean, rose from beneath his feet. Just then, the water shuddered, as if a small wave moved deep beneath the surface. He turned to look out over the lake.

The water shuddered again. He looked over and caught sight of something: the tail of a snake or long weed, shivering on the surface. He stepped carefully along the shore until he drew near it. No. It was something else. Neither reptile nor plant. He leaned forward and watched it for a moment. Something like a bit of cording or rope.

A growing dread rose within him. He wanted to leave it and go. Leave the entire place and walk away. Something about the strange object foretold of doom. And choices that would push him past the point of no return. But he couldn't. He couldn't leave the portentous cord there on the surface of the water and live the rest of his life wondering what he had refused to face. What final challenge had defined the extent of his courage.

He slipped off his leather boots and socks, rolled up his pant legs, and stepped into the water. It was cold, the bones in his feet and ankles aching in protest. The water's edge was slimy with algae and muddy weeds. Long tendrils, like thin fingers, stroked his calves. But he disregarded it all and pressed further. Suddenly the water dropped off and he nearly slipped under. He righted himself and stood immobile, knowing what he must do.

Slowly he bent down and took hold of the piece of rope. He knew what he would feel, what his sixth sense would reveal even before his hands touched it. Still, he grasped it. His sixth sense took over, filling in all of the dreaded gaps. Visions of water and blood flooded his mind. Some part of him shattered as it became clear. Every broken piece of him flew apart in a violent explosion of sorrow.

Eventually he waded back toward the edge of the water and huddled on shore. His shoulders shook with the pain and injustice. He pressed his face against his fists. It had come to this. What he had always feared. That Jan would go out into the wood in search of a nest of vipers, never to return. Worse, that he had sent him. That the youth's death was his own fault. It should have been his own. This would have been avoided if he had refused to allow him to play such a precarious part in this dark game.

So he sobbed silently under the indifferent moon. When his body stilled, the shattered pieces drew back together into a heated core of violent rage.

He rose and dressed. There on the hill, the house watched him and waited. But it would wait no longer. He strode, his steps lengthening until he jogged across the lawn and reached the perimeter. There was no longer any doubt as to what he would do. With the unraveling of the rope, it had all become clear.

Chapter Sixty-One

Lina wasn't really listening to anything the count was saying. Instead she was watching the crowd. Waiting. Waiting for all she had prepared. She smiled to herself. This night could make Edgar's death worthwhile. It could make him even greater in death than he had been in life.

One of the balcony doors stood open. Beyond it several men leaned against the stone railing, deep in conversation. Tendrils of smoke drifted away from them, hovering near the door instead of dissipating into the night air. The candles in the ballroom flickered and danced.

The spirits are with us tonight, she thought. Her lips broke into a wide smile. She was attired in a dress the color of pooling blood, trimmed in black. Her awareness of it gave her a sense of power, as if lightning surged through her body seeking a place to ground itself. *Soon,* she thought. *Soon I will give you a place to land. When everything is in place.*

The count took her smile as encouragement. He nodded, twirled his glass of wine, and launched into a discussion of the subdivision of power. Helene stood across the room, her hands folded before her, listening intently to two men. Lina could guess the subject of conversation. Those two were only ever interested in one humanitarian aim or another. They were almost certainly ingratiating themselves, seeking her approval. Lina shook her head in disgust. At which sign the count faltered and stopped.

She didn't notice. She scanned the room, looking for Berend. She needed him beside her tonight, of all nights. Where was he? She frowned. Come to think of it, she hadn't seen him for quite some time. Too long in fact.

Her eyes narrowed. Something was wrong. Something she couldn't put her finger on. But just then Lina caught sight of Helene, moving toward the toasting glasses. She was talking to one of the waitstaff behind the table. Lina broke away from the count and strode through the crowd to join her.

"You changed." Lina took in Helene's dark-blue gown. The earlier rose-colored one had called attention to her more readily. But this one, covered in tiny crystals that mimicked a midsummer night sky, set off her eyes.

"Yes," Helene said. "I managed to spill my entire glass of wine on myself. I can't believe how clumsy I am this evening."

"Hmm. That's unusual." Lina noted streaks of purple on Helene's arms, barely concealed beneath her white gloves. Helene smiled in appreciation, as if the comment had been a compliment. And then changed the subject.

"It looks like all is in order," Helene said, glancing at the table beyond them. "You must be so pleased."

"I'd be more pleased if Berend were here."

"Oh. Well, I'm sure he'll be along shortly. Have you seen Lotte or Horst? I thought they'd be here. You did invite them."

"Hmm. I hadn't given it any thought."

"It's so odd. And where are the wives? Since when does a Bavarian woman miss a ball?"

"I really can't say." Lina sipped at her wine and glanced around the room, struggling to suppress her smug expression.

"I have to say, this is really so gracious of you." When Lina's eyebrows shot up, perplexed, Helene clarified, "To honor Nathaniel. After all these years. And what with your somewhat strained relations.

It's really so exquisite. It's everything I imagined a homecoming party could be."

Lina pursed her lips and considered her shrewdly. "Of course. I'm expecting a magnificent appearance." With that, Lina walked away, leaving Helene puzzled. She stopped and pulled a heavy watch from her pocket. It shimmered in the reflected light. It was nearly time. She might have to go forward without Berend. Everyone else was present. Yes, it really couldn't wait any longer. With any luck he would appear shortly.

As if he had been summoned by her thought, Berend stepped through the ballroom door, his eyes intense. Lina froze. He wore a look on his face she had only seen one other time. They had been fifteen or sixteen when a foreign gentleman had come to her father's house. Berend had snuck into the carriage house to see the man's new Barouche Landau. There he had surprised his mother with the head gardener. Afterward, he had come to find her. His face had worn a stony mixture of horror and dark machinations. She saw that same expression in his eyes now.

He drew near, placed a gloved hand on Lina's arm, and leaned in to whisper something to her. She heard herself inhale sharply.

"I'll deal with her," he said.

"It's almost time. Are they put away?" Lina asked. They both knew what she meant. Berend nodded again, his lips tight, and turned. Seconds later he was gone.

Lina took a deep breath. She felt her pupils go wide, dilated. She blinked, waiting for her face to settle. But there was no time.

The door opened again. Nathaniel walked in, his step deliberate and thoughtful. Four other men, longtime guests she held in the strictest of confidence, hugged his side or followed close at his shoulder. Several guests bowed lightly or reached out a hand in greeting. Nathaniel bowed in return, his pose deferential, deflecting of attention. So unlike Edgar. Her lip curled.

"Ah! There he is, at last," Lina exclaimed, clapping her hands over the din.

A couple hundred eyes turned.

"Bring him here," Lina called to the men. "The man of the night."

The crowd shifted as Nathaniel moved forward until he stood in the center of the room. Several guests watched his approach with only scarcely concealed animosity. Most wore carefully guarded looks or averted their eyes to avoid his.

"Ah. Here we are. At the crux of the matter," Lina said, gripping him by the arm and pulling him into the center of the throng.

Chapter Sixty-Two

After she had carved a large enough hole in the wall next to the steel door, Clara crawled through it into the adjoining cavern. She avoided looking in the direction of the underground lake, where the young man's body still lay on the surface of the water. Then she took up one of the lanterns left burning there and made the long, winding trek back to the house. She had been unconscious when she had arrived, and now she had only the flickering light. But there was no choice to make. Only a long, wormlike tunnel. Eventually it opened into the passage where the tower door still stood ajar.

Passing it, she came to the recessed tombs. There she exchanged the lantern for a torch that she picked out of one of the sconces. For the second time that night, this time without Elise or any of her prior delusions, Clara made her way up the stairs to the sacristy, then down into the chapel.

She couldn't save them. Not on her own. She knew that now. It had taken Meike's death, and now the young man's, for her to understand. But there was one thing she could do that would free them all.

The chapel was still ablaze with candlelight, even though several had burned down. The smell of smoke curled around Clara in the cold air. She saw it hanging in the heavy gray moonlight that pressed against the stained-glass windows.

She left the chapel, stepping out into the eastern end of the ground floor. The first room was a storage one of sorts. The back wall opened onto a small flower garden. When she was young, her mother had used the room as a place to arrange the bouquets that she would deposit around the house. Constantly refreshing the rooms with lilacs and lilies and then peonies and azaleas. And roses, mounds of roses. At the time, Clara hadn't seen it for what it really was: a many-colored hypocrisy. Nothing more than grave flowers. The plants had imbued the rooms with an imitation of life meant to conceal the truth, to paint over it in false tones of mirth.

A prodigious quantity of vases still lined the shelves, but now the room also held extra tables and chairs, stacked against the walls. At least two area rugs, rolled and coated with dust, leaned against the far corners of the room. Clara touched the tables nearest to her. She couldn't remember where they had once stood, but it no longer mattered.

She moved down the hall. A billiard room lay still, the balls still racked, ready for guests. Perhaps even the month before, she would have heard the voices of her father's friends—especially Uncle Horst, who adored pool—all talking at once, their shoes scuffing the oak parquet flooring. She would have smelled the cloying scent of their cigars and hair pomade. Would have seen the light reflecting off oiled mustaches and gold and silver pocket watches. Most of all, she would have seen herself as a child, playing to their attention, basking in the glow of their hollow flattery. But now the space lay dead, its ghosts long gone. Clara's fingers brushed the shallow pile of the green felt, the dry worn oak paneling along the wall.

She moved to the library. Someone had recovered the sofas and chairs with white sheets, the room relegated to vanity, of knowledge coveted, consumed, and discarded. She sighed. To be here caused her pain. The rows and rows of books, standing fragile, vulnerable. She ran her hand over a section devoted to French history. Then one on Greek philosophy. She remembered immersing herself in them, not for the joy of learning but for the acclaim her grandmother anticipated and demanded. The approval of Lina's peers from the appraisal of such a studied and accomplished granddaughter. From wall to wall,

Clara ran her fingers lightly over their vainglorious spines, feeling them bristle.

She moved on. She needed to visit so many rooms. To say farewell to what had been her home. Loved for all the wrong reasons, now hated. A house full of things coveted, guarded, forgotten, unwanted. Her jailers. And in saying goodbye, she put each of them to death.

Chapter Sixty-Three

Richter didn't think, didn't plan, simply moved. In retrospect, he wasn't sure he had even felt anything. Between the flood of grief at the lake and his sense of bitter victory the next morning, his emotions receded deep within himself. To grow numb and quiet, allowing him to do what needed to be done.

He approached the front entry rapidly and from the side, using the shadows of the house as a cloak. When he tapped on the door, it opened to the surprise of a large, well-muscled guard. He couldn't have been more than twenty years old, and as he glanced from Richter to the gravel drive beyond, looking for carriage or porter, confusion registered on his face. Until Richter drove his dagger into the man's thigh and ripped to the side, severing his femoral artery.

The young man's leg gave out. He tumbled to the floor. Behind him a tall, solidly lean guard braced himself. Richter kicked him hard in the diaphragm. When the man doubled over, he stabbed him through the eye. His body convulsed then collapsed on the floor.

Richter turned back to the first man, who lay gasping and clutching his mangled leg. He sank the knife into the man's neck and tore it open. Blood poured onto his chest and over the floor. And onto Richter's hands. He stopped to wipe them on his jacket and pants. He almost felt bad for the two men. Neither one had been prepared for any real confrontation. If anything, Richter guessed they were simply well-built doormen meant to discourage prying eyes. More likely, Lina wanted to ensure that Clara didn't slip out during the festivities.

Rooting through the two men's pockets, he found what he wanted: the key. He had to drag both men farther into the hall in order to shut and bolt the door. He dropped the key into his pocket.

Silently he stepped past the empty receiving rooms and turned left down the axial hallway that ran the length of the house. The hallway Lina had showcased so proudly. As he did, he caught one of the waitstaff by surprise, upsetting a tray of hot hors d'oeuvres. "No. It isn't safe. Turn back, now!" he said, sending the ruddy youth rushing back to the kitchens.

Behind him, a pair of women in matching gray dresses followed with trays of small pastries. At the sight of Richter, his hands and shirt covered in blood, they froze. He put his finger to his lips and shook his head. "No. Quickly. Back now." They turned and bustled back into the expansive butler's pantry.

When the three pushed through the pantry door and into the first of several kitchens, Richter came face-to-face with the rest of the kitchen staff, who stood frozen and apprehensive. Clearly the freckled youth had sounded the alarm. Smoke filled the room, along with the smell of roasting meat and the sound of sizzling from the stoves. All eyes rested on him, wide with shock.

"Is there an exit?" he demanded. Everyone stood transfixed and mute. "Now! Quickly!" he shouted.

"Th-there. Through there." A woman covered in flour pointed back to one of the adjoining rooms.

"Okay. Everyone, quickly in there. Get out of the house. Get out as fast as you can. Get as far from here as possible. And don't look back. It isn't safe."

"We're not going anywhere. We'll be dismissed." An older man glared at him from under heavy eyebrows.

"If you stay, you'll die!"

It must have been the tone of his voice, for no one challenged the statement. For a second no one moved. Then several of the young people darted around the others and made for the back door. In their wake, the rest of the kitchen staff swelled toward the exit. Richter herded them all out of the room, gathering the residual staff from the side kitchens and shooing them along behind them.

"Quickly! Quickly! And be quiet. Get as far from here as you can. Now!"

When they were out, he shut the door behind them. There was no key. Most likely it had been on one of the senior staff he had just expelled. It was too late for that. Instead he shoved a heavy hutch from a nearby wall. It jostled and caught in the tile grooves, resisting his effort. Plates fell and shattered on the floor. But in the end he moved it into place, pressed firmly against the door.

The other exits would all be barred. He was sure of that. Lina and Berend couldn't keep the ship afloat with all the drains open. Other than the front door he had locked and this one, now barricaded, there should only be one available exit. Jan always had entered the underground cells via the chapel, which stood at the eastern end of the estate.

He ran back down the axial hall then stopped. In the distance, light burst from a door as it opened. A bobbing flame that confused and disoriented him. Behind the blaze the figure of a girl emerged, clutching a torch. She paused when she saw him.

"Clara? Is that you?" He moved forward quickly, reluctant to startle her but propelled by the gravity of the situation. She just waited without answer. As he drew near, he saw her eyes, settled and certain. He motioned her back into the room and shut the door behind them. The curtains were engulfed in fire, as was the upholstered furniture.

"Come with me. Quickly."

She looked him up and down then nodded as if she understood who he was. "I can't."

"You can. Now. It's urgent."

"There's something more I have to do." Her face radiated an immovable determination that he recognized. He reached into his pocket and drew out the stained piece of torn fabric. "I believe this is yours."

She took it, looked at it for a moment, then tucked it into her pocket. She reached for the door handle then hesitated. "The girls."

"Yes, I know."

She nodded, satisfied, then opened the door.

"Clara?"

She looked back, her face framed in flame.

"Do me a favor. Leave the receiving room—the green one with the crack in the wall."

She turned and moved off in the opposite direction. Richter didn't wait for an answer. He slipped out of the room and jogged the length of the hall, looking to the left and right.

At the end, he turned right down a narrow hall and nearly ran into the back of a tall, portly man. Coming up short, he slipped into a recessed doorway.

The man walked in great swaying steps, leaning to the left and right as if he took pleasure in the rhythm of his imposing form. He sauntered to the end of the hall, stopping before a door. As he turned to look behind him, Richter ducked back around the wall and waited. Several seconds passed before he heard the door open and close again. Even then he paused. He heard a second soft entry and subsequent latch.

Risking a look around the corner, Richter found the hallway empty. He jogged lightly across the thick red carpet and pressed an ear to the heavy wooden door. There was no way to know for sure. The door was too solid to hear anything. He waited and counted to sixty. Then he slowly eased it open. The chapel was empty but ablaze with candlelight. He slid through the opening and softly shut the door behind him.

The space felt cool and damp, as if it weren't attached to the rest of the house at all but rather stood alone at the top of a lonely hill. Glancing around the space, he saw no doors save for the one through which he had just come and the heavy double doors at the back of the nave. It was highly unlikely Lina had led her guests outside in the middle of the night. Still, Richter tried them. They were locked. Besides, Jan had insisted this was the way. At the memory of his enthusiastic assistant, pain gripped his heart, sending waves of cold despair through his body. He fought to press it aside.

Think. Think, he told himself. The exterior wall along the far side of the chapel stood even with the windows above. Thus unlikely to conceal any passage or stair to the area below. The same was true for the wall along the rear of the nave. That left only two others: the interior wall alongside the door from which he had entered, and the wall behind the altar.

Or above it.

He looked up at the loft high above. Then at the pulpit that hung below it. At eye level with the Christ figure that hung on the cross.

A narrow circular stair led from the side of the altar platform to the raised pulpit above. The walls behind the pulpit were framed in box molding. Consistent with the rest of the room. Yet the faintest sliver of light seemed to shine not *against* the wood from the candlelight in the room, but *from behind* the edge of the molding.

Richter dashed up the broad stairs to the altar's platform and over to the spiral staircase. He climbed them quickly, two at a time. Yes, it was clear. A room lay beyond this one. He pushed at the molding until a narrow strip gave way and the door sprang open. Adrenaline coursed through him. He threw the door open with one hand. The other gripped his dagger.

It was a small room, monastic in appearance. Nothing but a wood floor, small desk and chair, and a Gothic-style prayer kneeler. Upon its stand lay a large Bible. An intricately wrought iron lantern hung in the middle of the space. The room was otherwise bare. But to one side, a door stood open.

Beyond it, a lantern perched lit at the top of a staircase. Along its descent, other smaller lanterns guided the way. Heavy stone walls bordered the space, assuring him that ambush was unlikely. But as he descended, the walls seemed to close in around him, squeezing the air from his lungs. He concentrated on stilling his racing heart.

When he finally reached the bottom, he found himself in a narrow space, composed of stone walls on all sides. Ahead of him, a door stood open. Beside it, a heavy metal lever jutted out of the floor. He stepped through the doorway and edged around a heavy stone coffin. Before it, another lever protruded from the ground, presumably to open the door from the other side.

Richter was in some type of long crypt. To the right, a long hall lay cloaked in shadow. To the left lit torches lined the wall. He followed them until the hall ended. When he glanced around the corner, he saw that the hall jogged. He snuck up to the next corner, readied his muscles, and paused. There were faint noises but nothing that indicated who or what lay beyond the bend. Stilling his nerves, he shot a quick glance around the corner.

And found himself face-to-face with a grim-faced, black-haired man who stood more than a head taller than himself. Richter sucked in his breath and struck out with the dagger. But the other man was fast. Faster than his long-limbed, awkward bearing indicated. And strong.

The man deflected his attempt and retaliated with a fist in the center of Richter's chest. The blow knocked the wind out of his lungs and sent him staggering backward. He tightened his grip on the knife. Before Richter could determine a plan of attack, the man lunged at him. He was forced to dodge him and roll to the side.

Coming up quickly, he barely evaded the man, who crashed toward him then fell against the bars of a cell. Catching his advantage, Richter ran forward and stabbed his knife up under the man's arms, into the side of his ribs. The cut wasn't deep enough to be fatal, but blood seeped onto his shirt.

The man shoved back from the bars, his face an ugly mask of rage.

"Looks like you came to the party angry." Richter shook his head. "Never wise in a fight."

The other man glared at him, his teeth parting like those of a cornered dog. Richter made as if to stab forward, then came up short and twisted to the side. This time his knife found its mark, sinking into the side of the man's abdomen. Richter ripped it loose and watched as blood ran from the wound. But it didn't seem to stop or slow the man in any way. Rather, the pain seemed to spur him on, fueling his anger.

He lunged after Richter and swung, hitting him in the side of the head. The dagger flew out of Richter's hand and spun across the floor. Stars reeled before his eyes. His vision watered and the taste of blood filled his mouth. Before he could regain his sight, the other man collided with him, knocking him to the floor.

Richter wrenched himself free and rolled quickly, staggering to his feet. The room was unsteady, but he could see. There, fifteen feet away, the knife lay near a pillar between two cells. He started toward it, but the other man collided with his back, throwing him to the ground. Again. He had one arm around Richter's chest. With the other he pummeled him in the back.

The third shot caught Richter in the kidney. Pain seared through his body. He arched his back and cried out. Then, out of desperation, he shot his fingers back and jammed them into the other man's eye. The man screamed and covered his face. It wasn't enough, but it bought him time. Meanwhile, Richter slid out from under him and dove to where his knife lay.

Once again, the man ran after him and threw himself at him, as if to pin him to the floor. But this time Richter anticipated him. As he hit the floor, he clutched the knife and twisted. Since the man reached to clutch his torso, Richter's arms were free. And the man's head was undefended. Richter drove the dagger through his temple.

The man trembled and collapsed on top of him. Richter lay gasping for air, pain running up and down his legs from his back. Then he shoved the man aside, watching as his eyes grew distant, empty. His body lay still on the packed earth floor.

Chapter Sixty-Four

Ugh. Richter sat hunched over, pain radiating from the blow to his back. Several minutes passed as he listened to his labored breathing and tasted the metallic tang of blood between his teeth. When he looked up, he realized he had an audience.

Young girls stood at all of the cage doors, save for one. Sometimes two girls in one space. In one, the large ruddy man he'd followed watched him. His jaw hung open in stunned silence. His pants lay around his ankles. A sick roiling wave moved through Richter's gut. These were the ones who had been taken. And who still lived. At some level he had known they were here. He had believed the report at its inception. It had been too farfetched to have been fabricated. Combined with the missing children, it had been too coincidental to have been anything other than directly correlated.

But as he rose to his feet and took in the reality of the situation, he felt a sense of dissociation, as if the unknown had been more credible, more trustworthy than the reality. Still, there they stood, silently watching him. It struck him that the youngest ones, perhaps no more than six or seven years old, didn't cry out or whimper or beg for help. They simply stared, their eyes hopeless and empty. That alone filled Richter with an immense sadness.

He looked down at the brute of a man lying at his feet. One of the pockets in his coat bunched suspiciously. Richter reached inside it and withdrew a ring of keys. As he stood again, the room swam and spun. A blinding flash of pain shot forth behind his eyes. He doubled over, squeezing his temples as if to disperse the pain. Moments later it subsided into a resounding ache.

He stumbled to the closest cell and fumbled with the keys until he found one that fit. The heavy lock clanged. The door swung free. He moved to the next one. And the one after that. When he had rounded the room and opened each cell, he looked up. None of the girls had moved. They stood motionless—whether from shock or disbelief, he wasn't sure.

The man stood frozen as well. Even in the golden light, his freckles stood out sharply against his wan complexion. Beside him, a tall girl with eyes like stormy water watched Richter. He clutched at his aching back and moved toward her.

"You. What's your name?"

"Elise." It came out in a whisper. She looked from him to the body on the floor.

"Don't worry about him. Elise. Elise, look at me. We have to get all of you out of here. And I need your help."

"Who are you?"

"Don't worry about that either. Just know that I'm a friend. We're leaving this place now. All of us."

"What about the young man? And the girl?"

Richter felt a stab of pain through his heart. "They're fine. You can't worry about them right now. I'm here. And we don't have time." He almost told them the place would soon come down around them, but then he checked his words. And reminded himself these were children. Instead he softened his tone. "It's all right. You're all going to be all right. Elise, I need you to help me. Take the girls by the hands. It's okay. Girls, hold hands and follow me. Carefully but quickly. Everything's going to be all right."

Something in his voice shook Elise into motion. She raced out of the cell and gripped the hand of the girl next door. They rushed to the next one and the next. In seconds all the girls were trailing behind one another and moving back toward the flickering light of the long hall of tombs.

Richter jogged ahead of them. "Through here. And up the stairs." Then a thought crossed his mind. "Elise. Elise look at me." The girl stopped in the hidden doorway that led up to the sacristy behind the pulpit. "Take these stairs up. They lead to a small room. Pass out through the room and down the staircase. You'll be in the chapel. Get all the girls to the back of the church, near the outer doors. They'll be locked, but wait there."

"But—"

"I'll be right behind you. I have to do something first. Elise?"

"Yes?"

"It's going to all right. Be strong. For me. For them. I'll be right behind you."

She nodded, looked over the other ten girls, then turned and led them up into the light. Richter made his way back toward the hall of cages. As he rounded the corner, he took in the portly form of the disrobed man bending over the prostrate corpse. At the sound of Richter approaching, he rose and turned around. The look on his face betrayed his apprehension. He backed away.

The sight of him filled Richter with burning rage. His stride lengthened. The man's hair fell askance as he frantically looked left and right. There was nowhere to go. No way to avoid a confrontation. In the end he dove into the cell out of which he had come. He pulled the door closed behind him.

Richter bent and ripped the dagger from the temple of the gruesome corpse. Blood leaked from the wound and soaked into the dirt. He turned and started toward the cell. The man tried to hold the door closed, but without the key to lock it, it rested unsecured in its frame. Richter reached for the bars and tore it open. The man stumbled backward, holding his hands out in front of him.

"No. I can explain. It's not—"

Richter didn't wait to hear the rest. He kicked the man in the balls.

When he slumped over, clutching himself, Richter lunged at him. Though the man outweighed him by at least fifty pounds, he hit him hard enough to knock him backward. The man's heel caught on the edge of the filthy mattress. He tripped, struggled to maintain his balance, then fell hard.

Richter landed on him and drove the dagger into his chest. Again and again. The man tried to fight, but despite his size he was weak and clumsy. His heavy arms reached for Richter, to push him away, but Richter simply kneed his gut and stabbed at the man's arms and torso until he curled in on himself. He lay there, wrapped in a fetal position, his breathing labored. Richter heard his own breath coming hard. It was time to end it.

He drove the dagger into the man's throat and wrenched it to the side. Blood sprayed out onto the mattress and the wall beyond. Richter's arm and side were splattered with it. He rose and looked down at the man's form, curled on the mattress. In death he managed to mimic the sick parody of a helpless child. The smell of blood and loosened bowels made Richter nauseous.

He walked back to the cell door, pushed it open, and winced. His hand, coated in blood, bore several deep gashes. He tore a long strip of fabric from his shirt and wound it around his palm. Then he made his way back to the recessed tomb and up the staircase. When he emerged in the elevated pulpit, he heard several sharp gasps and took in the trembling forms of the girls crowded near the door. Elise was whispering something to them. Something insistent.

Richter raced down the stairs from the pulpit, ignoring the jarring pain that shot through his body. His hand was moving from sharp, searing agony to a throbbing ache. He struggled not to clutch at the railing.

The girls stood huddled beside the heavy exterior doors. As he jogged down the aisle between the rows of pews, most of them drew back, distancing themselves from him. In his mind he saw himself as he must seem to them: covered in blood, his jaw set in a hard line. They didn't move, though, and as he tried the keys and found the one that fit, several looked at him with the tremulous gazes of caged animals that desperately long to trust again but aren't sure it's safe. His heart swelled with pain and purpose.

The door swung inward, pulling with it the scent of dormant earth, long buried but brimming with the expectation of new life. They passed out through it and into a night long spent.

Chapter Sixty-Five

Dread rose in Helene's breast. And a sense of imminent destruction. It stemmed from the look on Lina's face. The look of a prowling beast creeping toward its cornered prey. Her smile was one of glee at the destruction of another. Helene's stomach cramped in anxiety as she watched, helpless.

Lina strode over to where the musicians played and signaled to them. The music fell silent. The conversations slithered off with a dwindling whisper. All eyes turned and looked at her. The men who had been on the balcony now clustered just inside the door, the smoke from their cigars spiraling up and intertwining with the candles that danced in their sconces.

Deeply satisfied, Lina smiled "Good evening and good morning," she called out.

"Good evening and good morning!" most of the room echoed.

"Here we are, together again. Edgar would be so pleased. It is my greatest hope and prayer that nothing will separate us in the future. That we will continue to celebrate as one as long as we all may live."

"Here, here!" called someone in the audience.

"To that end, I have gathered you all here for a very special purpose. We are here to honor someone we all love. Someone who unites us still, though he has been absent from us. And whose memory is so dear to us." At that point she paused and waved Nathaniel over. He came and stood beside her. In the candlelight, his auburn hair and beard glowed as if he were on fire.

"This, as you well know, is my first son, Nathaniel. The very image of my late husband, Conrad. God rest his soul."

Many people laughed; Helene looked around in confusion.

"Nathaniel. The savior of the people. Come home to us." Lina shot him a patronizing smile. Nathaniel eyed her without comment or response. As if he knew. "You know the Nathaniel of India. Gentleman farmer." She waved a hand in the air as if to brush off the triviality so that it wouldn't touch her. "Humanitarian and all-around do-gooder.

"But tonight I'd like to introduce you to the Nathaniel you've never met. The true Nathaniel hiding beneath all of that charity. That's right. In fact, let me tell you a story. And you'll have to pardon me. Creativity isn't my forte. So this story will be nothing but a truthful retelling, sad though it is.

"You see, there was a young boy who thought he had it all. As the firstborn, he stood to inherit home and title. And for a time, it appeared that such would be the case. That succession would follow tradition. Such was his father's intention, blinded as he was."

"Zealot," cried one.

"Hypocrite," said another.

"But I...I saw something Conrad had not yet. That it was Nathaniel's younger brother who bore all the marks of one born to lead.

"It was Edgar who had the sharp intellect, the ruthless mind for business, the sporting talent of huntsman and *playboy*." She grimaced in mock contempt. The room burst into applause and laughter. "And of course the charm. Charm with the ladies. *And* the gentlemen. Who among us hasn't felt the sway of his charisma? Hasn't pined for his approval and regard? You see, Edgar had it all. And in time even Conrad had to acknowledge it was his second son who really impressed. And that the first...didn't.

"Naturally we loved both our sons. As any mother would. But we chose to send Nathaniel to school in the north, where Conrad's connections were so strong. God forgive me. We had no idea at the time how much we would come to regret this. But then, who thought it would come to this?

"That wasn't the end of the story for our young man, though. No. It was there—in Prussia—that he acquired a taste for conquest. I know that now. His envy grew each year. He longed to take Edgar's place in the community. To win over the women as Edgar did. To be renowned in business, as Edgar was. To have the respect of those of you in this room. And of his father. In the end, that bitterness and jealousy drove him to take his brother's life."

Helene gasped. The sound of it swelled in the oppressive silence. But still Lina continued. Her voice rose, echoing throughout the room.

"Where, I ask you, do you think Nathaniel was on the night of my perfect son's fall?" She cackled, her voice shrill. This time she laughed alone. "Why, he was right here. Slinking around the town. Slipping into this very house in the dead of the night. And pushing my beloved son to his death. And I'm going to prove it." She spoke from behind her teeth, every word deliberate and laced with venom.

"Look to the north." All eyes followed her, every stance pivoted to face her as she circled the room. She came to a stop in front of the middle set of French doors that stood open. Every person in the room watched her. And waited.

She reached into her dress and pulled out a heavy gold pocket watch. At the sight of it, Helene gasped again, this time like the ragged inhalation of one who struggles to breathe.

"But that!" Helene said then fell speechless. The watch, a favorite of his, had been interred with Edgar. She had seen to it. *Where did she get it? No. How did she get it?*

Lina just laughed, her eyes flashing dark. She turned and faced out into the night. Lifting up the watch, her palms open, she screamed Edgar's name into the night. In the resonating silence that followed, the guests crowded closer. Then Lina began to speak, a low murmuring voice, the words indiscernible. Some form of ancient language. It rose and fell in a chanting rhythm.

A heavy cold fell over the room, wrapping itself around the guests, chilling body and spirit. Lina chanted a simple phrase over and over. As she did, first one voice, then another, joined with her, until most of the men called out in unison. Though many didn't understand the words, they knew what they were doing. They were calling for Edgar. They summoned the spirits of the dead, inviting them to walk among them.

As Lina held his watch in the air, Helene felt her spirit quickened by some unseen force. Just as Lina seemed to grow weary, a current of air twined itself around her. It lifted her hair and slipped its fingers down the back of her dress. Candlelight quivered violently. Many flames blew out, filling the air with the acrid smell of smoke.

Overhead, clouds scudded across the sky, obscuring the moonlight. The glass ceiling showed nothing but rapidly shifting shadows. In the background, as the voices chanted in unison, a high-pitched keening rose from a faint murmur to a wail. The air in the room reverberated. The walls seemed to pulsate. Even the glass above them seemed to breathe, drawing not air but spirit into itself.

The doors to the other balconies were sucked closed then slammed open with a crash. Lightning cracked in the distance. Then, before Lina, a dark pool grew out of the floor. It rose upward, elongating itself, taking form. As it did, the hearts of everyone present trembled with fear. But no one moved. As their spines crawled with a sense of evil unleashed, their bodies grew rigid, frozen. Every eye remained fixated on the unnatural being that manifested before them.

For though he grew and took the form of Edgar, his eyes shone with a vicious knowledge. And a desire for chaos, anarchy, and bloodshed. Everyone there, save for Lina, knew the one who stood before them was not Edgar. Rather, he was a harbinger of their own impending doom. If they could have run, they would have.

If anything, the spectral form was vastly more beautiful than Edgar had ever been. Yet his eyes were an abyss. His lips were curled just slightly askew, as if in anticipation. His gait was off. Rather than a swagger, the thinly veiled motion of insecurity, he moved with ineffable power. He smelled of fetid earth slithering with sightless, spineless creatures.

Edgar had been a man plagued by darkness. A man who had loved too deeply and had lost everything. A man whose reckless despair had driven him to unthinkable crimes. In his eyes and lips and walk, the ideal had mingled with defeat.

But not this one. This one was the *source* of that defeat and despair and darkness. Against him Edgar had had no power. And beneath his gaze, Helene's heart quailed. She took a step back, then another. In the corner of her mind she heard Lina whisper his name over and over. She cast an urgent, imploring look at Nathaniel, who calmly mouthed something she didn't understand.

"Edgar!" Lina cried. "Oh, Edgar."

The being, who thus far had stood, scanning the frightened crowd with an expression of hunger, turned his black eyes on Lina. For a moment she blanched and quivered as if terrified of that which only minutes ago she had so confidently desired.

"Edgar. Edgar say something," she pleaded. When he stared at her, not blinking, she trembled.

A low rumbling filled the room, a sound like a voice underwater. It was swallowed up by the cold, damp air that snaked around them.

"Edgar. Edgar. We've summoned you here to vindicate your name. To bring justice to your memory. You can understand that, can't you? You would want that."

His eyes seemed to recede before her. He gazed across the crowd. Last, he fixed his eyes on Nathaniel, who stood behind Lina, watching him as if he had tasted something particularly unpleasant. Yet, he alone seemed untouched by fear.

At the reminder of Nathaniel's presence, Lina regained some of her vitriolic composure. "Edgar, this is your chance. This is your opportunity to be heard. We're listening. You can tell us the truth. Finally. The truth about what happened." Lina's face appeared stretched, imploring, desperate. She pointed to Nathaniel. "Him. You can tell us. We know that he visited you that last night. That you fought. That he pushed you. Name your killer, Edgar. That's what we want. So you can rest."

But the beast she called *Edgar* simply turned back to Lina as if he didn't register her question. Or didn't feel any compunction to bow to her will. Instead he opened his mouth wide, horrifyingly wide. A deafening roar shook the room. Helene covered her ears and fell to the floor. In it she heard, without words, a dreadful pronouncement. In those few seconds, she begged for silence. Begged for it to cease. But when it did, when she looked up and saw his mouth still gaping wide, she cursed her own longing. For in the silence, in the aftershock, something was born.

Something crawled from his mouth and hovered in the air between them. A dark mass. It quivered with life. Lina leaned back, her eyes on the entity. Then, as suddenly as it had come forth, it split apart. The monster that had taken Edgar's form was gone. In its place, a dark current streamed throughout the room, drawing each of the men into its embrace. Lina clutched her chest. Tears of horror and anguish streamed from her eyes.

"Edgar. But Edgar," she whispered. "Who? Who stole you from me? If not him, then who?"

Just then, the ballroom doors flew open. They crashed against the wall, shattering the frozen horror within. The guests turned and exclaimed as one. There in the doorway stood Clara, her clothes in tatters, her face and body streaked with mud and decay and soot. She smelled of smoke and rotting flesh. Her face was resolute.

"I did."

Chapter Sixty-Six

Clara paused to take in the scene before her. A dense fog moved across the floor. Men were scattered throughout, their faces masks of terror. Around them and above them hung the ominous forms, like tongues of fire, shaded by mist and darkness. Apart from them, Uncle Nathaniel stood watching her with a barely concealed look of pride. Beside him, her grandmother's mouth hung open, her eyes wide in shock.

"You what?" Lina said. She pressed down on one knee, then rose with stumbling difficulty.

"I said, *I did*. I killed him." Clara turned back to her grandmother and strode forward. She pointed to her uncle. "This man is innocent. And you, Grandmother. You know not what you do."

"I—" Lina spat, her face contorted in rage.

"Clara!" Helene shouted, her voice laced with warning and a command to be silent.

"In your foolishness you called forth something you don't know. And can't control."

"I am *always* in control."

"Not this time you're not. Look."

The tongues of fire were dissolving, descending. And yet taking form. Arms emerged. Then legs. Willowy, ethereal wraiths of shadow and mist. They wrapped their limbs around the men and licked at their throats. Several men shuddered and tried to cast the spectral forms away. But the girls only laughed—a wide-eyed, toothy laugh lacking in mirth. And dug their nails into their arms and backs.

"You have no control over the dead. Your power died the day they did."

Lina's eyes narrowed. "You lie! You're no murderer," she hissed.

"Yes. I am. But I'm not the only one. You're a murderer too. You killed those girls. Over and over and over you killed. But unlike you, I repented for my crime."

"What is your aim? Did you hope to gain the sympathy of these?" Lina's arms swept wide, indicating the men who stood entranced. "Because you won't. They know what I am. They're no more innocent than I am."

"I know. I didn't come for their benefit. Or for yours."

"Preposterous! This is simply preposterous. That you...you...I've had more than enough of you. How are you even here? And where is Berend? Berend! Berend!" Lina called out for him, as if he were slinking in the shadows, waiting for her summons.

"I don't think he can hear you."

Lina rushed forward and seized Clara's shoulder, tearing her already mutilated dress. "You are *not* a murderer. This ends. This ends now."

"Mother!" Helene pushed forward.

"Helene. You stay out of this. You've never been able to control your daughter. She practically seduced my son. Her own father. A man who was already so troubled. Whose mind was unhinged. Then she has the gall to lament the consequences of her own behavior. And to claim she —a girl less than half his size—threw him from his own roof. It's preposterous. Absolutely absurd.

"I've had enough of her all around. No matter what we do to contain her, she manages to break free. I won't have this. I simply won't stand for it a minute longer." Lina clapped her hands, attempting to call the men in the room from their catatonic state. "I hereby open an auction. Like the old days! It's been so long." She shouted her intentions as if to drum up great excitement. The room lay ominously silent. Every eye watched her, including those of the shadowy wraiths.

"They can't respond," Clara said. "The prison they built brick by brick is complete. Now they're nothing more than slaves."

"What are you saying, you half-brained fool? These are free men."

"Look who holds them."

"I don't...I don't..." Lina said as she swung around, gazing from person to person.

"You don't what? You don't recognize them? Surely they look different from when you kept them enslaved, behind bars for years. But not that different. And possibly different from when you led them out as cattle to be branded and used. But not that different. How about when you tired of them? When you held them over the water and cut their throats, or drowned them, to satisfy your need for power. Are we getting closer? Certainly they look nearly identical to when you tossed their bodies in an underground cave and left them to rot."

Lina's mouth hung open as she took in each of the wraiths.

"Is it coming back to you now?"

"What are they...? Why are they...?"

"Clinging to them? Because they were invited. You invited them through your foolish attempts. And I joined my blood with theirs, so they were free to come. Now here we are, celebrating my uncle's homecoming. And yours. And mine. And theirs. Isn't that what we're doing, after all? Coming home? Coming back to the house each of us built brick by brick?"

"This is nonsense! The physician was right about you. You've lost your mind! What with your...your... And Edgar's death...Edgar! Edgar, come. Edgar, where are you?"

She clapped her hands again and called out to the musicians, who clasped their instruments and hurriedly launched into a discordant tune. The frightened men licked their lips as they were pulled into a brisk Viennese waltz. Wraiths and men, their faces fixed in masks of disbelief and panic, spun frenetically out of step with the music. Helene and Nathaniel pressed back near the doors to the balcony.

Chapter Sixty-Seven

Jutta's eyebrows slanted down in intense concentration. If she hadn't been so intent on the task at hand and had gazed up into the looking glass, she would have laughed. Her grandmother always had called her *kleine eule,* little owl, for that fierce gaze of hers. Her heart constricted at the thought of her family and her home. All that she knew she would lose. She breathed deeply and opened the carpet bag.

She tucked in the nightdress, her only pair of decent stockings, and picked up the brush her mother had given her. She raised it to her nose and inhaled the scent of the bristles. The smell filled her with warmth like an old blanket beloved for its memory of shelter and security. She was dressed in her traveling shoes and one of only two nonwork dresses she owned. She pressed the other one down on top of her few belongings.

Through the pocket of the bag she felt the hard edges of her money, everything she had been able to save over the last four years. On top of it all she laid her family Bible, the one from which her great-grandfather had read after dinner each evening. And then her grandfather after him. In the front, delicate, slanting writing noted each of the family members' birth, baptism, marriage, and death. Jutta stroked the worn leather, velvety soft but strong and thought of them.

Her grandmother. And the grandfather she had lost years ago.

Would they understand? Would they be proud of her? Anxiety filled her mind. And doubt. But deeper still, confirmation. They knew sacrifice. Understood the value of standing for something more than themselves. Certainly her father had when he had sympathized with the students during the revolution. Hadn't her grandmother said so on so many occasions? In her mind she saw the grief buried in the deep lines of her grandparents' weathered faces. But also the pride. Yes. They would understand.

She placed the last of her belongings in the bag and closed it.

Clara's rooms glowed with lamplight. Jutta crossed the bedroom and drew the leather bag out from under the bed. Of course she always had known it was there. Had seen the contents. Had even found the money and jewelry hidden in the bag's false bottom. There was no going back. She picked up the bag, took one of Clara's heavy woolen coats, and carried them both back to her room. She set them on the bed, beside her own bag.

A musky smell wafted into the room. Jutta clutched her throat and stepped back. There was no sound. No shifting of the light. No advancing of his shadow. No breeze snaking around her ankle, tightening its cold grip like a chain. Just his smell—the coppery scent of blood mixed with leather—and the sour taste of fear that filled her mouth.

Then he was there, standing inside the doorway, staring down at her with his angular face cut through with malice.

Berend.

He took in the bed, the two bags, the traveling coats, and her attire in one swift assessment.

"No, fräulein." He shook his head. His eyes shone with glee. His lips pressed together in smug satisfaction beneath his mustache. "No." He took one heavy step toward her. "I'm afraid your plans are canceled."

Jutta stepped back until she pressed against the cold wall, but there was nowhere to go. He took another step toward her.

Chapter Sixty-Eight

Clara watched the guests spin in delirious oblivion. Some faceless delusion had grasped her grandmother and now whirled her about the floor. More candles had gone out. The room lay in an eldritch haze. The more the unwilling dancers turned, the more disoriented Clara felt. Life and death seemed to coincide as if time and space had fallen away. Every allusion was cast aside, leaving nothing but truth.

The girls, their faces masks of sad satisfaction, twirled past her, their hapless victims held fast in their bony arms. In their expressions, Clara read a sense of vindication delayed but ultimately realized. Above it all, she heard the shrill glee of her grandmother's laughter, her elation unconfined by reason. Her mother stood to the side and stared at the scene in shock. Beside her, Nathaniel watched them all patiently as if he had expected this and already knew how it would end.

As the song wound down, Lina spun to a stop, clapped her hands again, then doubled over. When she caught her breath, she strode over and grabbed Clara's hand, pulling her into the center of the crowded floor.

"Well, that was the dance of our lives, wasn't it?" Lina said. It wasn't a question. No one responded. "Let's have the toast! Take a glass." She nodded to the table along the side wall.

The guests moved sluggishly, led by the wraiths. Each one crowded the table, clutched a glass, and moved back to the center of the room. Someone handed Lina a glass. When the movement grew still and all eyes rested on her, Lina raised her glass in the air.

"Let's toast to Edgar. To all that he lived for. And died for. That we might be together for many years to come. That we might always have a free Bavaria. And along with it, the ability..."

Her voice faltered. Clara looked at her perplexed. But her grandmother's gaze was on her mother. For Helene stood back, behind several men. As if to hide. Her hands were empty. Clara looked from one to the other. In her grandmother's eyes, she saw a spark of understanding awaken like a flame flaring up in a dark room. Followed by a wicked smile. She turned to Clara.

"But of course, it's only fitting that Clara should lead our toast. Seeing as she loved her father so much. Clara, here." Lina handed her glass to her and took another for herself. Clara looked into the dark liquid confused. Then she shot a look at her mother, who had in some mysterious way precipitated such a shift. Helene's face drained of color. Her eyes widened. Filled with panic.

"Clara, raise a glass with us," Lina said.

Out of the corner of her eye, Clara saw her mother propelled forward. The air in the room seemed to beat as currents of wind before the wings of a great bird. Then she was there, beside Clara. She grabbed the glass from her hand and held it away from her.

"Is something wrong, Helene?" Lina's smile never traveled to her eyes. Instead they grew darker, more certain of themselves. Clara looked from one to the next, confused. In her mother's expression she saw indecision and certainty warring with each other. Until finally something won out. Something resigned yet infinitely burdened. She wrapped her arm around Clara, leaned down to kiss her forehead, then lifted high the glass.

"To Edgar!" she called out.

"To Edgar," the crowd responded with their glasses in the air.

Helene hesitated for a moment then began to drink. The guests followed suit. When she had downed the liquid, Helene turned to Clara again with tears in her eyes.

"I love you," she whispered.

Then she fell. The glass hit the floor, shattering, cutting through the air.

Clara stared in horror at her mother, who lay huddled on the floor. Her heart leapt into her throat. She dropped to her knees.

"Mother! What...what?" Her mother's skin began to shift—from a pinkish glow to a sickly mottled tone, as if angry sores spread across her wan face. Clara attempted to pull Helene toward her. "No. Oh, no. Someone help her! Somebody! Mother, tell me. Tell me what to do."

Helene gasped for breath as if something had lodged in her throat. Above them, Clara heard the sound of bones creaking, then a raucous laugh. The smell of her grandmother's breath, ripe with sour grapes, enveloped her. "Did you think I wouldn't know? That we wouldn't find them? Wouldn't know what you had done? But we did. In time to switch the glasses. Of course we kept one of your own making for you."

Helene's eyes focused on the glass that lay in shards just beyond her fingers. She tried to say something, but her words were slurred, uneven. Her chest convulsed.

"I can't.... I can't hear..." Clara's words came out in choking bursts. Helene shook violently. Her eyes looked around her as if seeing something beyond the veil. She grew still.

Lina chuckled. "Cheers, daughter. Vengeance always cuts both ways."

"No. No," Clara begged. "Come back. Don't leave me. Please. Please don't leave me."

Clara crouched on the floor, her head hanging down. She heard a wailing that rose from deep within her, like a swelling sea that threatened to pull her overboard. With one hand she gripped her chest, as if she could still the heaving pain. Her eyes blurred. Her throat grew raw, hoarse.

Her mother's arm, stained with purple, lay outstretched beside her. Clara peeled off one glove and grasped the lifeless fingers. She saw in them her mother's intense concentration in the garden, stroking the intricately veined leaves of lemon balm, her journal lying beside her in the dirt. Clara had toddled up and down the rows, petting the long, feathered fingers of fennel, mimicking her mother's affection for her plants.

Her mother peered up through clouded eyes, her pupils immense, her face empty of the unease she had only barely disguised as she watched Clara's father jesting with other men on the veranda during a summer party. Empty of the quiet peace she wore beneath her mother-in law's constant scrutiny, the sunlight lying across her lap, highlighting a book whose page rarely turned.

Her mother's lips were tinged with a deep berry color so unlike the soft color of her smile when she had leaned against the mantel at her father's memorial. She had radiated a facade of hospitality, yet her soul had seemed to be drawn in tightly, held deeply within. Some part of her mother had retreated long ago, had always been inaccessible, concealed in a place where none would see what she really thought or knew or was.

And now it was too late to draw it forth.

Exhausted, Clara lay on the smooth parquet, her eyes swollen, heavy. Beyond her mother stretched a graveyard of statues and bodies. Most of the guests stood frozen, their eyes distant and clouded, held captive by the girls they had used and destroyed. Others seized in agony on the floor, victims of the wine Berend had neglected to change.

Someone bent low over them, resting his hand on a shoulder or a forehead as if speaking words of comfort. He rose and turned, moved to another suffering soul, and bent again. Uncle Nathaniel. Clara's body grew still. Her heart seemed to flutter lightly then stop, lying dormant within her. Her breathing ceased. She felt herself descend into darkness.

Then light flooded her eyes. Brilliant light. Everything was clear, clearer than it had ever been. She didn't just see her uncle—she knew him. Something about his movement spoke into her soul. She understood him. And she knew herself. Not just the parts she wanted to acknowledge but her entire being. In his face she saw her guilt. But also her freedom. She couldn't have articulated how.

Beneath her, the floor pulsated with warmth.

"You need to go."

Clara heard Cora's voice as if it stretched out into the distance. Instead she focused on her uncle. Joy flooded her heart as she watched him speak to those who minutes ago had derided him. Their hatred had fallen by the wayside, unable to penetrate or affect him. Unable to change his character in any way.

In that moment she loved him.

Beneath her, the house seemed to tremble and groan, as if it struggled to cast her off. She rolled onto her back and looked up through the glass. Though the night lay heavy and black above her, she pictured herself rising above the clouds. Ascending into a space where the moon and stars encircled her in stark brilliance. In her mind's eye, they shone down on her, calling her out and beyond, into wonder and awe. She sighed and closed her eyes.

Until she felt a shadow fall over her body. Then rough hands, hauling her up. She opened her eyes. The hands lifted her awkwardly from behind. And then shoved her toward the ballroom door. Clara stumbled and stepped around the men.

It wasn't until she had reached the ballroom doors and passed through them, pulling her attention back to her captor, that she knew the hands to be human. Fingernails dug into her arm, dragging her across the thick carpet of the hall landing. A voice sharp and brutal, sly and cunning, echoed in her mind. She gripped the heavy wooden railing and fought to resist. But it was too thick to hold. And her grandmother was so much taller and stronger. Clara's fingers slid across the heavily waxed surface. Her feet tripped over themselves. She stumbled down the stairs, rolling until she came to a rest at the next landing.

Lina rushed after her, grasped her arm, and ripped her to her feet. Together they descended the remainder of the long flight of stairs.

The air on the ground floor vibrated with heat and energy. The closed doors had kept the fire contained, had allowed the flames to grow slowly. With a gasp, Lina drew back from the hallway junction. Her eyes were wide, shocked at the sight of several doors wreathed in fire.

Clara watched her surprise then began to laugh. A low, easy, rolling laugh that grew until it shook her body. Tears streamed from her eyes. Her cheeks and sides ached. Slowly Lina turned and stared at her in horror.

"You! You...wretch! You ungrateful wretch!" she shrieked. But Clara just laughed harder.

Lina sneered at her, her teeth bared in a look of utmost hatred. Her fingers gripped Clara's arm like a vise, bruising the already tender flesh. She dragged her past doors and walls where flames licked the surface and raced along moldings.

Sweat formed on Clara's brow and ran down the insides of her disheveled dress. The fabric clung to her in patches. They rushed down the hall to the eastern staircase. As they rose up one flight of stairs then another, the heat grew, pressing down on them, warning them away.

At the third floor, they emerged to find the perimeter of the hall engulfed in flame. At the sight of it, Clara's humor died within her. Large sections of the wall had burned, exposing the rooms beyond. Fire spread across the ceiling, eating away at the plaster above. It rained down, lying strewn in ashy clumps across the hall's dense carpet. The cinders smoldered, orange heat mixing with white residue. In a short time the floor would be ablaze.

"It's not too late for you," Clara said. "You can leave. Go back. Get out."

Lina turned and looked at her, her face rigid with raw hatred. She clenched Clara's arms in both hands and bent until their faces were level, her rancid breath spitting in rage. "You'll die the way your father did. Thrown from his home. An inglorious end for a useless girl."

"The roof won't hold. It'll give way and kill you."

"Then let it!" Lina screamed from behind bared teeth. "You don't deserve to live. You're too depraved for anything other than fire. If it takes us both, then so be it! I'll happily die to rid the world of one such as yourself."

Lina propelled her toward the door at the end of the hall. Clara reached for it tentatively but it was far enough from the rest of the rooms as to be free from fire. The handle was merely warm under her fingers. As they ascended the steep, narrow stairway, a crash sounded behind them.

Chapter Sixty-Nine

Richter left the girls at the edge of the forest. He ran back through the chapel and into the axial hall that stretched along the length of the house. The heat was building. Flames had burst through at least one door. There wasn't much time.

He raced down the hall, past the front entry, and into the foremost receiving room. Clara had left it untouched, as he had asked. The painting of the hounds hung where it had on his last two visits. And to the left of it, the clever forgery he had gifted to Lina. She had moved several paintings in order to feature it slightly off-center but still prominently.

Richter climbed onto a chair, lifted it from the wall, and eased it onto the floor. From his coat he withdrew a small blade and cut the canvas away from the frame. Then he edged the knife into the back of the frame, and pried at the wood. It creaked beneath the blade but held fast.

"Come on," he gritted his teeth.

The wood continued to resist then gave with a crack. He peeled away the edge of the frame and then lifted out the back piece. There in the false frame, embedded in heavy linen, lay eight cylindrical glass vials. He took them out and lay them on the canvas. Then he gathered up the edges of the canvas into a stiff bag and stood.

The vials jostled, rattling against one another. His nerves shook. "Not yet. Not yet."

He clutched the bag and strode for the door. With every step, the glass seemed to shift. Beads of sweat formed on his face and neck. Holding the bag stiffly, he half strode, half ran for the ballroom staircase.

By the time he made it to the top, his hair was drenched, his arm muscles throbbing. The door opened before him.

"You're here."

Richter nodded to Nathaniel. "Help me with this. Is Clara...?"

"My mother took her. Most likely to the roof."

Richter opened the door to the ballroom and looked inside. A river of mist seemed to flow across the floor toward the open balcony doors. Hundreds of men stood throughout the room, their expressions those of fear and confusion. They shook themselves as if they had only just emerged from a stupor.

"We'll only have a few seconds." He didn't look to see Nathaniel's response. Instead he drew the canvas bag back then threw it as hard as he could. It flew through the air and hit the floor. The sound of shattering glass filled the air. Smoke began to rise.

They pulled the doors shut.

"A chair," Richter pointed to a row of chairs lining the wall outside the ballroom. Nathaniel sprinted to one and ran back with it.

"Here. And stand back." Richter took it and slammed it on the floor. Again. And again, until the legs swung loose. He grabbed a leg and twisted, tearing it away from the base. As he shoved it between the doors' handles, effectively barring them, someone inside the ballroom shouted. The doors shook in their frames, pressing outward.

"It won't hold." Nathaniel stepped back, his shoulders rounded, braced for impact.

"Leave it," Richter said. "The smoke will finish them long before they break through."

The two men raced back down the stairs. The edges of the hall were on fire. Flames were spreading across the floor and ceiling of the ground floor. Smoke filled the hall. They turned at the junction and dashed down the eastern hallway. At the end they paused.

Nathaniel thrust out his hand. "If I don't see you again, thank you. For everything."

Richter took it. "Just get her. And get out."

Nathaniel turned and sprinted up the staircase. Above him, fire rolled across the ceiling. Richter turned down the narrow hall to the chapel. The walls were engulfed in pulsing flame. He ignored the danger and raced out through the back doors.

When he reached the edge of the woods, he looked back. The doors of the church had caught and blazed like an eye giving witness to its own destruction.

Chapter Seventy

When Lina shoved Clara through the doorway and onto the roof, Clara's first thought was that she would fall. That the door would open onto a chasm of fire below. That she would step out into empty space only to plummet to her death. In fact, the darkness of the night and the cool, damp air that hung around her twisted her thoughts, giving her a sense of passing through death and into an impenetrable void.

Her arms wheeled, her scream coming up short as her foot set down over the threshold onto the roof's surface. Lina pushed her forward again as Clara struggled to gain her bearings. The night was dark. Oppressively dark. Heavy, crisp cloud cover hung low, clinging to the edges of the house, obscuring her visibility beyond ten feet. Below, the land lay shrouded in mist.

A loud crack beneath them shook the house, jarring the roof. Clara's heart sped. Horrifying expectancy froze her limbs. Lina's unflagging determination, however, forced her toward the edge. Her grandmother held her fixed to her side. Clara wrenched her arm but to no avail. They were no more than twenty feet from where the house fell away. Clara had no doubt that there would be no delay. That her grandmother would dispatch her with the same cold efficiency she had Cora and every other girl whose body lay in the underground cavern.

As she watched the drop approach, frantic desperation spread through her fingers. All of her senses, usually so quiet, hummed. Her eyes took in the vacuous space beyond the roof. The skin on her face, still warm from inside the house, tingled at the cold embrace of the void. Her ears flooded with the sound of the dense silent night. Clara closed her eyes and embraced her impending fall.

An explosion burst from the windows below them. A rush of flame and heat exhaled into the night air, tinging the mist with shades of yellow and orange. The shock sent them both stumbling backward. Lina's hands released Clara and instead flew up to cover her face. As soon as Clara realized she could move unimpeded, she turned and bolted for the door to the house.

It loomed before her, waiting. Then it opened.

Clara skidded to a stop, her feet slipping out from under her. She hit the roof hard, her palms scraping the rough surface. She looked up in shock. There in the doorway stood Jutta. And behind her, Berend. Blood ran from a gash across Jutta's forehead. Her lip was split and swollen.

Out of the corner of her eye, Clara saw her grandmother moving toward her, covering the ground she had lost in the confusion of exploding glass. Clara edged away, toward the other side of the roof.

"It's too late Clara," Berend called to her. "There's nowhere to go. The fire is moving up the stairs." He stepped toward her, dragging Jutta as he came.

The door opened again as Nathaniel burst onto the roof. Smoke and flames followed him. The door slammed behind him, pressing back the inferno. He doubled over, coughing up smoke and stomach acid. The smell of his singed clothes hovered in the mist.

Clara looked from Berend to Lina. Then to the conservatory at the other end of the roof. Now it was the only exit. Berend saw her focus shift and edged sideways toward the garden door.

"Berend. What is this?" Lina called out.

"A rat. I promised you a rat. And here she is. The one person who had constant access to Clara. Who comes and goes from the house on a regular basis. And who has been conspiring with him." Berend shoved Jutta towards Lina and pointed a long, accusing finger at Nathaniel.

Lina gawked at the two then over to where Nathaniel stood. He still bent over, his hands on his knees, inhaling deep breaths of the cold clean air. But his eyes were fixed on Berend. Lina scoffed loudly.

"She's practically a child. How...what are you saying?"

"Call her what you will. But I guarantee this one...and he...are the rats." He turned to Nathaniel, his gaze accusing. "Deny it. Deny what you've done. Let's hear it from the liar himself."

"I've never lied to you. To any of you."

"Don't change the subject," Lina said. "Are you, or are you not the one who has been carrying information about this household—this family—to those outside? To the likes of that youth...Diedrich?"

"I am."

"And are you or are you not conspiring with this girl," Lina gestured to Jutta, "in order to...to... What is it you're planning?"

"Jutta has aided me on occasion. She's been most loyal."

"Loyal? To whom? Not to me, she hasn't been. What were you planning on doing? Ruining us?"

"Don't be dramatic, Mother."

"It'll never work."

"It will. Even now, forces are moving in. They will be here tomorrow at the latest. I only wish they had been sooner so this catastrophe might have been avoided."

"Ha! Likely story. It's more likely that you, the rejected son, wanted this very end. The home you could never have—destroyed. The community who would never have you—lying dead. The family who didn't want you—torn apart. Very likely to die in a matter of minutes."

"No, Mother. It was I who wouldn't have your home, or your community. And it was you who tore this family apart. With your obsession with Edgar. Your condescending disdain for your daughter-in-law. Your abuse of your granddaughter. All to serve your desperate need for the approval of one man who thinks less of you than he does his hunting dogs."

"I—" Lina shrieked, but Nathaniel cut her off.

"Your depravity severed this family long before I entered the scene. You made sure of that! And what are you left with now? A son who doesn't want you. A granddaughter who now knows the extent of who you are. What you are. Who wouldn't take you back under any circumstances."

Clara stared at her uncle. She should have seen through her grandmother's words. Should have known a woman who could idolize Edgar and Heinrich, who could kill and maim and destroy for her own self-serving purposes would only despise one who was the exact opposite of herself. Who reminded her of everything she was not. Whose very existence shone a light on her darkness.

"You were feeding hatred to her. Telling her to despise me. To think me evil." Lina pointed a finger at Clara, her vicious gaze still fixed on Nathaniel.

"You did that yourself. We told Clara nothing."

Lina turned and looked to Clara, took in her bewildered look and faltered briefly. "We? Who's *we*?"

"If you must know, it was myself. And Helene. And Jutta." Nathaniel paused for a moment then added, "And Edgar."

"No! No! You liar. That's all you are. Edgar would never conspire against me. He was the son I always wanted. You. *You* were the worthless one. The one no one wanted."

If she had intended to bait Nathaniel, to force him to defend himself, it failed miserably. He stared at her unflinching and instead forced her to hear it all.

"It was. It was Helene who had the courage to contact me in the first place. She told me everything. What Edgar had done to Clara. The reason for all the missing girls. That you were using them, using Clara, to obtain and then maintain power."

"Everything I did, I did to protect my son. To protect Edgar." Lina was huffing and shouting. It did no good, though. The heavy cloud cover absorbed her words and cast them aside. They came out weak, pitiful. In contrast, Nathaniel's voice resonated in the air around them.

"You didn't. You did it to hold power over everyone around you. You wanted to be esteemed, revered. You wanted others to succumb to your will, to come at your beck and call. You wanted to be their god. To control their every move. To hold them under your thumb. And Helene couldn't stand it. Couldn't stand *you*. She pitied Edgar, but she despised you. And she despised what both of you had done to her daughter."

Nathaniel turned to address Clara. "Your mother's greatest regret was that she hadn't been able to do more for you sooner. That she hadn't known enough, about who her husband was, about who her mother-in-law was. That she wasn't able to stop them. And protect you."

Tears streamed down Clara's face as she pictured her mother's last words to her. Her arm around her in sad resignation. Her body torn and broken on the floor. Her delicate fingers, stained with purple, outstretched.

"And it was Jutta who posted Helene's messages to me in India. Who coordinated the meeting between myself and Inspector Richter. If you must know, it was Jutta who took up the gauntlet for Clara's cause. And it was Jutta who established the plan to shut you down.

"But it was Edgar who met with me. Who agreed to go to the authorities farther afield. Those you can't control. And it was Edgar who insisted we expose not just you but all your colleagues."

"Never!" Lina said.

"Yes. You said it yourself. I *was* here the night of Edgar's death. We met here. On this roof. It was Jutta who admitted me into the house, who guided me here. I confronted him and he confessed everything. His part in this. And yours. And he begged me to do what he could not. To expose you. To save him from himself. To take his daughter away from him. Far from him, where he wouldn't be able to hurt her any longer."

Clara gaped at Jutta, her mind full of the image of Jutta's dress still splotched with rain when she had tried to stop Clara from her futile attempt to flee that night. The night her father had died.

"It was Edgar who realized you had murdered his sister. Had made him into a monster. A monster to serve at the altar of your vanity. And he was too weak, too vulnerable to your devices. Too ensnared. There was no way for him to walk away from what held him so tightly.

"He tried poison. He took the soporific that he recognized and increased the dosage each time it didn't succeed. He didn't know which ingredient would kill himself instantly. Didn't have the knowledge to know that the deadliest plant, the one Helene used, was right there all the time. Still, his body grew weaker daily. I'm sure the doctors told you his system was full of it. That's how much he wanted to be free from you. He despised you. Know that before you die."

Clara's heart shattered in a thousand pieces. To hear that he had wanted to save her from himself. Had enlisted the brother his family hated to rescue her from his clutches.

What have I done? What have I done? She sobbed. Her chest and throat, already sore, screamed in agony. *Let my heart burst*, she thought. *Let it break. Let them tear into pieces. Let them die. With the rest of me. Let me have what I deserve.*

Lina was screaming at Nathaniel. Calling him every vile name she could conjure. At some level, Clara was aware that her grandmother had lunged forward and grasped Jutta's arm. That she was dragging her toward the edge of the roof. There was nothing Nathaniel could do. Berend blocked her uncle's access to his mother.

"She'll die to pay for what you've done. And what she did. And what Helene did."

"No!" Clara screamed at the top of her lungs, then rose to her feet. Her chest was on fire, her eyes swimming with tears, but she strode toward her grandmother regardless. As she neared Berend, he grasped her and held her fast. "She's innocent. I'm the one who pushed Edgar. I'm the one who took him from you. I'm the one who's guilty. I'm the one who deserves to die. Take me! Take me!"

Lina's face froze in shock. Then the faintest smirk turned up the corner of her mouth. It widened, twisting her face into a hideous grimace. Her head rotated slowly. She cast a triumphant look at Nathaniel. "So you won't run after all? Okay. Come then. I'll take you in her place." Lina nodded to Berend, who loosened his hold on Clara.

"Clara! No, Clara!" Both Jutta and Nathaniel were yelling for her to stop, but she disregarded their words. She understood now. Understood so much more. Only death could erase her guilt. Her death. The one who truly deserved to die.

In her mind she still saw her father hunched over and disoriented where she had found him on the roof that night. Saw his troubled mind turning over and over in the dark. She felt the hatred, the bitterness that had risen within her. The determination she had held—to be free from him, to punish him, to see him suffer.

She had expected it to be difficult. But it hadn't been. It had been easy.

When he had seen her approaching, he had risen, with surprise on his face. And a sheepish expression she hadn't understood. Now she knew she had nearly caught him there with Nathaniel. That her uncle had just departed. That they had intended to save her. That her father's death had been unnecessary. It was her grandmother who had stood in the way of her freedom, who had kept her close as a means of controlling Edgar. It was Lina who never would have allowed her to leave without sending the hounds out after her. No. Clara knew too much. Remembered too much. Shutting her down was the only answer. Her father and uncle and mother had understood that.

But she hadn't. She had been so self-centered, seeing only her own suffering. So she had approached him, had lured him to the edge. It had been easy to silence her conscience, to still her doubts. In the end, he had fallen easily, willingly.

And so had she.

"Jutta." It was Nathaniel, calling to the girl. She twisted, distraught, from Nathaniel to Clara, but didn't move. Lina had relinquished her grasp on her. As Clara drew closer, Lina pushed Jutta away. The look on her face, a mask of disgust only faintly concealed her glee to nearly have her son's killer in her power.

A crack sounded behind them. The roof buckled then cracked again. An awful whoosh of heated air rose behind her. Clara flew forward and fell to the roof, shielding her head from the source of the explosion. When she twisted and looked behind her, the roof where Berend had stood was gone. In its place, a gaping hole exposed the raging fire beneath them.

The shock had thrown Jutta to the side. Nathaniel ran forward to help her up. As he did, the roof buckled again. Clara staggered to her feet as the surface shook and bulged upward. Another crack split the air. She cast about frantically, but nothing looked solid. Nathaniel was too far away. At the last moment, she leapt toward the edge.

The roof fell away beneath her. She came down hard, her arms and chest landing on the raised edge of the roofline. Her feet dangled above the open space where the roof had been. Burning heat licked at her feet and legs. She smelled the acrid scent of singed fabric. And skin.

She clutched at the edge and pulled. She heard herself whimper and grunt as her slender arms, strengthened by desperation alone, hauled her body up until she could swing one leg over the edge. And then the other. She felt the heat wave against her back as she sat there looking out into the mist. To where she knew the house fell away. Death beckoned on either side. Her thigh muscles trembled with stress and exhaustion.

Another blast of heat lifted her hair. A stone lip protruded from the face of the house a couple of feet below the roofline. Clinging to the edge, she turned and slid over the front of the house. In her mind she pictured herself continuing to slide. Then fall. Out into nothing. Her breath caught in her throat. But then her foot felt the lip. She rested her toes on it and looked back across the burning wasteland that had been the roof.

Beyond the waves of smoke, she barely made out the figures of Nathaniel and Jutta. They had backed along the other side of the roof, where the floor was still intact. Jutta was running for the door to the conservatory. Nathaniel was circling the gaping hole and calling to her. She couldn't make out anything he said over the roar of the fire.

Movement caught Clara's eye. Lina hung just below her, inside the gaping hole. Her long fingers clutched at the stone that edged the roofline, trying to pull herself up and away from the heat and flame. Clara watched her striving, hanging there out of reach. There was nothing she could do for her.

At the perimeter of her sight, Nathaniel was beckoning to her. She understood. If she leaned over the edge and walked her toes along the outer lip, she could bypass the portion of the roof that had collapsed. She shut her eyes against the fear then opened them. Slowly, carefully, she slid along the edge, moving toward him.

Until she came to a protruding stone obstacle. A large chimney or bay window below. The lip followed the jog in the stone, but the roofline rose. She could no longer lean over the edge . She had to cling to the house by the tips of her fingers and pray she didn't lose her footing. Or fall back into space. Her arms shook.

There was no alternative. The roof had bulged and cracked again, another portion falling away to fuel the fire below. Gritting her teeth, she moved away from the tenuous security of the edge. Her heart raced. She refused to look down. Thankfully the heavy, low fog obscured much of the view to the ground below her. First one step. Then another.

Don't think. Don't overthink. Just do, she told herself.

The next few minutes felt like hours of terror. Clara rounded the other edge of the protruding section and pressed back up against the house. Once again she could lean over the roofline. Nathaniel was close. Merely ten or fifteen feet farther. Suddenly the ground beyond him buckled. He stepped back, his eyes wide with fear. Clara froze. Then his gaze returned to her. He called out. Now she could just make out his words.

"Quickly! Don't stop. Keep going!"

With a nod, she pressed along the roof. Moving closer and closer to him. Until she felt his hands reaching over her. Gripping her under her arms. Pulling her over the edge and onto what was still solid surface. Her legs trembled and gave way. But then he clutched her tightly to himself and half carried her. They ran—a loping, weary limp—to the door of the conservatory, where Jutta waited for them. Her face was tight, drawn. But then the roof shook again and a wave of fire burst through. It was moving closer.

"There's no way out." Jutta shook her head, reconciled to their fate.

"Actually there is." Clara's voice trembled. "This way."

The roof buckled again as she turned and made her way toward the back of the conservatory.

Chapter Seventy-One

Down they descended, through the darkness, into the belly of the house. Around them, Clara heard walls and floors quaking and caving in. Rats raced up and down the stairs in terror. The walls crawled with the creatures that dwelled in the darkness, forced to the surface. There was no way to grip the stone without grasping something that slithered. It was as if the fire were simultaneously exposing and destroying life. Clara cursed herself for her prior skittishness.

Behind her she heard Jutta squeal. Nathaniel followed them, his tread urgent and confident. Clara focused on the sound of it. At the bottom, she pulled the lever, springing open the door to the tunnels.

They were pitch-black. And cool. Still unaffected by the raging inferno above their heads. Clara looked to the left. The narrow tunnel. She knew where it led. The darkness seemed to constrict and pulsate. She turned right and headed down the familiar route.

Nathaniel hesitated. "Are you sure this is the way?" She looked back at his shadowy profile. He was glancing away, to the left.

Clara shook her head. "This way." She turned from him and walked down the right-hand tunnel. But premonition crawled up her spine. If she had been willing to say it, she would have said she feared to take the other way. She knew what it would require.

They moved through the long, dark passages until they reached the hall of tombs. There, light shone from within the recessed alcove. The door stood open. Clara approached it and peered up the steep stairway. Lanterns bordered the way. Two had gone out. The others stood silently, breathing in the restricted air.

She paused and looked toward the end of the hall. There was nothing there but the cells. The house above her creaked and trembled. The walls groaned loudly. Her mouth felt dry. They didn't have long. On trembling legs, she pressed up the stairs as quickly as she could. Twice she hesitated, her muscles quivering and threatening to give out.

She knew what they would find before they reached the top. The smell of smoke drifted into the stairway, hanging in the air near the top. Clara passed through the tiny sacristy. She already could see the reddish glow beyond. Still, they clustered together within the pulpit and gazed down. The chapel lay engulfed in flames. At the end of the aisle, a twelve-foot high pulsating blaze blocked the open doors. Below them, a rolling sea of orange heat consumed the altar, the floor, the pews. There was nowhere to go.

"What do we do?" Jutta whispered.

"We go back," said Nathaniel.

Clara looked into his eyes and read assurance that she didn't feel. She swallowed hard and nodded. "We go back," she echoed.

Nathaniel and Jutta turned and reentered the sacristy. As they did, Clara paused and looked back at the chapel. She felt around in her pocket. It was torn but still intact. She withdrew the piece of fabric. It felt stiff, caked with dirt. Still, she knew what it was. She remembered. Remembered her father, in the fraction of a moment after she had pushed him. He had grasped for her, managing only to take hold of her sleeve. It had torn away, falling with him.

She looked at it in her hand. Then let it go. It rode the waves of heat and smoke until it landed on the altar. There it rested for a moment. She watched the fire glow through the heart of it. Then the flames spread, and it was entirely enveloped. In less than a minute, it was gone.

"Are you coming?" Nathaniel peered from around the doorway.

They took one of the lanterns from the stair. It lit their way back through the tiled hall. Past the entrance that led up to the rooftop conservatory. Then down through the long, cramped passageway where she feared to go.

As they rushed down the long, winding worm hole, Clara clawed through her mind, searching for a different outcome. Anything other than what she pictured so clearly. All she saw was darkness.

She smelled the stench of the bodies before she emerged from the tunnel.

Ahead of her, Nathaniel pressed through the gap into the subterranean cave. Jutta skidded to a stop. All three of them stared across the cavern to the dark pool of water, its black surface broken only by the young man's body. They covered their noses and mouths. Gently Nathaniel steered the two girls forward.

The wall beyond the pool of water stood as it had before, impregnable, interlaced with tree roots and rock. Clara looked toward the room of bodies and the small hole she had dug in the wall. Even if they each squeezed through the tiny opening and took up a bone, the house probably would crash down around them long before they could dig through the exterior wall. A silent scream rose in her chest.

She turned and looked back toward the lake. The black water lay as still as an open grave. Clara stood some distance away, her feet anchored to the ground. Nathaniel and Jutta moved toward the edge then stopped to peer into its inky depths.

"Where does it lead?" Jutta asked.

"Presumably to its source. If I were to guess, the lake you're familiar with lies just beyond here." Nathaniel gestured to the wall then touched the surface of the water with his shoe as if, in the disturbance, he could see a way through the depths.

As he did, the ground shook. A crash like thunder sounded from the direction of the house. A cloud of dust hung over the entrance to the tunnel.

"We can't go back," he said.

"Why?" Clara's voice croaked.

"The house is dead. It's falling." He pointed toward the tunnel. "The force is impacting the land around it. The tunnel is collapsing as the ground shakes."

"But this room?" Jutta looked up at the ceiling as another crash reverberated in the distance. The walls around them trembled, sending dirt and rocks crashing to the ground. One of them hit Clara in the face, gouging her from cheekbone to jaw.

Nathaniel already had removed his shoes and jacket. He rolled up his sleeves. "There's no other option. Let's go." He and Jutta sat at the edge of the lake, plunging their feet into the water. She inhaled sharply then slipped under. He turned to look at Clara and extended his hand.

She felt her eyes widen in the darkness. Beside her the last lit lantern flickered weakly, the candle nearly extinguished. A light sweat covered her body.

"I'm coming." She took a step forward then stopped. Licked her dry lips. Nathaniel still stared at her. "I'm coming," she repeated.

He gazed at her in question, nodded to himself, then slid into the water. Clara took another step forward and peered down into the water. The ripples grew still. There was no sign of them. No way to know.

From the corner of her eye, the shadowy corner moved. She spun around to face it. For a second, Clara didn't recognize her. Her skin was mottled, blackened, and blistered red in places. Her head was bald, the hair singed to nothing. As she drew closer, Clara smelled smoke and burned flesh. She gagged reflexively.

Her grandmother tried to speak, but her voice cracked as if her vocal chords were charred. It didn't matter. Clara understood. "I should have brought you here long ago. Should have drowned you when I had a chance." That was what she tried to say.

"Why didn't you then?" Clara asked. "Why did you spend all those years, all that effort just to keep me a prisoner? To risk discovery when I could, at any moment, have said something? I'll tell you why. Because my father would never have allowed it. Sick though he was, he loved me in the best way he knew how. That's what really chafes at your pride.

For all your worship of him, you know he never truly loved you. He loved Cora. And he loved me."

Lina's eyes bulged. She bared her teeth and lunged. Clara stepped out of the way and watched her fall. As she did, Lina cried out and squeezed her fists tight. When she opened them, Clara saw that several fingers were charred. Two were missing, blackened stumps, most likely burned and torn off in her attempt to climb out of the burning roof. For some reason, watching her curled on the floor, Clara felt empathy welling up in her. It surprised her.

"It's not too late you know." She gestured to the lake. "We're leaving. You can still escape."

"That's ridiculous!" a familiar voice said.

Clara turned to see a faint image of Cora standing next to the lake, her features veiled. If Clara hadn't known that voice, her dress, and those few remaining strands of long auburn hair, she wouldn't have recognized her. The girl before her was an emaciated skeleton. Yet her voice was strong. As strong as it had ever been. She held out a jagged rock.

"She deserves everything she's going to get. Look at her! Hands she used to kill. Deaths that never touched her conscience any deeper than what she could easily wipe away. Those hands are blackened with guilt. All the soap in the world can't hide them. And her hair, her pride. Gone. Exposing her for the vulture she is. Feeding off the carcasses of the vulnerable to feed her reputation. Let her burn! Let her go to a nameless, faceless grave. Where no one will remember her. Here." Cora thrust the rock forward. "End her!"

Clara ignored Cora and turned to help her grandmother to her feet. Lina grunted and gasped as she stood. As she did, she raised one hand and crushed a stone into Clara's temple. Clara cried out and stumbled backwards, fingering the blood that ran from her head.

"Why?"

"Why? Why wouldn't she?" Cora circled the two, jeering at Clara. "You know who she is. What she is. You should have killed her when you had the chance. What did you expect, you fool? A glowing change of heart? That the woman who lived only for herself suddenly would care about you?"

"A change of heart..." Clara whispered the words. "I'm leaving. You can follow me or not." She strode toward the lake, determination winning out over her fear.

"What is wrong with you?" Cora tried to scream. But her voice had faded to nothing more than a hoarse whisper, her frame vibrating under the force of her words. "What happened to the girl who knew Lina had to be destroyed? Who would have done anything to end her?"

Clara looked back over her shoulder. "She died." And then she stepped off of the edge, into the water. It was as cold as she remembered. She bobbed to the surface and gasped for air. The lantern had gone out. The cavern lay in darkness. But Lina was close, leaning out over the water. Toward her. Another rock, a much larger one, in her hand. But as her arm swung wide, a tremor shook the air around them.

The cave's ceiling groaned and cracked as a rain of dirt and stone ricocheted off of the ground. Clara ducked under the water and swam away. As she came up near the wall at the far end of the pool, a portion of the ceiling tore away and collapsed. When Clara opened her eyes, all she could see was the far edge of Lina's foot. Layers of stone and earth pressed her under the water. If the rockfall hadn't killed her, she would soon drown.

Clara expected Cora to laugh, to rejoice, but she didn't. When she looked up, the apparition was glaring at her, her eyes like burning embers.

"You know, you weren't all that different."

"I know. I *was* her. And becoming more so every day. But not anymore." Clara smiled faintly and looked toward the wall. She remembered her uncle and Jutta waiting on the other side. "That part of me is gone. With you."

When she looked back, Cora had disappeared. The ground trembled again, rocks bouncing along the floor, crashing into the pool just feet from her. She drew in a deep breath and plunged below the surface.

It took her breath away. Not just the cold but the darkness. There was no way to see. Fear gripped Clara's heart as she used the tree roots protruding from the wall to pull herself down. Farther and farther into the unknown.

The temperature fell as she descended. She pictured icy fingers from strange creatures that dwelt in perpetual obscurity taking hold of her and pulling her under. She imagined them clutching her to themselves, binding her in oblivion. In a place where she was lost to herself forever.

If she lived, what would she be? What would the water take from her? What had the house already taken? If she rose to the other side, away from her family, her history, would she be nothing but a shell of herself? A girl without an identity, her nature lost, left behind, scattered like chum on the surface of the water? An empty vessel, nameless, faceless?

A current swirled around her. In the midst of it, the memory of the other girls rose. She half expected them to encircle her again. That their souls might be trapped in this place in which they had swum free of their bodies. That she might soon be like they were. Her heart raced as the darkness wrapped around her. Tremors of fear whipped through her limbs.

Her lungs burned, screaming for air. Her fingers felt the ground meeting the wall of roots. It was solid. There was nowhere to go. She walked her hands along the edge, desperately seeking an inlet. Frantic, shaking with exhaustion and anguish, she closed her eyes. Then she let go. Let go of the fear. Let go of the past. Let go of who she had been and who she might become. She ceased striving.

Nathaniel wriggled through the gap in the wall and felt about him. There was nothing but water. And a solid, impenetrable blackness that chilled his soul. Above him he felt debris float down, settling around him on its way to the lake bottom. The entire cave was collapsing. Before long, Clara would be lost.

He propelled himself from one side of the subterranean lake to the other, his arms outstretched, sweeping the depths. Then he felt it. A hand, floating lifelessly in the water. He gripped it in his own. Pulled her arm toward him until he could clutch her close to himself.

He swam for the gap. Shoved her through. And followed. They rose quickly, sending water spraying into the air. Jutta was leaning on an exposed tree root, peering into the water. Richter and the girls clustered at the edge of the boathouse, waiting.

"Here!" Nathaniel said. "Quickly."

Jutta jumped from her perch, into the edge of the water, where the muck rose around her ankles and threatened to hold her fast. She wrenched her foot free and reached out over the water, catching at Clara's arm. They dragged her from the water and laid her out on the frost-covered lawn.

"Is she...?" Jutta's eyes were wide.

He didn't answer. Instead, he set to work turning Clara and slapping her back. Turning her on her side to try to coax the water from her lungs. Fluid burst from her mouth. But still she lay unmoving, her eyes closed.

The air was lit with a burning glow that gave everything around them an unearthly semblance. Smoke hung in the air to the west. Where the house had once stood, a ruinous shell bordered the raging inferno. Gaping holes in the walls exposed the structure to the rising sun. No secrets remained.

Nathaniel bent low and took Clara in his arms. "Come back to us, Clara. Come away from the edge. This isn't the end. It's only the beginning." As he rocked her limp figure, the sky behind the ragged form of the house grew light, tinged with the rosy glow of sunlight. A light snow began to fall, covering them in a blanket of white.

Chapter Seventy-Two

Richter sat motionless, waiting. The man behind the desk held a page in his hand. He read it, turned it over, set it on top of the ones he'd already read, and picked up another. Then another. When he had set down the last one, he removed his spectacles and rubbed his eyes. He set his elbows on the desk and steepled his fingers before him. Then he looked at Richter. They sat for several minutes merely looking at each other in silence. It seemed as if nothing more was necessary. As if they both understood all that could be said.

"Damn foul business, Gerhard. Damn foul," the man said.

"Yes, sir."

"The children?"

"One or two families were hard to locate. But in the end, we found them and returned their daughters. It was a great relief for them...but there were the others, of course."

"Of course," the man echoed. "Can we say that this is comprehensive? That this settles the matter?"

Richter shook his head. "At this point, I'm hard put to make such a determination. I certainly hope that is the case. But many of the... bodies. There was simply no way to know who they were. I hope we've accounted for all the missing girls. But—"

"But the number is incomplete."

"It is."

"This variable could be attributed to singular incidents."

"It could. Very likely some are just that. There are always runaways and singular acts of violence. But…"

"But what? Off the record, Gerhard. What are you thinking? What does your intuition, your experience tell you? About the men involved. You listed names in your report."

"Yes, sir. The place was a war zone. Bodies everywhere. Some we could identify; others we can infer simply by virtue of association. And their wives' reports they are in fact missing. But how many of their associates might not have attended that night? For any reason whatsoever—prior business engagements or personal disinclination."

"You think there are others?"

Richter paused and measured his words before speaking. But there was no way to soften it. "I think we would be fools to assume this is anything other than the tip of the iceberg."

The man leaned back in his chair and looked to the side, out the window, to where thick snow covered the ministerial gardens. In the foreground, a regiment of horses and their riders marched along the drive, headed out of the main gates. He turned back to Richter without speaking.

When Richter left the building, he did so as he always did: a nameless entity devoid of notoriety. Few people looked up to acknowledge his passage. Some recognized his face. But even those who did knew little about the nature of his business there. It had never troubled him. He didn't do the things he did for acclaim.

It would never have bothered him if it hadn't been for Jan. Someone had notified Jan's parents. He hadn't. It would have compromised his position. He knew that. But Jan's sacrifice deserved to be proclaimed. His family deserved to know what he had done. That he had been a hero. That he had done everything right. That his actions were part of what they had accomplished.

What had they accomplished? A notable house, burned to the ground. A good portion of the local leadership decimated. Some form of closure for so many families whose young girls had disappeared without a trace. Would the outcome have been the same without him? Without Jan? He couldn't say. Yet it troubled his dreams, chased sleep from his eyes, and haunted his waking step.

He had never before had such uncertainty about what he had done; it left a bad taste in his mouth. As he passed windows, he turned to see his reflection: that of a man whose face bore a strange, twisted grimace. One so unlike his former self. When he gazed on himself in the glass, his eyes had a dark, recessed quality. As if he had eaten of the tree of good and evil. As if, at the most intimate level, he now knew things he could never un-know.

He remembered what he had told Jan. *That it's the man who battles injustice who goes home to his family and his hearth with a heart of gratitude. He knows how much there is to lose and so he takes nothing for granted.*

He brushed snow off of a bench beneath the bare uplifted arms of a sycamore maple. And sat. He hardly noticed the cold. Around him, the snow rose lightly in the wind and filled the air with a sparkling quality. Beneath it, the land lay dormant. Some of what had thrived and bloomed had died. Much of the rest slept, gathering strength for the spring. Waiting for the ground to thaw so that new life could come forth. Above it all, the snow spoke of something greater. Something beyond the cycles of life and death. Something that transcended it all, clothed it all in white.

A deep peace settled over Richter's soul. He reached into his coat and pulled out a file with his next assignment.

Chapter Seventy-Three

The dawn rose in shimmering waves of warmth. Enveloping waves that soaked into the skin and bones and filled one with a sense of ease. The rich scent of lemons and sandalwood hung in the air.

Clara opened her eyes and rolled over. She ran her hands over the white linen bedding, feeling its rough texture. Cotton curtains that hung from the mahogany bedstead fluttered in the breeze. She sighed deeply, taking in the warmth of the gentle Indian breeze. Across from her bed, two sets of doors opened onto a deep, covered veranda. They stood open, as they usually did. It had taken months before her nightmares had subsided. And sometimes she still awakened in the night, bolting upright, clutching the bedcovers to herself, her body covered in sweat.

But the sight of the doors, flung wide to the rolling hills beyond, filled her with a deep and settled reassurance. Often she went out in the depths of the night and stood on the veranda, listening to the trees sway in the darkness. Feeling the warm, moist night air. Hearing the crickets chirping in the fields. Once the dark form of a tiger had moved through the shadows; her breath had caught in her throat. It had turned and fixed her with two glowing round eyes. Then it had moved on, disinterested.

Clara hadn't flinched. Hadn't fled for the security of her room. Instead she had laughed lightly under the golden moon. Nothing here could harm her. Not in any sense that mattered. To live here was to dwell in a land of eternal light.

She opened the armoire and smiled. She had fewer dresses than before, but each one was something that she had chosen. That she loved. She pulled out her favorite: a yellow dress covered in white-and-pink embroidery. After stepping behind the intricately carved screen, she pulled off her nightgown and pulled on the dress. And flat beaded sandals. They slid wonderfully across the dark wood and tiled floors throughout the house. As if she floated here and there without a care.

She passed through the central living room, listening to voices drifting in from the far end of the veranda. Her step quickened as she moved under the hanging punkah toward the open doors.

Her uncle and Jutta looked up in greeting.

Clara pulled out a chair and sat between them. A bowl of rice and yogurt sat in the center of the table. As her uncle served her and Jutta poured her some tea, Clara basked in how different her life was. How long had they been here? Seven months? Eight? The weather was turning rainy.

She ate some of the rice and took in the rolling green hills beyond the lawn. Clouds hung in the distance. She smelled the moisture in the air. Usually she walked through the fields with her uncle, helping the workers. But soon they would pause and wait for the autumn flush of tea to come in. They would sit inside the plantation, Nathaniel reconciling his ledgers, notating their crop production, and reading farming journals.

Jutta loved to knit and embroider. She wanted her hands full and her mind at rest. She would sit quietly working, singing softly to herself. Every once in a while she'd look up and smile at Clara. When they weren't in the fields, she and Clara would head out in the mornings, arm in arm. Sometimes they walked along the rhododendron paths in the shade of towering hollong trees. Other times they wandered into town and sat beside the lake, watching the birds preen in the sun.

Usually they talked of India, carefully avoiding any discussion of what had happened in the past. Other times they sat in quiet, heavy silence, each one feeling the weight of all they remembered. Occasionally they spoke of it. Usually in the night, seated side by side on a settee on the veranda. There was something about the dark stillness, the night vast with stars, redolent with the smell of the earth, that seemed to insulate them from reality. That seemed to whisk them away from all that had occurred, to a place where nothing and no one could touch them.

"*Sahib*." Amar bowed to Nathaniel and placed a silver tray in front of him. The morning paper rested on it.

"Thank you, Amar."

Nathaniel shook it open to one side, quickly perusing the front headlines. Clara sipped her tea. Jutta was saying something about Clara's art.

Her latest drawing was of a lotus flower. It rested on the surface of the water. Around it, lily pads floated. It had taken her considerable time and effort. For she had wanted to capture the fuchsia-tipped petals at just the right moment. When the light seemed to glow from its core. As if it were alive with energy and an endless source of life.

Sometimes, when the past hung low over her mind, she'd stand beside the nearly-finished drawing and gaze at it. She'd reach down and brush her fingers across the radiant-white light in its center, and she'd know she would never again suffer as she had. The past was dead. And with it, part of herself. But in its death, something had been reborn. Something greater that the past could never touch. She smiled softly to herself.

"What is it?" Jutta was gazing at Nathaniel, her face tilted to one side. The faintest sign of conflicting emotions played about his eyes.

He set the paper down and looked at both of them without words. Clara reached for it. A photo adorned the lower right side of page seventeen. In it, a beaming face she knew stood out. He was surrounded by several other men in official dress. The caption below it read, "Midsummer Gala Hosted by Duke Heinrich von Ehrenschau."

"We don't know. It may not mean..." Jutta's voice trailed off.

Nathaniel didn't answer. He was looking out into the distance, at nothing in particular. Eventually he said something softly to himself.

Something she didn't catch yet understood as if she had. That seemingly endless desire for a closure that never truly comes.

Clara had seen the front cover when Amar had set it down. Bismarck had defeated Austria. "It's only a matter of time."

Nathaniel looked surprised to hear her say it. Then a smile broke through his frustration. He reached over and squeezed her hand. "Yes, yes it is. Not quite the way you mean it. But yes. It is only a matter of time."

They passed the rest of breakfast in quiet, easy conversation about nothing in particular. As they stood, the storm clouds that had been building suddenly unleashed a downpour that swept all but the closest portion of the gardens from their sight. Clara went to stand at the edge of the veranda, where she felt the warm rains blow over the railing.

"Are you coming in?"

She turned to see her uncle standing in the doorway, watching her expectantly. "Soon. But not just yet." The water washed over her. Soothing. Clean. She understood what he had felt and thought. That some things couldn't be cured by a fire or a war. They would have their way regardless. The Linas of the world would continue. For the time being. But it was only a matter of time.

Meanwhile, she was beyond their reach. More important, she was beyond herself. The house had burned to the ground and herself with it.

Thank you so much for supporting my work. I hope you loved *The Death of Clara Willenheim*. This is my debut novel. It came about as a series of strange dreams—each one about a girl who retreated through some form of doorway or small opening into a secret place in a house. In each dream the house and the hidden rooms were different.

The dreams lacked what many dreams do: plot. However, I loved the symbolism and the depth of possible psychological and spiritual meanings. I couldn't resist crafting a story around this girl and why she's exploring the hidden areas of her home.

Right now I'm hard at work on my next writing project. In the meantime, I'd love to have your help. Reader feedback is one of the best ways to encourage Amazon and other retailers to promote my work to other readers. Reviews also give those readers more confidence in choosing this story. You can do this by leaving an honest review wherever you choose: Amazon, Barnes and Noble, Goodreads or at other sites.

Thank you again. I look forward to hearing from you and bringing you another great story!

About the Author

Charlotte Lesemann has been an avid reader and writer since early childhood. She fell in love with the Gothic genre as a child when she read Rebecca by Daphne du Maurier.

She has two degrees in Business, a past career in Finance and Accounting, and a degree in and passion for Interior Design.

She lives in the Pacific Northwest with her family and her beloved pets where she writes full-time.

www. charlottelesemann.com

 x.com/gothiccharlotte

 youtube.com/gothicliterarysociety

www.ingramcontent.com/pod-product-compliance
Lightning Source LLC
Chambersburg PA
CBHW031836310726
48972CB00005B/1297